In The Beginning...

Harding McRae

In The Beginning…
by Harding McRae

Print Edition
ISBN 978-09858494-1-2

e-Book Edition
ISBN 978-09858494-0-5

Please visit:
www.HardingMcRae.com

Other works by Harding McRae:
Always/Never

Forward and Acknowledgments

The forward to this book basically wrote itself. Why? Because I have been intrigued and fascinated by the premise and questions it raises for at least 35 years. For most of my adult life I have asked virtually everyone I know for their answers to the questions. Bring out the wine and I found much better answers! The questions? They are the themes of this book; that is, if humankind were given an opportunity to "start over" knowing all we do to date, **who would we choose for that task?** And would we "get it right," or even get it different? One can answer from the heart, from a philosophic viewpoint, or religious and many other perspectives. After all, we are all colored by our own life experiences and people we've met. Those at the least influence our answers. I've also found that the answers change over time for some and not for others. Why, I wonder?

The first book of a trilogy, *In the Beginning…* proposes one answer to the question *"Who would you choose?"* The questions *"Would we turn out differently?"* and *"Would our supposed wealth of knowledge gained through the years make any difference?"*…I'll leave those for the Parts Two and Three down the road.

I've found that *candidate-professions* divide into several camps— those which most will agree on and others which most will argue strenuously over. While the questions are serious, I would encourage you to ask yourself and your friends. But don't take the answers too seriously. It is the asking of the questions that I consider more important.

I originally wrote the first edition in 1997-98, but kept it on the shelf until it was taken off for a possible movie treatment. When that ultimately didn't happen (long story), I picked it up again, rereading it again after about ten years. I decided to update it a bit in 2012 and publish the second edition. *I was pleasantly surprised at how much didn't need revision and how many of the technological predictions came to be. I also realized how little some things had changed after ten to fifteen years, especially in the big picture.*

Acknowledging some of those who have been instrumental in my musings is important to me. They have had to suffer through the process of writing a book along with me. While I say "suffer," there was joy as well. They have experienced the same emotions and, for a few, some additional ones. First, among all others is my wife, Lynne. Without her I would not have survived, physically or emotionally. And, of course, Babraham Lincoln— those who know, know why. Special thanks goes to Wrennie Landau, my friend, agent, lawyer, and provocateur, not necessarily in that order, depending on her mood!

As I wrote the first edition, Lynne Richardson, my erstwhile assistant and long-time friend, was invaluable. Chardonnay, too, for her unwavering love (again, those who know, know it's not the wine). Alan Hollingsworth, MD, my friend from undergraduate and medical school, and an excellent author himself, offered timely and thoughtful advice. Thanks to *Hasbro* for their permission to use their board game *Risk*®. There is "some" truth to the rumor it was played during medical school.

Then there are the real-life friends and family upon which several characters are based. *Tatman* is modeled after my father, a retired trauma surgeon, whose family really was a Tatman. Dad never verbalized wanting to go to space, but he never walked away from a challenge. I have no doubt he would have relished the opportunity, but likely wouldn't have left his family. Could any of us? John McRae, my brother inspired more than the name.

Watching him grow and thrive has been an inspiration.

Tom Conroy is a friend and former Air Force major turned actor. The late Mark Houston was my musical writing partner for many years. An idealist, he would have loved trying to improve humankind on this Earth or anywhere. Believe me, there really is a David Chapman, *Chappo* to most, down-under in Australia—and the world's a better place for him. He and *the real Damien* have terrorized that continent far and wide for decades, and I am proud to call him friend.

Through my last thirty years or so (closer than I'd like to forty), Thad Mercer has been there for the highs and the lows. A stock trader by profession, through those years he has been—at one time or another—my therapist, collaborator, co-conspirator, business partner, limo driver, limo rider, adviser, mentor, and many, many other things. But most of all, he has been a friend. Thank you, Thad.

Then there is Marvelous Mel Siverts. Another thirty-plus-year "veteran," Mel has been my problem solver through it all. Loyal—should you want the definition—look it up under Mel. My two computer programming friends, Brian Hart and Ron Evanko, have taught me much about life—perseverance, not taking things too seriously, honesty no matter what others think, and a general joy for life I had lost. Thanks, guys. Oh, and Ron is the webmaster for my website, too.

Extra special thanks to friends and family who gave me their time to read this revised edition. Their critiques and suggestions pale in comparison to their friendship, including Roger Harding, Susan (Chase) Kay, Jennie Corella, Elaine Dodd, Ty Richardson, and Paul Ake. Thanks to Max Herr, who took the lead and acted as the head wrangler for my willing team of editors, and who also put the finishing touches on the manuscript as well as the cover and interior book design.

Serious questions, but enjoy. Life is for living, after all. Still, *Is there a deeper meaning? Could we do it better? Could we get it right if we had the chance for "do-overs"?* I leave as I started:

Who would you choose?

Prologue

On September 12, the Jupiter probe *Challenger II* decelerated and began its orbit of the Jovian planet. The Galilean moons of Europa, Io, Callisto, and Ganymede, as well as the other twelve smaller moons were quickly identified by its vast array of scanners and monitors. Launched just a year earlier, it was the most recent in a series of deep space probes beginning some sixty years earlier, in 1960, with the launch of *Pioneer 5*, which weighed only about one hundred pounds; her successors, *Pioneer 6* through *11*, were the first U.S. spacecraft to explore the solar system. *Pioneer 10* and *11* were the first nuclear-powered deep space probes and the first to investigate Jupiter and beyond. Though not designated a *Pioneer*—named instead in honor of the ill-fated 1980s space shuttle, *Challenger*—this much more sophisticated collection of man's technology made a pioneering discovery. Hidden from the Earth's view and circling in a slow, eccentric, and nearly polar orbit around the largest of Jupiter's moons, Ganymede, was a new moon...code named "Genesis."

This was no ordinary, everyday discovery. It represented one of the few moons of Jupiter discovered by a spacecraft after *Voyager I* and *II* in 1979. Technically a moon of Ganymede, it was a moon of a moon. As exciting as discovering a new moon or planet is, that isn't what made Genesis unique. What did was finding an atmosphere, water, gravity, and natural resources unlike any moon or planet previously found in our solar system. All indications were this Jovian satellite would support human life without cumbersome equipment or long-term artificial life support systems. To be sure, it was no garden of Eden. Still, the possibilities were astounding. Until now, there was no compelling reason for sending astronauts into deep space. Unmanned missions were cheaper, safer, and gathered more than enough data to occupy man's curiosity. Genesis changed the equation.

If it would sustain human life, was mankind not obligated to go there? If it would support human life, would it not be reasonable to think it could support other life? Was there life there already? Or are we alone in the solar system... in the universe? Could man plan and execute a mission to such a distant site? Who should go? What characteristics of mankind in general, and of individuals, specifically, should the team possess? Were they explorers or settlers, colonists or refugees, nomads or permanent residents? Didn't earthborn humanity now have compelling grounds for answering these questions?

Who would you choose?

I

As the entire team regained consciousness, and struggled to find the wherewithal to stand, each was vaguely aware of having been unconscious, in a fog, now trying to remember.

Trying to remember what?

Only a moment earlier, each had been lying on the cold ground, awakening in an environmental suit. A pounding headache was all each had as a memory of the most recent events. Surely there was more. Each member of the team gradually became aware of the others.

What was going on? What had happened?

As each one's mind slowly cleared, realizing the presence of the others, they fumbled to just touch one another—confirming their own existence, confirming they were alive.

Alive, but where?

One by one they found their feet and, soon, also found their way to the entrance. Jockeying for position, each squinted in an effort to see through the opaque night. All anyone could see was smoke. Thick, acrid, dense, particulate-matter smoke.

Opaque? Not exactly. The exterior was a swirl of winds, intermittent lightning and thunder, and just plain noise. No, this wasn't opaque. It was becoming more and more clear, as each member began to grasp the view. Their instruments quickly began to scan for radiation, temperature, winds—atmosphere. All their devices were working, but the team didn't like the readings. There was radiation, higher than expected. And winds...with occasional gusts over 150 miles per hour. And the temperature was considerably lower than anticipated. But mostly, there was smoke.

"Everyone make sure your helmets are fastened correctly!" Tatman screamed into the headset communicator. "Let's not deal with things we can prevent. Anyone break anything?"

"Look over there! Nkata's not up." They stumbled over to Nkata. He was conscious, but dazed. Tatman began surveying him for injuries. The trauma surgeon's work ethic obscured any need to deal with thinking about what had happened.

"Everyone! Listen," Svetlana commanded. "We need to check out our equipment and each other. Melissa, is your haptic interface working properly?" she asked, fumbling with the suit in an effort to help. "You and Chappo check out the instruments. We have to confirm that the readings are accurate. They must be out of calibration. Then, we have to go outside."

She was right. They *had* to go outside. There was no escaping it. That was what they had to do and each one knew it, no matter how hard they individually tried to put it out of their mind. Each member checked his own suit, then checked someone else's. Then, they checked another—they checked and checked again for at least thirty minutes. To check was to postpone. They needn't check each other's pulse. Racing didn't describe the pounding, or the empty feeling in the pit of one's stomach, a gnawing, hollow sensation, as they prepared to enter their new world. As each stared into the stark, barren surroundings, together they were a composite of emotions. Confused, disoriented, exasperated, angry, scared. But fear of the unknown is the worst of fears.

"The instruments are calibrated correctly. The readings are correct. Radiation levels are way above baseline." Melissa Sturmbourg's matter of fact scientific voice hid her fear.

If there were radiation out there, what caused it?

"Nkata's got a broken arm, but he's alright otherwise," Tatman notified the group. "Where the hell are Eric and Hayes? And Al? They were…" His voice trailed off. He'd nearly verbalized what the others were thinking.

They were what?

"Before we go outside, I think we all need to get our heads on straight," Najibul broke the momentary pause. "I think we all know what happened, or have a pretty good guess. If the three of them are out there, we're no good to them in here. But we're no good to them unless we deal with some realities."

"The first reality is we have to concern ourselves with the main objectives," Chappo began. "Those remain the same. Food, water, and shelter."

"With one additional complicating factor," Melissa added. "My haptic interface works now, but who knows for how long? We are all incredibly dependent on technology. I don't want to be a burden—"

"We are most dependent on each other," Mariani corrected her. "Without each other there will be no technology. Life is about people, not technology. Machines are replaceable or repairable. People aren't."

"People are repairable, too," Tatman added. "To the limits of our technology and knowledge of how to apply it. There is a—"

"Excuse me," Xiao interrupted, perturbed by the conversation. "We can debate philosophy later. Right now, we need to find our three missing comrades and see just exactly what we are dealing with. You're all jumping to conclusions. We need facts, not speculation." That meant they had to go outside.

"Help…me…up," Nkata insisted, in the haltingly, hoarse voice the team had long ago become used to— his voice synthesizer was not working at the moment. Tatman had splinted his arm and placed it in a makeshift sling. "I…did…not…come…this…far…to…be…left…behind…because…of…a…broken…arm. I…want…to…see…for… myself…what…new…prison…we…are…confined…to."

The first person to step out of their cave, Chappo, was blown to the ground by the unexpectedly strong winds. The next, Svetlana, learning from her predecessor's mistake, grabbed onto something, but she, too, encountered problems. The unexpected cold penetrated her suit; so cold, in fact, as to cause her gloved hand to stick momentarily to anything hard and smooth she touched.

And so it began. Each person finding a tentative new bearing in a new, foreign surrounding.

But was it really foreign?

One by one, each scanned the horizon looking for something—something usual. The supposedly familiar, now unfamiliar. The hoped- for ordinary, extraordinary. The common—prayed for, but found to be uncommon.

As each of the nine found a place on the ledge overlooking the land below, they gently held hands. Not only to steady themselves physically, but mentally as well. What they saw was a vast wasteland, devoid of vegetation, in the midst of a perpetual, but stationary, tornado—and cold, so *very* cold. As far as one could look, there was darkness, but a visible darkness, an illuminated darkness. The smog of all smog, the haze of all haze. And the wind. Blowing in a swirling, pulsing, random pattern. Then, suddenly, a lightning storm—but very much unlike "normal" lightning. The billion-volt-plus electromagnetic pulses, with surges reaching peaks well-above 50,000 amps, were arcing across miles of sky, rarely striking the ground, and left eerie, luminous trails in the sky—oddly similar to those irridescent trails left by meteors.

How would they survive? How could they eke out an existence?

"I've got a reading on the smoke. It's actually fine dust. Particle sizes of less than one micrometer in diameter. The average number of particles in the atmosphere is in the 2.7 grams/cm^2 range." Sturmbourg's calming voice helped.

"Can't...grow...anything...in...that."

"What do you mean?" Najibul was neither being accusatory nor questioning Nkata's statement. He, like the others, just didn't know what Nkata meant.

"With...that...kind...of...optical...density...sunlight...will...be...filtered. That...will...drop...the...temperature...below...what...it...takes...for...plants...to...photosynthesize."

"So we need to find temporary food and shelter until I can set up a hydroponics lab for you." Chappo wasn't going to let his mates dwell on the negative. He was an engineer. There was a solution to every problem. All he asked for was time. "Any sign of the others, mates?"

"Why is the temperature so much colder?" Mariani trembled.

"It is down more than thirty percent," Melissa answered her query specifically. "I'm reading -23° Celsius. The windchill makes the effect of the temperature worse."

"How long will the cold stay around?"

"At least four weeks." Tatman answered. "Then much cooler than normal, with continued subfreezing temperatures, for at least several more months."

"What about radiation?" Natarajan had been quiet through the entire catastrophe, until now. "Where are we on exposure now? And what can we expect?"

"Our immediate threat is gamma radiation," Tatman explained to his fellow travelers. "Without the suits our exposure would probably be in the 50 rem range from gamma radiation and another 50 rem from ingestion of beta and alpha particles. With the suits, we should be able to minimize that exposure. Right now, I'm measuring minimal internal radiation. The problem is in the environment. We have to keep it that way."

"And chemicals? There are probably toxic chemicals." Gagarin checked her scanners. She was right. "The atmosphere is a veritable soup of pyrotoxins including cyanide and carbon monoxide."

"We've got high levels of dioxins and furans as well as bizarre organic compounds," Tatman added.

"So no one eats or drinks anything until it's checked," Chappo added. "Everyone stays in their suit for the foreseeable future."

"And what is 'the foreseeable future', Mr. Chapman?" Xiao had more than a tinge of irony in his voice.

"The foreseeable future is our only future." Nkata was emphatic. And his voice synthesizer was once again working, too. "We have to decide here and now. Do we want to try our damnedest to survive or do we roll over and let God or whomever do with us as they please? Right now, sir choose. All of you! Choose now! What will it be?"

"My love," soothed Natarajan to Xiao. "None of us would pick this as our future. But apparently it is. Not only ours, but our child's." patting her growing abdomen. "What has changed? The future is still our history to live, our rules to write and our legacy to create." She grasped her husband's hand. "This, for better or worse, is our destiny."

  What hath God wrought? Or was this man's folly? What heaven or hell had they found? What had they gotten into?

  They were of one mind.

  They found a place without form—void of all apparent redeeming value. A place without day or night, morning or evening. There was no division of light from darkness. No greater or lesser light. Although there was soil, there was no seed, no grass, no tree, no fruit, no fowl, no beast of burden.

How did this come to pass?

II

Four drops of blood splattered his fresh white T-shirt. "Damned general," fumed Sheppard out loud. "He's gotten to me already." Though there was no one else in the room, he addressed his mirror as if his image were someone else. "How is this gonna look to the President of the United States. I can't even shave without becoming so clumsy and flustered over a two-bit, tin star of a bastard general, or is that general bastard," he thought to himself, while trying to apply pressure to his bleeding neck. "Now I get to walk around with a piece of toilet paper stuck to my neck," he lamented. This was not a good start to a predictably bad day—a cold January day. Sheppard never got used to the Washington cold. He was a warm weather kind of guy.

Dr. Eric Sheppard, the President's civilian science adviser, was being summoned to the White House for a meeting. Unfortunately, or so he thought, rumored to be in attendance as well was General Beauregard Calhoun Adams. A military moron in Sheppard's eyes, there had been minimal interaction between the two through the years. When they were forced together, the two had agreed on virtually nothing. Now Eric was pacing in the oval office of the White House waiting for the President of the United States to finish a videophone call to his daughter. General Adams was sitting comfortably on the couch, flipping through a briefing statement, obviously enjoying Sheppard's nervousness.

Why was he here anyway? This was a scientific issue, not a military one, he smoldered. The General's friends called him B.C. All Sheppard could think of at the moment was, why? Was it because he was from the Jurassic period or just thought like it? Was it because he acted like a Neanderthal? Was it...

"Excuse me, Doctor...can we begin?" the President interrupted Sheppard's flight of ideas. "Dr. Sheppard, could you give us an update on this newly discovered moon?"

This was his first significant White House meeting. Choking on his first words, the presidential adviser's voice cracked as the first words spilled from his mouth. "The new moon, code named Genesis, is in a polar orbit around the Jovian moon Ganymede, meaning it is hidden from the Earth and the Sun for approximately nine months." He cleared his throat. Why should he be intimidated by Adams? The President was his audience. Not the Pentagon. To hell with the General. He continued, more assured, "It had previously been thought to be a space anomaly, or comet—not a new moon. It is inclement for those nine months, then it emerges, maintaining a very mild climate for the next nine months. There is an atmosphere, water, light, and soil. In short, Mr. President, I think we have found the first extraterrestrial planetary object in our solar system capable of supporting human life."

Sheppard surveyed the room. The President was more interested than normal concerning scientific matters. What was up? He wondered what "Beauregard" had to do with it? He had to sit down, no more pacing. Why doesn't one of them say something? He was starting to feel nervous again. Both the President and Adams sat quietly, waiting for him to proceed. Their eyes were squarely focused on Sheppard. Eric snapped back to the briefing, took a deep breath and continued. "I believe a manned mission to explore this new frontier should be given the highest priority by our space program. A launch within the next few years should be possible."

Sheppard rocked back and forth uneasily. There was complete silence in the room for about two, very long minutes. All he could think of was, 'Did I screw up? Did I say enough? Too much? Did I make myself clear?' The President and the General were each pondering the possibilities. Sheppard had definitely made himself clear.

General Adams broke the quiet by ruminating about military objectives. "A mission launched this quickly will need to be carried out as a military mission, in secret, and with—"

He was cut off by the President, "No, General, no. We will study our options for now." President John Franklin Stone was thinking about the possibilities. As he looked to the ceiling, this former college economics professor of a President from Iowa was also thinking about the problems such a mission would entail. Sheppard was squirming in his seat.

"What I meant was—"

"General, if you'll let me finish without putting everything into a military context," Eric glared at Adams.

"Let's not jump to conclusions about this being military or anything else. We haven't decided we're going anywhere, yet. It's options I need for now." This President had little interest in the military. He was forced by the times to tolerate them. As a matter of fact, Stone had little tolerance for much of what General Adams, or many of his military cohorts, said.

Unlike Dr. Sheppard, he realized that he was stuck with the General, for political as well as *realpolitik* reasons. And the military advice Adams had given this President had been good counsel in spite of Stone's fundamental anti-military feelings. It wasn't so much what he said, but the way he said it, that bothered Stone. This General was one tough soldier.

A grunt in 'Nam at seventeen, having lied about his age, Adams was the first foot soldier to advance to the position of Chairman, JCS. That's Chairman of the Joint Chiefs of Staff at the Pentagon, our nation's top soldier. Stops in Lebanon, Grenada, Panama and that nasty little conflict in 2013 off the coast of China helped make him a legend. And let's not forget the Congressional Medal of Honor to the former Colonel Adams in the Persian Gulf War. That didn't exactly slow his meteoric career. Now at 70, older than any other chairman, he was nearing the end of a long run. No lasting legacy to be remembered by the public. No Marshall Plan kind of fame. Only a career easily remembered by his military, a military he had served well. And the reverse. It had served him well, too, as a springboard not only for his talents, but also his ego.

Legacy was far from President Stone's mind. "Gentleman, I have a country to run and a planet we're all very familiar with. One with its fair share of ongoing problems. What I need from both of you is cooperation." Stone knew too well these two advisers were less than complimentary of the other. They radiated hostility. Their animosity was a distraction. Stone knew though, this habitable planet was a nice distraction. It allowed him to think about other worldly things for a time. An escape from the realities of a planet with too many problems and too few problem solvers. All Presidents find distractions. One can't deal with secular, domestic, and foreign crises for long without praying for a distraction.

Stone short-circuited his daydreaming and returned to his two advisers. Distraction or not, he needed input from both. "I'm appointing the two of you to head a task force to consider the possibilities. Things like how to choose appropriate team members, undertake their training and preparation in anticipation of a possible launch. Also the logistics of the mission. Not just who goes, but when. And is it technically feasible? We need more data on this moon before we can make any kind of an intelligent decision. I like the idea of flying off to another planet.

Hell, there's a congressman or two I'd like to send along."

A launch for what purpose? The President thought back to his early years and another challenge by another President, this one John Fitzgerald Kennedy, to land a man on the moon before the end of the decade. And land they did in 1969. Those were the "good ole days" of the space race. Back then, it was a race between the Soviets and the Americans that captured the world's attention. What he had in mind was another stretch of technology. An endeavor the world could get behind—like landing on the moon—but one each individual could dream about. Stone was thinking on a grander scale. This launch would have a different purpose. A more lasting legacy. Not General Adams' legacy, but mankind's. President John Franklin Stone envisioned just such a mission to explore this new habitable moon. "Gentlemen, your objective is to consider the options for permanently colonizing this place, not just a trip there and back," Stone ordered.

Sheppard and Adams were speechless. What did he mean by colonize?

"Colonize, Mr. President?" Sheppard finally sputtered.

"Colonize, Doctor. You know, stay there, forever. It's damned expensive to get people there and back. Think of how this will captivate the imagination of the world. Think big, boys. Think of the possibilities." The President was gazing upward, reflecting not on Earth but the heavens. His mind was absorbed with the possibilities.

Adams and Sheppard were considering more than mere celestial possibilities. Was Stone serious? Had he thought about this, or was this just a fantasy. Their minds were racing, too. Racing through the staggering task of organizing such a mission. As the two advisers tentatively began questioning the President on various points, the meeting was interrupted by the National Security Adviser, C. Trumball Williams.

His daily appointment was now and Williams seemed agitated. He interrupted the science meeting in progress, whispering to the President. "The Taiwanese and the Chinese are at it again," Williams murmured. "I have to talk to you about the hostilities in the Straits of Taiwan." The Taiwanese were increasingly hostile since the People's Republic of China reneged on its promise of a free Hong Kong after it reunited the colony with the rest of the mainland on July 1, 1997. And of course, Williams wanted to discuss the Secretary of State's impending Middle East trip and the President's upcoming NSA weekly meeting. Williams paid little attention to Adams or Sheppard. "Now, Mr. President," he insisted.

"In a minute, Trump," Stone responded to his National Security Adviser. He'd known "Trump"—as everyone called him—since his days in the Senate. So much for the "distraction" Stone groused to himself.

"General Adams. Doctor Sheppard. We'll meet in two weeks for a report on your progress. Let's burn some midnight oil preparing some contingencies. Colonize, gentlemen. Colonize," the President stated again for emphasis. Two weeks until he could think about something Utopian. Two weeks until he could talk about the future. Two weeks until he could hear about a "Brave New World."

The walk from the White House to Sheppard's office in the old Executive Office Building is short. But as Sheppard and Adams walked the distance to his office, all the science adviser could think about was how long a distance those few short feet were. Long, when one is enduring the blow torch rhetoric of his new task force partner. General Adams was pontificating about one of his issues, leadership. "The first member of any team must be the leader," he insisted. "The other team members fall into place around a strong leader. I remember back in—"

"You are kidding, aren't you?" Sheppard rolled his eyes in strong disagreement. He was full of disdain for

Adams. It went back several years, not really over a single incident; it was about the man's attitude in general. An attitude of superiority Eric thought was undeserved. Arrogance and impertinence. Where did this superiority complex come from? In his opinion, this general made it into the gene pool while the lifeguard wasn't watching. Just because Adams was a general didn't make him a good leader. He challenged him on leadership, quickly responding, "General, what is a leader anyhow? What is leadership? It isn't important who the leader is. What is important is why they lead. And on what basis. By what authority? Or whose? One is a leader by a continuing mandate from their constituents. Leadership is derivative, not anointed. That's why we don't elect politicians for life." His contempt for the military and Adams specifically was barely contained.

General Adams, of course, couldn't object more strenuously. "The military knows how to pick leaders. You do the grunt work right, you make Lieutenant. Then, you prove yourself on a little larger project and make Captain. Then, on up the ranks. Proving yourself at each step. Leadership is about getting the job done—and done right. That's why we don't hold elections for promotion. We reward success. We recognize getting the job done, not how you go about it. You rise through the ranks, with promotion being the reward for a job well done." Adams grunted, dismissing this *civilian* who knew nothing about leadership, command and control, duty, or mission.

Sheppard interrupted, "So when your colonel reaches the level at which he can't handle the job, you stop promoting him, leaving him in a position he's now proved he can't handle? Is that how you pick leaders, General? And what if a really good colonel comes along but doesn't get the job done because someone on his team above or below him fails? You stop promoting the guy because of somebody else's screw up? I think you pick a few winners that way, but you surround yourself with a group of people who've fallen by the wayside, unhappy, unsuccessful and not very well motivated.

"No, the leader will evolve from the team. It may be a changing leader, too. On the trip there one person may be in charge. After arrival, someone else. A team has experts in different fields recognized as a leader in their particular area of expertise, not just for the title. Before we even have a leader, we have to choose a team. And what type of team?" queried Sheppard.

"If the goal is to permanently colonize this place, then the team members must be capable of surviving without mother Earth. That means care placed in choosing the team members. What vocations, sex, race, disabilities? There are a host of criteria to be examined before a single member is chosen, and we've got multiple obstacles to overcome." Sheppard thought he knew the problems. He wasn't at all thrilled with having to pick this team using any input from this uniform, or any of his type.

"I say we stick to known astronauts first," Adams shot back. "They are mostly military. They have some experience with leadership and command. As for sex, are you worryin' about sex? We don't want a space version of 1960s with all that free love. We've got a bunch of good, red-blooded American men and women astronauts to choose from. Why are you talking about sex?"

"I didn't say sex, I said of different sexes. But let's talk about it. You're right. We've got American astronauts, who you believe wouldn't pair off or anything? Even on a two-year mission to a new moon where they would live for essentially forever?"

"Well," the General paused. "I guess it'd be alright if they had babies. As long as—"

"As long as they were good old, red-blooded American babies, General? Get real. Who says this is an

American mission anyway? What if the best engineer is from Holland?"

"The Dutch are okay by me. Just don't go turnin' the world over lookin' for every weird scientist with an axe to grind against the U.S." Adams was a Texan with a Texas-sized chip on his shoulder. It came long before his paranoia was worsened by his stints in the Persian Gulf and "the Straits." He was particularly peeved about the Chinese. "Look, Sheppard. I'm sure you've got your ideas about this whole thing. And you can be damned sure I've got mine. The thing is, I've got to keep control. There are lots of issues you don't know squat about. Like dealin' with Congress and the politics of this town."

"You said, 'I've' got to keep control'?" Eric asked. "Didn't you mean 'we've' got to keep control? And who decides? Not just the two of us. Who goes? Who makes the decision? General, those are issues we, not you, have to come to grips with. We've been handed a hornet's nest of problems, each choice fraught with controversy. So what do you say you and I try to get along?" Eric knew full well he was trying to convince himself as well as the General. "The initial top priorities for survival are food, water and shelter. That means we should concentrate on team members for those priorities first. And the logistics that go with them. Can we agree on that?"

Adams was reluctant to buy into anything this *civilian* said. He considered "civilian" a four-letter word. But he was enough of a pragmatist to realize the importance of the project. It was important to the President, his Commander in Chief. No matter whether Stone and Adams disagreed on certain issues, one thing was certain about this soldier. He was loyal without fault and knew who was boss. It wasn't a pencil pushin' bureaucrat of a scientific adviser to the President. It was the President.

"Yes, Doctor, I think we can both agree on détente in the interest of the mission." If his commander wanted him to work with the science boys on going to space, by God, that's what he would do. "You just remember one thing. This is about getting them there and getting them there safely. It's not about you and me. Hell, I can get along with you or anybody else. If I push, push back. If I piss you off, piss back, damn it. I'm really just a big wind bag full of.... Well, you know what I'm full of."

And so a general would become a diplomat and a scientist an ambassador. As they started down that road, both were still mindfully pursuing the mission options, each from his own perspective and in terms of his own interests. Détente may have "broken out all over" but Adams remembered Mikhail Gorbachev and Ronald Reagan jousting for position back in the 1980s. Reagan said, *"dovyeray, no provyeray,"*—trust, but verify. A little self-interested verification never hurt any project. And he was just the man to have all the G-2 intelligence on this amateur space jockey. He'd know Sheppard's every move before Eric knew. Before this novice made a move Adams would know he was going to make it. This was his ball game and Adams was the pitcher, catcher, manager and cleanup batter.

Eric sat studying his coerced, new partner. He could live with this warrior. That didn't mean he had to fight him. Know your antagonist. Learn his strengths and his weaknesses. Exploit both. Sheppard was no military expert. But he did know people. He wasn't appointed by the President because he didn't get things done. He was appointed because he did. And if that meant working with the Pentagon, then so be it. Besides, he had a staff, too. Maybe they hadn't played the game as long as Adams, but Eric and his staff were fast learners. And they were smart. This science stuff was their ball game and Eric was the quarterback, wide receiver, punter and coach. He also knew when and how to play defense. He knew the rules and what it would take to play by them and when to bend them a little.

What was coming was not a war of the worlds but a clash of two giant egos over that new world. The two grudgingly agreed to divide the project into several arenas. Sheppard would begin working on potential team members while Adams concentrated on the logistics of the launch and mission. This seemed to fit both men's personalities, interests, and spheres of influence. After all, the military would probably be responsible for the actual launch. This would allow Adams to "lead" the Pentagon types planning the project. Sheppard could control the personnel by his initial choices, even if Adams had some role in the final cut. As they adjourned, they were both excited, albeit for different reasons. There might just be a bit of "legacy" in this for everybody.

III

As the scalpel laid open the subcutaneous fatty tissue below the skin, tiny bleeders bubbled to the surface and were just as quickly "zapped" and coagulated. C. Thomas Tatman, MD, did not come by his craft of the last twenty years without having seen it all. As a trauma surgeon, teacher, and pioneer in medicine, this was old hat. As a matter of fact, it was almost boring.

The only thing that kept him interested was knowing that a human being lay beneath the layers of drapes, instruments, monitors and noises. This was his arena, his center stage, his passion. Helping fix another person's broken parts is the mechanical aspect of being a surgeon. Tatman was wanting more. More challenge, more than just a mechanic. More impact on that person's life, more impact on life itself. *Zzzzzttt!* the cauterizer stopped another group of bleeders as he divided the muscle layers of the abdomen lying between the *linea alba*, the white line signifying the midline of the abdominal wall, opening it deeper and deeper. No, what he wanted was to branch out—a bigger role.

The intercom crackled to life, the circulating nurse startled out of a boredom that only years of routine can create. "Dr. Tatman, there's somebody named Bone or Rhome, or something on line three. He's calling from Washington. You know, in D.C., something about from the house, or something I didn't understand. I don't know. Says he's got to talk to you immediately—I know you're busy with your case, so I took a message. Now I've misplaced his number...sorry. Do you know him? 'Cuz you probably oughta call him back."

C.T. held his fire, having dealt with this kind of thing on almost a daily basis. But a house...and in Washington, D.C. ...*Naw*, he thought. *She couldn't mean the White House. I don't know anybody at the White House.*

"Try calling Washington, D.C. information and getting me a number, Janet," hoping against hope she wouldn't lose her way to the phone or lose the number if she was successful.

The peritoneum entered, the organs of the abdomen almost spilled out into the field. This pouch held his patient's abdominal organs, as well as his patient's problem today. Because, without even being a surgeon, anyone could see that the mass protruding from the anterior surface of the liver was not normal. Nor were the smaller, but just as abnormal, lesions surrounding the larger one. Why hadn't it been seen on all the high tech tests this poor soul was subjected to before suffering the ultimate indignity of having his belly slashed open? If it had been discovered to be this advanced, we could have sent in the microscopic engines to destroy what it could of the tumor with chemotherapy delivered directly to the tumor, he grumbled. He was angry, disappointed, and dissatisfied.

"Take it off, damn it," he muttered impatiently. He lifted his shoulder to help shrug off the virtual retinal display cradled on his head just as the circulating nurse reached for it, a combination of frustration and exasperation. All this high tech equipment wouldn't change the outcome, including this or any other display. The VRD, or virtual retinal display, projected the patient's MRI into this surgeon's eyes allowing him to superimpose those images on the surgical field. Since this tumor had eluded detection by technology, no display, gamma knife, CT scan, or MRI would change the consequences of his findings.

No, this wasn't normal, but it wasn't the primary site of the tumor either. He'd seen it all before. A grade IV colon cancer with liver metastases. Meaning that this tumor had already spread widely, to the liver. Chemotherapy would buy his patient six to twelve months statistically. Even the newest tumor markers, interferons and tumor vaccines wouldn't be sufficient. The microscopic kamikaze engines would deliver their lethal payload to the site of the tumor's spread, but even that wouldn't change the outcome by much. Technology had progressed so far—or had it? Surely there was more to life then this, he thought. How frustrating to not be able to impact the world on a grander scale. This was one patient, one life, one tumor. Important to the patient and his family, but what wide-ranging impact? None. What about influencing all of civilization?

Locating the primary colon tumor, he excised the right portion of the colon containing the tumor and biopsied the liver so the "poisoners" from chemotherapy would be able to tissue type and analyze the tumor. He allowed his resident to close as he scrubbed out of the case to try and find Janet. Now he was frustrated about the patient and more. Frustrated and angry about life in general, but still curious about the call. *Bone or Rhome, huh...a house, huh? I don't know anyone, anything about, anybody who....*What was this all about, anyway?

"If it's the White House, either I'm in big trouble or this is something strange. Bet it's about the IRS problem I had a few years ago," he muttered under his breath. Locating the scrap piece of paper with a telephone number Janet miraculously found, he gambled and called. The number looked official enough. One with lots of zeros at the end. "This is WHO?" Tatman instinctively stood. "Yes, Mister President, I'll hold." That's *STONE*, Janet, not Rhome or Bone. *STONE.* He burned. As in, *President Stone*, the head of our government. The man. The big fish. The man in charge of all things that could make or break his life. This wasn't about the IRS.

President Stone returned to the phone and continued, "Doctor, I'd like you to talk to my science adviser, Dr. Sheppard, about something very important to both of us, to our country. To the world, for that matter. Dr. Sheppard...."

The other end of the phone was soon buzzing with questions. What was his schedule over the next few days? Could he come to Washington? It was the last question, an open-ended one, that caught Tatman off guard.

"Am I interested in *WHAT?*" the surgeon shouted into the phone in disbelief. "Could you say that again? Am I interested in going to work one day and never coming home again—all for the good of mankind? Doctor, you'd better explain what the hell you mean before I hang up!" It was a good thing the President wasn't on the phone then, or maybe that IRS thing might have been reopened.

So began Dr. Tatman's introduction to Dr. Eric Sheppard. Less than six hours later he found himself on an airplane taking a red-eye to D.C., either to hear a better explanation or to break someone's neck. Who cares if the ticket's paid for by the government. What's all this about the "good of mankind"? He had to admit, he was more than a little curious. This appealed to that part of him that was admittedly bored. Maybe he'd get to actually meet the President of the United States.

Tatman was fairly apolitical. He couldn't even remember whether he'd voted for Stone. Probably didn't vote at all. Most likely, he was doing a case or two that day. Still, it isn't just anybody who talks to the President. He could get used to that. Maybe become a presidential adviser, or something, himself. Who knows what Washington held for the future. Even if this guy, Sheppard, was a typical bureaucrat—government-type nut case—being flown to Washington for consultation at the White House would make for a good "sit around the bar" story.

Ever since growing up in Estherwood, Louisiana, Clarence Thomas Tatman, C.T. to his friends, C. Thomas to his profession, Tommy to his family, *anything but Clarence*, had dreamed of getting out of that small town.

Little did he know just how far out he'd actually get. Try Harvard Medical School, sent there because of Vietnam. Growing up in the '60s, he hated that war. For that matter, he hated all war. He even became a bit of a pacifist. But it was war that brought him to Boston. During the late 1960s and early 1970s, as part of the military preparedness for Vietnam, a program for financing and choosing the military's doctors was put in place. In place, even in the 1980s, when he was ready to matriculate to a university of higher learning in pursuit of a medical career. Ironic, because not only did he hate that war, but he was an active protestor at Louisiana State Normal College. That's where his academic career started, at a "normal" college, or what is now called a teacher's college. God knows Tatman was never normal.

Coming from Estherwood, no one, not even his parents, thought of him as normal. Estherwood wasn't a one stoplight town. It was a *no stoplight* town until "Joe Bob" Thibodeaux ran for mayor. "Joe Bob" was the high school janitor until he hit upon his new career as a politician. His "platform" was bringing a stoplight to Estherwood. He figured if the truckers off the interstate stopped at the stoplight, then greater commerce would ensue. And so it did, at least until the first trucker came barrelin' through and encountered the new stoplight, then in the red position. The trucker being unfamiliar with the situation, slammed on his brakes, locking up the entire eighteen wheels, causing one hell of an accident. Joe Bob was recalled by acclamation the next day. Yeah, that was the kind of town C. Thomas grew up in…and from which he wanted to escape. He was destined for bigger and better things, or so he thought.

He damn near didn't make it out of high school because of the Frugé twins. They were dirt poor, but that didn't stop them from thinking they owed each of their classmates a graduation present. So they drifted over to the next backwater town and robbed the local jewelry store of its finest graduation-type gifts for their nine fellow graduates. Unfortunately, the state police also attended the ceremony, confiscating not only the gifts but the "giftees" as well. So, C.T. had to enroll at Louisiana State Normal College—sans graduation gift but at least a free man.

After drinkin' up most of the experimental alcohol as "lab projects," lo and behold, the United States military enlisted his services in the war effort. Unfortunately for them, and lucky for him, the war he despised was over, but not the program transferring him to Harvard at their expense, although expense is a relative term. There he helped the dean of the medical school learn about drinking too much and tattoos. Seems that medical school graduation was just around the corner. Another graduation, another fiasco. To celebrate, C.T. and a few friends invited the dean to accompany them on what they called a Cajun pub crawl, so named in honor of Tatman's academic and non-academic achievements during his tenure in Boston.

Unfortunately, they crawled right on up to a tattoo parlor next door to one of the many establishments frequented that night. Apparently graduation was a dangerous time in C.T.'s life, what with the twins incident, and now, the dean. Just as the dean was about to sport a new tattoo on his otherwise balding frontal scalp, the local gendarmes arrived to prevent what surely would have altered his medical career. Through it all, he managed to do well enough in the more traditional aspects of his training to land a surgical residency back in more familiar territory at New Orleans' world famous Charity Hospital. His exploits, and the damage left in their wake, went on throughout the next five years. Slowly, r-e-a-l-l-y slowly, he came around to a greater calling and began taking the lifesaving thing pretty seriously. He became an accomplished surgeon and a well-rounded human being to boot.

Now he was bored and looking for that old thrill again, and on a flight to our nation's capital. The thrill of a challenge, the thrill of doing something new and unique. Picking up and leaving wasn't a problem since he currently was unattached, having gone through his fair share of the fairer sex. None of them seemed to appreciate his view of the world or his life and their apparent lack of a significant role in it. So being rather able to pick up and go anywhere only required getting a partner to cover his patients for the weekend, an easy task, as that's what junior partners are for, he thought.

Washington can be intimidating and awesome, especially for anyone with a sense of patriotism. All the monuments, memorials and other historic sites. Throw in traffic circles designed to confuse and that premise is exacerbated. Tatman rented a car at National airport, renovated in the late 1990s to more comfortably accommodate passengers in our nation's capital. He rented one of the many generic cars available. With all the auto mergers of the early 2000s, cars all looked the same to him. They pretty much were all the same.

The beginning fuel revolution, now in its infancy, precipitated the mergers. Manufacturers needed to unite in order to afford the massive capital outlays required for conversion of their industry. Conversion from fossil fuels to fuel cells, energy efficient, clean, and environmentally benign. But very expensive to engineer and produce. The infrastructure of fuel delivery made their initial introduction problematic. With gasoline, there was a century old network of fueling stations offering the whole gamut of gasolines on almost every street corner.

Right now, Tatman could care less what fuel cars ran on. It was navigating the Washington streets which currently confused him. He was resisting use of the on-board guidance computer. Maybe it was male ego, but he believed he should be able to drive to his hotel, not be guided there. He had never figured Washington out, even though he'd been there many times. Maybe it was the traffic circles. Nothing seemed to ever get anywhere. All the streets seemed to go in diagonals or circles. All he wanted to do was go from point A to point B, a nice straight line. Not in Washington. He had to convert his surgical way of doing things, the quickest way to go between two points is a straight line, to a round about way. Convert to diagonals and circles, in other words.

Converting the oil companies from fossil to electricity generated by fuel cells was a hard sell. These companies were used to gas. They had lived with it for over a hundred years. They knew how to explore for it, drill for it, refine it, and market it. They had to be dragged, kicking and screaming, into the twenty-first century with its twenty-first century technologies. But even the most shortsighted oil companies now saw the future. And it wasn't fossil fuels. They were too polluting, expensive and finite. No, electricity was the future. But they fought it and would continue to resist total capitulation as long as there were oil thirsty consumers. It would be a long conversion process. The United States, as with most new technologies, would lead. Others would eventually follow, but over decades, not a few years.

Arriving at the Washington Hilton at six a.m. allowed him enough time to clean up and take a "Beta Bath" as he recalled from his college days. A little deodorant under each arm and a splash of bad cologne. No wonder the Beta's never had dates. Since this wasn't a date, he took a bit more time and actually jumped into the shower this morning. No, it wasn't a date. It was a meeting near the White House...at eight a.m. Eight in the morning and no sleep. Sounds like the good old days. At fifty-eight I'm getting too old for this, he thought. A fresh shirt, underwear, and a suit later and he was ready for the big time. Running on adrenaline was *no problema* for this *hombre*.

Finding the Hilton hadn't been too big a problem at six a.m. An hour or so later, as he started to leave for Sheppard's office during morning rush hour, the situation was different. Rather than deal with maps and one-way streets and the other idiosyncrasies of driving in a strange city,   this time he chose to engage the on-board traffic computer for guidance. Guidance and peace of mind. With the help of geostationary satellites and built-in sensors in vehicles, Tatman could punch in his destination's coordinates and the car would take him there with almost no additional human input. No problems with traffic circles this trip. Spacing, velocity and route would all be handled for him, freeing him to look around and wonder about the upcoming meeting. The immediate task was inputting those all important coordinates. As he fumbled through the list of "Washington Destinations" in the online menu, trying to locate the Old Executive Office Building, he wondered how he had been able to see anything on his previous trips to DC. Especially on his first trip. That occasion was his honeymoon back in the 1980s.

Now that was a time to come to Washington. After Vietnam, Watergate, the oil crises, and medical school, but before his residency, he had taken the plunge with his high school sweetheart from Estherwood. It was "Morning in America." Reagan was in the White House and the country was rediscovering faith in itself. The West was on the threshold of defeating communism. A victory for which we took complete credit, in spite of the reality that included many other factors. There was a rebirth of optimism unbridled by reality. It was a time of infinite possibilities before the mood was spoiled by global realities.

Realities such as Iraq and Kuwait in 1991 and again ten years or so later. Budget limitations and limitations in projecting our power. We hadn't yet learned we couldn't fix everything broken. We spent too much, bragged too much, indulged in excess, and thought too little about commitment. Commitment to each other, to the future, or to anybody other than ourselves. It was the time of the "me" generation and of self-indulgence. This surgeon-to-be wasn't immune from the extravagances of the decade. He, too, bought into the fantasy of superficial love. Although they had nothing in common, other than knowing and dating each other in high school, C.T. married. It seemed like the right time. After college and medical school, before his surgical residency. Unfortunately, the timing was right, but the other details weren't.

Medical school forces you to grow up, not necessarily to mature. It's impossible to confront issues of life and death without having to define those issues within. If you don't, you are consumed. How many doctors are there who should never have made it through medical school? C.T. was convinced their problem was an inability to internally resolve those issues. Since they hadn't answered the questions within, they were incapable of helping others with similar issues. They completed the course work but, ultimately, were failures as physicians, as healers. Well, he'd learned about all the life and death questions and had resolved them within. He was confident and self-assured. That's probably what also gave him the surgeon's swagger. Resolution and living in the self-centered 1980s certainly was compatible with his hell-raising lifestyle. Although it was for the wrong reasons, he married a truly sweet high school darling, Marissa Thornton. Married her, ignored her, and left her to grow up on her own. Medical school forces you to deal with issues. Marriage doesn't. It should, but it doesn't force you to. So Marissa grew, too. But in a different direction from her high school paramour. They never fought. They didn't have enough in common to fight about. After three years, C.T. decided the only mature thing to do was to split up. He explained to an incredulous Marissa, that he wanted a divorce now, while he still liked and loved her in his own way. He would not wait for some trivial event to precipitate what he saw as the inevitable.

He dedicated himself to his career, not unlike many others of his generation. His practice prospered, even in the face of the overindulgences of "managed care." This was the medical economics lesson of the 1990s and early 2000s. A lesson taught to physicians and administrators by Wall Street and business. What business didn't appreciate was that consumers wouldn't get particularly exercised by a faulty widget. But mess with their health and a public relations fiasco ensued. People wanted all the health care someone else was willing to pay for. Wall Street wasn't going to pay for Rolls Royce medicine and citizens weren't going to accept a Chevrolet. What evolved was an uneasy compromise between government, the public and insurers. Evolved over ten years or so with lots of starts and stops along the way, now in the late-2010s, the pendulum was swinging back toward more physician and patient control. Good doctors will always do well if allowed to practice good medicine. And C. Thomas Tatman was doing well.

While medicine was his vocation, medical politics became his avocation. He held an adjunct professorship at the local branch of his state's medical school. He was an integral part of Louisiana's medical establishment—a past president of the State Medical Society and, nationally, on the board of the American College of Surgeons. He wasn't sure what this guy Sheppard was talking about, but it probably involved a move up the prestige ladder. Maybe a government position, like say, Surgeon General. No, they basically outlawed that after Clinton's problems finding anybody capable or willing to serve. Besides, as tough as some jobs were in Washington, at least you came home sometime. What was with this "never come home" line they'd given him, anyway?

His vehicle stopped in the passenger discharge lane at the Old Executive Office Building. No more speculating. It was time to find out what this was all about. Prior to exiting, he punched in his retrieval code. This would allow him to signal the car to return and pick him up. God, I love technology, he thought. Exiting the vehicle on the left and climbing the stairs to the lobby took less than five minutes. He was directed to a third floor office. After entering the outer office, he was led into the inner office of the presidential science adviser, Dr. Eric Sheppard.

It was a large room, crammed with books, computer printouts, and charts strewn on every bookshelf and covering most of the floor. Tatman studied Sheppard, who was talking on two telephones. One was audio only, the other a videophone. Sheppard was mid-50s, he speculated, graying and distinguished. He looked like a science adviser. Probably six feet tall, but hard to tell while sitting. Clearly he didn't exercise enough, a sure sign of the Washington work syndrome. Looked a bit like Carl Sagan, Tatman thought, with pudgy face, heavy eyebrows and a constant energy about him.

Tatman didn't realize that Eric was summing up his guest, too. Even though he was on two phones, that meant only one eye and one ear were occupied. With his right eye he evaluated his visitor. A perpetual motion machine, thought Sheppard. Typical surgeon. Thick brown hair with tinges of gray at the temples. Reminded him a little of an old tennis player, Jimmy Connors, from the 1980s. His steel-blue eyes stole focus from the early bulge at the waist. He didn't really look fifty-eight even though Eric knew that was his age from his bio. Athletic, in some ways like a jungle animal. Muscles always tight, ready to pounce, never still, with eyes constantly moving. Studying, evaluating, planning. They were alike in more ways than one, though Eric had a few years on him.

He soon ended both calls. "I'm Eric Sheppard. I'm sorry to have sounded so vague on the telephone yesterday. There's a tinge of secrecy to what we were talking about. I hope you understand."

"I understand the vagueness. But not what we're discussing, Doctor. Let me be blunt. Why am I here?"

"Spoken like a true surgeon, Dr. Tatman. I expected nothing less. You have every right to know what this is about. But I must warn you, some of what I tell you is sensitive. For now, it mustn't leave this room."

"I understand." Tatman responded with less animus. It appeared he wasn't going to be the Surgeon General. "Look, Dr. Sheppard—"

"Call me Eric. Do you mind if I call you Clarence?"

"Yes, I mean, no...how about C.T.? Don't ever use the name Clarence even on one of your secure phones. Please."

"I've got a few names I don't like, myself," Sheppard laughed. "I know this was sudden. And you're mad about our initial phone introduction. I'm still learning how to do this thing, too. It's new to me, also."

"So what's this about, Eric? Are you sending me away, you know, up the river? Did I do something the government wants to thank me for or do they want to shoot me?"

"Neither, actually. Although that 'send away' comment isn't completely off target. What do you know about 'Genesis', C.T.?"

"Never heard of it."

"I didn't think so." Sheppard began running down the proposed mission. He updated Tatman on the known specifics of the moon and the tentative mission. He could see his guest beginning to fidget in his chair.

"Geez, Eric. Why me? What if—"

"You're it because I've studied your style. You come highly recommended. You like being challenged by problems and are obsessed with finding their solution. You've got more energy than most. Look at you. You can't even sit still. You're a doer. We both know there are two kinds of people in medicine. Those who make errors of commission and those who make errors of omission. I can't tolerate someone sitting around wringing their hands while the opportunity for resolving the problem slips away. You know, the internist approach to medicine. They'll think about an answer until the patient's in the grave. This mission can't tolerate it either. We need a physician of action. Sure, you'll make mistakes. Errors of commission. But you'll be working hard on the solution and you hate failure. You're also a control freak. You have to be in control."

"You think you've got me pegged pretty well, don't you." There was a long pause. Quiet, but still Tatman was in motion, pacing across the carpet. "Well...you're right."

"And you're bored. We talked to several of your colleagues and one thing was clear in all their statements. You're frustrated. Bored and dying for a challenge. Well, brother, I've handed you the biggest challenge of your life, or anybody else's. You have three primary priorities. First, to maintain the health and welfare of the team. It's to be a small, highly integrated team. There's no room for backup members."

"But the law of averages says somebody will get sick, Eric," countered Tatman.

"True enough, C.T. Your job is to make them survive. Survive long enough to complete your second priority."

"Which is?"

"Training other team members. This trip is going to take some time. During travel to this moon, everyone will begin cross training in areas outside their expertise. It'll take the better part of two years to get there."

"But Eric, medical school is four years with residency after that. And medical students are concentrating on nothing other than medicine. Not engineering or tap dancing or whatever."

"C.T., you can't tell me you were totally committed to medicine while in school. Hell, you were in your 20s. Nobody ignores their hormones in their 20s. Least of all you, from what I've heard. I found time for other things during medical school."

"Okay, so let's say I need to operate on someone in the first three months. What then? And what do you mean 'I came highly recommended'?"

"You'll have more on-board, high tech stuff than you can even dream about. It's a challenge, C.T. But you're up to it. I won't tell you who, but several associates gave you a thumb's up. Both in Louisiana and nationally. Actually, several from overseas, too."

"So what about number three. You said I'd have three top priorities. What's the third?"

"To help train the next generation. The offspring of the mission."

"You mean we're taking little ankle biters on this trip? Hell, I hate the little rug rats. I've got—"

"You've got nothing to worry about now. What? No pediatric patients in your practice, Tatman? Relax. There are no children going. But there will be kids after arrival."

"What'd ya mean, no kids going? How will they, when will they...I don't get it."

"Trust me. Your third priority is way down the road." Eric wasn't going to tell him they hadn't figured out the specifics of what he just alluded to. "Some details have to wait for the future. C.T., this is a work in progress. You'll have a lot of input about how it evolves. From your background check, you don't currently have any significant others?"

"You've got my bio, Eric. You probably know more about me than I do. Look, I'm the kind of guy who can't sit still, remember? I'm constantly finding new things that interest me. Medicine is my true love. Not just the practice of it, but the politics of it, the social interaction. Everything. What woman wants to always be second fiddle? Everyone I've ever met wants to be first chair. I don't blame them."

"Maybe you'll find more on Genesis," Eric suggested to his medical ally. "I'm beginning to mellow. I used to be the same way. Governmental medicine and policy was my life. I'm starting to look for more now. Maybe it's because I'm a little older than you."

"Is that why you're not going, Eric?"

"I've never really thought that was an option." Sheppard hadn't ever considered it until Tatman asked. "No, I think I'm ready to settle down here. Find someone to curl up next to on a deserted island somewhere."

"You'd get bored," Tatman countered.

"No, C.T., you'd get bored."

Just then the door flew open and a man in his early fifties strode through followed by an entourage of about 10 people. He had a warm smile and an extended hand, "I'm John Stone, Dr. Tatman. We're glad you could make it to Washington," shaking C.T.'s hand firmly. "I'm sure Dr. Sheppard has briefed you on the specifics you'll need to help make your decision. Is there anything I can do to make your decision easier, Doctor?"

"Mr. President, you did, just coming by. Thank you, sir," Tatman grinned, standing quickly.

"Sit down, please. By the way, Doctor. There's no IRS on Genesis." The President knew more about him than C.T. had expected. "We'll just talk to the folks over there about you not filing for, say, the next thirty or forty years. Does that sound about right?"

"Yes, sir. That would be fine," an embarrassed Tatman answered.

"I consider this mission to be of paramount importance to our country. The world, for that matter. A seminal event in our history. What an opportunity. Do you have a sense of history, Doctor?" asked the President.

"Can anyone not, given the magnitude of the event? Dr. Sheppard and I were just discussing the details of this daunting responsibility. I'm not at all sure I'm worthy of your choice."

Eric couldn't believe the humility in the surgeon's voice. A first, he thought. A humble surgeon. "We believe you are our physician, Dr. Tatman."

"Yes, Doctor. You are our physician," echoed the President.

"If you don't mind my asking, Mr. President," C.T. asked in a hushed voice not typical of his style.

"Of course, Doctor."

"Would you go, Mr. President. Would you go, if you could, sir?"

IV

Make your briefing long on detail and short on opinions, Colonel." So commanded General Adams to this anonymous associate, one of many a Colonel whose career advancement depended on attention to detail during frequent briefings similar to today's. This one was for the benefit of the Chairman of the Joint Chiefs of Staff, and some other uniforms with stars, brass he didn't recognize. Three generals, and an admiral, so this briefing had better be a great one. He didn't have the luxury of introducing himself to the four, though he wanted at least to know who the female general was. There was a fifth uniform in the room that didn't seem to fit even though he wore a Colonel's eagle, too. This guy seemed too relaxed, too informal.

Knowing how to press their subordinates to do the legwork and one's own presentation skills breaks many a wannabe general. But not today's briefing Colonel. General Adams had picked him to brief this select group and he wasn't leaving anything to chance. He'd cajoled, bullied and stroked his staff of sergeants, majors, captains and lieutenant colonels over the last few weeks and he was ready. Bring on the stars, boys, thought this Pentagon prognosticator.

As the lights were lowered, the first computer-projected image appeared on the screen in front of each member of his audience.

"Today's presentation will be divided into several components, the first of which is background. Our *Challenger II* spacecraft traveled 483.6 million miles in just a little more than a year, at an average speed of roughly 40,000 miles per hour, and now maintains Jovian orbit about 112,000 miles above the planet—approximately the same distance from Jupiter as the moons Amalthea and Thebe. The largest Jovian moon, Ganymede, discovered in 1610 by Galileo, orbits at approximately 665,000 miles from the center of Jupiter. The German astronomer, Simon Mayr, also lays claim to the discovery of Ganymede and gave the moon its name. Ganymede has a diameter at its equator of 3,270 miles and orbits Jupiter in just over one week. It has an icy surface and a rock core approximately twice the density of water. However, it is a satellite of Ganymede that is the subject of today's briefing.

"*Genesis*, as the new satellite is called, is considerably smaller than Earth, yet has a slightly greater mass. Although smaller, its increased mass corrects for what would appear to be too small a diameter. This allows for an atmosphere similar to Earth's. Small planets cannot retain an atmosphere, like many of the other Jovian moons. Without an atmosphere, no planet can sustain human life without artificial means, an example being our current moon station. Bodies too large become gaseous, like Jupiter itself.

"Genesis orbits Ganymede at a very slow speed. This sluggish and unusual orbit allowed it to remain unrecognized, hidden from our scans while essentially in the shadows of Ganymede. *We weren't looking for a moon of a moon.* Interferometry and photometric astronomy on board this latest probe allowed us to discriminate its form from Ganymede. Frankly, General, the folks at JPL were so focused on Europa, no one paid much attention to Ganymede. Scientists knew Ganymede couldn't sustain life and quickly turned their curiosity to the other satellites. The long orbit of Genesis also carries it away from the Sun and the Earth's view for a 274-day period. Then, during its temperate period, it is bathed in reflective radiation and the Sun's heat for 273 days. Thus, a 'year' of 547 days. The surface of Genesis is mineral and organic. Its atmosphere is slightly less dense at 0.89 times that of Earth's. So one's daily walk would carry a lighter step, making bipedal travel easier."

"Sounds to me like this place is life compatible," came an anonymous voice from the audience. "If we can live there, Colonel, why can't someone or something else? Have you thought about the possibility of life already existing there?"

"Well, while that is a consideration, no signs of life have been found by our scanners. Certainly, there isn't complex, sentient life. It would be primitive, microbial life. And—"

"Primitive...but life just the same, Colonel," interrupted Adams. "Right?...Think about what that would do to the philosophers and kings?...Continue your briefing, Colonel."

"Yes, sir. There is water on Genesis, although its abundance is not clearly known. However, Ganymede and other Jovian moons have large supplies of water in the form of ice. Because energy is reflective from Jupiter and Ganymede, harmful radiation received is minimal during the climate period but markedly elevated during the inclement time. The radiation dangers are similar to those expected after thermonuclear war but, unlike war, are predictable and last a finite time. Winds can be hurricane force during the winter but tropical and mild during the summer. In short, there are two definite seasons, the winter being inclement and inhospitable and the summer with mild earth-like living conditions."

"So why is its mass so much denser, Colonel?"

"We don't know at this point, General Adams. It is currently under review, sir." He paused while Adams muttered something under his breath to one of the other audience members.

"So is it habitable during the winter period?"

"Survivable is more accurate. With environmental suits the crew could operate in the winter environment for extended periods, say weeks to months. They would need shelter from the elements."

"In order to maximize that first summer, they'll need to land at the end of winter," came this assessment from another anonymous voice from the dark.

"That means training the team in survival techniques. Right up your alley, Jack," again from a voice not seen.

"They'll need survival training anyway. It's a long trip from here to there. Lots of time for something to break."

"Who are these people anyway? You're not in on this are you Leahy?" The six briefing beneficiaries began discussing among themselves. Finally, a soft, female voice asked, "B.C., are you picking this team?"

"Let's just say I've got operational control, Anne," Adams grunted. "There are some science types doing the screening right now. The President wants the civilians to have a role in this thing."

"I don't know, B.C. What the hell do they know about space?" The room broke into more undecipherable debate until Adams signaled to the Colonel to continue.

"Unless there are additional questions, I will divide the remaining time into the logistics of getting a team to Genesis, supplies for the journey, initial 'winter' arrival logistics and priorities after arrival". General Adams grunted his approval.

"As you know, for several years we have had in place a long-term mission to the moon, primarily for geological purposes. A similar life support module would be modified for the Genesis mission. We already have one, built initially to be deployed as a second base on the moon. This is currently undergoing the appropriate modifications. Also, a mock-up of that module is available for training right now. Getting the module into Earth orbit is nothing new. We've done it twice for the moon missions.

"A modified Titan VI rocket would be the launch vehicle. An offspring of our long line of Titan missiles, the Titan VI has five first-stage engines each developing thrust of 300,000 pounds—a total of 1,500,000 pounds of thrust. This would carry the mission into Earth orbit where a much smaller energy source would suffice. Additional missions to orbit other components is also anticipated. These would take the personnel to the orbiting long-range transport vehicle.

"The actual journey to Genesis would begin from Earth orbit. The Titan VI engines would need to be modified for additional lift rather than traditional storable aerozine-50 and nitrogen-oxygen propellants. Long range fuel would be at issue. For the journey to Genesis, a nuclear power plant would offer the advantages of more thrust, lighter and more efficient fuel, much greater range and essentially infinite burn time. This degree of thrust is more than capable of propelling a large, long-distance expedition. We can't go nuclear in our atmosphere because of the risk. Once in orbit, the downside is extraterrestrial or space contamination in the event of an accident, that is, a nuclear accident in space. Three Mile Island goes to Jupiter!"

"Colonel," cautioned Adams, "the facts, not comedy". As the briefing droned on Adams drifted off to a "briefing'"of his own. He remembered Galileo. But not the same one the Colonel was talking about. The Galileo he remembered was a three-fingered drifter of a cowboy in his hometown of Buford, Texas. Man, that boy could ride. Unfortunately, "could" was the operative word, not "can" since two of his fingers went west when a horse went east a few years back. That precipitated a rather abrupt career change from rodeo-rider to philosopher-drunk. That cowboy taught young B.C. a lot, some by good example, some by bad. Beauregard Calhoun Adams was a whiney little piece of bully bait until Juan Galileo showed him how to stand up for himself. Gal was living out his fantasies through his newfound associate. It seems the Adams family thought B.C. had fallen out of the family tree. They didn't pay much attention to him. Galileo did.

Sometimes, though, he stood up and acted tough when he didn't need to, the downside of "the Gal's" instruction. The tough guy image had served him well in the military, but B.C. was struggling to let his softer side be seen, a hard sell in the Army. *Damn it, I have feelings, I care!*, he burned. That had always been the problem. He burned. He burned with passion, burned with patriotism, just burned in general, until he WAS a general. Now he wanted it to be somebody else's fire.

"What about transportation from orbit around Genesis to the surface, Colonel?" Adams could reminisce and pay attention to the briefing at the same time.

In stationary orbit 22,300 miles above the Earth, a KH-17 satellite zeroed in on the western Pacific Ocean. Deep within Cheyenne Mountain, four miles outside of Colorado Springs, Colorado, at the headquarters of the North American Aerospace Defense Command—NORAD—a diligent Air Force major was startled out of the monotony of staring at his monitoring console. Every three seconds a cool synthesized voice repeated the message. The message was anything but routine:

> ***Warning. Launch detected in the western Pacific.***
> ***Warning. Launch detected in the western Pacific.***

The major stiffened in his chair, swiveled to his left while talking into the phone covering his left ear, "Systems. I need authentication. Now!" As he spoke, a new message was being generated:

> ***Warning. Three additional launches detected***
> ***in the Gansu province of China.***

"Damn, that's one launch and three potential responses," the major muttered. "I need authentication now, Captain." He picked up another phone and placed it to his right ear; a few seconds later he was talking into it. "General Cummins, we have a launch of an SLBM 200 miles southeast of Shanghai, target unknown, source unknown, suspect Taiwanese. We have three, repeat, three counter ICBMs tracking from the mainland, target unknown, presumed to be Taiwan."

"Major, do you have authentication?"

"Yes, sir. Just now. On the one sea launch and the three land-based."

"Do we have subs in the area?"

"Only a *Los Angeles*-class attack sub one hundred miles east, sir."

"What the hell are they up to now?" Cummins wondered. "Alright, Major. Notify me of any targeting data. I'm calling Washington." With that, General Cummins, CINC-NORAD—commander in chief of NORAD— slammed one receiver down and immediately picked up another. This one was red and was immediately answered on the other end.

"General Adams here. What's up, Joe?"

"Four missiles, B.C. Sir, we are tracking one hostile sea launched missile apparently headed to mainland China and three retaliatory missiles from the mainland. Targets unknown at this time."

"God damn Chinese. Both of 'em. I'll notify the President. Joe, this is real, right? I don't wanna get the politician's shorts in a bunch over a computer glitch."

"It's real, sir."

Adams placed the phone back on its cradle and left the briefing for an inner office to call the President of the United States. It was his duty to notify him of this nuclear exchange. This was no bump in the road. It might signal nuclear world war. "Mr. President..." he began.

High school was a bump in the road on the way to Adams' underage enlistment in the Army. Vietnam actually appealed to this Texan of a rebel—he became a rebel with a cause. First Air Cavalry was his first assignment after basic training and infantry school. He couldn't wait to kill Cong. And kill he did. Land mines, bungee cord, and punji sticks couldn't stop this one man, commie-hating, wrecking crew. He even had cards made to put in the mouths of dead Viet Cong, propping open the teeth with cards that read:

Death From Above…
Kill 'em All, and Let God Sort 'em Out!
Compliments of B.C. Adams
First Air Cavalry
United States Army

Reckless was his middle name. And valor and bravery. But all good things come to an end. After several tours of duty in 'Nam, he was shipped state side, having already decided to make the Army his career and picking up a field commission as a second lieutenant during his last tour. By the time he arrived at Ft. Bragg, North Carolina, he was a legend, and not just in his own mind, being eyed for bigger and better things by his superiors.

"General Cummins, incoming SLBM, target is Shanghai, ETA to impact is three minutes. Three responses are inbound, target is confirmed to be Taiwan. All three have independent re-entry warheads and are beginning to separate. Target in four minutes. Hold that! General…"

There was an interminable pause that was, in reality, only eight seconds.

"The SLBM was just destroyed in space without nuclear detonation. Well I'll be…the bastards were just testing them."

"Major, what about the three Chinese ICBMs?"

"General, we have confirmation of their destruction, too. What do you make of that, sir?"

"I don't know, son. But that's not my idea of how to spend a night on the town." Cummins broke off his call with the major and called Adams. "General Adams, Cummins at NORAD. The damnedest thing just happened…"

"The re-entry vehicle had better be reusable, Colonel," came another shadowy audience participant. "Our space plane technology should be applicable."

"We're working on that, ma'am, and, yes, it will be reusable for multiple trips between the moon base and the circling mother ship."

"Tell us more about the actual flight module design." The colonel thought the question was from the one the group had called Leahy. Now he remembered who he was. He was Admiral Jeremy Leahy, former astronaut.

"Yes, Admiral," the colonel continued. "The module that goes up on the Titan will have several components. Power station, living quarters and work areas are the primary elements, along with the docking port and transport vehicle. There are provisions for backup systems for every major system."

"When you're a couple a million miles from Earth anything that breaks is major, Colonel. I've had some experience with space repairs. You're aware that none of the manned space hardware we've previously sent up has had a shelf life measurable in even months, let alone years? Better send along a lot of spare parts and someone trained in fabrication. You never know what you need until you need it."

"What about resupply?" came next from the dark.

"As to the durability of the vehicle, we've had hardware on the moon for over a year. With respect to resupply, we think there are several options here," the colonel continued. "First, there could be a dual launch roughly at the same time. One a supply vessel and the other carries the crew. Advantages are an escape opportunity in the event of trouble. Second, periodical unmanned resupply missions with supplies anticipated by Earth. The advantage is we can control the schedule. The obvious disadvantage of either plan is we don't know what they'll need. Third, we just wait until they get there to tell us what they need and send a customized shopping cart back to them. The downside here is the delay—the first resupply would probably not arrive earlier than their third or fourth year on Genesis."

Adams had slipped back into the briefing and picked up on the conversation as if he'd never left. He'd notified the President of the game of chicken carried out over the Pacific between the two Chinas. Now it was back to this space mission.

"I say go with a dual launch, B.C."

"Sure you do, Jack," Adams shot back. "You don't have to pay for it, do you? These are the kind of issues I need position papers on from you. Do you know what we're spending on these moon bases? It's not going to be easy to find a spare hundred billion dollars layin' around waitin' to be used for a mission to Jupiter." Adams was clearly unconvinced about the rationale for the entire operation. "Hell, it won't be my decision. I'll have input, but I can guaran-damn-tee the President will have some thoughts on it. And probably the civilians, too."

"The power station is nuclear?" queried another anonymous voice.

"Correct, sir. The plutonium fuel is being taken to the space station in small increments—small self-contained pellets for safety. That began even before this mission was conceived," the colonel added. "There is some interest from JPL in sending along a backup ion propulsion system."

"Now what the hell is that, Colonel?" rang out B.C.'s familiar voice.

"It's basically a solar powered engine, General. It was first used in 1998 on the Deep Space 1 mission. They're safe because nothing can explode and they're very efficient."

"But they aren't very fast, B.C." Leahy added. "The acceleration is from a steady stream of ions, usually xenon. They can accelerate to over 70,000 miles per hour. But it takes an eternity to get going."

"For backup, General," the colonel persisted. "They're only in case of catastrophic power failure."

"If there's a catastrophe, speed will be their least concern. Go on, Colonel." B.C. settling back into his chair and his fantasy again.

Adams had advanced quickly, primarily because his senior officers knew if they had a tough one, he was their man. He never said, "No," never hesitated, and rarely ever failed. If he had, he'd have been dead three or four times over. The military's War College is an elite training facility. Not only did he attend it, he placed first in his class and stayed on as faculty. Not bad for a high school semi-drop out. An instructor! Would his old high school teachers roll over in their graves if they saw him now? B.C. probably put a fair number of teachers in those graves during his teenage years. Yeah, he was being noticed by higher and higher-ups.

"Stand down the alert, Major," Cummins ordered. "We've had our Chinese thrill for the day." Although the Taiwanese and the People's Republic of China had been hostile previously, never before had either side played this kind of roulette with the world. Now it was up to the politicians and diplomats to sort out the reasons for the escalation and to attempt prevention of a recurrence. The United States and her allies had been struggling to understand Chinese strategy and policy for years with little success. The stakes had suddenly been raised. Getting this one right just became something of paramount importance.

"So let me see if I've got this right." Adams was suspicious. He listened to the colonels at the Pentagon with a jaundiced eye. This one was no different. Adams might not know the details of this project, but he was a pretty good judge of horse flesh and other things emanating from a horse. "The plan is to blast these poor sum bitches into Earth orbit, have 'em rendezvous with a big ass Titan carryin' the main payload, and after hookin' up with it, get the hell out of Earth orbit usin' a plutonium-powered nuclear reactor to send a barely tested moon module crammed full of a lot of bullshit you don't know whether or not works on a two- year trip to some moon you really don't know shit about. Is that about it, Colonel?" Damn, B.C. knew how to sum things up.

This wannabe general-of-a-colonel swallowed hard and stared right at the CJCS, "Yes, sir. You've pretty much got it right." The room was uncharacteristically quiet.

The General had recaptured some of his Vietnam glory by leading a brigade of Rangers on a night mission in Panama. Even though he thought the whole operation was a disaster from the start because Noriega, "that cruddy little pineapple of a general" as B.C. called him, evaded arrest for so long, Adams came out of the conflict with more accolades. Stints in other far flung places followed. But it wasn't until the first Gulf War that he became a household name. While Schwarzkopf and Powell were on TV, it was Adams who actually made the end run of artillery and infantry that broke Saddam Hussein's back, not to mention that of his republican guards. He was quoted as saying, "It was the only time in my live I've beaten up a bunch of republicans".

The two commanding generals recommended, and Congress approved, the awarding of the Congressional Medal of Honor, for an incident that brought him to the forefront. He was leading the point tank column that was savagely attacked in a desperate attempt by the Iraqis to counter-attack the advancing coalition troops. He charged his M1A1 Abrams tank into thirteen Soviet made Iraqi T-62s, incapacitating seven, destroying four, and accepting the surrender of the remaining two. Even his own troops were "stunned, shunned, and outgunned," as he outflanked the line. The picture flashed to every newspaper in the civilized world showed B.C. standing on his tank holding two 1880s Colt .45s pointed, Texas style, at the heads of a couple of frightened Iraqis. "Now that's how to get stars, boys." That was his first star.

"This star quest is chock full of logistics problems. But I still think we have to make it work," came a voice in the dark. "You know what this is all about? I'll tell you. It's about a chance to fix our human mistakes. Think about what you'd change if you could start humanity over."

"Aw, Dupree, you don't know jack shit." B.C. was obstinate. "Leave that mumbo jumbo, change the world crap to the civilians. Whether it should go is for the politicians. We're here to figure out how to make it fly. Hell, can it fly?"

"Should it fly?"

"What does that mean?" B.C. asked. "Come on, Anne. What'd ya mean, should it fly?"

"Do we really know what we're getting into here, B.C.? We're asking a group of people, military, civilian, who knows who, to commit their lives for the benefit mankind. Would you do that?"

"I did, damn it. It's called the United States Army," B.C. struck back. "And so did you. So does every person I know. Just in a different arena. How many doctors do you know that didn't go into medicine to benefit their fellow man? Or dentists, or fishermen. Hell, even lawyers think they're here to benefit somebody other than themselves. Sure, there are exceptions. But are we going to be ruled by the exceptions? I think not, General Hayes."

"Yeah, but this is different, B.C.. You knew what you were committing to. How can we ask these poor souls to commit to something this big when we can't even define it ourselves?"

"We'll tie up the loose ends. We always do. Did you really know what you were getting into when you first signed up?" B.C. wasn't going to let up. "I believe most people know the difference between right and wrong. They just have too many temptations distracting them from making the right choice. I've spent my whole career making sure there's enough proper motivation to keep 'em on the track to righteousness."

"You're a saint, B.C.," Hayes responded sarcastically. "Our other task is to make sure these folks are truly what we want representing our future."

"Damn it, Anne. I hate it when you go philosophic on me." But B.C. knew she was right. So here he was, Chairman of the Joint Chiefs, sitting in a briefing hearing about a bunch of people going to another planet or something, interrupted by his memories and a hostile Chinese missile launch—*or four*. One moment, he was briefing the President about how the world may be coming to an end, then, only minutes later, had to call him back to say, "*No, it's not true.*" All this was just a typical day for the CJCS, a country boy from Texas. God, I'd like to be going with them, he thought. Of course, he couldn't say that to the others. He had his reputation to preserve. But damn, you talk about a legacy! *Hell,* he thought, *too bad they don't need someone with shootin' experience.*

V

Think of a homogenous cup of coffee—of essentially infinite density. There is a sudden and rapid heating causing rapid expansion, as if the coffee were dropped into a cosmic blender sending forth each molecule of coffee in every direction at a velocity nearing the speed of light. A split second later, just as suddenly, it is cooled, like placing the exploding "goo" into a freezer. Well, that coffee is still expanding today in all different directions. Only the speed has slowed," explained Dr. Sturmbourg during her opening remarks at the World Congress of Physics. "That's the 'Big Bang Theory' with a bit of 'Inflationary Theory' thrown in." From her wheel chair at Hamburg University, she could barely see over the podium, even though it had been lowered to the minimum level.

As Dr. Sheppard listened, he couldn't help thinking how simple an explanation he'd just heard of one of the most incomprehensible of ideas. A cup of coffee, huh? Even so, how was the universe created? And how long ago? From the restricted vantage point of a wheelchair, Melissa Anne Sturmbourg was far from imposing. Yet, she was director of the most world renowned SETI project—Search for Extra-Terrestrial Intelligence. Today she was presenting data gathered from several of the latest generation space telescopes. In 2004, the SIRTF, or Space Infrared Telescope Facility, began sending back millions of bytes of information from its thirty-three-inch mirror. Capable of peering ninety percent of the way back to the Big Bang, it expanded man's knowledge of the universe's origins by gathering infrared radiation. But it was the Next Generation Space Telescope—NGST—that had scientists excited. After rocketing away from Earth in early 2007, this twenty-five foot wide composite of mirrors was changing the way astronomer's viewed the possibility of extraterrestrial life. This was Sturmbourg's arena, her operating theater, her stage.

A brilliant physicist in her own right, she was mentored at Cambridge by none other than Stephen Hawking in the early 1990s. How ironic that several years later she, too, would be wheelchair-bound. Sturmbourg as a result of a skiing accident; Hawking from ALS— amyotrophic lateral sclerosis—commonly called Lou Gehrig's disease. Like Hawking, it didn't stop her from excelling. The laws of physics state that matter is neither created nor destroyed. She was living proof. As her physical strengths seemed destroyed, her mental prowess became enhanced, a transformation of energy, without creation or destruction. And what energy.

At the end of her lecture, Sheppard approached her and asked, "Dr. Sturmbourg, might I have a moment?" As he began, he was trying to figure out how he was going to sell the General on this diminutive woman in a wheelchair. "I'm here to talk to you about a new moon you may have heard about," he continued.

"Everyone is quite excited about this new discovery," she asserted. "First, we concentrated on Titan. Then, it was Europa. Now, Genesis." She, like most of the scientific community, not only knew of the discovery, but had her own ideas about it. Secrets don't last long, Sheppard logged into his own cerebral database.

She was referring to the Saturn moon of Titan, its largest moon, discovered in 1655 by Christiaan Huygens. Cold, but Titan had sufficient quantities of carbon-based compounds to make primitive life a possibility. Possible until the *Huygens* probe, named after the discovering astronomer, surveyed this moon in 2004 after its separation from the *Cassini* probe. It was thought to be the extraterrestrial body holding the most promise for life. Disappointment there was followed by the launch of *Challenger II* to scrutinize Europa, one of Jupiter's moons. In the late 1990s, the *Galileo* project circled Jupiter analyzing Europa and several other Jovian moons. This small moon was next in line with promise for life. *Galileo* only hinted at Europa's possibilities. The purpose of the *Challenger II* mission was to further explore Europa in the quest for extraterrestrial life. That was its initial purpose until it uncovered Genesis. Europa had long been considered a possible life-sustaining body because of the abundance of water. And water there was, and is. But not life, or a life-sustaining environment.

"What we know of the so-called 'winter period' is that temperatures on Genesis range from -90 to -25 degrees F. There are tremendous winds, reaching gusts of up to 200mph. It is dark for lack of sunlight with high gamma radiation during this time." Eric thought he noted heightened interest on Sturmbourg's part.

"Radiation from where?" she asked.

Sheppard had already decided internally that he was going to insist the team be chosen for their talents applicable to the project, and not limited by a worldly disability. It sounded good, but this one was going to be a tough sell. This petite, blonde had a presence unlike any Sheppard had previously encountered. She was poised, articulate and quite pretty. In her early 40s, her dynamism was contagious. If you looked her in the face and let the wheelchair drift from memory, she was what every parent wanted for their son. No, even with the wheelchair, any parent would be blessed to have Melissa Sturmbourg as their daughter-in-law.

"We're not sure about the radiation. It's a winter phenomena. When the moon emerges from this 'winter', an equal nine month 'summer' period begins with temperatures ranging from +30 to +85 degrees F. The moon is drenched in sunlight for the entire period with tolerable radiation levels, and an atmosphere similar to Earth," pausing to let what he'd said sink in before adding the hook line. "We're organizing a mission to colonize the moon."

"Colonize, Dr. Sheppard? Did you say, colonize? Not explore, but a permanent presence on this moon?" Now he really had her attention.

"Yes, colonize. You're a scientist looking for life outside our planet. Well, there's going to be life somewhere else. Only, it will be mankind transplanted from the planet Earth."

"And you're telling me this, because...?"

"A basic scientist understands the fundamentals of how and why things work. Working with our team, planning, testing and understanding this new environment is that basic scientist's goal. I believe you are our scientist. I want you to go along, Dr. Sturmbourg."

"Have you run this—me—past your President?" Sturmbourg demurred. "I'm flattered, but you've got to be kidding? Do you really want me to take your offer seriously?" She waved her arms across her wheelchair. "I am comfortable with my disability, but that's here on Earth. I would want...no. I would expect no special treatment. But the reality is, I do have special needs. Have you considered that thoroughly, Doctor? And what is my role? Yes, a physicist searches for, and explains the natural laws of the universe. But what role could I play in constructing a shelter, or planting food, or searching for water?"

"That's just it, Dr. Sturmbourg," Eric persisted. "Searching for water, building shelter. Not searching for it, or building it, but *where* to search for that water, and *where* to build that shelter. That's part of your role. A scientist studies the environment, breaks it down into its components to understand how best to utilize the assets. You can't utilize something until you understand it. Do you think an engineer knows where to look for water? No. He knows *how* to look, but not *where*. There are also phenomena unseen. Radiation, sunlight, thermodynamics, solar winds. A physicist can anticipate problems of the solar system. Problems others can't see, or fathom."

"Follow me!" Wheeling her way through winding corridors reminded Eric of the Pentagon. With her head start and wheel power, Eric was having trouble trailing this dynamo. She finally turned the last corner and voice activated the security door, allowing both to enter a darkened room with infrared lighting. At a computer terminal, Melissa spoke a few cryptic words and a giant forty foot screen lit up the south wall. The image was obviously from space, most likely from a space probe. "Do you know what that is?"

"No. I'll assume it's from one of the probes you were outlining in your lecture."

"This is what I am searching for," she emphatically answered. "What you're looking at is a cluster of stars forty light years away. That's about 250 trillion miles from Earth. Somewhere in this constellation, I believe we will find sentient life."

Eric was quiet. He studied the image and the physicist. "What is so important to you about finding life on another planet?"

"It changes everything," she replied. "We are such an egotistical species. We take the gift of life for granted. Maybe if I can prove life exists elsewhere, mankind will stop abusing the gift and this planet."

"You mean, if you prove we are not unique?"

"Exactly. We act as if nothing will happen to us because we are unique. We wrongly assume we can control our fate. I'm not so sure. If I show the world that we are an infinitesimal speck in the cosmic soup, that we are subject to the same rules as the rest of the universe, maybe we will have a chance to survive each other." She paused for a moment, scanning the image on the wall. "And if I were to go, who would know of my work? For whom would I toil? For the inner glory? I think not."

"No, Melissa, if I may call you Melissa. No. You would be the backbone of educating an entire new world. You would hold the key to explaining the universe from an entirely unique perspective. From another planet, from another vantage point unlike any other. Think of the vantage point you would have in evaluating questions of the universe. You would have the most unique observatory in our culture. Think of the universe. How old is it? Do you know definitively?"

"Not really. But I can make a pretty close guess," her dark brown eyes sparkling. "Are you familiar with the Hubble Constant, Doctor?"

"Call me Eric. Both civilizations would be in communication with each other. You, the team, wouldn't operate in a vacuum. Slow for now, but communication is possible. Your discoveries would be shared with all of humanity. That isn't inner glory. That is a unique, unprecedented opportunity. Think of the improvements in technology generated by this project. And not just in communications and video uplinks. The Hubble Constant?"

"Edwin Hubble was the discoverer of the expanding universe. A hundred years ago, he postulated the age of the universe was calculable by dividing the speed of the expansion by distance. Sounds simple enough until you start trying to measure distances accurately. This equation arrives at what is called the Hubble Constant. We've been getting closer to the age of the universe since the telescope your government launched bearing his name came on line. In the late 1990s, it was thought to be about eleven to twelve billion years old. With NGST, we believe that number is closer to thirteen point seven billion years. Maybe fourteen billion at the outside." She was studying Sheppard, looking for a sign of insincerity. "I'll admit, I'm intrigued by being able to measure distances to other stars from the new moon. We could then triangulate my measurements and those from Earth and arrive at a much more accurate figure."

"Will the universe last forever, Melissa?" Sheppard had studied the paradoxical questions physicists had been pondering over for centuries. He knew how to pull her chain.

"Do you mean, is its expansion slowing, or is it constant? I don't know. Our best guess is that it will expand forever."

"But what is forever, Melissa? Is life forever?"

"Why should I go to another celestial body when I can search for life from Earth?"

"You believe there is extraterrestrial life, Melissa? That's what you search for on Earth. Do you really believe? If so, what are the odds?" asked Eric.

"Statistically, yes, I believe there has to be. I feel like an astronomical name dropper, but, have you heard of Frank Drake, Eric?"

"No, but let me guess. He had something to do with life out there?"

"Drake actually came up with a formula attempting to estimate the possible number of civilizations capable of communication. The long and the short of it is there are seven factors involved. After working through the formula, we've estimated there are at least forty intelligent civilizations in our galaxy alone."

"Forty?"

"It gets better," now she was enthusiastic. "There are at least 100 billion stars in 100 billion galaxies. That's 10^{22}, minimum! Some say as many as $10,000^{22}$. Given those kinds of numbers, even with an error rate of 10,000, there would still be 400 million communicating civilizations in the universe. And you want to tell me there isn't life out there? There has to be, statistically speaking."

"So how do you try and talk to these folks?"

"First of all, we don't talk, we send and search for radio waves. We send out signals all the time, both intentionally and unintentionally."

"Unintentionally?"

"You think they like listening to *Saturday Night Live*? That's been going out to them for thirty-five or forty years, since the 1970s. They should've gotten some of it by now. Or, maybe, those old Rush Limbaugh broadcasts? We don't broadcast them to the universe intentionally, but they're out there just the same. These radio waves travel fast, at the speed of light."

"So how fast is fast? I remember from college the speed of light is 186,000 miles per second. Put that in context."

"Well, to give you some perspective. It takes light a little more than one second to travel to the moon. It takes about eight minutes to get here from the sun, the length of time we have to predict solar flares. That's pretty quick when you consider it takes four years to receive light from the nearest star. Or 100,000 years to travel across our own galaxy, the Milky Way."

"Light travels fast, but the distances are extraordinary, almost inconceivable. That pretty much excludes a visit I would think. Given they would all be dead of old age when they got here."

"Given our current technology, travel even within our own solar system, as you propose, is a stretch. I'm sure you're considering many of the logistical problems of space travel. To go outside our solar system is unrealistic. And there are about a 100 billion stars in the Milky Way alone. That's a lot of travel...if we could. And the closest spiral galaxy to us, Andromeda, is two-and-a-half million light years or so away!"

"So searching and trying to communicate by radio waves is the next best thing?"

"Currently, it's the only thing. For our lifetime, anyway, Eric. Given the current political climate of the world, we don't have much time. That's why I'm obsessed with my projects."

"Wouldn't you want to explore the universe from the unique perspective of Genesis? Think about the questions you will answer and the ones you will ask. Not just about helping to establish a colony on a new world, but the universal questions. Don't you want to help ask and answer the questions, Melissa?"

They talked on for several hours. As she talked, he was engrossed by her enthusiasm. She really believed. This was not only her profession, but her passion. What a platform for an observatory. Melissa wanted to be sure Eric was serious. Due diligence, to assure herself of the intent. And to make sure he wasn't patronizing her.

Tough sell, I guess. Not only to the General, but to the President, too. There would be special needs. For Sturmbourg and probably others. Tough sales would soon become Sheppard's norm. This was the first. How better to push the technological envelope than to have a necessity for developing a new piece of equipment. Say a suit for a paraplegic that allows her near normal movement? Yes, she and the technology derived would push the envelope.

Melissa Anne Sturmbourg grew up in Israel although she wasn't Jewish. She was actually of Germanic ancestry. She was the daughter of two archeologist parents who traveled extensively. Extensively, until they seemed to permanently land in the Promised Land, not only of several religions, but also of archeology. With the wealth of digs, materials, and artifacts in the Middle East—especially in what is now Israel—the two scientists were in heaven. This was the world Melissa lived in as a pre-teen and throughout her high school years. She was athletic and an outdoorswoman who loved horseback riding and kayaking. But it was skiing that became her passion. Passion and tragedy.

As a post-doctorate fellow at Oxford, she gave herself a birthday present. A trip to the Swiss Alps, and onto a steep slope she had jumped from a helicopter, intending to powder to the bottom. She made it to the bottom, but on her back. On her back for about half a mile that she remembers. The ski patrol kept her on her back and immobilized for the rest of the trip down the mountain, on a backboard. A T-10 paraplegic now, she redoubled her efforts as one of the world's brightest astrophysicists.

"So what are you concerns, Melissa?"

"My major concern is you may be pushing the natural timeline too rapidly."

"What do you mean?"

"Well," she paused, wheeling herself to the whiteboard. "Unmanned space exploration hasn't reached its full potential. We've only been at it for about sixty years. One of the primary reasons it hasn't been all it was hoped for is the inordinate cost. It's cheaper now than twenty or thirty years ago, but still incredibly expensive. As the various technologies advance and become cheaper, a natural evolution can be expected. That leads us to manned space exploration. I wouldn't have predicted this kind of a mission was feasible for about sixty or seventy years. Not until around 2075." She was drawing a graph with two lines. One was time and the other technology. "I wouldn't have thought these two lines would intersect much before then."

"What you're saying is that it's too soon to go?"

"I'm just not sure the technology is there to support the mission yet. And I'm sure the expense is massive." She was doodling on the board as she thought.

"I'm assured we have the financial commitment," Eric declared. "If we wait until 2075, that may be too late, but today is not too soon—for mankind. Certainly, it will be too late for you and me." He stared directly at the physicist. "As to the technology, my very strong feeling is what better way to expand technology than by the need to solve specific problems. We have the attention of a wide variety of people who are instrumental in making this project happen—the President of the United States, the American military, the scientific community. Who knows if that coalition will ever come together again? Or how long we can hold it together. And soon, this mission will capture the imagination of the world."

Paraplegia at the T-10 level means no feeling or movement below the bellybutton. Resulting from a crushing of the spinal cord contained within the bony spinal column in the mid-back, her sensation was impaired but not her feelings, her intensity. Melissa's passion for exploration of the outdoors would never be the same. Or so she thought prior to meeting Eric Sheppard. She pushed herself forward in her wheelchair, listening more intensely.

"You think all these different telescopes are impressive. Wait until you see what's planned for this trip," Sheppard was effusive. He looked to the stars splashed across the sky.

"Go on," she answered with increasing excitement. "What about new technologies for paraplegia? If you've had me in mind, I can't believe you haven't thought about my disability."

"We have several haptic interface projects in the pipeline."

"Haptic interfaces?" asked Sturmbourg with a peculiar look on her face.

"You remember the gloves movie makers wore in the 1990s to create lifelike movement on computer-generated images? You'd put on a glove and oppose your thumb and forefinger and the stick character on the screen mimicked the same motion. We're using entire body suits. They'll be combined usage, doubling as an environmental suit and programmable for different tasks, too. The user can program, let's say, eye movements to lift the legs, or experience tactile sensations, transmitted to the brain through the haptic suit. Sure, this would be more important to you because of your paraplegia. It will also be extremely beneficial to others without paraplegia."

He saw her eyes glisten with a hint of moisture. Maybe she would walk again. That technological advance would make her participation worthwhile. Dr. Sturmbourg would be the first test of Sheppard's concept of a world complement of cast members as well as a test of his will. Women, disabilities, foreigners. Boy, he thought, I sure know how to push the General's buttons.

VI

Sheppard summoned his staff. He was two days away from his meeting with Adams and he wasn't about to be outgunned. "Tell me about other potential candidates. I've got to have more than this."

Dr. Mark D. Houston began a wild dissertation about attributes he was looking for in potential mission members. Eric couldn't help but laugh inside. What was he talking about? He'd seen it all before, and for many a year.

Markey Dwayne had been with him since their college days in Oklahoma. *Mad Dog* was Markey Dwayne's nickname for the MD. It also meant Medical Doctor. They were classmates in medical school, too. They went way back. So did most of his staff. That was important to Eric. But Mad Dog wasn't just his handle, it was his life. Give him a project and he bit it off like a mad dog. That's why upon being named White House Science Adviser, the first person Eric Sheppard chose for his staff was Mark. If madness was the mother of invention, then he was the mother of all mothers and maddest of all madmen. And the most reliable and loyal. Loyalty cannot be overrated. Mad Dog was totally loyal to Sheppard.

It probably started over *Risk*®. In order to play the game of *Risk* all day during medical school, the two had to come up with a scheme to get lecture notes. Actually listening to the lectures was considered a waste of time, so the two came up with an idea and enlisted about eighty people in their class to get together to tape the lectures. One person was responsible for taping each hour of lecture and transcribing the tape, then turning it over to Eric, who printed copies and distributed them to each of the other members. This way, everyone only had to attend one out of every eighty lectures or so. The theory was, now you could go and "just listen" to the oratory at hand.

Thus, you could spend all day playing world conquest and domination, also known as, *Risk*. What made Houston really angry was when Eric took someone else's notes and got an "A", while the original note taker got a "B". Billy Bob Sipes and Mad Dog were the two best *Risk* players. The two best, next to the "King of the World," also known as second year medical student, Eric Sheppard, MSII. No one could start with the continent of Australia more often and so quickly expand into Asia, leading to ultimate world domination like Eric.

"What are our criteria for picking candidates?" Eric asked his group. "I say we pick the team by profession. That's my plan. But I've got to be able to defend our decisions to the General and his people. We pick the best possible candidate by job description. The best engineer, doctor, lawyer…forget lawyer." They all laughed. Anybody got any ideas?"

"What about nationality? Is this an American mission? A NATO mission? Who decides?" The question from his colleague was pertinent.

"And how many get to go on this little space vacation?" queried Houston. "If we choose by job description, what jobs? What do they need? You say no lawyers, why not? Who's to say what a mission like this really needs?"

"And race? Are we obligated to make this mission into a rainbow? Aren't we gonna catch hell for having some foreign-born soul to the exclusion of one of our own?" added another.

"And why can't they come back sometime? Can we communicate with them? Even ET phoned home, Eric," came the opinion of one of his troops.

"You seem to have decided disabilities aren't a problem with Sturmbourg. But what about others? Do we really want to send all the genetic defects from our gene pool?"

"Wait just a country minute," responded an indignant Sheppard. "Dilution of the gene pool? Give me a break. Who among you doesn't have deficiencies? And some more than others."

"Not me boss," shouted Houston in mock denial. Again, all laughed, but with an emerging thoughtfulness.

"I don't know. It seems to me we pick the best qualified candidates and let the chips fall," Sheppard concluded. "Let the number evolve. Surely not more than a dozen. Let's draw up a list of job descriptions we definitely recommend and I'll run it by Adams. Don't let superficial or first impressions dissuade you from a good participant. I know something about exceeding expectations."

Eric was the last person accepted into his medical school class—and accepted only when they expanded the class by five students—just three days before his class began its studies at the University of Oklahoma Health Sciences Center, in Oklahoma City, Oklahoma. He had applied after three years of undergraduate work, and hoped to get his degree in basic sciences upon successful completion of that all-important first year of medical school. Who could forget that first day of class?

Everyone, arrived early, so as not to miss anything. No matter how early you arrived, each student saw the same thing. Standing transfixed and catatonic at the lectern was this stone figure of a man. With bushy sideburns that nearly met at the chin, beady eyes covered by rounded scholarly spectacles, disheveled and uncombed graying hair, stood this professor-type, staring straight ahead, both hands grasping the podium. No movement, no sound, transfixed, like a marble statue.

As the bell rang, exactly at eight, he bellowed out, "Man is inevitably curious about himself." Each and every student feverishly wrote his every word. "Through the ages man evolved from the molecule, from the parasite, from the most primitive of life forms. Throughout time, the bacteria evolved from the molecule, the insect from the bacteria, the reptile from the fish, the bird from the reptile, the mammal from the bird, the higher primate from the lower mammals"—working himself to a heightened, frenzied pitch, finally screaming—"FUCK THE MOLECULES!!!" This clearly psychotic instructor next began licking his hand...after spitting into it. Finally, reaching a state of frenzied maniacism, all anybody in the room could think of was "what am I doing here?" Billy Sipes nearly died when he bit through his pencil and swallowed half of it.

So began their medical careers, with their introduction to G. Grunfeld Deacon, Chairman of the Department of Psychiatry, who liked loosening up new students this way. They had just served as Deacon's guinea pigs during their first lecture in his course, "Man and His Environment." They had reacted just as he knew they would—exactly as all the others before them had always done. Uptight, and clean out of sight! Designed to integrate and initiate new medical students into serious study, Deacon also structured his course to help them loosen up. Life isn't just academics. This was a study in people as humans, not anatomy, physiology and molecules. He went on to tell them about how each would faithfully attend every lecture, terrified that, if they didn't, they would certainly fail. All dressed in clean shirts, with coat and tie, until the first test came back. Once they realized they weren't going to flunk out, things would change. And change they did.

Hence, how the *Risk* game came about. Billy Bob, Mad Dog and Eric all passed that first test, and didn't wear ties or coats anymore. They barely wore shirts and T-shirts at that. That is, when they showed up. That was their first two years of medical school, the basic sciences part, not the deal with patients part.

Risk, for the uninitiated, is a board game in which the object of the competition is to conquer the world. There are six continents on the board: North America, South America, Africa, Europe, Asia, and Australia. As one consolidates their pieces into continents, more armies are awarded. The more territory, the more armies, until someone takes the entire world. One is "at risk" with each move because, to take a country, you inevitably take it from someone. They probably don't like that and may try to take it back, or take something else from someone else, making them equally mad. So the game progresses with everybody making everybody else mad at them. Politics 101. Or is it physics? *For every action, there is an opposite, but not necessarily equal, reaction.* Or so went their bastardized version of a Newtonian law. Sheppard never liked that saying. He felt it should have been, "For every action, there is an equal and opposite criticism."

"So our tentative list of necessary job descriptions are a physician, a physicist, an engineer, and someone who knows something about growing food." Eric was at a whiteboard making the list.

"It's a short list," Houston observed. "What about one of Adams' soldier boys? Isn't he gonna insist?"

"Let him try. In a new society what would a military type do?" Eric asked. "We're talking about the essentials of a new society. I don't see building an army as a top priority."

"What about someone to write about the day's events?" someone asked.

"I'm not sure they need a writer," questioned Sheppard.

"But they might need a historian," Mad Dog offered. "Someone to chronicle their journey—"

"And teach the past to the next generation."

"A writer, huh?" Eric stared off. He and Mad Dog got off on a songwriting kick during their junior year. That led to Houston getting his master's degree in music and theater just after medical school. Just what the world needed, a singing doctor. He dabbled in songwriting to this day. He'd had a Number One country single in the early 1990s with a hook line, "Honey, when you sling mud at me, you're only losin' ground." Sheppard gave up songwriting to pursue other "risks.'

Playing the game of *Risk*, Eric's organizational skills flourished. Soon thereafter, he was senior class president and one of the top five in his class. Along the way he may not have attended many lectures, but it soon became obvious he had a knack for medicine.

He also picked up an interest in academia. After residency, he completed a Ph.D in public policy from the University of Washington. Maybe it was being around the university environment, but Eric needed the stimulation of the seminar. The questions and answers of teaching, the repartee. He always felt in a discussion group it was a toss-up who learned more, the students or the instructor. The competition of staying one step ahead of his inquisitive students stimulated him. Several prestigious teaching positions followed until a phone call from the transition team organizing JFS's presidential appointments changed his life.

"So let's all think hard about who else to add to the job description list. As to communications with the group, it may be possible," Eric suggested. "But we need a contingency plan for a mission with minimal or no communication. Otherwise, do you abort because you can't talk to them? And at these distances, time delays become a significant factor. Can they ever come back? Hell, I don't know. Maybe. We can't send them with a return vehicle. It's just cost prohibitive. And we don't want to create false expectations. All these questions are open issues as far as I'm concerned. The President may provide some guidance and I'm sure General Adams has some thoughts," this last comment resulting in hoots and hollers from his entire staff.

"That General," started Houston. "Most people try to drink from the fountain of knowledge. He just gargled." The room erupted. Houston wasn't just a songwriter. He was a country lyricist. He sure knew how to peg the General.

"Our job's to make him swallow," came from the back of the room. Laughter, again.

"Now, now. We have to work with him, people," Eric interrupted. "He makes me as crazy as the rest of you. At least you don't have to sit in a room with him. Anyway, let's cut him a break."

As Houston droned on, Eric began to drift away. As challenged as he was by the mission, he was beginning to have feelings he'd never experienced before. He'd been a loner his whole life. Dedication to his work used to be enough. But not lately. For the first time in his life he wanted to share what was left of it with *a somebody*, not *a seminar*. But how do you start to date when you're in your late 50s? And when you're at work all day? And night. Or on an airplane traveling to some strange place looking for the next candidate. Maybe he needed to find an airline pilot for a soul mate. That way he could incorporate his work into his pleasure. Naw, what he really wanted was to get out. For the first time in his life he was getting tired of the governmental rat race. He was younger than his years. He had some catching up to do. Typical. Doing things out of order. Most people go through this phase when they're younger, then on to a career. Eric was going about it in reverse. He was snapped back to the discussion by a subordinate.

"God, Eric, you can't send these people off to Never Never Land and completely cut them off from the Earth."

"I know, I know. But we have to plan as if they don't need us for anything. Surely, with all the technology at hand, we should be capable of at least audio communications. And probably video links, too—eventually. Right now, I don't want to commit to specifics. That's for later. We've got time to think about it."

He went back to his own thoughts. He was half listening to Mad Dog rattle off names of potential candidates to literally be thrown out of the Earth's little fraternity. He and Houston had talked about the other team members by job description. No doubt, Adams and the Pentagon would add to his list of job descriptions. What he needed his group to do was find the right candidates and he'd close the bargain. He had enough problems finding people to fill the previously designated positions. The group was debating various names—names that represented another trip to Eric. He was struggling to stay focused, constantly being torn by recurring thoughts of getting out. He had to pay attention. Something this important warranted his full attention. So as Houston went on, Eric tried to listen more closely.

"Houston, we have a problem," he interrupted. Everyone laughed, but Sheppard had been pondering a previous question and wanted his staff's opinion. "Someone already asked it, but we didn't get a clear answer. Is this a U.S. mission? Can I sell the world participation theme?"

"Sturmbourg is German as well as paraplegic. Seems like you've answered your own question."

"Yeah, but she's also a member of the European-American West. What happens when I pick an African, or an Asian?" Eric asked.

"Seems to me you just answered your own question again. When I pick, not if I pick," answered Houston.

"Okay. I'll buy that. What about procreation? Since there are only going to be a handful of team members, you can't have them all going around 'procreating' all the time."

Houston was anticipatory, "We've got a solution. I'll go as a sex surrogate," he volunteered, always the comic. "Actually," becoming serious, "*in vitro* fertilization. Just because there are a small number of team members doesn't preclude taking a large quantity of eggs and sperm."

"But Mad Dog, who picks the eggs? Are we taking American eggs? Russian sperms? Chinese boys and Japanese girls? Who picks?" Sheppard responded. "It's solvable," Houston answered.

It's solvable, he says. He had heard that one before. Mad Dog Houston had a nickname. All Sheppard wanted was a nickname back in college. It was during their songwriting days that he got his, and he got it from Houston. When he complained about not having a handle, Houston had responded, "It's solvable. Give me some time."

So there was Eric, singing at the top of his lungs, a very complicated lyric. Standing in front of about seventy-five drunken students in a bar, singing his heart out. That's when he blew the words. He mangled a very fast-talkin' song called, *Talkin' Candy Bar Blues*, by Paul Stookey of the 1960s folk group "Peter, Paul and Mary." What came out was a horrible rendition of the original:

Bought a Candybar the other day, only ate half, gonna throw the rest away, when I saw this kid playin' in the street, I said, hey kid, you want somethin' to eat, he said…what? I said, the Candybar, and he started to run…half a bar of chocolate runnin' down my fingers.

On and on he sang, until he put the third verse before the second, and the next thing you know, the story's really messed up…just like the chocolate. Mad Dog looked up from his apparent indifference and said, "That's it, no more beers for the Dwarf." Eric Sheppard now had his nickname, *Dwarf.* He liked it!

Though he wasn't particularly short at 5' 6", next to the 6' 2" Houston, "Dwarf" worked. And it stuck. In private, associates still called him Dwarf to this day.

"We also need some help from the Pentagon people on some of the tech problems," injected Sheppard. "Sturmbourg was very excited about the haptic projects. I think that's what sold her on the mission. As important as technology will be to her, its uses to the others will be just as consequential."

"And we need help on the ark," volunteered Houston.

"Huh?" Eric responded.

"The sperms and eggs. If we're going to send them along, we need answers to who picks them and what do they choose."

"Ah, yes. The ark. You've heard of Noah's ark," Eric sarcastically answered. "Now we have Houston's ark. Noah's was 300 cubits long with a breadth of 50 cubits and a height of 30 cubits. Do you know what a cubit is, Mad Dog?"

"No sir, I don't. But I'll bet it's bigger than the space you're giving me."

"You got that right, partner. You have the advantage of puttin' a lot of little sperms into a bunch of flasks, or beakers or whatever, and blastin' 'em off into space. Has anybody thought about what happens to sperms and eggs in space over time? We need to protect our Earthly offspring from radiation, and who knows what else. Let's assign task forces to answer some of these questions, people." The Dwarf was thinkin' out loud.

"Who incubates these space critters, Eric?"

"Or, are we picking a team of young, nubile virgins to do nothing all day but eat grapes and hatch babies?" came the sarcastic comment from a female staffer.

"No, no, no, people," Houston exclaimed. "Age is no object. Or sex, for that matter. We do not need the female uterus for incubation purposes anymore. That's the old fashioned way. Thanks to modern science, we can fertilize and nurture all our little sperms and eggs outside the human body."

"How romantic!"

"Look," a serious Houston continued. "The trade-off is we get to choose more experienced parents as team members. We're not excluding the old fashioned way. Science has been raising other mammals totally *in vitro* since the 1990s. This is just a guarantee for success, with the added benefit of members who have lived life and have careers. Who—"

"Who have a daunting job ahead of them," Sheppard interrupted. "They'll have their professional work and, when the time comes, a communal family to help raise. Demanding and daunting, because they get to do it either in space or on a foreign planet." His thoughts drifted off again.

Today, it was the work that seemed to dwarf Sheppard. He wished he was somewhere in the world scuba diving. Both he and Mad Dog still saw Billy Bob from time to time. All three still went scuba diving when they could get the time. How he'd like to be in the water off some tropical beach right now. But the more he thought, the more Mad Dog and Billy weren't who he wanted to be with on that beach. It was time for this loner to settle down. As soon as the mission was over, Sheppard resolved to leave government service and take his pension. Take it to some far away beach. Hopefully, with someone by his side. For now though, he needed a plan.

What he had to do was come up with a game plan for dealing with General Adams. And he only had two days. He needed to run their tentative criteria past Adams, and get help on the technical side. Also, find out what his people were up to. While the staff continued the discussions at hand, Dwarf Sheppard picked up the phone and called Adams. "General, how would you feel about a game of *Risk*? My office, on Wednesday, seven p.m. Good. I'll see you then."

He still knew how to conquer the world. All you have to do is roll over one general.

VII

"Grab a beer, pull up a chair, General. Choose a color." Eric ushered Adams to the small card table he'd set up next to his cluttered desk. This would be the most important game of *Risk* Sheppard would ever play, or was that the most risky game? He was playing for his version of the mission. He figured a little liquid inspiration might help.

"So how do you play this game?" Adams snarled, popping the twist top off the bottle of the local micro-brew, making a mental note of the fact Sheppard at least didn't offer some watered down, piss beer. B.C. grew up on Coors in Texas. He soon graduated to real beer, not that high school version. "Tell me the rules again."

"The object is world domination," advised Sheppard. Was the General trying to sandbag him? Eric wasn't sure. Did he really not know how to play, or was he a poker player in disguise? All Sheppard could do was explain the rules, all the while trying to read his opponent. As he detailed the objective, he decided Adams really did know how to play and was just sizing up his adversary.

"So, General, I've chosen several team members. I'm enthusiastic about several other potentials." He told the General about Drs. Tatman and Sturmbourg, putting his best spin on the General.

"I'll be blue and you be commie red, Doc. You can go first, since I own the advantage being of military background." B.C. wasn't about to let this civilian dictate the ground rules. "Mind if I loosen my tie? You civilians don't give a damn about uniforms anyway, do you?"

As he let the insults pass, now Sheppard was sure Adams had played before. Sheppard rolled the dice for the first time, asking Adams for any objections to the two choices just detailed. "Any thoughts about Melissa and C.T.?" He had initial troops on Eastern and Western Australia, just the way he liked to start. After throwing the dice he quickly consolidated his good fortune, taking Indonesia and New Guinea, thereby gaining possession of the entire continent of Australia.

"So, Eric. . . may I call you Eric?" B.C. was deferential, or patronizing, Eric couldn't tell. "You've left me with a dilemma." He took a long, slow chug down to the end of his beer. "Do I fight you in Australia, from a bad tactical position, or move on to my own offensive strategy? It's early, after all, and why fight over preliminary choices made by one's opponent?"

As the General rolled for his first moves, he swept down from Siam, taking Indonesia, then New Guinea, to disrupt Sheppard's continent of Australia. This left both sides in their original start positions. Well, I guess we know how he plays, thought Sheppard. No walking away from a fight.

"Are we fighting over Australia or my choices, B.C.? Do you mind if I call you B.C.?" Sheppard countered, deciding a frontal head-on attack about his choices was his best approach. He drained his brew. He wasn't going to be intimidated. "Another beer, B.C.?"

"I'm concerned about this woman physicist, what's her name, Steamburg? Why do we need her? Isn't she in a wheelchair, Eric? For God's sake, son, are we gonna have to build a handicapped ramp to the spaceship or what?" So the General *had* done his homework.

"Are you concerned about her being a woman or because she's a woman in a wheelchair, B.C.?" Eric was ready for this one.

"Both," Adams hesitated for a second. "Shit! man, I can get past the woman thing. After all, the boys will have to have some diversion," the General laughed. He slugged back his beer.

Not much of a woman's libber, thought Sheppard. Score one for the good guys. He had won the "woman" issue. The son of a bitch probably doesn't have a woman within fifty miles of his own staff. "B.C., this is the best physicist for the project. Hell, she's probably the best in the world. And anyhow, in the weightlessness of space, who cares if she's in a wheelchair on Earth? She isn't going to be on Earth." Sheppard prayed he'd buy it. "Besides, we're working on some environmental suit that may make the whole issue moot."

"Yeah, maybe so." The General was being exceptionally agreeable. That bothered Eric. What was he up to? "I know about your haptic project, Doc."

As the General took his turn, Sheppard had barely paid any attention to the game and it showed. Not only did the General have the entire continent of Australia, but half of Asia already.

"Eric, I want you to promise me something. No more disabled folks without us talking about it in advance. And another thing."

Here it comes, thought Sheppard.

"I'd like you to sign-off on keeping the majority of the team from the United States. We gotta maintain control." Adams was looking for some kind of a trade-off.

Sheppard hadn't really thought about it, but yeah, he could support that. What was with this control stuff? Both Adams and the President seemed to be hung up on control. Sheppard really didn't care. Besides, what did it really mean? "Sure, B.C., no problem."

"And another thing. Let's keep the mission our little secret. No reason to let the Chinese know more than they can find out on their own," Adams confided.

Sheppard didn't really care about secrecy, because, in time, it wouldn't matter. He didn't care if the General got this one. Looking at the board, the two were just about even, with maybe a slight advantage to the General, on the board at least. Sheppard had changed directions, concentrating on South America and then North America. The downside was that B.C. had all of Australia, more than half of Asia, and controlled the Ukraine, the gateway to Europe.

"How do you feel about race and nationality? It's my feeling that this thing should be a reflection of the world, although my first priority is to choose the best qualified." So how does the General feel about affirmative action?

"Yeah, pick the best. You can have a few foreigners. But remember, it's the United States that has control of the mission," countered B.C. It seems affirmative action isn't as important to this General as is control. "Can I have another brewsky, Eric?"

"What's so damned important about control, B.C.?" Eric wasn't probing, he really didn't understand, popping open another beer for the General. "Don't you think we'll lose control once they leave Earth?"

"Yeah. But it's gettin 'em away from Earth that I'm worried about," Adams slurred. "If we can just hold on to control of this thing without it gettin' outta hand..." Adams' words drifted off. He sat silently for about a minute. "There's a lot of shit goin' down in the world you don't know squat about, Doc."

"You think I'm not aware? Why you—"

"Pissed off, Doc?"

"Yes. I'm as aware of current events as anybody."

"So you think. I like to see you get riled up, Sheppard." B.C. had a big, shit eatin' grin on his face. "You just think you know about current events. This little project will do more to educate you than sittin' around bullshittin' with your scientist pals." He finished another bottle and popped the top on another. "So my staff and I have been thinkin'. If this place'll support life, what makes you think there isn't some already there?"

"I hadn't thought too much about it, B.C." Seems his counterpart's staff was brainstorming, as well.

"If there's something alive up there, you'd better not mess with it." The General was chuckling. "We wouldn't want to contaminate the environment. Maybe ya oughta take along one of them Greenpeace, freak show types."

"We oughta at least make plans for the possibility of pre-existent life. A containment area—or the team has to stay in suits until they're sure there are no bugs. We could—"

"Look Eric," the General slurred. "I'm sure your boys have already considered it and have a plan. If you don't, after my suggestions, you will by next week. We've got some other ideas. Maybe we oughta put our two staffs together to work on this thing? What'd ya think, Eric?" With his speech slurring increasingly, the General's Texas accent was becoming more prominent.

"Sure, B.C. Another beer?"

As the two divided up the world, they really were getting on smashingly. And smashed was also where they were headed. As they talked, they began to swap stories, laughing all the while. Sheppard learned he had more in common with this general than he'd thought. Both came from the southwest, from mediocre backgrounds and less than prestigious schooling, to a position of authority in Washington, D.C. Both worked their way up "through the ranks" to their current positions, advancing on the basis of accomplishments, not pieces of paper written in Latin, hanging on the wall. Even though Sheppard still didn't trust Adams, a grudging respect was beginning to emerge.

The game was coming down to who controlled Africa. As they traded countries back and forth, it became obvious to both that a coexistence was probably the final outcome. The winner certainly would be determined by something other than skill.

The phone rang, abruptly halting their repartee. The General's body and soul snapped to attention. He was being summoned back to the Pentagon. "Something going down in Asia again," mumbled Adams. "Eric, I think I could actually like you, if you'd just quit stabbing me in the back. You play *Risk* better than most of my cronies." Laughing at Sheppard, "By the way, we play on Saturdays. Maybe you'd like to join us sometime? Anyway, I've got my sources on you and I'll bet you've got them on me. Instead of competing on this thing, maybe we really oughta pool our resources."

Sheppard was right about the General knowing how to play. *The bastard's trying to hustle me, thinking as he spoke.* "Are you serious, or trying to sucker punch me, B.C.?" Eric thought he could get on board, but just wanted to hear it again from the General.

"What, you don't trust a country boy of a general? Hell, Eric, I'm harmless. All talk and bluster. You oughta hear what them sum bitches back at the Pentagon think of you. They're really cruel. I might have to change their thinking about you. By the way, when are you headed off to Africa?" Adams queried. "And another thing, boy," now sober as a judge, Adams fixed his eyes on Eric. "She might not need a wheelchair in space, but your paralyzed little physicist ain't just goin' to space, son. She's goin' to another planet. A planet with gravity. That moon won't be weightless. You'd better bring along some extra wheelchairs for Steamburg."

"It's Sturmbourg."

"Whatever."

So Eric hadn't just slipped Sturmbourg past the General. But he bought her inclusion. And the General knew all along that Sheppard's next trip was to the dark continent in search of the next team member. Just like the board, the next moves were in Africa. Like the game tonight, there was no winner. Only a draw, or was it? A mutual existence might mean everyone wins. Maybe this Adams guy wasn't so bad after all. Eric thought long and hard, could he trust him?

"Gentlemen, I've got problems with the logistics on this project," began the President. It was too early in the morning for Sheppard to answer any questions. He was more concerned about whether his heart was beating. His head certainly was from the night before. The coffee had helped, but it wasn't enough. "For one thing, whose mission is it anyway? Doctor, it would appear you've chosen someone other than an American. So, is this a world mission, or what?"

"Mr. President, I'll let Dr. Sheppard address that issue," deferred General Adams. He was no dummy. Let the civilian take the heat. The General was dressed in a perfectly creased fatigue uniform, with a green beret decorated with four small stars glistening brighter than his spit polished paratrooper jump boots.

"Mr. President, this should be, must be, a world mission. If it is a venture to colonize a new planet, then by what right do we as Americans claim supremacy of our existing planet?" His brain was beating like a hammer on an anvil. How was Adams uninjured? What was his secret? Why was he sitting there like last night's beer bash hadn't happened?

Sheppard summoned all his energies to spew forth his defense of the mission. "Yes, we have resources unavailable to other countries, but are our people superior? I think not. Just the lucky recipients of good fortune. As an example of world peace, why not go forth with the world's best, not just ours?"

"You're point is well taken, Doctor. Spoken like someone who doesn't have to deal with a skeptical Congress. So why should the United States pay for your world mission? Congress is going to have a field day with this. Why not have some help from others?" questioned the President.

"It is precisely because we have the resources that we must use them. We are still the wealthiest country on this planet. If others wish to help, so be it. But we must be willing to go it alone," argued Sheppard.

"You think we have the resources, Doctor. Let me tell you about the economy. Since 2008, we've been climbing back, but we're still deficit financing. We've got—"

"I'm in agreement with the Doctor, sir," interrupted General Adams, somewhat to Sheppard's surprise. "This is a mission from the Earth, not the United States. This *is* the only country with the resources, sir. I've been a soldier all my life. Who better to know when to fight and when to coexist? We train all our careers to avoid a fight, but if forced, we'll fight to win it. This is a time to build consensus, to bring along the peoples of the world. It is a world mission," he looked Eric straight in the face. "Although I do believe there are certain parties that should be excluded. I see no reason why the last bastion of communism should be allowed to grab the glory of this mission. What do we need the Chinese for anyway?"

"But General, are the Chinese not part of the world community?" asked Sheppard. Giving his newfound friend a break, he didn't mention that this wasn't about glory. "How can they be excluded from this and be expected to get along in our world? From the distance of space, are we not all the same? We aren't Americans, or Chinese. We are human beings, all from Earth. No, I think the Chinese must be included. We can all hope they see this as a reason to join the world stage, on this, our current planet," argued Sheppard.

"What you're saying is there is a political rationale for including even the Chinese. Get them to re-engage with the rest of the world." Both could see the President's mind going in high gear. "I like it. I like it a lot. Dr. Sheppard, you may include other nationalities. If qualified, Eric. Only, if qualified," concluded the President.

The General grimaced and leaned into Sheppard, "I thought we decided you'd stop stabbing me in the back, Eric?" Quietly whispering in his ear, "Did you HAVE to pick the Chinese?" Then, to the room the General asked, "What if they don't want to play on your world stage by our rules, Doctor?"

"First of all, I haven't picked anyone from China. Our goal is to pick the best qualified. If that satisfies some worldly geopolitical balance, then, all the better. As to rules, who says that we make the rules, General? Are you talking about rules *for* the team? Because I say the rules will evolve *from* the team. Who goes is important, but I'm a realist. Look at it from a military standpoint. If you include the Chinese, you can control them. Exclude them, and a potential saboteur is unleashed."

"Doctor, *we have to maintain control*. We have to set the rules. The Congress will eat me alive on this if we lose control," answered the President.

"Yes, sir, I understand. We can suggest rules, even influence the rules. But ultimately, it is the team that will determine the rules. Just as in our country, they will evolve a democracy based on the rule of law," countered Sheppard.

"What if the Chinese convince them to vote out democracy. Like the damned French have done about ten times over the last fifty years?" scoffed Adams.

"The French never did it, General. They only threatened to. Threatened it for political advantage," chastened the President. "If the team throws democracy to the wind, I for one will be surprised. But if they do, they'll be a couple of million miles away and we'll be incapable of doing anything about it."

The room was quiet. Good point about sabotage, thought Adams. Besides, the closer they are, the easier to observe. "As to secrecy, Mr. President, we at the Pentagon feel that secrecy is less important. We're in favor of declassifying the project. That doesn't mean we have to advertise it. But, sir, everybody'll know about it soon enough. What's the point in keeping something secret that's for the good of mankind? Anyway, Sheppard's already told half the scientific community."

Was this the General Adams Sheppard despised just a few short weeks ago? He'd let the comment about telling the scientific community pass. He leaned towards Adams, "When did you become a flaming liberal, B.C.?"

"Don't push too hard, Doc," came the rapid fire answer. "Look, I know what's right. And besides, now you owe me...*Dwarf.*"

Oooh, the General did have good intelligence, smiled Sheppard. "I expect we can have the team completed in the next few months, Mr. President. I'll need input from the General on several candidates," Sheppard returned courtesy in kind to Adams.

"Mr. President, as to the logistics of the actual mission," continued Adams, "the Pentagon recommends a dual launch. The first vessel launched four weeks in advance carrying supplies and matériel. It would also be capable of becoming a backup ship in the event of an emergency. There's also controversy over what fuel to use. The most efficient and cost effective is nuclear fuel. But in the event of an accident, Earth-orbit contamination would be problematic."

"General, I don't want a nuclear catastrophe, but as I understand it, conventional fuel would be heavy, expensive and limited in supply, am I right?" The President had also been doing some research. "We've been using nuclear power plants for decades. And a nuclear reactor would be small and reusable, making control and containment in the event of a problem more likely. Nuclear is the way to go."

The President continued, "As to the two-ship question, I'm not sure it matters. With the nuclear reactor for energy, the additional cargo area can be maximized to carry supplies. I'll leave that up to your experts. What does matter is this must be an all-or-nothing project. Psychologically, I think it is important that those committing to this project have no expectation of returning. I don't want a second ship to create doubt, complacency, or even anticipation of a return. Members must concentrate their efforts on the success of this mission, not whether they have a space lifeboat. I know you're concerned about the team returning to Earth. That is for the future. This mission is about the present. There's an old saying, 'Nothing focuses your attention like a hanging'. You know, an atmosphere of crisis, of drama, of importance. And this is damned important. A second ship must not steal focus. Gentlemen, I expect our crew to be well-focused."

"Is this a crisis, sir?" Eric was confused.

"No, but it could be down the road. For now, I have my work cut out on this project with funding and Congress, not to mention the rest of the world," the President worried. You two get this thing ready to go and the people chosen. If they cut the mustard, the Chinese are in. And anybody else well-qualified."

The President concluded the session, "Let's speed it up. Maybe this is the kind of thing that will bring the world together. Like the race to the moon, but this time we all race on the same team. God knows we need something, what with all the bickering going on. One thing for sure, you can't hold a coalition together for any purpose too long. Bush forty-one proved that."

As they adjourned, both Adams and Sheppard were trying to figure out who the President was thinking of hanging. They agreed to reconvene in a month. At that time, with the team in place, training would begin.

If there hadn't been a hanging in the meantime.

VIII

John Stone hadn't always been the modern savior of the Republican party. But after "Slick Willie" and the "Gore bore," both Republicans and Democrats were devastatingly alike. Even the black president who was heralded as, "The Change We Need," couldn't deliver on that one. Neither party offered an interesting candidate until Stone. His Midwestern ethics and pristine political record made the contrast obvious. Being a widower and having single-handedly raised three children in Iowa, now grown, hadn't hurt either. Interestingly, having gone to college in New Hampshire during the 1980s increased his political capital. It also made both the Iowa caucuses and the New Hampshire primary pretty much in his home court.

Stone held a master's degree and Ph.D in economics, making him the first President of the United States with the ability to understand what his economic advisers really meant, not just what they were saying. Keynesian economic subtleties and supply-side gobbledygook didn't impress or intimidate him. His Ph.D was from the University of Iowa, where he stayed on to teach until the downturn in the economy of the early 1990s propelled him to the governorship. Still in his early thirties, everything seemed to be perfect until his wife found that mass in her abdomen. Three years—and a lot of chemotherapy—later, she died a long, public, but dignified death. Gilda Radner raised awareness of ovarian cancer, but Jennifer Lynne Stone sanctified it. She had testified before Congress without hair, given speech after speech at rallies, counseled others with the disease, and still—always—maintained her legendary smile both in public and in private. That's what attracted John Stone to her in the first place, that smile.

He was a doctoral candidate and she a third-year law student when they met, dated, confirmed their love for each other, and married. The twin boys and a daughter followed over the next few years. She never practiced law, instead devoting her time to public advocacy of issues close to her heart. Issues like the environment, family values, safety for children, and some other not-very-Republican issues, such as equal pay for equal work, women's right to privacy and choice.

The difference wasn't the message, but the messenger. Her style was unique in public and politics. She believed in turning down the volume and listening to her opponents, rather than ratcheting up the rhetoric. Arguing with facts, logic, and a quiet voice were more effective than invective, emotion, and anecdote. And she practiced what she preached. After the divisiveness of the 2000s, she was a breath of fresh, non-partisan air.

Their marriage wasn't one of convenience. It was true love, with two equal partners holding up "the pillars of the temple," in the words of Kahlil Gibran. Their sometimes differing views strengthened, not weakened, their feelings for each other. Both knew the one person they could always count on was only a heartbeat away. A heartbeat away, because they were practically inseparable. When her husband became governor, she didn't use his position to gain advantage, but she certainly knew how to utilize it. It didn't hurt his chances having such a well-regarded mate standing next to him on the dais.

After her death, instead of withdrawing into a shell, JFS decided to dedicate the rest of his life to public service. What made him different was he really didn't care if he ever won the next election. He was issues-oriented and never sold out to special interests, though he certainly had special interests of his own. He was a consensus-building governor, not a divider. If he had honest disagreements with his opponents, he tried to understand their viewpoint. If he wasn't convinced, he argued the issue, not turning the debate into a personal referendum. Everyone knew he wasn't for sale. Although everyone in politics has to spend their time raising money, he seemed to attract more money and spend less time doing it than anyone could remember. After the governorship, he was a two-term senator when his party nominated him as their candidate for the presidency. He won in a landslide.

John Stone was alone in the early evening on a gorgeous spring Washington night. Even through the barely cracked window in the oval office, the sweet smell of cherry blossoms blanketed the room. This Iowan always liked spring. It signaled a rebirth of ideas, momentum, and energy. Tonight was different. Stone couldn't relax and enjoy the springtime renaissance of color, fragrance, and life. He was waiting for a videophone call from his NSA, Williams.

The Chinese again. Now in his early sixties, his tolerance and stamina were beginning to wear thin. Thin didn't describe his waistline. He used to jog every day, lift weights and do sit ups. Now his exercise consisted of coffee cup arm curls and lifting copious quantities of antacids. At six-feet-two, he was one of our taller presidents. The distinction of being one of the more portly ones he intended to leave to William Howard Taft. Asian hegemony wasn't what he'd planned on dealing with on this spectacular night. He was tired of waiting. He picked up the phone, pressed a button, and was connected to his adviser within seconds.

"So what's going on?" he impatiently asked Williams.

"Mr. President," Williams responded., "the Taiwanese and the PRC are at it again. They've both been shooting at each other's aircraft over the Straits of Taiwan."

"And we've moved in an aircraft carrier, again," the President answered in a matter of fact, I know this is routine way. But it wasn't routine. Aircraft carriers in that part of the world hadn't been routine since 2013. "Do not, I repeat, do not let the PRC take out another carrier. I don't want another *Kennedy* incident."

"Yes, sir." Williams knew exactly what his boss meant. No one in the government wanted another *Kennedy* incident, nor citizens outside government, for that matter. "We've got all available assets, satellites, U2s, and human intel concentrating on this area. The *Stennis* carrier group has some new anti-nuclear technology the *Kennedy* didn't have."

"And, Trump," Stone added, less stridently, "I want the press briefed—and briefed accurately. Nothing gets withheld unless the Commander-in-Chief of the Pacific Fleet approves it on military grounds." The President had learned that lesson. "The American people have a right to know where and why their children are put in harm's way. Where's General Adams? Let's see what the Pentagon thinks about all this. Have him find me."

Stone felt like the world's problems were increasingly insurmountable. Like many a president before him, he was frustrated by his attempts to change the world for the better. Trying to impose America's desires on the rest of the world had previously been a difficult task. Now, in the twenty-first century, the cataclysm hadn't arrived with the millennium. What had was a world much different than the twentieth century's.

To use Samuel P. Huntington's title, the "clash of civilizations and a remaking of the world order" was going strong. Where there were two polarized divisions during the cold war of the last century, there was now a reversion to "civilizations" that were becoming more influential, more so than traditional nation-states. These crossed national boundaries to exert spheres of influence. Where before each country aligned with the West or the East, with few non-aligned nations, there were now at least six civilizations pulling the world in different directions. Where problems could be analyzed by their impact, their cause and effect on the two camps of the cold war, there was now a certain "Lebanonization" of the world's problems, what with so many cultural and civilizational influences.

If a conflict pulled one side in one direction, it generated five or six dissimilar views, not the twentieth century's traditional one opposing adversary. The civilizations vying for position were, with no particular weight to the order, Japanese, Hindu, Sinic, Islamic, Western, African, and Latin American.

It was into this fray President John Franklin Stone ventured on pretty much on a daily basis. Trying to get consensus between two or three of the parties, let alone all parties, was rare, if not impossible. Ironic, since this economist was elected because of the economy or, more accurately, *to fix* the economy again. Now we were all living in a worldwide global marketplace that made "the haves and have-nots" more divergent and the cultural camps more volatile as each jockeyed for position.

"Mr. President, General Adams on line two," the anonymous voice announced.

"General, what d'ya make of all the Chinese volleying? Trump's given me the standard party line. You got any better idea what they're both up to?" The President was starved for information. Like most decision makers, he wanted as much data as possible before taking decisive action.

"The damned bastards," Adams huffed. "Yang's fingerprints are all over this." The Chairman was referring to the leader of the People's Republic of China, Vice Premier Yang. "My guess is they're trying to distract our attention away from some other area. I'll bet their real objective isn't Taiwan this time. But you never know how the Taiwanese will respond. If they buy into the provocation, we can't control events. I suggest we get on the horn to the Taiwanese and counsel patience. After all, so far both sides are shootin' blanks."

"What?"

"Neither of 'em has hit anything they've shot at," Adams scoffed. "Candyass rice eaters. I wouldn't give a—"

"General! We're trying to find out what's happening and stop it from escalating."

"I know, sir," the General was more subdued. "Some back door diplomacy with the Chinese to find out what they're really up to might help."

"All good ideas. I'll get Richardson working on the PRC first. Let's see if we can prevent them from playing with their nukes again. If the world knew what they did...I can't believe they actually fired on each other, I shudder to think what people would do if they knew." Stone hung up. As always, Adams' counsel was helpful. Still, his mannerisms and tone grated on Stone. Tone was the least of his problems. He could tolerate tone as long as there were tangible results. There were domestic problems, European problems, Middle Eastern problems. Now, again, Far Eastern problems. The problems first begun in 2013 seemed recurrent.

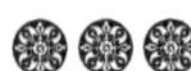

"B.C., General Cummins at NORAD. Have your Pentagon snoopers been noticing the troop movements along China's northwestern border?"

"*Troops*, Joe. But not much in the way of heavy weapons. Can't start a war without artillery," Adams answered.

"General, call me a crazy old fool. Look at your monitor." Cummins flashed a satellite photograph from his screen to B.C.'s. "See those mountains near the China-Kyrgyzstan border?"

"Damn it, Joe. Talk English!"

"In Central Asia, B.C.," Cummins persisted. "The Tian Shan mountains. See anything different?"

"No."

"Neither did we—at first. But the infrared signatures indicate a lot of machinery's been through there in the last few weeks."

"So what? You said yourself you don't see anything."

"Maybe they're hiding something under the mountains. We haven't paid any attention to that region because of our preoccupation with hot spots. But I'll tell you—"

"Joe," Adams interrupted. "If the Chinese are up to anything, it'll be tryin' to get to the Caspian Sea. And you know what? We don't have diddly squat in that area to stop 'em. The President's not gonna defend a country Americans can't even pronounce. I'm gonna let the Russians know about it. It's their neck of the woods. Course those chickenshits won't do anything for fear of havin' the Chinese or the Muslims climb up their ass."

Adams hung up, then called to his aide. "Get me General Petrov at the Russian Defense Ministry."

One of the lessons learned in the Persian Gulf in 1991, and again a decade later in Iraq and Afghanistan, was to commit to a specific course of action and don't get bogged down, either militarily or politically. Sell it to the public and then, once committed, utilize all available resources and use them to the maximum. Public opinion will tolerate losses when they understand why.

What the public won't stomach are vague commitments with open-ended timelines. Get in, get the job done, and get out. Clinton got away with vagueness in Bosnia. Got away with it because of minimal American loss of life, unlike Reagan in Lebanon. Of course, when the U.S. left in 1999, fighting quickly resumed. The American troops' presence had little lasting effect because they didn't go after the war criminals. That was the safe way, the Clinton way. Take a poll and see which way the wind blows. He was also being pragmatic. To his credit, he realized there was no generalized public support for sending troops there in the first place, let alone placing them in danger trying to track down Balkan war criminals. The people of the United States do not tolerate deaths of their citizen soldiers well. This was a European war and deserved European attention. Unfortunately, the Europeans weren't interested in becoming bogged down either. It might be their geography, but this was a generations-old conflict.

Bosnia was the first modern conflict along the fault lines of three different cultures. Each of the combatants were surrogates for larger nation-states. There were the Catholic Croatians, the Muslim Bosnians, and the Orthodox Serbs. This confrontation had been a smoldering conflagration that rekindled every few generations, and each time—after the participants had caught their breaths—they all rearmed and repopulated for the next round. What had changed over the years was their relative strengths and their weaponry, not the centuries old hatred.

The United States was slow to enter the melee for very good reason. Since joining the world diplomatic stage during and after World War I, America tried to be different. Different by attempting to maintain the fiction of being above the fray, maintaining her presence only as a mediator to facilitate all the parties' interests. That wasn't the case then and it wouldn't be throughout the rest of the twentieth century. More blatantly with each new conflict, the United States became increasingly frustrated with the various parties.

Historically impatient, American actions also became less subtle. She began imposing solutions on the parties with increasing regularity. Her frustration level was understandable. Understandable, but shortsighted. What the U.S. created was a situation where ALL resented her help and ALL parties now had a common enemy. They resented the imposition of terms for resolution of various conflicts throughout the twentieth century. Lessons America would learn painfully in the new century in new places like Iraq, Afghanistan, Libya, Iran, and the Taiwan Straights.

America was a new and naïve player in the diplomatic arena championed by countries, religions, and cultures much more sophisticated at the game. After all, they had been at this for centuries.

The roar of the explosion was deafening. Then another, and, quickly, a third. There were human body parts, debris, blood, and grime littering the Shanghai sidewalk where a high-rise, high-security building once stood only moments before. Police and ambulance sirens wailed inharmoniously. Over the din of the sirens, the screams of the injured and dying prevailed. These weren't terrorists' bombs. They came screaming down from above.

"General Cummins, Guam AWACS tracked three low level bogeys from an undersea launch platform into Shanghai. Detonation was two minutes ago in their downtown. Conventional, not nuclear. Initial indications are the target was the Chinese Defense Ministry."

"Damn, what now?"

"Taiwan, again, sir?"

"Can you confirm that, Major?"

"No sir. These were cruise missiles. Too low to track their heat signatures. Hell, they could be ours for all I know."

"They're not ours, son, trust me. Keep me informed." He picked up his Pentagon phone and General Adams was immediately on the other end. "B.C., they've done it again."

A President must make clear to his constituents, as well as to other countries, just what American policy is. What we will tolerate and what we won't. In the face of equivocal pronouncements, other countries have little choice but to test us to determine what our limits are. Whether you agreed with Reagan or not, you knew where he stood. Bush-one drew a line in the sand and made it stand. Even Bush-two was a known foreign policy quantity.

No one ever knew where Clinton stood. He professed to standing for things, but rubbed away the line. What he stood for was constantly changing. Obama was slippery. John Stone, like Clinton, was basically a domestic President. But the world's stage doesn't go away just because you aren't interested in it. Obama learned that. And all presidents retreat to foreign policy. After all, Europe doesn't vote.

"Secretary Richardson on line one, Mr. President." Again, the faceless voice came through his intercom.

"Rich, I'm sure Trump briefed you on the China situation." The President considered the Secretary of

State and Williams his two closest advisers. Richardson and Stone met while both were in the Senate, though Richardson was eight years his senior in tenure there. Richardson had taken the newly elected senator from Iowa under his wing, arranging for his appointment to the committee he chaired, the Foreign Affairs Committee. Stone had turned to Richardson for advice on foreign affairs for years. It was only natural to appoint him Secretary of State.

"My sources at the embassy in Beijing can't figure this one out." Richardson was cautious. "It doesn't make sense to precipitate a crisis now with the world's economies rebounding. CIA tells me the Chinese economy is recovering well. Taiwan's, too. We have two choices, as usual. Be tough and challenge them publicly or do so privately through back channels."

"Challenge who? I want the Taiwanese ambassador's butt in your office, pronto. If they did it, he'd better have a damn good explanation. And if they didn't—"

"Who else could it have been? Not everybody has cruise missiles."

"For now, I think the back channel route sounds best and the safest. We've got to approach the PRC, too. See if you can keep them from blindly assuming it's the Taiwanese and doing something stupid. I'm still issuing orders to move additional aircraft and ships into that theater. They sure know how to wreck a growth curve. This could ruin our short term recovery."

JFS knew he could handle the economics. Like any good red-blooded American, he was also sure he could handle foreign policy. It is human nature to think the world revolves around you, and that the world holds a special place for your thoughts and opinions. Most presidents have held that conviction. John Franklin Stone was no different. He was convinced he could bring about change where others had failed.

And like so many before him, he had been given an education with ample portions of disappointment. One of the weaknesses of the American system of government is the perpetual re-education of our leaders, especially as it pertains to affairs of state. Each comes to the office assuming he is God's gift to international relations only to discover their lack of history, lack of sophistication, and the paralysis of the moment. Each is obsessed with making his mark in those four or eight short years with continuity between administrations. Like American business, they are only measured in the short term. Long-term gains can be debated by historians. Presidents think in terms of "Can I be re-elected?" and "Will history remember me well?" How sad when most must learn from the mistakes of his predecessor. And sadder still, when they don't.

The steady alarm and synthesized voice startled the major, diverting him once again from his paperwork:

Warning, launch detected. Warning.

and repeating every three seconds.

"Now what?" asked the exasperated NORAD officer. "Am I ever going to have a shift without a crisis," he murmured.

Warning, launch detected. Warning.

Turning rapidly in his chair, he reset the launch detection computer. *"I need validation, here!"* He was furiously writing in his log book. "Systems," he asked into his headset. "Are we authenticating another launch?"

"Affirmative. All systems have been validated. We have dual confirmation."

"Damn! When is this going to stop?" He grabbed the other telephone. "General Cummins, we have another launch detection. Far East, but we can't pin down the location this time. We didn't pick it up until it had altitude."

"Confirmed?"

"Yes, sir."

"I'll call Washington."

"General. We have a carrier group in the area with intercept capability."

"B.C.," Cummins was clearly rattled. "We've got another launch. Since it's probably a retaliation, I doubt they'll detonate it before impact like before. The *Stennis* has shoot-down capability."

"That would put us right in the poop chute of this thing, wouldn't it?"

"If this goes nuclear, the whole world's in it."

"Authorize the shoot-down, Joe. I'll notify the President. We can take one out. God help us if there are more."

There are no minor leagues in American politics. Oh, there's the Congress. Still, the Executive and Legislative branches of government aren't comparable. The rules of conduct for each are unique, as are the stakes. If you lose in Congress, you live to try again another day, on another bill. The loss isn't taken personally. Congress compromises, negotiates, and rewrites.

Or at least it's supposed to. It is the ultimate committee: Congress is domestic. It has foreign affairs responsibilities, but advice and consent and treaty ratification isn't glamorous. The glamour resides in the Executive branch. Most of Congress is running for president most of the time. In our modern era, there are no declared wars. Only a declared winner. If Congress has time to debate whether or not to go to war, there is no imperative.

Today we have limited police actions, War Powers Act invocations, or whatever we or the media choose to call them, but all-out war is no longer a declared phenomena. The Presidency is both domestic and international. If you fail in foreign policy, there are immediate and long-term consequences. And worse, it is very much personalized. Personalized by the Congress, the public, other governments, the media. A President speaks with one voice. The Congress with 535. The only politician not running for President is a second term President. And the *only* reason he's not is because he can't—it's been prohibited by law since 1951, following FDR's reelection to a fourth term.

"Mr. President, NORAD is tracking a nuclear-tipped missile targeted at Keelong on the northern tip of Taiwan," Chairman Adams advised. "The *U.S.S. Stennis* carrier group is equipped with tactical anti-ballistic missiles capable of intercepting and destroying this threat. I have authorized the commander of the battle group, Admiral Gruenwald, to attempt just such an intercept."

"Jesus H. Christ, General!" the President was incredulous. "Why wasn't I informed about—"

"Sir, in order to have a rat's ass chance in hell of shootin' this bird down, I had to act immediately. Any delay, and we wouldn't be able to get to the missile."

"General, we're up to our ass in alligators if the PRC comes after us."

"Yes, sir, I'm aware of that. If we can keep this thing from lightin' up half of Taiwan, we've bought a little time for you politicos to keep the rest of the Chinese arsenal in their silos."

"When will I know whether you've been successful?"

"In less than two minutes, sir."

It was into this partisan psychosis that the two-term governor and two-term senator from Iowa had voluntarily entered. Like many before him, John Franklin Stone, too, believed he could change the world with his ideas. He soon learned that ideas cannot be foisted upon unwilling souls. Fixing the economy meant playing on a world stage. Our domestic economy was inextricably linked to the economies of virtually every other country in the global economy. All politics may be local, but add up the various localities and there are thorny issues strewn across the globe. So, the economist from Iowa was now required to practice world class, big league diplomacy—and he really didn't much care for it.

"The *Stennis* has launched its package, General Adams," Admiral Gruenwald reported to the White House, the Pentagon, and NORAD. The multiple link communications channel was open for all to hear. "One minute to predicted intercept."

"Bogey is descending through 80,000 feet," NORAD warned. "The warhead will arm at 30,000. Thirty seconds to impact."

"Fifteen seconds to intercept."

"General, I can't—"

"Quiet, Mr. President!" Adams shouted.

"Ten, nine, eight, seven, six—"

"We have intercept! We have intercept!" screamed a radio operator on the *Stennis*. "We confirm a kill...I repeat...we have a kill!"

"General!" the President persisted. "Get your Chinese counterpart on the horn and call this thing off! Trump, get me the Vice Premier, ASAP!" Several very long minutes passed until the crisis finally subsided.

"Mr. President, the Chinese have held further fire and the Taiwanese have assured them they did not launch the cruise missiles. The Chinese confirm they were not nuclear, they were conventional explosives," apprised Richardson. "Vice Premier Yang is furious and blames the United States for the attack. I have guaranteed him—"

"How dare he accuse us of this," Stone seethed. "Doesn't he know we just averted Armageddon?"

"No sir, he doesn't see it that way," Richardson replied.

"Damn it, Rich! There's got to be a better way," answered a disheartened Stone. They both took several deep breaths and regained their composure. "Great, more antacids," the President complained, swallowing several.

Stone disconnected from Adams, the *Stennis,* and NORAD. "You know what drives me crazy?" The President waxed philosophically to Richardson. "I'm so used to teaching. Students want to listen and learn. With this thing today, I was so busy preaching dogma I forgot I wasn't the only player. What really drives me crazy is that I can't control the situation. In the classroom I had control. Now, supposedly, I am the most powerful man in the world, and I feel helpless, Rich. I've lost control."

"You're doing fine, John," came the reassuring reply. "You need some rest. Good night, Mr. President. The world will look different in the morning through rested eyes."

Stone appreciated his friend's perspective. He did need rest. But he also needed to control something. "Good night, Rich. And thanks. The world dodged one helluva bullet tonight."

That's why this Jupiter moon project appealed to him. No persuasion of others or diplomacy needed. Not on the same level. He was in control. He regulated the branch of government capable of carrying out just such an endeavor. Just find a few people willing to go and send them up on a rocket. Sure, he needed Congressional approval for this or that, but they'd understand. It was only funding. That shouldn't be a problem. This felt so unilateral. Only minimal consultation, no arm twisting or consensus building. No United Nations vote or Security Council authorization. Who would argue against such a grand and noble scheme, a mission to colonize a new world? A mission to advance mankind, a mission of such higher moral value? So what if a few were to oppose him? This mission didn't require a U.N. vote. The U.S. could do it on its own.

Or could it? Damn, he flinched inside. Where's the antacid? He began considering a few of the logistics. *Who will pay for it? And if Congress goes along, do they get oversight? What about telling others, is it secret? If they find out about it, are they included? What if they're opposed to the idea? Is it a U.S. mission? Only for the military?* No, Stone churned, not again! Complicated problems with more questions than answers. This job just doesn't catch any breaks.

Where's Sheppard? Misery loves company. John Franklin Stone wanted company, and he wanted it now!

IX

Kwasie Mutumba Nkata hadn't always been a vegetarian. During his fourteen years of incarceration in apartheid's worst prison, he survived on rollypollies, beetles, and roaches. The dank, moist walls and floors of his solitary cell were an ideal culture medium for the soil-creatures that ventured into the night in search of food themselves, soon to become tomorrow's prison repast.

On a good night, Nkata captured enough *Orthoptera* species to use as "meat" between two chunks of dark, molded bread given up as his first meal of the day. First of two, and the more nutritious. He'd close his eyes and try hard to pretend the crunching sound of exoskeleton chewed in desperation was really fried chicken. The fungus growing on the bread was at first an insult, stomach turning. It soon became his passion. The *Penicillium chrysogenum* fungus grew wildly on the bread served in this squalid environment. The uneducated knew it as bread mold. Nkata knew it was penicillin. And from that fungus he was able to derive the antibiotic that helped him survive the repeated bouts of pneumonia acquired over the years.

He had always been a survivor. A long-time African National Congress operative, this quiet man went to apartheid's prison primarily because he was black, like all the other ANC leaders in the 1960s, '70s, and '80s. Some had been imprisoned in the 1950s, although most had died in prison by the time of Nkata's release. Yes, he had been an activist. But what is activism? To oppose a regime that suppresses one's being and one's people just because of the color of their skin was not a valid reason for incarceration. So he fought. Nonviolently primarily, but he fought. And he was enough of a purist, an idealist, to get caught quickly, not like many more realistic, real world agitators who ran. He stood his ground, and was captured. He stood on principle. He hadn't been there as long as others. But prison isn't measured in years alone. It can be measured in diseases and loneliness, despair and hopelessness.

One year, he was nearly consumed by "consumption." Consumption, beginning in the 1600s, and known today as tuberculosis, spreads through institutional environs quickly. And prison was the ultimate "institution." Created to suppress and oppress the opponents of the white governmental regime of apartheid, the prisons of South Africa were not designed to rehabilitate, but to punish. At least the South Africans were honest about it. There really are only two purposes for prisons, punishment or rehabilitation—and this was definitely not for rehabilitation. Death is the ultimate punishment, and if that occurred, the white ruling class thought, so be it. Nkata defied that fate, unlike many others.

So the bugs made him a carnivore. They also made him a survivor. Battered but not broken, his body was certainly worse for the wear. He survived long enough for the prison conditions to improve in the few years before his ultimate release. The few years before regaining his freedom, three meals a day, and regular medical care became the norm. He guessed the regime was feeling guilty. In fact, his country was about to undergo a transition to majority rule the likes of which our world sees rarely. Rarely, because it was peaceful.

By the time of his discharge, his tuberculosis was in remission, but it had devastated his body. He no longer could eat "meat" *or* meat. Now he identified with the hunted. One doesn't have to hunt asparagus or oranges. Such items are also a delicacy, not available in South African prisons. Not a bitter, caustic man, but a more cautious and reserved one. A vegetarian and humanitarian.

He actually began to change during his incarceration. He quit being embittered about his lot in life and became one of the world's foremost authorities on botany, specifically, hydroponics. As conditions improved, he was allowed access to books and journals. He was given a small area to set up troughs of plants, all grown hydroponically. Hydroponics is the practice and science of growing plants in a liquid medium, not soil. This was ideally suited to a controlled environment. The water content, sunlight, and nutrients are artificially controlled. Again, prison was the ultimate controlled environment. And just as quickly as his bitterness was consumed by science, his circumstances changed.

With the dawning of freedom in South Africa during the 1990s, and no longer a political radical, his groundbreaking botanical achievements soon became well-known. As Chairman of the Department of Botany at Capetown University, he now received recognition previously denied. Today, he was receiving Dr. Eric Sheppard from the United States. The American State Department seemed quite "hush, hush" about this visit. So he was curious. Curious about why a scientist from the United States wanted to talk to him. Curious, but not intimidated.

After his years of confinement, nothing intimidated this small, giant of a scientist, his voice barely a whisper. You…could…barely…hear…his…slow…plodding…but…meticulously…accurate…speech. He spoke this way, not intentionally, but because of a laryngeal injury caused by being hung by his neck, just off the ground on a yoke, enough to choke, but not enough to kill. This chronic pressure around his cervical region caused permanent paralysis of the laryngeal nerves, creating his dissonant voice. This "stretching" made him taller, mentally, not physically. Prison made him a survivor—a survivor with scars. And a survivor with dignity, veracity, and honor. Incapable of being intimidated. No, not this raspy-voiced, gray-haired, 110-pound, 5-foot-4-inch giant of a man.

"Welcome…to…Capetown…Doctor. Would…you…like…some…root…tea?" came the barely audible question from Nkata. Sheppard was not taken by surprise at meeting the diminutive botanist. He'd come prepared. He knew Nkata had no formal degree. Sheppard knew that was a liability or an asset, depending on who was providing the critique. If the university accepted his real world credentials, why couldn't the universe? What is a degree anyway? Nothing but a ticket affirming a minimum standard, not excellence, perseverance, not scholarship. It didn't measure enthusiasm, creativity or passion.

"Root tea? From what root, sir?" Sheppard asked.

"A…shrub…unique…to…my…country…graciously…named…for…me… It's…called…Nkatamorus. Quite… tannic…at…first…taste…but…it…grows…sweet…at…the…finish. He poured Sheppard a cup of his namesake and sat down very close. He was studying Eric's every facial twitch. This was a man who couldn't be rushed. Finally, after a solid ten minutes of silence, broken only by the soft slurping of tea drinking did Nkata speak again. "Why… have…you…come…Doctor? What…do…you…wish…of…a…simple…botanist?"

Sheppard briefed Nkata about the planned mission. As he came to speak of Nkata's role, his voice seemed to soften to his host's level. "The three primary needs for survival are food, water, and shelter. Since the quality and quantity of the soil on Genesis isn't guaranteed, hydroponic growth of food en route and once the team arrives is essential. You are the best and most creative hydroponicist alive. You will be in charge of sustenance for this most important mission," concluded Sheppard.

He had done his studying on hydroponics. Sheppard knew that the complex interaction between temperature, nutrients, and light determined the success or failure of hydroponically grown food. That is, whether there is sufficient growth of vigorous, healthy plants. The ingredients for success are commonplace—water, light, carbon dioxide, organic carbon, nitrogen, oxygen, phosphorous, and sulphur. Common chemicals, readily available. And transportable. What wasn't so common, was someone to "stir" the brew into a life-sustaining, viable flora. Sheppard thought he had his brewmaster.

"Do...you...know...how...many...species...of...plants...there...are...Doctor? Approximately...250,000. And... how...many...do...you...propose...we...take? And...who...decides...which...ones? Surely...we...can't...take...them... all."

"Or can we, Mr. Nkata. With modern technology, maybe we can take all 250,000 species. I don't know. But you will help decide what goes and in what quantities, sir."

"And...what...of...the...70,000...fungi...and...30,000...algae...and...the...15,000...earthworms. Not...to... mention...the...750,000...insects...and...the...125,000...arthropods?"

"Earthworms?"

"They...aerate...the...soil. We...have...an...entire...ecosystem...here. To...leave...any...part...would...disrupt... that...environment."

"They all have a shot at going, or at least their DNA. Let me tell you about the ark we're taking." He could see Nkata's eyes brighten and his head tilt slightly with confusion. "Not only team members are going to Genesis. DNA samples of all creatures will be traveling with you. As you can imagine, choosing what DNA sources to send is daunting. If you want earthworms, sir, you'll get earthworms. You just may not get them until you get there. Earthworms crawling throughout the habitat might not be the best idea. Once you get there, fertilization of the various samples can begin whenever you like."

"Fascinating," drinking his tea. "And...what...if...life...already...exists? Will...it...coexist...with...Earth's?"

"You're not the first to suggest that possibility. I can't give you a conclusive answer. But I can tell you this. This mission is to further life. To expand its reach to a new moon. It is not about destroying life. Ours, theirs, or anyone else's." Eric felt strongly that what was evolving was a chance to correct some bad habits mankind had developed over the centuries. Killing and blind destruction were several concepts that immediately came to his mind.

"What...if...I...fall...ill? I...am...not...a...young...man. I...have...had...more...than...my...share...of... disease...Doctor. Not...only...me. What...happens...then?" He was in his fifties. No one knew exactly how old. Nkata was born in the late 1950s when records of black births weren't accurately kept. Most weren't born in hospitals.

"During the trip to the moon each team member will help train the others in their particular area of expertise." Eric was quite aware of Nkata's past. "You are young in spirit, sir. Your mind is as keen as it was thirty years ago."

"Am...I...expendable?"

"I'm not sure I understand."

"Since...I...have...no...family. Is...that...why...you...chose...me?"

"Your family is all of humanity. Soon you will have new, close family members. This is a team effort."

"You…say…the…mission…will…be…a…chance…for…man…to…start…over? Are…you…a…violent…man, Doctor?"

"I don't believe I am," Eric answered. "Why do you ask?"

"Are…you…sure?"

"Well, I—"

"How…do…you…think…this…new…moon…will…affect…life…expectancy? Not…only…mine, but…others?"

"There is no way to predict that I am aware of." Eric hadn't thought about that directly. "The trade-offs are more technology versus increased environmental impact. I see no reason why you can't live to be an old man."

"I…already…am…an…old…man…Doctor. At…least…my…body…is." They both smiled. Nkata had a sense of humor about his experiences. "And…why…should…I…or…anyone…want…to…leave…this…planet? As…you… may…know…I've…had…some…experience…with…a…living…hell, Doctor. What…is…my…reason…for…going…to …another…possible…prison?" As his speech pattern quickened, Sheppard hoped that it signified not just interest, but excitement.

"Mr. Nkata, you are a humanitarian and a scientist. I, like many others, know of your background. Who is more qualified to struggle with the elements, to survive, and to do so with dignity and humanity, than one who has already triumphed? But this time, your previous circumstances will be your advantage. Your mission is for the good and betterment of all mankind.

"If our world is a prison, who better to break the chains of that oppression? If our world is morally bankrupt, who better to create a new one than one who has seen such corruption from the inside? If our world shackles the human spirit, who better to cast off the bonds than one who knows of them, first hand? You sir, are not only qualified by your life experiences to go, but compelled by them. If you truly believe there can be a better life, you must be instrumental in establishing its parameters."

Sheppard finished with his head less than two inches from Nkata's. Close enough to feel his host's almost labored breathing. Close enough to hear his heart quicken. The seed was planted. But did it take root?

"Come…with…me…Doctor," rising as he spoke, Nkata walked to a small door. As they passed through into a large garden, Eric noticed Nkata was cradling a large, hand carved walking stick in his hands. They walked quietly through the tropical gardens to a clear area approximately ten feet square with a stone wall against the back. Sheppard was admiring the many different species of plants when he glanced over toward Nkata just in time to see him lift the walking stick over his head.

He turned to face Sheppard and quickly swung the walking stick at Sheppard's knees, barely missing them. Eric jumped back several feet in the direction of the stone wall. Nkata drew the staff back and swung again.

"What the hell…what are you doing?" Eric screamed, only to be forced backwards by another blow nearly landed. He was now forced to the edge of the wall with his back against it. There was no further possible retreat. As Nkata raised the staff like an ancient mace, ready to strike a final blow against his supposed adversary, Eric lurched forward, grabbing the end of the wooden weapon.

"That," Nkata softly spoke. "That…is…what…I…worry…about." The end in Eric's hand rested under his chin. This diminutive man was quite strong. He lifted the end ever so slightly, pushing Eric's head upward. "Every… man…has…his…breaking…point. Each…can…be…pushed…only…so…far. Then…they…fight…back. You…want…

to...change...man's...ways, Doctor? Are...you...sure? Are...you...sure...it...can...be...done? Are...you...sure...you... really...want...to? Does...anyone?"

As he lowered the staff from under Sheppard's chin, both were breathing quite rapidly. Nkata turned toward the small door and walked to it. Upon reaching the door, he turned back to Sheppard, who was standing with his head down thinking about what had just happened.

"Think...about...whether...you...want...an...old...revolutionary...on...your...journey...Doctor. I...have... already...been...pushed. I...have...proved...I...can...turn...the...other...cheek. But...what...of...the...others? Have... they? Can...they? Remember...you...like...the...rest...of...your...team...are...nonviolent...Doctor."

Eric walked towards the door. He didn't know what to say. Both men studied the other's face for several moments. Nkata broke the impasse.

"Life...is...precious, Doctor," a somber Nkata declared. He lightly hugged Sheppard. "It...also...is...finite. We...cannot...waste...it. We...do...not...have...much...time. I...will...go...to...this...garden. Whether...it...is... Eden...or...Gethsemane. Choose...the...others...carefully...Doctor. Choose...well." Nkata disappeared through the door and Eric found his way out. He was fascinated, confused, exasperated, exhilarated.

X

A flight from South Africa to Malaysia normally is rather direct. Unless you are trying to hide your route. That is exactly what General Adams had scheduled for his intrepid partner. A route taking him first from Capetown to Nairobi, Kenya, then on to Bahrain, the island archipelago chain in the Persian Gulf. No time to see the wildlife of Kenya or the nightlife of Manama, the capital of Bahrain. Sheppard had read about both and had hoped to someday see them. Not this trip. No doubt the General was more than mildly amused by Sheppard's trek.

Next on to Islamabad, Pakistan, where he stopped long enough to sample the local cuisine. Just long enough to get a major case of the runs, too. Major Conroy, the attaché B.C. had generously assigned to help him, became his lifesaver here. Attempting to rehydrate his charge, the Major plugged Sheppard into an IV solution and dumped a couple of liters of saline into his traveling companion. He'd learned a bit of medicine during his combat survival courses. This was certainly combat as far as Eric was concerned. Conroy was his nurse, doctor, and pilot. So much for international travel, thought the cramping, diarrheic adviser.

From there, one must avoid even coming close to China or its allies in the region. Since the conflict in 2013, American diplomats and military personnel tried to avoid the area for fear of becoming a pawn in another international incident. The Chinese still didn't play by rules the West understood or agreed with. Avoidance of China was definitely in order. So it was on from Pakistan to Rangoon. Had he not still felt so ill, this cuisine capital would have held great appeal. But not after Islamabad. Solids were not yet on Eric's plate—agenda. After a brief stop for fuel, they were off to their final destination...Kuala Lumpur, the old capital of Malaysia.

Although this city of one-and-a-half-million-plus was populated by native Malay, almost fifty percent of its population was of Chinese ancestry. Those of Indian descent comprised an additional twenty percent. Two people, a husband and wife, one of Chinese derivation, the other Indian, were those he had come to see. But first some sleep. As he literally stumbled off his small diplomatic jet into the city at the confluence of the Kelang and Gombak rivers, solid ground, solid American-style food, and a solid eight hours of rest were his only interests. As he sat alone in his room in the American embassy, drinking a bit of cabernet and downing a burger and fries, he couldn't help wishing he'd paid more attention in geography class. He wasn't sure where he was, or how he got here, but he knew one thing. He'd come a long way to get a short distance. Cabernet and fries...what a combination. And such a well-balanced meal for a physician. Also, a meal he had lived on since his early years, at least the burger and fries part. The cabernet came in residency. After all, there wasn't a lot of wine, cabernet or otherwise, in Purcell, Oklahoma when he was growing up. Moonshine, for sure, but no wine.

Now the country boy-science adviser was in Kuala Lumpur, a city founded by those plying the mining trades in the mid-1800s. Tin brought the early miners and settlers. It also brought the British empire, from whom the Malay gained their independence in 1957. Since then, a business center and vital trans-shipping point in the world economy, this Pacific Rim port city was a mixture of sorts. A mixture of races, nationalities, businesses, politics, and intrigue, a fault line of cultural existences. Sheppard's new hosts were a mixture of all of the above.

Dr. Xiao Deng Wu was quite outgoing for a Chinese expatriate. He was born in Beijing in the late 1970s. Educated at Beijing University during the 1990s, he did not directly participate in the student uprisings at Tiananmen Square. But he did not escape them either. He was a sympathetic observer, but observe was all he could afford to do. He was always being watched, even while he slept.

He studied philosophy, both Eastern and Western, eventually receiving his Ph.D in philosophy, but not from Beijing University. He was a student sympathizer. His grandfather, Deng Xiaoping, was the ruler of China during many of those formative years. So he was watched. The ruling party couldn't have the grandson of the paramount leader galvanizing his fellow students against their leadership. Deng was an icon. They didn't need another one. So Xiao was tolerated, but barely. Tolerated until the death of his grandfather. Then he was persecuted. Or would have been, had he not had the foresight to know what was coming.

Historically, the Chinese have not treated the surviving relatives of their recently departed leaders very well. After the death of Mao Tse-Tung, his widow and daughter were jailed. Upon the death of Deng's immediate successor, Chou En-lai, in 1976, his family was forced into internal exile and has not been heard of since. With the death of Deng in the mid 1990s, Xiao Deng Wu didn't wait to discover his fate. He fled the country in the waning months of his grandfather's life. Immune while Deng lived, Xiao was a sure target upon his death.

He studied in Paris at the Sorbonne just after leaving China. It was from this originally theological campus that he received his Ph.D. The University of Paris, as the Sorbonne is now known, evolved from the medieval schools of Notre Dame. Today, the thirteen universities are consolidated under the name University of Paris. However, it is the Sorbonne that has been synonymous with theology since its endowment in 1257 by Robert de Sorbon. Since it was established in 1170, and to this day, this bastion of liberalism and philosophy remains a prestigious moniker.

It was there he met his wife. She, too, was a refugee from her country of birth, India. Not so much a political outcast, but of the caste system. She was Harijan trying to gain a higher education. She and her parents believed that education was the key to bettering one's station in life. Her parents could not escape the caste system of India.

Parvathi Natarajan was determined not only to escape, but to prosper. Harijans—children of God, according to Gandhi—are the *Untouchables*, the lowest of the low, in a cruel, oft misunderstood archaic system. Castes began around 1000-800 BC and have evolved throughout the centuries. The original four castes divided along their functions in society. The Brahmins were priests, the Kshatriya warriors, the Vaishya traders, and the Shudra craftsmen.

As time evolved, so did the castes, adding numerous new jati, still preoccupied with Hindu concepts of how each caste dealt with the problems of purity and pollution. The lower the caste, like the Harijan, the more "impure" one's occupation would be, such as disposing of excrement and other waste. She was but one of the 75 million Harijan, and yet unlike the others. She, instead, was determined to defy the Hindu concept of karma, which holds that all are reincarnated, and that if one has been obedient to the rules of their caste, they may be reincarnated into a higher caste. She was determined to escape the stigma of her caste's traditional societal role. She would not wait for reincarnation. She wanted to rise now, obsessed by changing her status. She was also obsessed with history.

This obsession probably grew from her repugnant view of the caste system. In order to beat an opponent, you must understand your adversary. From the studies of her caste sprang an insatiable quest for how she not only came to her current station, but how mankind arrived there also. Since caste discrimination in education had been outlawed in 1949, she received a modest primary education in India. Having run away from home for the fourth time in her continuing attempt to attend a preparatory school for eventual college, her parents finally gave up and let her go.

She wound up where many Indians of the 1980s and '90s landed, in Malaysia. After working as a house maid for a Malay businessman through what would be the equivalent of high school years in the U.S., she attended school at night and weekends, saving enough money to travel to a country without castes. She hoped to find a place of enlightenment and academia. A place where one is judged by the content of their thoughts, not their unlucky birthplace.

So she, too, arrived in France in late 1995. Working at night, she soon took the university placement exams and was admitted to the University of Paris to further her hunger for history. She was well fed at the table of this historical institution. Eight years and a Ph.D later, she taught there, as one of its most popular instructors. Her specialty was comparative history, a study of how different societies evolved, their similarities and differences. She met Xiao Deng Wu while both were attending a seminar on the comparative philosophy throughout history.

They were married less than two months later. An interesting ceremony, between this Hindu-bred, Harijan Indian outcast, and a communist-bred member of atheistic Chinese aristocracy. It was attended by many academics and several government ministers befriended during their time in Paris—a secular event, just the same. Xiao joked about how he wasn't sure he was really married since he didn't understand half of the ritual or most of the words. Parvathi laughed, because in her eyes there was no ritual, only a French judge presiding. The magistrate was so confused by the two, he read something by Albert Camus, which only added to the confusion. Knowing Camus was born to poverty, he thought it would appeal to Natarajan, and that as the best known French moralist, it would also appeal to Xiao. Unfortunately, this and the rest of his rambling colloquy was completely lost on everyone else. To sort out the various customs being ignored, alone, would have taken the United Nations.

After agonizing over it, the decision to return to Malaysia was made easier when they were both offered teaching positions by the government at the new university in Kuala Lumpur. Perfect culturally, geographically, and academically. They had prospered in the years since leaving Paris, but neither felt fulfilled. There was something missing. So on this night, the two professors from Kuala Lumpur University were being visited by a stranger from the United States.

Sheppard arrived by taxi, alone. Conroy needed the night off after the nursing, doctoring, and piloting of the last forty-eight hours. Their residence was modest. Material possessions meant little to the expatriates from the East by way of France. However, they had succumbed to one vestige of materialism: a large, two-person swing suspended from their front porch, including a state-of-the-art surround sound music system, complete with individual headsets.

Eric was met on the porch by his two hosts. They were relaxing in the swing, with their four extremities entwined. As he arrived, they extracted their arms and legs from each other and stood to greet him. Dr. Natarajan was about five feet tall, with long, straight, jet black hair. She was dressed impeccably, wearing a western styled bright red, pants suit. Xiao, on the other hand, was not at all what he had expected.

He was tall, especially for a Chinese—easily 6 feet tall—thin, and had short, crewcut hair beginning to gray at the temples. Xiao had on a long, flowing robe draped from the shoulders, similar to Indian attire. He had a constant, infectious, sly smile. This gave him an appearance of seeming to question everything. With his lips upturned at the corners, he seemed ready to dispense a joke at all times. Both were in their late thirties, chronologically, yet seemingly much older in experience. Eric hadn't really known what to expect since they were such a mixture of different cultural influences.

"Dr. Sheppard. We have been looking forward to your visit," greeted Xiao. "Please, sit down. May we offer you some tea?" They gestured him to an adjoining hanging swing.

"Thank you, yes. All the travel has my stomach turning in circles," Eric replied. He began to gently sway back and forth. The evening was perfect. No wind and a temperature in the low '70s. Their porch was hidden from the street by gardens of ornamental flowers.

"We know of the reason for your visit," came the soft voice from Natarajan. "We are curious why you are considering us for your mission."

"Because the mission isn't about surviving, it's about thriving," Sheppard began. He was enveloped by a sweet smell of jasmine. "What separates man from other animals is his ability to think. To ponder the ramifications of his actions. To learn from his experiences. To change what he does and why he does it." He was settling into his wicker swing, quickly adapting to his hosts' style. "The role of a historian is twofold: to chronicle the present and to teach others of the past."

"Ah, but Dr. Sheppard, all history is seen through the prism of the storyteller," replied Natarajan. "Who determines what is told and from what viewpoint?" She leaned over to a small table and lit incense.

"May I call you Parvathi?" The blend of jasmine and incense was powerful, as was her question.

"Please do."

"Parvathi, I agree, all history is political." Eric was now totally relaxed. "As will be this mission and its history. Look at the world today. There are certain fundamental truths. Facts and events that aren't disputed. What you will carry with you is the history of mankind. As interpreted by you with the help of many references and communication with Earth."

"Why should I want to carry the history of humanity, with its oppression, persecution and evil, to another world? All facts and events are disputed—at least from each participant's point of view. It is usually the victors, not the defeated, who write the histories of mankind. And whose history? Indian history, as told by the English? Mongol history, as told by the Chinese? Australian aboriginal history, as told by the Europeans? History is nothing more than an argument without end."

"Why?" Eric countered. "Because it is also the record of triumph, achievement, and knowledge. Only through knowledge of our past, can we learn from it. As you say, it is an argument. It is also a dialogue. Who best to examine the premise?"

"Why go to another part of the solar system to answer such basic questions?" she asked, casually leaning against Xiao.

"Mankind has a natural, innate drive to explore," continued Sheppard. "Why have we explored the far ends of this Earth from the beginning of time until our recent history? Yes, to find new resources necessary to sustain or enhance life. But also because of our need, our passion to expand our knowledge."

"And what of the history of other peoples?" The pale light from the moon highlighted her sharp facial features with high cheek bones and deep, dark eyes. "Since interpretation of history comes through the eyes and experiences of the historian, what of the experiences of others I am unfamiliar with, or uninterested in? Am I to be an expert on American history?"

"Because you personally have known persecution and oppression, who better to translate those experiences than one who has lived them also? I believe history must be written and viewed dispassionately, but that doesn't mean the historian is indifferent. Just because you have no interest in something today, doesn't exclude interest tomorrow. You have an unquenchable thirst to understand. You may not be an expert on America, but you could be, if you wanted. History is an infinite body of interpretations of the events of our past, a diary of our species. From that discourse springs knowledge."

Eric noticed Xiao was sitting quietly, with his smirk showing. He hadn't said anything throughout the discussion. He leaned forward and spoke, "Is knowledge immutable, Eric? Is the quest for it unchanging? Is not the individual the most important source of knowledge? Each of us have our own ideas, emotions, and reactions to past events. We only validate those perceptions against the perceptions of others. We each write our own version of history. We rewrite it as our experiences change and as we are changed by those experiences."

"Spoken like a true philosopher, sir."

"A true philosopher? Philosophy is truth, or the search for it, Eric. Where is the truth for including me? What is your reasoning?" Xiao was stroking Parvathi's hair as he spoke.

"As an historian interprets history, the philosopher asks the fundamental questions about life." Eric's demeanor matched that of his surroundings, peaceful, quiet, thoughtful. "The difference between reality and perceived reality, the definition of good and evil. You ask the questions that we all must answer internally. I believe the philosopher must be the moral conscience of the group," concluded Sheppard.

"Or, offer the moral choices and let each member decide?" asked Xiao.

"Better said."

"Answer internally or eternally?" Xiao laughed. "Values reside in each of us. But our choices are defined by our experiences. I've studied all the standard philosophical questions, Eric. I'm willing to offer my opinions, but, frankly, we each answer those questions within. No doubt, you will choose a team whose members have previously considered these questions. What fascinates me about this mission are the new, unique challenges and questions. You are aware, that this mission threatens man's view of himself and his egocentric place in the universe?"

"Meaning?"

"Man feels he is the center of the universe. The world was created for mankind. If life can exist on other planets, maybe our human experience isn't unique. That is, what if there is life other than on Earth? If that is the case, it complicates the age old question, *Who invented whom? Did God invent man, or did man invent God?*"

"Isn't that for each of us to decide?"

"Yes," the philosopher continued. "But one's previous belief may be drastically changed as a result of this endeavor. If there are other celestial civilizations, is there a God they created, also? Or, if God created man, did he also create other planetary life? A philosopher must ask the old questions in a new way. And new questions as well. On Earth, our philosophical questions have a religious component.

"Even for the atheist. If there is no God, or if there is, but we are not created in his image as we have believed since the beginning of time, the core beliefs of our humanity are challenged. How can two civilizations both be created in God's image? Or, one hundred civilizations? Or, a billion? Is there more than one God? This mission will inevitably create turmoil for the individual team members, and for the society you hope evolves."

"And uncertainty and anxiety," added Eric. "I see what you mean about changing the fundamental concepts of our existence. That's enough to invoke some intense emotions in anyone."

"Yes. And fear," Xiao predicted. "Fear of the unknown is a most primitive emotion. It was, and continues to be, the prime reason for the existence of religion. It provides us explanations for the unexplainable. It allows society to codify its ethics and beliefs. Religion is nothing more than a code of conduct that allows people to survive, enforced by mythical reward or punishment," concluded Xiao.

"Sounds to me like you're in the "man created God" school. Does that mean there is no role for religion?"

"On the contrary. There is a paramount role for religion. It is, and will be, what sustains the members. What I am concerned about is the transformation in our religious beliefs. A transformation I believe is inevitable. How will mankind and each individual handle their religion within this new context. I do believe man created God for his own use. However, that does not exclude the existence of God. I believe in the existence of a supreme spirit. I also believe science and religion are compatible." Xiao expected his guest to be confused.

"How can you reconcile science and religion?" Eric questioned.

"Because science is constantly discovering new answers," Xiao replied, unphilosophically shrugging his shoulders. "Explaining the unexplainable, now suddenly explainable. But there will always be unanswerable questions. Or unprovable answers. Is there a God? Possibly. But will it ever be proven? Not unless God is revealed," replied Xiao.

"To the believer, God has already revealed himself," Eric countered.

"Truly revealed, or perceived, Doctor?" They both paused.

"This mission is also a reverse evolution," Natarajan stated.

"Reverse evolution?" questioned Sheppard. "What do you mean?"

"Throughout history, societies evolved from small bands of hunters, to tribes and then into small kingdoms," she explained. "Initially, all members were responsible for gathering or hunting food, including the head of the tribe. No different job descriptions. Everyone had the same responsibilities. Only after societies became large enough did specialization develop."

"What you are saying is, we are sending ten people or so, who are already specialized?"

"Yes," she continued. "This goes against evolutionary history. Specialization only occurs as a society has become sedentary and stays in one place, or moves infrequently. Society evolves to one of farming, not hunting. Since fewer members are involved in food production, the others are free to become specialized. You are proposing to send a small band of specialists. Are they all equals, Eric?"

"Yes. I believe they are. I mean...I hadn't thought about ranks in this mission."

"As a society evolves, with more and different kinds of specialized citizens, different classes develop. In my country of birth, India, this is how the caste system evolved. Which of your members will be considered less useful to the others? Or, maybe equally necessary, but less prestigious?" she asked.

"I hadn't thought of the members from that standpoint," Sheppard worried. "Since we are starting anew, couldn't this societal stratification be avoided?"

"Not if history is our guide," responded Parvathi.

"And who is to say there isn't a tyrant among your team," Xiao interjected. "You believe because you have been careful picking these people, they aren't susceptible to the same failings of all humans. Power corrupts. History is filled with good men who committed horrid atrocities. Mankind has survived by the law of survival of the fittest. Not necessarily individual men."

"But in such a strange environ, won't they have many common reasons to work together to insure their mutual survival?" Eric asked.

"Yes, initially," answered Parvathi. "However, anytime two or more humans interact, there is inevitably a conflict. Since all know each other, all have an interest in resolution of the dispute. Thus, the group members will be forced to choose a side. Alliances develop and over time, as the group becomes larger, resolution requires an intermediary, or—"

"Or, what?" asked Eric.

"Or, the conflict is resolved by violence. Are you planning on taking weapons, Doctor?" came the question from Xiao, with Parvathi nodding agreement.

"I hadn't thought about it. If no weapons are taken, will that not be an impetus to resolve disputes peacefully?"

"Again, initially," answered Xiao. "Man did not use weapons on his own kind first."

"They were used to hunt game," interjected Natarajan. "But man soon realized the advantage it gave him in dispute resolution."

"So here we are using the same tactics..."

"With much improved spears," smiled Xiao. "How can you prevent this team from taking them if they decide there is a valid reason? This isn't your mission. Only yours to prepare. How do we change man's inclination to use the spear? Merely not sending it along isn't the answer. No, what we must do is modify our behavior."

"Renounce violence, as Mahatma Gandhi? He was killed in spite of his own convictions," Parvathi quickly answered. "It simply isn't acceptable for one to renounce violence and the other, not. How do we modify mankind's behavior? All men. Not just a few. It is an age old question. What makes you think the chosen few on this journey will be any more successful than their earthbound predecessors?"

"You're asking, how do we change a character trait that served us well in surviving early on, but now threatens to doom us? Maybe we screen for it, by choosing personalities that are nonviolent. And also look genetically at what predisposes someone to violence," responded Sheppard.

"And who among us wouldn't become violent if their survival depended on it, Eric? Which otherwise peaceful man or woman?"

They sat silent for a few moments.

"As I had expected, you both give me more questions to ponder than when I came. Good questions. Important questions. Questions that are just as important on Earth as they will be on Genesis. More so, because this is an opportunity to start over. I need your insight. The mission members need it. Will you consider going?"

"We did before you arrived, Eric," came Parvathi's whispering voice.

"Yes, Eric. We have given it much thought," followed Xiao. "We needed to know you were serious and thoughtful about something this momentous."

"I will be your historian."

"And I, your philosopher."

The three put their tea cups together in a toast. All realized the courage this would take. They sat silently appreciating the beautiful night with moonlight licking the veranda as they sat taking in the fragrances, the sights and the sounds of Earth.

"Why did you arrive at your decision to go before I came?" Eric wondered.

"We had not," Parvathi demurred. "What we had concluded was there is nothing holding us to this Earth."

"Neither of us has a family, Eric," Xiao added. "We are both frustrated by mankind. We have been persecuted, expelled, harassed and heckled by our fellow man. We only have each other. We are alone. We have struggled to enlighten and inform our students of the value of differences. Mankind seems hell-bent on eliminating others because of the differences rather than celebrating and learning from those who are different."

"We are tired of the fight," Natarajan interjected. "Not tired of the struggle. Tired of the participants. We need new challenges."

"We need to be appreciated for our differences and for our thoughts," concluded Xiao.

"Can you leave Earth that easily?" Eric asked.

Both sat quietly for several minutes. Finally, Parvathi asked, "What are we really leaving, Eric?"

They each intermittently looked toward the black night sky, punctuated by shining white twinkles of the stars. So vast was their universe. So in need of exploration. So in need of explanation. Xiao broke the seriousness. "Are you sure you need a Chinese communist?" he laughed.

XI

Arlington, Virginia, is only a short drive from the Executive Office Building across the Potomac River, but Sheppard always seemed to get lost. And now at twilight, he was in Washington's nightly rush hour. Lost, in stop and go traffic. What a combination. Maybe it was in anticipation of getting really flustered by the corridors of the Pentagon, his destination tonight. Why hadn't he gotten one of those computer guidance gizmos?

Built during World War II, the Pentagon supposedly has more halls than any other building within its "footprint" of 6,700,000 square feet, and of which 3,700,000 square feet is office space. The five-sided concentric "rings'" were fabricated in only sixteen months in 1942–1943, during around-the-clock construction. Eric could barely put together a team of ten in a similar period of time. Times had changed. So had the circumstances.

As he entered the building, he was determined not to get lost finding General Adams' office. But the best laid plans.... Before he knew it, he was being escorted by a uniformed soldier to the security checkpoint for entry into the Chairman's cluster of offices. A bit more luxurious than his small cubicle, he thought—with more than a touch of envy. He was doing all the jet-setting while Adams lounged in his suite. As he was escorted through the door, his musings were interrupted by B.C.

"Welcome back, Sheppard. I presume you've rested since your around the world tour?" B.C. couldn't contain the twinge of amusement.

"Rested," Eric muttered. "You call sleeping on one of your Air Force jets, resting? Let's just say I'm awake, B.C...but barely. What's the rush to meet?"

"Well, Doc, I knew you'd want to hear about our progress as soon as you'd set down. Besides, tonight me and the boys are playin' *Risk*, Pentagon-style. None of that diplomacy stuff you and I played. This is real world conquest, and you're our special guest. You in, Eric?"

Guest, he thought, or entrée? "Sure, if I can just set my head down for a few minutes, I—"

"No time for rest, son. Game starts in half an hour. We usually play around my conference table. It's intimidating to my junior officers...just the way I like it. Reminds me of Schwarzkopf's table in his bunker back in the Gulf. Alright, so I requisitioned his table when I became Chairman. It reminds me of the 'good ole days' back in Saudi.

"Ever been to Saudi, Eric?" B.C. continued. "Pretty inhospitable place. Hot, damn desert, and camel dung everywhere you step. Just as you're about to step over the stuff, somebody starts wailin' and everybody drops to their knees prayin'. I didn't know whether to stand at attention, or drop to my knees, too. Ain't like Texas, brother. I was just a bird colonel then. Am I borin' you, Doc?"

Without waiting for an answer, the General never missed a beat, "Naw, didn't think so. Speaking of camel dung, Eric, what's this I hear about you getting a Chinese philosopher—and the kin of a Deng to boot? I thought I asked you not to include the Chinese unless absolutely necessary. I know I sort of said OK about 'em, but one of their old leader's relatives? What's with that, Eric?"

"B.C., he's no more a Chinese leader than I am," Eric was tired and in no mood for this. "He left China just before his grandfather's death. He was enough of an historian to know nothing good was going to happen to him if he stayed. Besides, he and his wife are a perfect team. She's an Indian, or, hell, you probably already know that, don't you, General?"

"Yeah, I heard. Not exactly a Brahmin, is she? Bit of a firebrand, I hear, too. Rabble-rouser type. Well, she's your problem, if you want her. It's the Chinaman I'm worried about. You sure he's not a plant from those commie rice-eaters?"

"B.C., this guy's a philosopher-extraordinaire. We talked late into the night about religion, history, ethics, logic. I gotta tell you, he's not a communist. Or, an 'anything'. He asks more questions than he answers."

"That's my problem with him, too. You can't pin him down on anything, Eric. You know, I think he was in the Square back in 1989. If he's no communist, how come they didn't throw his sorry ass in jail with the rest? How can we trust someone who won't give you a straight answer? He answers your question with a question: 'What is real, and what is presumed real?' What's that mumbo jumbo shit, anyway, Eric?"

"B.C., this mission is about taking the values, all the values of Earth, to another world. Not just your values, or my values, but all the different virtues this planet has to offer as well as the history of our civilization. All civilizations. Not just Western, or Hindu. Not just the good, but the bad, too. How else do we learn? We study the past, chronicle the present, and teach both to the future. If the two convinced me of anything, it is that we must think historically and philosophically about what we are, have been, and what we want to become as a people and a civilization...or culture. They are the key to the second generation of this mission. After the first survives, living will evolve during the second. And living has to do with questioning one's existence, as a person, civilization, and culture. Planning, learning, studying. Laughing, crying, hurting, and triumphing. That's life, General. Not just survival. OK, General, you've kept me awake...actually gotten me somewhat worked up. So what've you been doing while I sampled the cuisines of the world?"

"From what I heard, you didn't sample much, Doc. You need to travel more, Eric. Get your old stomach tuned in to more exotic rations, you know, sample real food. While you've been seein' the world, we've been makin' a few arrangements about this little trip. Ever heard of Area 96? No, of course you haven't. Well, after the Russians and the rest of the world found out about Area 51 outside of Vegas back in the '80s, we developed a new secret facility. Area 51's where all the stealth technology was first developed and tested. Well, remember back in 1996 when Clinton all of a sudden declared the whole damn southern part of Utah a national park, or something?"

"Yeah, Grand Staircase-Escalante National Monument."

"Well, that was just a cover. 1.7 million acres of oil and prairie dogs. And access to seein' the prairie dogs was already sort of restricted out there. There's not much to see, anyway. So we took it. Nothing but pretty skies and sage brush, with a mule or two thrown in. And hot. Let me tell about hot. Except, of course, in the winter when it's colder than a...well, you know, cold. But underground. That's another story. We'll be goin' out there soon enough. Anyway, the food's more to your taste. Those damn Pakistani's and their curry. Never much cared for that crap either, boy."

B.C. pressed a hidden button and a screen dropped from the ceiling, revealing a complicated timetable. "We also have a launch solution calculated. We project launch capability in twelve months, with a window of about two months in which to launch, once we're ready. Every thirteen months we get another two-month launch window. Course, that assumes you'll have a team ready and trained. You still pickin' customers? How many more?

They're gonna need at least a year for training, Eric."

"I expect to have the team in place after one more trip. When do we brief the President, B.C.?"

"All good things in time, son." B.C. was being fatherly. "Now Doc, tonight's game will have some characters you don't know. In *Risk*, everybody knows what the object of the game is, you just don't tell your compatriots your strategy for success, if you know what I mean. I think you'll find these people helpful on the project, but don't let them steal your thunder. Stand up to them. Ask questions, but listen to 'em, Eric, *comprende?* We talk to the President when you come back...when the team is complete. I'll be ready with the logistics for him then. Listen tonight. And listen hard."

While he was talking, Eric noticed the General's hand slide under his desk. Just as he finished his counsel, the door opened and several uniforms entered, all with lots of scrambled eggs on the brims of their hats and even more ribbons on their chests. Four men and, to his surprise, one women had come to the General's wing ding. A female, two-star general. Maybe there was hope after all for Adams. "Ladies and gentlemen, this is Dr. Eric Sheppard from the White House. He fancies himself a *Risk* player. I think that's enough of an introduction...and a challenge, for now. Be seated and in deference to our guest, we'll let him choose first...he seems to likes RED."

As the board was initially divvied up, Eric studied the room. An Army colonel, one three-stripe Navy admiral, a Marine Corps lieutenant general, and some other general, of the one-star, brigadier-in-the-Army, persuasion. And, of course, Air Force Major General Hayes, or so he thought. Her Pentagon security badge was his informational source. Thank god she was wearing a small Pentagon ID badge. Generals don't wear name tags. Eric had learned that from B.C. They're generals. They don't have to. What an interesting mix.

Sheppard noted the pilot's wings on General Hayes' chest and a Distinguished Air Medal or two. This was no ordinary general. A woman, a pilot, and a general. Quite a combination. He really wanted to hear her story. The colonel rolled first, which meant he also talked first.

"So, Doctor, we've been hearing a lot about your project? When do I get a *Risk* card, sir?"

"Oh, Jim Bob, you know it isn't formal at my game table," interrupted Adams.

"Yes, General, but I still derive a certain pleasure from kicking your East Texas ass and calling you sir as I do it...sir," drawled the colonel in an obvious Texas accent similar to Adams, having just knocked the Chairman out of two countries in South America during his roll of the dice. "Eric...do you mind if I call you that? As we understand it, the primary needs of this or any mission are food, water, and shelter...the fundamental needs for survival. What if the surface isn't capable of sustaining plant growth for a period of time? What if the launch window puts their arrival in the winter for more than anticipated?"

"Colonel, Mr. Nkata advises me that hydroponic food growth will be self-sustaining and self-replenishing throughout the trip to Genesis. That means, theoretically, this hydroponic food source is infinite." Eric knew he was being tested. Hell, they probably knew half the stuff he was gonna tell them tonight.

"That's a lot more beans and sprouts than this Okie would want," Sheppard continued. "It'll sustain life, but not a very pleasant one, to my way of thinking. That's why taking DNA samples of not only humans, but animal DNA is the answer. Sort of a Noah's ark in Petri dishes. As the colony gets established, the plan is for *in vitro* reproduction of animals for food as well as work stock. Why do you ask, Colonel Dupree?"

He was wearing a name tag. "I believe the colonel's due a card now, B.C.," Sheppard gloated after the colonel knocked the Chairman from several countries. *Damn, I hope they leave me Australia*, Eric worried about his standby favorite.

"The colonel's trying to decide what and how many chickens and cows to take, Doctor," General Hayes responded in an almost matter-of-fact way. "It's my move, if I'm not mistaken, B.C."

"Be careful, Eric. Anne Hayes has shot down a lot more than just aircraft in her time. She seems to be lining you up in her sights for something," laughed Adams. "Beer anyone?"

So it's going to be not only a sleepless night, but a beer drinking one, too. *Ooooh, I don't like tomorrow already today*, thought Sheppard.

As Hayes began walking around the room to study the board, that wasn't all she was assessing. She was thin, about five foot eight, but stood ramrod straight, no slouch to this woman of about forty-seven. Forty-seven! How many people make general by forty-seven, Sheppard wondered. Can't be too many...of either sex. Blonde with early streaks of gray, she obviously worked well in this equal opportunity environment. She knew when, and when not, to use her femininity.

She rolled the dice, "Who's going to pilot this vehicle, Doctor? You've got the mission planned out once the team arrives, but it has to arrive first, and in one piece. Then you've got to get around in a less-than-ideal environment. First landing sites usually aren't the best. We know that from moon landings in the 1970s and our more recent 2013 landings. You need a pilot with lots of contingency experience. Someone who can make a decision...and without stalling. You know, quickly and dispassionately. And once you get there, you may have to move around. Have you thought about that, Doctor? A military pilot fits that bill, wouldn't you say? B.C., it looks like we're all ganging up on you tonight. Card, please."

She took Australia. *How could she do that to me?* Sheppard smoldered. Even though he'd just met her, he was indignant. Who was she?

"And working in suits. Have you considered the ramifications of prolonged life in environmental suits? At least until a safe habitat is constructed," piped Admiral Jeremy Leahy, the three-striper from the Navy. "My expertise is working in uninhabitable environs, with a wealth of experience not just under the ocean, but in space as well. I can tell you, it's not as easy as it looks on TV. The suits are cumbersome, hot, prone to nitpicky-type breakdowns and generally miserable to stay in for more than a few hours. We need to fix that for a prolonged mission."

Now Sheppard remembered. Leahy was an early space shuttle astronaut. That is, after a decorated career as a Navy SEAL...the acronym for Navy's elite, covert commando teams. He did time in the Gulf, Afghanistan, and the China Straits, even after going to the MIR space station in the late 1990s. "We need to resolve several issues, Doctor. Speaking of uninhabitable, B.C., consider yourself booted out of Europe, as well," as the Admiral took control of several countries, he smiled at the Chairman. "Card, please."

What is this? Who are these people?, thought Sheppard. And why are they ganging up on the General... and me? "I...we...have considered your points, and we will take all the help we can get. Give me a beer, B.C. It's gonna be a long night." If he only knew. The suffering had just begun. "Is it my turn, yet?"

"Not just yet, Eric. It's General Abraham's turn. Have you met E.J.? E.J. stands for Ezra John. Hell, he's the only Ezra I know...at least that I know I can trust. Named after the Bible, am I right, E.J.? More beer, anyone?"

chimed Adams, always the perfect party host.

"Doctor, Eric...I'm a nuclear physicist by trade and, I guess, somewhat of a stargazer, too. Seems I'll just have to take Afghanistan," moving his pieces into that strategic spot between the Middle East and the rest of Asia. "Too bad the Russkies couldn't in the '80s, eh, General?" the brigadier chuckled, also pouncing on Adams' previously held Asian territory.

"Well, they gave us a pretty bad time, too. Looks like all you'll be doing tonight is being our waiter, B.C., or is that bus boy...sir? You see, Eric, my biggest concern is radiation. What kind of instrumentation can we design to warn the team about radiation? Prolonged low level radiation, then surges of high intensity stuff, on occasion. Thought any about that? Card, B.C. And another brew, too."

As he took his card, Abraham nonchalantly loosened his tie. "And temperature. This place sounds cold to me. Colder than you may think, and I'll tell you why," continued Abraham. "The radiation will heat the surface temperature, but when it's gone there's nothing to hold that radiant heat within the biosphere. At least not enough, not enough atmosphere for me. No, sir, I'm sure you'll need the artificial environment for longer than you think while you're on the surface. The team can't stay in the suits all the time. Never get any work done that way. Grimes, I believe it's your turn. Remember, 'Get B.C.' is our motto."

"Doc, I'm a Marine. Marines are trained to live off the land. Hell, I ate grub worms in Grenada and drank goat's milk in Panama. Met that pineapple of a dictator, Noriega. Damn near ate him for lunch one day. I knew the food in Panama was still something of this Earth," so Eric was introduced to the Marine two-star, General Jack Grimes.

"Attack Jack" as he was known to his friends, because retreat wasn't in his vocabulary as a combat officer over his thirty-plus-year career. "I'm concerned about where they'll live, what they'll eat, where they'll find it, when they eat it, and what'll happen to them. Son, we need to talk. B.C., get the hell out of North America, too. Card."

"Well, Doctor, I believe it's your turn. As Chairman, naturally I'll defer to you and go last. But don't cut me any breaks. I've chewed on better than you for tack," quipped Adams. "You listenin' to what they say, Eric?"

"Yes, General—B.C.—I am. Interesting points they all raise. My guess is they have others, too. Guess it's back to Africa for me. I'd like to have my team coordinate with all of you...talk about your concerns. You obviously have experience thinking about these problems we've never considered before. My people are scientists. But theoreticians, not real veterans. So from East Africa I take North Africa and...B.C., looks like you're gone from the continent of Africa, too. Guess I'm done. Card."

Done in more than one way. Tired, lightheaded, dirty, beginning to get drunk, and generally ready for anything that had to do with closing his eyes. "You shitheads think you've got ole B.C. don't ya? Well, think again, people. I could...," he began to throw the dice, but stopped.

"It seems our guest looks like death warmed over," the Chairman smiled. "Reminds me of an Iraqi type, huh, Jim Bob? You remember the desert don't you, uh...Colonel? Anyhow, maybe we should continue the game some other time," the General concluded, but not before taking a picture of the board—in case they resumed at another time. "And don't think I'm lettin' y'all off so easy. This game'll be resumed later, believe you me."

"Eric," Adams said, after pausing for a brief moment, "you ever heard of the Joint Military Task Force on Extraterrestrial Life? We call it JMT-EL," putting his arm around Sheppard's shoulder. "It's a Joint Chiefs operation that's been considerin' the problems of somebody else comin' here and how to prepare a place for them to live. Or, at least help 'em some. Been around for about fifteen years, or so. They've been considerin' what some space creature would need to survive here. You know, what would those little buggars eat and drink? And what kind of atmosphere do they need? All that kinda crap. Well, it seems their knowledge works in reverse, too. Preparin' people to go there instead of them comin' here."

"Never heard of it, B.C. Can I meet with them?" *But please, not tonight*, thought Sheppard.

"You just did, son. You just did. I LET them kick my butt at *Risk* just so they'd have somethin' to impress you with. They're the best thing that ever happened to you, boy, and to this project. But don't let 'em fool you. They don't know it all. They've just thought about it. By the way, the colonel ain't a colonel, exactly. He's CIA," laughed Adams. "We just let him wear the uniform to get through the door. He was a card-carryin' soldier an eon ago. Hell, probably was an officer...but never a gentleman, right, Anne? We tolerate him now 'cause he knows his stuff."

The newly revealed team reintroduced themselves to Sheppard, shaking hands and laughing at their inside joke. Now he knew why a "Colonel" was hanging with the big boys...and girls. And probably why there was such an air of informality. Hell, half of them probably weren't in the military. Naw, he thought, the others probably were. So what was General Hayes' story? Was she "available"? Is it kosher for a White House civilian staffer to ask a Pentagon general out on a date? He was just drunk-tired enough to want to find out. No, he was just tired-drunk enough to want to go home to bed...alone.

As these JMT-EL people had their laughs at his expense, Eric knew one thing was true about tonight. They surely were the best thing that could happen to him. He made a mental note to find out more about them, especially General Hayes. He knew something else, too. No more games without a full night's sleep.

XII

The longest commercial non-stop flight in the world is from Los Angeles to Sydney, Australia, at about fifteen hours. Unfortunately, Eric wasn't on a commercial flight. He was, once again, on a U.S. Air Force jet, a T-43, the military version of the Boeing 737. It was a new plane built in the early 2010s, but still an aircraft originally designed in the 1960s. Because it wasn't a 747, or other bigger plane, it didn't have the fuel capacity to make it fifteen hours in one jaunt. So refueling every eight hours or so meant Eric got to see more of the world than he had ever dreamed of. And Australia was where he was headed. Not to Sydney, but to a small, insignificant dot on the map called Roma.

Australia is the world's smallest continent and has the largest proportional amount of desert of any country in this world. Geographically about two thirds the size of the continental United States, it was the last continent to be explored and settled by Europeans, other than Antarctica. Its name is a Latin mixture "terra australis incognita," meaning "unknown southern land," a confusion with Antarctica. It is, to this day, the only continental nation-state.

First sighted by the Dutch in the seventeenth century, it was claimed by Captain James Cook in 1770, for his majesty, King George III of Great Britain. Used initially as a British penal colony, it is the driest of all the Earth's continents, making preservation of natural resources a top priority, including comfortable shelter. Most of its geography is uninhabitable, or ought not be inhabited. As you get more than forty or fifty miles inland from the coast, the terrain is desert, with few exceptions. The population lives primarily along the coast. Even now. in the 2010s, its inhabitants only number around twenty million or so. But the coast was not Eric's destination. Roma is about two or three hours inland from Brisbane, but not by T-43. Even that aircraft was too big to land on the small asphalt runway just on the "outskirts" of Roma. The whole town was outskirts.

The oil and gas industry provided the jobs. The pubs provided the distractions. So, on a hot, summer afternoon in December, Eric Sheppard found himself in the southern hemisphere, headed towards Roma, Queensland, Australia, looking for an engineer named Chapman. In Brisbane, he and his military attaché, Tom Conroy, rented a single engine, six-passenger Cessna 210. At least it had retractable landing gear. Tom had hoped to pilot the craft, but the Aussies talked him out of it.

In the U.S., there are all sorts of navigational aids for pilots, radio vectors, VORs, DMEs, ILSs. None of that exists once you leave the coast of Australia. As you go farther inland, the only thing you've got for navigation is dead reckoning. Or a GPS, a global positioning system. In the 1980s and '90s, the United States sent into orbit a constellation of satellites in geostationary orbits around the globe. Using even a handheld GPS device, one can find his position as the device receives electronic pulses from three of those satellites and vectors your position by triangulation. They're uncommonly accurate. You can preprogram the GPS with a certain position, using its longitudinal and latitudinal coordinates and literally fly to that exact position.

And flying to Roma's coordinates was the plan. It sounds easy until you get out there and start looking down and all you see is flat, hot, indistinguishable desert. So, if you truly have faith in your GPS system, or, more accurately, faith in your ability to program your GPS, flying to your desired location is a piece of cake. Of course, if you programmed it incorrectly, you're in the middle of a very large wasteland without a paddle. Even if you had a paddle, there's no water. There is only sand and rock. Hot and hotter. So, it was off to Roma to look for Chapman with a rent-an-Australian pilot. If they got lost, at least he knew the territory. Eric was damned sure not going to trust B.C. and his boys on this one.

Looking for Chapman was problematic, because unlike all the other potential team members, Eric had no idea where he was. This guy was in Australia *somewhere*, but no one could tell him exactly where. Oh, plenty of people could tell you where he'd *been*, but not where he *was*. He did seem to leave a rather wide wake upon his departure. Great, thought Sheppard, I've picked a Crocodile Dundee-type. Little did he know...

Chapman was an engineer's engineer. He improvised. He cajoled. He prodded. "Can't be done" wasn't in his vocabulary. Partying was. After matriculating at Adelaide University to study engineering, allegedly study, that is, he realized all he had missed in his youth. He was hell-bent on making up for lost time. Founded in 1874, Adelaide University had produced three Nobel laureates to date and was considered one of Australia's more prestigious centers of learning. Prestigious, mates, until *Chappo* appeared on the scene. To say he turned this proper school on its ear was to minimize Chappo's influence.

The fifth largest city in Australia provided plenty of "mates" to party with and "sheilas" to party over. In between pub crawls, he managed to obtain one of several advanced degrees in computer science and civil engineering. That he survived was, in and of itself, a miracle. That he thrived, was to be expected. This was no ordinary party animal. He was a finely tuned, rally hound, of the first order, single-mindedly bent on tapping into festivity central, party headquarters...his natural place of residence.

After graduation, he landed a teaching position in Melbourne, a damned British traditional city, quite fit for a proper university. To say he didn't fit in was an understatement. His extracurricular activities made the prissy, higher-ups at the University uncomfortable to say the least. They said he had a "reputation." Thus, with his honor and name discredited, he resigned—by mutual agreement, and to one faction's unending relief. Moving on to Flinders University back in Adelaide, on the occasion of the opening of its engineering school, he seemed more suited to this less than conventional environment. He excelled there and became not only an outstanding researcher and professor, but bored. So, once again, he lit out across this continent-country to make his mark, in a less conventional sense, but his mark on his terms.

His specialty was designing and building structures from the existing environment. His genius at insulation generated several patents, making him quite able to afford his pub bills across this large country. After designing several buildings for the oil and gas industry in Roma, he adopted the town as his base of operations.

Landing uneventfully in Roma, Sheppard and his aide checked in to a sparse but clean hotel, the Club Hotel on McDowell Street, in "downtown" Roma and headed for the pub to try and pick up the scent of David Anthony Chapman.

"Chappo? Haven't seen 'im, mate. Hey!" screamed the bartender to the bar patrons, "anybody seen Chappo lately?"

"He was here about a week ago, Yanks," shouted an anonymous Aussie. "Said something about heading up to the gorge to try out a new something or other. That Chappo. Always coming up with some crazy, new stuff." Turning to Eric he said, "Any idea where the Carnavon gorge is, mate? 'Bout one hour flight time from here. Land on Peabody's strip and hike on in. That's where you'll find Chappo. Beautiful place, the gorge. A bit hot this time of the year."

"If you find that scrum-breaker, tell 'im he owes me for two tables and three chairs from last weekend. And three sheilas are looking for him, mate. Tell 'im to be on the lookout," so cautioned the barkeep.

Great, now we get to go even further into the outback, a resigned Sheppard thought. "Major, let's find our pilot and head for the gorge. Hope he can plot the position into the GPS for the Carnavon gorge...wherever that is."

After locating their pilot in another part of the pub, they diplomatically dragged him away from two lovelies to get some sleep. Judging from his pub bill, this wasn't the time to fly and certainly not at dusk. There is no light in the outback to use for navigation. So, almost all general aviation flight is done during the day.

The next morning at six, there was a loud pounding on their hotel door. "Morning, mates. Ready to fly on this gorgeous morning?" beamed their previously incapacitated pilot. Incapacitated, no more. What's with these Aussies? How can they bounce back so quickly? The two Americans struggled to wipe the sleep from their eyes and readied themselves for the next leg of the adventure in a short, thirty minutes. Soon they were airborne, headed northwest from Roma in the general direction of the Northern Territory.

The GPS said they were getting closer and closer. When it pinpointed the coordinates of the landing strip, all they saw was grass. They began circling lower and lower. Gradually, they noted that the grass seemed shorter over a linear area. There were kangaroos everywhere.

"Hold on, mates. Gotta buzz the strip to chase off the 'roos," shouted the pilot into the radio headset. As he came in low across the alleged runway, kangaroos scattered in all directions, like pogo sticks gone wild. On the next pass, the Aussie aviator pulled back on the yoke and the 210 settled onto the long grass.

As they slowed to a stop they noticed an old wind sock. So this really was a runway. Soon, a weathered woman of 30, looking all of 50, came out to the plane. "Morning, mates. That'll be twenty dollars for the landing and tie-down. Hiking up to the gorge today? Bit on the hot side, I'd say."

Hot. Dry hot. Hotter than these fair weather Yanks were used to. Stuck in the middle of nowhere with no trees, no buildings, no shade anywhere, anytime. The runway lady was nice enough to drive them five miles to the Carnavon gorge entrance...for an extra five dollars. But even from there it was a still a bit of a trek on foot. "Just a few miles," the bartender in Roma had said to them as they were leaving the night before.

"I'll wait here, mates. Good hunting," waved their pilot. Hopefully, they would see him again.

The Carnavon gorge is the "Grand Canyon" of Australia. It isn't very grand, and not much of a canyon. More like thousand-foot walls whittled by a stream. Its attractions are the wall drawings. Aborigines from before the time of Christ had been putting their artistic impressions on the walls. They also built a primitive outdoor amphitheater.

The science adviser and his attaché saw all of it, but only after hiking about five hours through rocky paths minimally cleared for passage. They saw a few other tourists. But not Chapman. On arriving at a campsite seventeen miles into the gorge, they discovered he'd been there trying out new equipment, some kind of a portable living structure. But not for about three days. Someone said he was headed for Lightning Ridge. Where...what... was Lightning Ridge?

So they marched back seventeen miles out of the gorge. Exhausted and aching everywhere, the two were beginning to understand the attraction of the pub to locals. On arrival back at the plane, they downed three beers each in record time, all the while keeping their pilot from joining them. They wanted to get back to Roma, to their garden spot in the desert, as soon as possible. No delays to quench his thirst. Airborne again, they made the flight back to Roma without event, arriving just as the sun set. There was a God.

The next morning, at the crack of *0-dark-thirty*, it was back in their trusty 210 for the trip down south, deeper into Queensland and Lightning Ridge. The flight was without incident. Lightning Ridge wasn't.

Lightning Ridge is a small town that looks like it has been invaded by human gophers. There are holes in the ground everywhere. Not deep holes. Gopher-like holes about three feet deep, and two feet wide. If somebody went walking at night they could fall in a hole and die and nobody'd notice. It, too, was hot. And had a pub or two. The best one was the RSL.

Black opals. Lightning Ridge is where most of the world's black opals are mined. Mined, if you call digging a test hole a few feet deep to see if there's a vein of the gem, mining. Hence, why there are craters everywhere. Everyone wants to be a miner in this place. After looking around a little, it was obvious where they needed to start to find Chapman. The pub, or, in this case, the RSL.

RSL stands for Returned Serviceman's League. What it was, and continues to be, is a watering hole in a town full of holes. This truly was the best hole of all. And air conditioned, too, with real food, not vending machines. But it was the bar where they knew they'd find Chappo, or information on him.

As they entered, they could hear a loud commotion. There, standing at the dart board next to a rather large bloke, HAD to be Chapman. He looked like a Chapman, acted like a Chapman, and everybody yelled their cheers of approval each time he threw. "Hooray, Chappo! Good on ya, mate!" screamed the crowd.

A thin, wiry, ruddy-faced bloke of about five feet, eight inches, he was not imposing, physically. But a personality! A raconteur extraordinaire and everyone in the room seemed mesmerized. The mass of a man next to him turned out to be a best buddy. His name, they surmised, was Damien. They picked this up between chants of "Damien, Damien, Damien, Damien rules," with each throw he'd make.

They made their way over to the pair and started to introduce themselves when this "Damien" mumbled something in a low, growling voice neither could understand, "Hun't eh? Inaway, mates. Chappo's 't'rowin'". They stood back, assuming the previous guttural noises were, in fact, a warning of impending injury. With that, Chappo landed a perfect bullseye to conclude the match in victory. Monies changed hands all across the room amid cheers and calls for more Four-X.

"G'day, mates. Come to have a spot o' tea with Chappo? Or maybe buy him another Four-X, boys?"

So began their opening with the much ballyhooed David Anthony Chapman, Chappo, to most anyone he met, present or future. As they sat around the RSL drinking copious quantities of Four-X, the favorite beer of the region, Chappo regaled all, including his newfound American friends, with story after story of his exploits. It was obvious from the outset he wasn't interested in hearing what the Americans had come to say. Not now, at least. They agreed to reconvene their powwow in the morning. Hopefully, over coffee, Eric prayed.

Evening, at last, ended at two a.m., closing time. Eric's today began a few hours later with a hard series of knocks and a loud grunting, "Chappo says ya better hurry up t' bar."

What hell on Earth was he in? And who is this guy, Damien? Or what? He was six-four and 325 pounds easy. Chappo's friend and confidant was a mate whose occupation was excavation with large, earth moving equipment. This came in quite handy when Chappo was building the latest whatever. Apparently, today, he also was a messenger service and wake-up caller rolled into one.

Speaking of rolling, he rolled his own cigarettes or at least rolled something. What did make it between the paper had the worst smell Sheppard had smelled since leaving the farm in Oklahoma.

Damien had a Four-X in his hand, the hand not pounding on the hotel door. Maybe Damien really wasn't pounding, but Sheppard's head certainly was. The 1812 Overture—complete with cannons—seemed to reach its climax as he pulled himself into the shower.

After shaving, he found himself sitting next to Chappo, who was relatively quiet, relative being the operative word. He, too, had a beer, so Eric thought, what the hell, hair of the dog and all, and popped one open for himself. By the second one, he didn't feel too bad, actually kinda good in an *I like a beer buzz in the mornin'* kind of way. He ran down the mission for Chappo, with brief interruptions from Damien mumbling something about his attaché.

Chappo was interested, especially the part about creating new living environments. He set down his beer, and a focus Sheppard didn't think possible came over him.

"I'm concerned about people not having fun on this, mate. You're all business and no pleasure. That isn't my cup of tea, sport. Life is for living, you know. What do we do for recreation? How do we let our hair down? I have somewhat of a vested interest in the question. Seriously, sport, is someone in charge of that?"

Eric really hadn't thought about entertainment or recreation. He mumbled something about checking into it as he made a note to take back to his team concerning Chappo's suggestion.

"So who's in charge of this trip you've been organizing, Eric?" Chappo belched under his breath and popped another Four-X. "Hold that thought, mate. Chappo's got to choke 'is chicken."

"You've got to what?" Oh. Eric realized what he meant as Chappo danced away from the table to the bathroom to give back some of the Four-X. He was gone over thirty minutes. Eric watched him from across the room. As he would pass a table in route back, someone would gesture Chappo over to their table, throw their arm around him and engage him in conversation. By the time he made it back, Eric counted two dart games, three additional beers purchased by his mates, and two more by sheilas, uh, women.

"Sorry to be so long," Chappo grinned. "Seems my reputation precedes me. You were saying?"

"I'm coordinating the—"

"Na, mate. Who's the chap I'll be answerin' to? The leader?"

"There's no designated leader, if that's what you mean," Eric explained. "This is the team's mission. You'll all make the decisions together that affect you as an individual and as a group."

"Good. Because there's not a Buckley's chance in hell of me takin' orders from some pissant of a soldier or other." Chappo and authority clearly didn't mix well. "Sounds like a grafter could get ahead on this little outing."

"A grafter, Chappo?"

"A hard worker. No politics, only hard work. Never been a good ass kisser, Eric. But I'll work my butt off if I'm interested. And that means hard play. Now I'm back to the first question. What about pleasure? No bull Eric, I want dinkum now."

"Chappo. This is a team of about ten people. I think you'll find an audience to talk to and some suckers to beat out of their earnings at the dart board or poker table."

He was quiet. Too quiet, Eric thought. Had he lost Chappo? What could he say to get his interest back? Maybe he could—

"Styrofoam-like composite modules is my idea of how to travel," asserted Chappo, shattering Eric's train of thought. "Broken down into small, repeatable components. Resistant to heat and cold, light weight, and capable of being stacked, if designed right. Another beer, mate?"

He and the General were definitely co-conspirators, thought Sheppard. "Sure, what the hell. The day's gone, anyway." He looked around for the major and finally saw him. There, in all his splendor was Sheppard's attaché, Major Thomas Conroy, with his head down on a bar table three booths over. Asleep, passed out or whatever, but mercifully down. So that's what Damien was mumbling about.

"What about water?"

"There's plenty of it there, we think," Eric was venturing into an area he wasn't well-versed in.

"You think, mate?"

"Well, we know there's water there. We don't know in what form. There's also plenty on Ganymede and some of the other moons."

"So how do we get it? Is it drinkable?"

"You will have a water purification system on the spacecraft," Eric continued. "But you're right. At some point you'll have to find it on the moon. Or get it from somewhere close. We're designing a reusable vehicle to use for transport between the ship and the surface. There's also a physicist going who should be able to help you find water."

"Is it a he or a she, mate?"

"A she. Melissa Sturmbourg. Heard of her?"

"Na," Chappo laughed. "The better question is has she heard of me?" They both laughed. Now it was Eric's time for relieving himself of Four-X. Funny. It only took him about three minutes, but Chappo was nowhere to be found on his return. He finally spotted him at the dart board with two sweet young things. Sheppard figured the only way to continue their discussion was to play, too. They divided into two teams, one male and one female on each.

"What about food? Chappo's been known to down a steak or two, you know?" He threw another dart, this time landing a "double-20."

Eric threw a "double-1." "The plan is to grow most of the food on the trip hydroponically. That means—"

"That means Chappo can kiss his steaks goodbye. Nice throw, mate. I believe you're up, my lovely."

"Only during the trip," Eric countered. "There'll be supplemental rations sent, too. Once you arrive, you'll be taking DNA samples of cattle to raise as a protein source."

The four completed their game and the two men adjourned back to the table. Chappo ordered another round. He sat motionless for about ten minutes, barely breathing with his chin resting on his hand. Eric welcomed the silence. It was the first break mentally or physically in about eight hours.

Suddenly, Chappo came alive again, arms waving and mouth engaged. Eric could almost feel him thinking aloud. "Plug in, interchangeable auxiliary packs for energy or environment. Stick them into a standard port built into each module. Use them when and if you need to. That means you're gonna need some equipment. My guess is you're sending us out with some fairly sophisticated toys. Am I right?"

"You could say that. An abundance of computer hardware, haptic interfaces and communications gear. You'll probably be helping to design the software and responsible for systems maintenance."

"Right up my alley. I'll assume there will be others going who can help? Another game, my lovelies?" He was looking around for the now departed women.

"Chappo," Eric was quiet. "What about family?"

"What about it, mate?"

"Would going be a problem for you in that regard?"

"My parents were both killed in a helicopter accident when I was in primary school." This was the first time Eric had seen Chappo without a grin on his face. He sat tranquilly for a minute or so, with a blank stare. "They were my only family. My line of Chapmans dies with me. I'm an only child." He sat for another minute, then his mischievous grin broke out again, "I suppose they'd be right proud of their little Davey helpin' create a new world."

They talked from that morning late into the night, alone some of the time, at the dart board on other occasions. Eric explained the schedule to Chappo and the estimated departure date. They went over his expected role at least five times with Chappo refining his questions each new version.

Sheppard found Chappo to be engaging, smart, charming, and a scoundrel, but highly ethical. The problem was, he really liked talking about the mission. Talking. He would philosophize, opine, lecture and discuss, criticize and examine. What Eric couldn't figure out, and what Chappo wouldn't directly say, was whether he wanted to go.

XIII

"Targets acquired...I have a visual contact on one," crackled the radio. "Three bogeys...in bound at six o'clock...altitude two-three thousand.... I've got them, I've got them!"

"Tango one, Tango one...break right on my mark...three...two...one...break! Come about to two-five-zero and maintain current altitude..."

"Two bogeys on my six, range one-five thousand!...breaking left!...I've got visual...I've got tone...Fire one...Fire two...."

"Hostiles at two-three thousand, approaching Mach II at nine o'clock..."

"I have them on screen...Fire one...fire two!...Splash one, splash one! Two contacts dead ahead, no visual."

"Tango one, climb and maintain two-niner thousand...bogeys are two F-18Es at two-three thousand..."

"Targets acquired...I have—"

"Svetlana! You have guests. End simulation."

"No!" she screamed into the headset. "Who dares interrupt a dogfight where I triumph over the Imperialist, capitalist dogs! Who—"

"Sveta...END SIMULATION...NOW! It's the American."

Yes, it was the American. The American, Dr. Eric Sheppard, world traveler, calling on another country, and another one of its citizens. This time to Russia, more specifically, to Plesetsk, the premier Russian space Cosmodrome, about 800 kilometers north of Moscow.

To get from Lightning Ridge, Queensland, Australia, to Plesetsk, Russia, is certainly not a nonstop flight, especially not aboard his T-43. General Adams seemed to have placed the jet on permanent loan to Sheppard. After leaving Lightning Ridge in their rented Cessna, Eric and his intrepid attaché journeyed back to Brisbane, reconnecting with their T-43 and jetting north. First stop, Papua, New Guinea, 1,300 miles to the Northwest.

Eric had been to Papua before, on a live-aboard, scuba diving with Billy Bob and Mad Dog back a few years. It was the first place he ever saw a manta ray. Gliding through the water, such a gentle giant of an animal.

Then it was west to the Philippines, another 2,300 miles, where Eric bought new shoes...not from Imelda. It seems all the hiking in the Carnavon gorge left his shoes in disrepair. His traveling companion, Major Conroy, wanted to sample the local cuisine, but Eric reminded him of the lessons learned in Islamabad last trip. Instead it was peanut butter and jelly sandwiches on board their less-than-luxurious vessel.

From there, it was a "short" 2,950 miles from Manila to New Delhi, India, where they mercifully had eight stationary hours of land-based rest before traveling northward again.

Rested, as it were, they made another quick jaunt to Tehran, a mere 1,575 mile trip, in only three and a half hours. The capital city of Iran was a much friendlier place in the 2010s. With the moderation of its government and people, westerners could at least travel to Tehran without fear. Although more moderate, it was emerging as the core country in this Islamic region. That emergence still tended to polarize Iranians into pro-western and anti-western cliques. Before, all were more or less forced into the anti-western camp. At least since 1979, when radical cleric Ayatollah Ruhollah Khomeini finally overthrew Shah Mohammad Rezi Pahlavi, forcing him to flee to safety in the U.S. after several years of fomenting insurgency, and was able to return from exile, spent mostly in Iraq after being sent to Turkey in 1964.

The Middle East, however, is a region with no historic core country to its civilization, unlike the United States is to the West. Iran was certainly an anchor country of Islam, but still existed uncomfortably in the twenty-first century. As it had in the latter part of the twentieth century, Iran continued to struggle politically and socially, juggling the technology of the West and the principles of Islam. Less fundamental now, its government was still not particularly fond of western values. And there were other, more subtle, factors evolving, making Iran more multi-factional rather than simply pro- or anti-West.

As China awakened to lead the other Asian tigers, so awakened the Islamic realization of these eastern powers. Islam, and Iran in particular, was being squeezed now from three directions. Russia to the north, China to the east and the older threat from the western cultures. This required a more global policy and politics to match. At least the travelers could refuel without fear of being captured.

Then it was on again northward to Moscow, only 1,530 miles and this leg of his journey was complete. A mere 9,700-plus miles in about two days. Routine. No problem. What time is it? And on what day? Was that a simulator, or a real jet attack? Or, maybe a traveler's hallucination?

Sheppard was embarrassed to intrude. As the simulator hatch opened, he fully expected to take a blow to the head or, at the very least, to be read the riot act. Instead, a tall, lissome woman climbed down from the simulator. As she brushed back her long blonde hair after removing her flight helmet, Sheppard found himself aware of the erect hair follicles on his body.

She walked smartly and directly to him, removed her gloves. Extending her hand, greeted him warmly, "Doctor, welcome to Russia. I am Svetlana Yuryevna Gagarin. I am in receipt of your correspondence and am here at your service," her textbook English perfect, in a stilted way.

"*Gospozha* Gagarin. I come to talk with you about a matter of great importance." Sheppard found himself inadvertently mimicking the stiff enunciation of his host. "May we adjourn to a more comfortable place to continue?"

She gestured toward what Eric thought was a nearby conference room. "*Gospozha?* Doctor, who told you of this term? Do you know what it signifies?"

"It is a term of respect to an important person, is it not?" responded Sheppard as they walked. He'd done his research on Russia and was briefed prior to the trip about customs and practices. "It is my belief that you are an important individual to your country and our project…to the world, for that matter." The room was not a conference room, but a dressing room instead

"Have you ever been in a high performance aircraft, Doctor?" I thought you might like to see our facility from the air." She gestured to a locker and began helping Eric out of his clothes.

He was again sensing the hair follicles on his arm becoming erect, again. *Just exactly what was she doing?* he wondered. She pulled his shirt out of his waistband and gently unbuckled his belt. Eric was confused and was worried that an international incident was in the making. But Svetlana knew exactly what she was doing, and quickly turned away, tossing him a pressure suit as she turned. "I will be outside," she announced. A smile crossed her lips, "If you don't come quickly, I'll be back to get you."

After getting his emotions back under control, he dressed and walked through the door, finding himself on the tarmac of a runway.

"Good. You have stomach as well as brains. Come with me!" Walking briskly, she led him about forty yards to a two-seater jet fighter parked on the runway, then helped him climb into the rear ejection seat, and strapped him in securely. A technician assisted in fitting his flight helmet and securing his oxygen mask. The technician fumbled through the emergency checklist in broken English, pointing out his ejection release pull, an air sickness bag, and several other items Eric thought he was instructed not to touch.

"I've never done this before." The canopy closed above their heads "What do I do?"

"Nothing, Comrade Sheppard," she laughed. "*Gospozha.* So, you think I'm an important person, Doctor?" She seemed flattered but remained on her guard. She might be important, but who was he to tell her?

As Sheppard became more comfortable in the cockpit, he also took in the surroundings. Clearly, time had not been kind to this facility. Although it was the Russian flagship, it had suffered from budgetary constraints during the 1980s and '90s. Now, in early 2009, attention was again being paid to Plesetsk, both monetarily and scientifically. He noticed much that was new in this sixty-year-old facility. Much new equipment, but no one had gotten around to painting it in a long while.

This facility's existence wasn't even acknowledged prior to 1983, during the Soviet era, despite the fact that Western intelligence sources knew of its existence as far back as 1957. In this time of new openness and cooperation, the Cosmodrome had begun to recapture its former glory. The Russian state predecessor, the Soviet Union was the first space nation in the 1950s. Its early successes spurred the Americans into a competition, a space race. The West's greater resources assured its victory, but the old Soviet program was not without achievements.

Svetlana taxied the aircraft to the end of the runway. There was pilot babble in Russian between the tower and this cosmonaut/pilot. Without warning, Eric was suddenly thrust into the back of his seat as if a heavy weight slammed into his chest. He was breathing rapidly and heavily, as if there were no oxygen. The aircraft accelerated down the runway, and in only a matter of seconds, they were pointed nearly vertical and climbing fast. Eric's head was spinning, or would have been if it weren't pinned against the headrest by the incredible G-force of the climb. He was perspiring through his every pore.

"Calm down, Doctor," she commanded with an air of confidence, not superiority. "Are you choosing me because of my father?" coming right to the point, leveling off at fifteen thousand feet.

"I'm considering you in spite of your father," Sheppard surprised his candidate.

"Please, explain." She rolled the left wing over the right and the aircraft pitched into a steep dive, screaming toward the ground.

His stomach and its contents were also rolling...and tossing and turning. "This is a team mission, Svetlana. If I may call you Svetlana," he strained just to talk. "No one member can be better than another. There are no ranks. We don't need to include a previous hero resting on her laurels. We need someone experienced, but not burned out. Accomplished, but not sedentary. Energetic, but not foolish. What aircraft are we flying?"

At that, the plane resumed level flight, this time at an altitude of just eight thousand feet. She nudged the aircraft's nose upward and they began a gradual ascent.

"I have proved myself before. I do not need to prove myself to you. My character and my skills are well known. I am flying a MIG-31, a high performance tactical fighter. It never went head to head with your American combat planes." She wasn't hostile. More self-assured. She was interested in his mission, but it was clear she wasn't going to beg Eric. The MIG had climbed this time to twenty-eight thousand feet.

"Tell me about your mother." Eric had studied her face before leaving the ground. She had soft facial lines with just a hint of age lines forming around her eyes. He hoped she couldn't sense the nausea that was sweeping through him.

"She was a hero of the Soviet Union," she exuded with pride, performing three tight rolls in her honor. "She died three years ago. No one remembered her. They only remember my father." She wasn't angry, although clearly hurt by her country's dismissal. "She raised me and my brother, Sergei."

"How is your brother?"

"As you know, he is a government minister. In the Ministry of Defense. He was a young Soviet general. Now he supervises space launches from Kazakhstan. He's fifteen years older, but we are close. Have you ever been to Kazakhstan, Doctor?" She gently banked the airplane in a generally southern direction. "We can be there in a matter of minutes with afterburners." There was a sudden kick as the plane lunged forward ever faster, and Eric was pinned hard to the back of his seat once again.

The Soviets were the first to launch an orbiting satellite, *Sputnik 1*, on October 4, 1957, and the successful launch of the much heavier and mammalian-occupied *Sputnik 2* just a month later demonstrated the Soviets' initial superiority. Though it carried a living dog, it was really the beginning of the end, even at that early stage. American technology would far surpass that of the Soviets, and it did so rapidly

But it was economics that ultimately prevailed. Like other aspects of the Cold War, the Soviets couldn't keep up with America. The U.S.S.R. spent countless rubles on its futile efforts to match the American desire for space supremacy. That only hastened the government's eventual collapse. The ultimate ball-breaker was Reagan's "Star Wars Initiative"—the space-based anti-ballistic missile system which, following the collapse of the Soviet Union in 1991, was later discovered to be a complete fraud, intended only to force the Soviets into bankruptcy by causing them to spend virtually every last ruble they had in competition...with nothing.

"Star Wars" was a masterpeice of deception, and the media were comletely duped—taking the bait hook, line, and sinker—spreading as the gospel truth the well-crafted disinformation being fed to it by the U.S. government. And it changed the way the media dealt with the government. At least for a while

The Soviets learned a lesson the hard way. ***Those who have the gold, make the rules.*** Yet the human spirit of their cosmonauts endured.

Today, Sheppard was meeting with the daughter of a legend, Svetlana Yuryevna Gagarin. Not a Russian legend, but an international legend. In Russian, the suffix of the middle name, "evna," means "daughter of." This was the daughter of Yuri—Yuryevna.

Yuri Gagarin, the first Soviet cosmonaut in space. Not only the first Soviet, but the first human, period. When he rocketed into orbit aboard *Vostok 1* on April 12, 1961, a legend was born. Even his American counterparts were envious. Major Gagarin's tragic death, at age 34 in 1968, came two months before the birth of his only daughter, Svetlana. It also ended the Soviet competition for getting to the moon first. Though never acknowledged, his death set Soviet efforts so far back, they were not even preparing for a manned attempt when Neil Armstrong took that "One small step for man...."'"

Although she wanted desperately to follow in her father's footsteps, this was not a career path open to the daughter of a legend, and not to any woman in 1968. She had longed to fly for the Soviet Air Force, just as that force all but went away. By the mid 1980s, women were being admitted into the Soviet military, but its ranks and operations constricted dramatically during the transition from Soviet communist to Russian democratic authority. There were few slots available to anyone, let alone women.

"We...don't...have...to...go...to...Kazakhstan," Sheppard labored to speak, and was thrown forward into his restraints as Svetlana came off afterburners. He couldn't take it anymore, tearing off his mask, he bolted forward burying his face in the airbag the technician had thankfully pointed out.

"Did you know, Doctor, that over eighty percent of all people going into space vomit?" As he leaned forward, continuing to give up his last meal, she put the MIG through a series of three rolls. Eric barely noticed. After completing his gastrointestinal chores he sat up, clearly feeling better. He was actually getting used to the aerial experience.

"So how did you become a cosmonaut, Svetlana?" Eric knew when and why. But he didn't know how.

"Not because they wanted me." Gagarin was laughing. The kind of laugh indicating victory. She knew she had won. "My brother Sergei." Her voice tightened and she regained her steely presence. "The bourgeois pigs. Sergei used his influence. But I showed them." Three more triumphant barrel rolls followed.

She had opted for a civilian alternative. Flying since her youth, she was an accomplished pilot and instructor by the time of her college years. Beginning with Aeroflot, the Soviet civilian air carrier, she quickly broke the mold of stereotypes in Russia. A woman in a Soviet man's world, she was allowed to train and fly with the military, probably because of who she was, or more accurately, who her father was.

Breaking the formula, and turning more than a few heads with her excellence as well as her stunning beauty, she managed an appointment for cosmonaut training. Soon thereafter, it was on to Baikonur Cosmodrome and, eventually, her grudging acceptance to the space program—the first civilian to become a cosmonaut.

And in so doing, she became the most decorated and honored pilot, civilian or military, to command the Soviet, now Russian, *MIR* space station. Launched in the 1980s, *MIR* literally changed hands in space, with cosmonauts rocketed into space as Soviets, and returning as Russians. Beginning as a *SOYUZ* pilot in the 1990s, she was quickly recognized for her skills. *SOYUZ* modules carried supplies, both human and other perishables, to *MIR*.

History, however, hadn't hurt her. She began her training at Zvyozdniy Gorodok, affectionately called "Star City," and was assigned as a ground controller in Kaliningrad, a suitable task for a woman, her superiors thought. Again, they underestimated her determination and perseverance, not to mention her piloting skills. Fast moving on to Plesetsk, where sixty percent of Russian commercial, research and military launches occur, she distinguished herself as a pilot and leader. Several trips into space followed. Her skills were consummate. She swiftly became a legend of her own making, with no need to stand on her father's. However, it was her beauty and nationalistic rhetoric that endeared her to the Russian people. As Reagan gave his country an ability to be proud again, so too, did this second generation space hero.

"Why do you want to go, Svetlana? You are a credit to your country and mankind. You have nothing to prove. Why go to Genesis?" His voice was more steady as color was returning to his face.

"Why not, Doctor?" She barrel rolled the MIG with Sheppard having no problems this time. He was becoming acclimated. "The better question is how can you go without me?"

"Can you leave Sergei behind? Or the rest of your countrymen?"

"I'm not leaving them behind, Doctor. I'm taking mother Russia with me, her values and her spirit. I'm leaving nothing behind."

Eric hadn't noticed but the ground was nearly under them. The MIG's landing gear lightly touched down at the west end of the runway and Svetlana taxied to their starting point. As the canopy opened, Sheppard climbed out with a swagger he didn't know he possessed. With his helmet under his left arm, the oxygen hose dangling from his chest, he thought he had the right stuff. She locked on to his eyes and refused to disengage. He felt pinned against the airplane.

"You cannot afford to send such a mission without someone you absolutely know has the will—the courage—the determination to succeed. I have that determination. I have proved it several times before."

Next on her curriculum vitae, had been the joint venture known as the International Space Station, a project of most all space nations. Developed and built in the late 1990s and early 2000s, the ISS went through many growing pains. Building it expended a lot of capital—political and economic—in each of the participating countries.

Because of the accidents aboard MIR in the mid to late 1990s, Russia's prestige took a hit. Attention to detail had been ignored. The lack of funds and the loss of morale was infectious. Their entire space program was in disarray. They could have folded shop, but instead chose to excel rather than falter. Russia's public standard bearer was Svetlana Gagarin.

Challenging her countrymen to dare to be great again, she led the charge back to her country's former prominence. The government redoubled its efforts, not to mention more than "re-doubling" the cash commitment to this cash-strapped agency. New flight simulators, computers, hardware, and, most importantly, new personnel. She was the natural choice as lead Russian cosmonaut during the many trips taken to the International Space Station.

Her heroism was confirmed when she rescued two astronauts, one American and the other French, by making an emergency space walk when their handheld transport packs malfunctioned and they began to float into the never ending void. Had she not acted quickly and without hesitation, they would have drifted too far for rescue and run out of air, becoming the first in-space casualties to suffocate for lack of oxygen, not a pleasant way to die. Think of the pictures on the evening news of motionless bodies in space, a memorial for all time and for all to see. But neither died, and all three received medals and commendations. Svetlana also received the undying life-long loyalty of the two.

"This will be different, Svetlana." Eric could feel the heat as she pressed him.

"In what way?"

"On your trips into space before, you knew you had assistance and help on the ground," Eric explained, pretendeding to inspect the MIG they had just exited. "On this mission you and your comrades will have to depend on each other. There will be minimal Earth-bound assistance."

"Do you think the ground controllers made the decision to rescue my two friends when their propulsion units failed?" She held her visual lock, her eyes piercing his. "Do you think they risked their lives? I am committed to caring for my friends, then and now. The Russian space program doesn't have all the redundancy of your American system. We depend on people, not machines." Eric detected pride not envy.

Svetlana was part of a new breed of Russian, a civilian, but one with military ancestry and deportment, evolving with pride in her country and fiercely independent—entrepreneurial and not dependent on the state. Her non-military career path wasn't for lack of desire. She would have, if she could have. To that end, she trained on and flew any and every aircraft she could, including military, like today.

She liked the MIG-31 because it was highly maneuverable and allowed the pilot to fly the plane, rather than the plane flying the pilot. It also afforded her the opportunity to live out her military fantasies of dogfights against her country's old enemies, primarily the United States and its Air Force. She engaged in every variety of simulated combat in her MIG, with F-14s, F-16s, F-18s. She even took on the F-22 and F-35, which weren't around during the Soviet era. An unreconstructed nationalist, she still believed the Soviet Union, her mother Russia, would have prevailed had an actual conflagration occurred.

She chose to ignore history. The fact that the Israeli Air Force, flying U.S.-built, stripped-down aircraft, downed over ninety top-of-the-line Soviet combat planes, yet lost only one of its own planes during the 1967 war with the Arab consortium, was completely lost on her. The undeniable fact that the Iraqi Air Force flew away rather than risk annihilation during the first Gulf war made little difference to her. No, had she been there, things would have been different.

Sheppard knew her history, aerial and political. It was her "can do" attitude and her independence that gave her a shot at his final cut. It was also that intense nationalism. Nationalism by any other name might be called patriotism. It was the belief in her people, culture, society, whatever one wants to call it, that made Eric know she would be an asset, albeit, an inflammatory one. Who needed a patsy, he thought.

"Your role as pilot will not only be to supervise the flight to the new moon, but transportation on the surface after arrival as well. Surveying and planning landing zones and choosing the habitat location will be critical. We need someone who isn't afraid to improvise, someone—"

"Like me," she interrupted. Her eyes had Eric targeted, locked and ready to be fired on. "I am afraid of nothing. Nothing except others interfering with my mission."

"Madame Gagarin, may I remind you, it is a team mission. You will have your say, but ultimately, decisions will be made for the good of the team, by the team itself," Sheppard cautioned.

"I've never been much of a democrat, Doctor. My philosophy has stood me well," she answered. "So, why me? You have your choice of many others. Why this poor Russian girl? What is your reason for my inclusion?"

"Because you have a fire inside, a passion to do great things. We need your intensity—we need your skills. And deep down, through all your bravado, you know what the right move is and aren't afraid to make it. To stand by it and defend it. You also aren't afraid to admit when you're wrong, which isn't often, but you are obsessed with success. You aren't afraid to say you're wrong if it improves the success of your mission. That's why I want you," he concluded emphatically pounding on the titanium fuselage of the MIG-31. He wasn't at all sure that he didn't mean, "I want you right now," follicles and all.

As she stared into his eyes, an optical game of chicken was again being played...who would blink first. She could fire at will, and Eric was locked in her sights. He was captivated by her. The corners of her mouth gradually turned up into a smile as she remarked, "You think you know me pretty well, don't you, Doctor?" Not only was she walking around the plane, but around Eric as well. Her eyes captured every aspect of the moment.

"Svetlana Yuryevna Gagarin will be your pilot. And I will make you proud."

"Not make me proud, Svetlana. Make the world proud."

XIV

Flights back home always seemed to take longer. Maybe they weren't, but they sure seemed so. That was certainly Sheppard's attitude. The adrenaline was gone, the unknown now known, or something. It seemed to take an interminable length of time to go from Moscow back to Washington. It was a trip of only 4,850 miles as the crow flies, but T-43s don't fly like crows. So it not only seemed longer, it probably really was. At least he could talk on a secure telephone back to his compatriots at his office. Mad Dog was lining up new possibilities even as he called.

"Hey, Dwarf, I got a call from the Pentagon today. They want to set up a meeting as soon as you get back—between us and the JMT-EL group. The ones who ambushed you," laughed Houston.

"As long as it isn't tonight, I'm game. Delete that! Not game—let's not play any more games with those folks. No more *Risk* games or mind games or any other kind of games. I can't take any more of their kind of excitement. Try to set it up on our territory if you can. Did I tell you, we named the plane after you? The *Flying Mad Dog* we're calling it. We're due to land in about three hours, and I'm heading straight home, so don't call me, please," pleaded one very tired world traveler. Was there a recurrent theme here? Tired. Always tired. Hell, I'll sleep next trip, he thought.

It's amazing what the human body can take. It's amazing what it can't. At some point we all have to pay the price for our abuses. Even physicians. Eric was fond of describing himself as, "A finely tuned machine, like a high performance racing car that runs on high octane fuel." Except his body ran on junk food. "It's used to it; I'm used to it," he convinced himself. "Take away the leaded fuel and it wheezes, coughs, and sputters; change my fuel to sprouts and health food, give me exercise and regular sleep, and I'll wheeze, cough, and sputter, too," he rationalized. No one was sure if he really believed it. He undoubtedly lived it, though. This was his justification for the cheeseburgers and fries, irregular hours, and all the other bad habits he had acquired. And most of them long before the White House gig ever started.

So, on this beautiful Washington tomorrow—glancing at his watch, it was no longer today—in three hours, Eric Sheppard, the President's science adviser, would be laid up in bed. This finely tuned machine was wheezing, coughing, and, generally, sputtering, with a temperature of 104 degrees.

❀ ❀ ❀

He was bound and determined to pull himself out of bed for the JMT-EL meeting. His body was not so resolute. A grown man pouting is not a pretty sight. And a grown doctor? They're even worse. Not only do they pout, they are the worst of patients. They don't listen to anyone's advice and they question everything. "Do I really need Tylenol for my fever? I'm feeling better. I don't need to drink more liquids." And so on. Turnabout is fair play.

Mad Dog loved it. Now he got to play doctor for real and there was nothing his old buddy Eric could do about it. Nothing other than complain loudly and repetitively. Houston made an early morning house call to his colleague.

"I'll suffer quietly….as per my normal," Sheppard lamented. No, Houston wasn't letting him off that easily. No, there'd have to be blood tests, and maybe an x-ray or two. He even threatened Sheppard with sigmoidoscopy, but let him win that round. He made him take antibiotics and cough syrup, acetaminophen and throat lozenges. You know, the whole routine. And just as in previous times, what he really needed to get better was time, "tincture of time."

So, phlegmatic, depressed, frustrated, febrile, and nauseous to boot, this "finely tuned machine" was forced to make a pit stop, to take it easy. After awakening at six a.m., he tossed and turned until after noon, with the occasional interruption from Houston for the aforementioned poke-and-grope session. In the depths of feeling sorry for himself, he was buoyed by the phone ringing. At last, a respite from illness.

"Eric...Anne Hayes. I hear you're not doing too well. I thought I'd stop over and bring you some home cooking."

Maybe I can get used to illness, the chivalrous scientist reflected. "No, you don't have to do that, Anne... When are you coming?"

"Give me an hour or so. Maybe we can talk about your last trip. I heard you met Svetlana. Don't you move a muscle. What you need is intensive care, Doc."

Was he dreaming or did he hear her correctly? Oh, he wouldn't, move. Every time he tried, it felt like something was going to break off anyway. "You're the best, Anne."

He drifted in and out of sleep for the next three hours. He awakened to see General Hayes in civvies, carrying a tray covered with lots of goodies. Out of uniform, he could also now see her well-cut figure. She was one good looking woman. "How'd you get in?"

"I'm not only a damned fine fighter pilot, but highly experienced in breaking and entering. It's kind of my specialty. Goes way back to the Academy. The guys tried to pull stuff on the girls. So I broke into their rooms and sabotaged their plans with a little shaving cream. Do you know what happens when you take a can opener to the bottom of a can of shaving cream? It comes out in a large V-shaped pattern for about fifty feet in all forward directions. What a mess. So don't mess with me, Doc, or I might cream ya." At the moment, he wasn't capable of messing with anyone or anything. He wasn't sure if Anne was a mirage or the angel of death. "Try the soup first. Here. Let me fluff up your pillows. So, what d'ya think of Svetlana?"

What did he think of Svetlana? What did he think of Anne Hayes? This was one fine lady herself. From the first time he saw her, he wanted to know her story. Well, now seemed the right time to find out. "She's fascinating. I think she's made the cut. Bit of a cage rattler, isn't she? She won't be a tough sell to B.C." As he ate, he couldn't keep his eyes off Anne. "You're too good to me. Can I marry you," he teased.

"You don't know what you're getting into here, Eric. You'd be in over your head. I thought you'd like her. That's why I recommended her to Houston. Eat. Not so fast, slow down. I said, slow down," she commanded. "I'm married to the Air Force and she's the jealous type. Of course, what she doesn't know—"

"YOU called Mad Dog about Svetlana? Eric was surprised. Bet she didn't know about the pants incident. Svetlana had intrigued him. Anne was the real thing. Anne made those hair follicles do more than stand erect. Wonder why Houston didn't tell me about the Hayes call, he thought. "Are you propositioning me, General? Or, just flirting?"

"I told you we needed someone like a military pilot. She's as close as they come without being the real thing. I'd kill to be going. Wouldn't you?"

"Not really. I have enough trouble navigating this planet."

"So I've heard," she giggled.

They bantered back and forth like this while Eric ate. This was the best meal he'd had since before Lightning Ridge. Absolutely, positively the best...and the warmest. And he was serious about getting serious with her.

Anne Hayes was right about her relationship with the Air Force. But she also had concluded that it no longer held the same fascination as before. Maybe there was more to life than an F-22 screaming down from the heavens to tree-top level. She really didn't know. But this was the kind of guy she wanted to test the theory with.

He was smart, in a disorganized way. He was ambitious, but not desperately so. He was driven, but preferred the slow lane to the fast. Thus, his illness was fortuitous. It gave her the chance to get to know this science adviser on a personal basis. She, too, was attracted, and they seemed very compatible. Both were old enough to have tried what they didn't want, but still young enough to now know what they needed, and not just settle for someone less than ideal. They had both done the "I can fix your problems" routine. And the "we'll grow up...together" and "we can work it out" phases. Both had also sowed an oat or two.

There's a necessary bravado that's part of the mandatory ritual of being a fighter pilot—that *Top Gun* attitude. After all, you don't want someone up there flying a high performance, damned expensive, government-issued F-whatever, and *not* have them think they're God's gift to the military. Anne Hayes was one helluva fighter pilot. And not just a fighter pilot, but an ace.

Air Force Academy educated, she graduated in the early 1990s, like all cadets, into a second lieutenant's uniform. She was not only an officer, but a soon-to-be a fighter pilot. The equal opportunity Air Force of the New Age was perfect for rapid advancement. That was the time just after Reagan's military buildup. The fall of the "evil empire"—and the several limited conflicts that followed—guaranteed to advance a pilot who excelled. And excel she did. The first female F-117 Stealth fighter pilot, she trained over the desert space of Nevada.

The Gulf II war was just what advanced a career. She flew multiple sorties over Baghdad and that plane and its pilots were the glamour of the skirmish. Rising rapidly from rank to rank, she was an F-117 wing commander by 2010, a 'bird' colonel with only a bit more than fifteen years of service. Then, in 2013, hostilities broke out in the Straits. The world had been perking along so nicely. Economies growing everywhere by leaps and bounds after the downturns of 2008. Trade flourished, everyone was happy.

Until 2013. It was probably inevitable. A misunderstanding, a miscalculation, a misjudgment.

The People's Republic of China, or PRC, was euphoric over the return of Hong Kong in 1997. One hundred forty-two years of embarrassment and humiliation under British rule ended with the reunification of this city-state and the mainland. The PRC was committed to a free economy, but not committed to political dissent. When such discord quickly raised its head after the first of July in 1997, they just as quickly suppressed it. And suppressed it as harshly as in Tiananmen Square nearly ten years earlier. Fewer deaths, but with much more publicity. The world was revulsed.

Even before the Clinton administration, United States policy toward China was predicated on the premise that politics would follow economics. The Chinese economy flourished, but political changes lagged significantly. Democracy was, and is, an aberration in China—in all of Asia. Democracy is anathema to Confucianism. In fact, they have more than five thousand years of nondemocratic history. It was naïve to think China could—or would want to—change that history.

After the agreement negotiated with Great Britain for the reunification, Portuguese Macau was scheduled for a similar fate in 2000. It was a less auspicious transition. And next? The PRC was on record as early as the 1980s, saying that Taiwan would be next. They were also on record as stating that a Taiwanese declaration of independence would be met with military action, swiftly and decisively.

That is exactly what happened. In early 2013, Taiwan's freely elected legislature voted a resolution declaring their independence. It was really a vote of frustration. Increasingly isolated, this economic tiger felt it was a lamb awaiting slaughter. Taiwan once believed it had two choices: reunification with the mainland (and inevitable subjugation), or, in the alternative, independence. After sixty years of democracy and several years observing the fate of its brethren in Hong Kong, they now felt they had no other choice. They wanted political recognition comparable with their economic station in the world—with a U.N. seat and traveling rights for their diplomats. No more exclusion from the U.N. because of PRC objections. So, they opted for independence over the strenuous objections of the United States and others.

What followed was predictable, but surreal, nonetheless. How could either side allow their differences to spoil their economies, or for that matter, the world's? This conflict reiterated the premise that, once a policy gains a life of its own, the reasons for its origin are lost. Neither side could possibly prevail. Neither side could back away. Nor could the United States and her allies. The Japanese and the other economic tigers of the area were in a quandary. To support the Taiwanese meant great harm to all, especially economically. Not to come to their aid meant even worse. It was a classic no win situation.

Both sides sustained significant damage. The collateral damage on the world's stage was worse for the PRC. It forced each nation to choose sides. The East Asian countries bowed to the lead of their historical warlord, China. Japan and Korea both tried to remain neutral. Neutral in a dogfight is like sitting on a fence when both sides are throwing rocks. Both sides remember your stance in less than flattering ways. They both throw at you. This left only the United States to act against China in a region where it was already overextended, politically and logistically.

In spite of the clash, the world's economies rebounded. Some faster than others and some with more vitality. The PRC was the largest Asian marketplace before the dispute. Not so in the aftermath. It was slower to recover because it was, again, the odd country out. A pariah amongst nations, China became more paranoid. It was a no-win war, except for the career advancement of all survivors of the conflict. As in all wars, some go home in boxes, others go home heroes. It was a hero playing nursemaid with whom Eric was exchanging flirtations today.

Most of the conflict was aerial. As with all modern confrontations, it was over quickly. Quickly, yet costly. She lost three good friends and her wing executive officer. But Anne Hayes had survived. Survived and came home a hero with a star on her shoulders, one of the first female combat to so advance. Her unit had taken heavy losses in combat with the People's Liberation Army and its Air Force. She had become an ace, downing five PRC aircraft in one day. In the course of her glory, she also saved several pilots in her wing.

Today the question at hand was whether Eric Sheppard would survive? Would he prevail over the virus or whatever he had contracted? Not exactly as dangerous as the Straits, but he played it to the max. And Anne Hayes was ready to accommodate his theatrics. She hadn't played the role of a woman in a long time.

"Tell me about JMT-EL, Anne. How did you get involved? How long's it been around?"

"Slow down again, Doc," she soothed. "All good things in time. After the Straits of Taiwan, I was brought back to the Pentagon. I'd known of B.C., but I didn't really get to know him until the Straits. He was the task force commander in my region. A four-star already and a real pistol. For all that gruff exterior, he's quite sensitive to the needs and anxieties of his subordinates. After I made ace, he found me to congratulate me. I guess he sensed I wasn't really into that kind of a deal. Neither was he, so we bonded pretty swiftly. When he came to the Pentagon, I came with him. I've always been interested in space exploration. Did you know my degree from the Academy is in astrophysics? Anyway, this task force on extra-terrestrial activity has been around for fifteen years or so. He appointed me Director. It's part of a bigger picture, but you don't want to know about that."

"Well I'll be damned. You know more about what I'm doing than I know, and you knew it years before me," muttered Sheppard, thinking out loud.

"Not exactly. Remember, we've been planning for them coming here. Your guys are planning to go there."

"Some of the problems play either way. Food, water, shelter. Every engine's gotta have fuel."

"Yes, it does. And you haven't taken in enough yet, Doctor. I force fed two younger brothers, so don't make me—"

"Alright, already! I'll eat. But I'm fascinated by JMT-EL. Are we still on to meet, soon?"

"Just as soon as you have medical clearance. What about sex?"

"What? I couldn't...I...I...we..." he blurted.

"No, not us, you goof. The team. What do they do about sex? You've got girls and boys going to summer camp in outer space. You can guess what will happen," she had come a little closer to look at his consumption progress.

"It's probably inevitable that someone will pair off, or something. But it's not a requirement. Don't forget about Mad Dog's Petri dishes. We've already got one couple, the historian and the philosopher." He paused before asking his next question. "Anne, would it be copacetic for a White House civilian to date a Pentagon general?"

"What a romantic thought—inevitable, but not a requirement. You're a real lover boy, aren't you. The historian and the philosopher. Sounds like a Disney movie." She paused. "Eric, I like you. I like you a lot. Can you tolerate the abuse we'd get? I don't want to get you into trouble. Not just from B.C., but from the President on down. I'm ready for a little adventure. Are you?"

"I'm up for it, if you are."

She gently kissed his cheek, "Get well, soldier. We'll talk about this and everything else later in the week. I'll check on you tomorrow."

As Anne Hayes bussed his tray and let herself out his back door, Eric was thinking about his prospects. He was feeling much better already. You might even say ready to get up.

XV

It took Eric a little longer to recover than he expected. Physically, that is. Two trips to Bethesda Naval Hospital and a lot of antibiotics later, and his pneumonia was on the mend. Who knows what or where he'd acquired bilateral lower lobe pneumonia. Probably in one of the bars in Australia, where he'd gone from scorching hot to air-conditioned cold one too many times. Anyway, he was improving. His lungs were still way behind his heart in the healing arena.

Anne had almost stopped his heart a time or two. They had become constant companions during his three-week recovery. He was certifiably in love. Now it was time to get back to the business at hand. Eric was actually ambivalent about having to go back to the office. It would cut into his time with Anne. At least she was part of JMT-EL. But there was something about JMT-EL she wasn't telling him. They'd talked about many things during his convalescence. He just couldn't overcome a nagging feeling that there was more he didn't know.

"Welcome back, stranger. Read any good books lately? Or, have you been occupying your time elsewhere? Been to any good restaurants?" So harassed his friend, physician, and associate, the one and only Mad Dog Houston. "Get ready to knuckle down and work, brother. We're meeting with the JMT-EL people tomorrow. I guess you know one of them already, huh? Here's my agenda so far. Feel free to add anything you want." Mad Dog's agenda was as follows:

1. Update on team members
2. Remaining potential team members
3. Discussion and justification of criteria for team selection
4. Target date to begin training
5. Location of training
6. Estimated time of departure
7. Reproduction—food and livestock
8. Philosophy
9. Communications
10. Return capabilities
11. Update on food, water, shelter

"I was thinking of adding a policy prohibiting sex between JMT-EL members and our staff. How would you feel about that, Eric?"

"Cute. Real cute. What time tomorrow and where? God, I hope it's here. Please tell me you talked them into coming here, Mad Dog."

"Your wish is my command, Herr Doktor. Actually they didn't care. So it's here in the conference room at ten a.m. Will you and the General be up by then, love lumps?"

"I'll ignore that if you promise not to bring it up tomorrow. Anne's sensitive about the public display of affection thing. So lay off, OK?"

"I'm just pimping you, pal. No harm, no foul. But watch your back. Others may not be so charitable," counseled Houston.

The door opened and in strolled General Hayes in full dress uniform. "Ready? We're off to the White House for lunch with the President, or didn't Eric tell you, Mad Dog?"

"I should've known something was up. He's in a suit. Not a well-fitting one, but a suit. Try to dress him better, will ya, Anne? And where'd he get that tie? A bit of color coordination might help. He's hopeless, General."

The two left Houston to prepare for tomorrow. As they walked, they hardly noticed the traffic or the accident a block from the White House. They were both too busy doing and saying all the little love things people do in the beginning of a good relationship. They stumbled into several people on their walk from Sheppard's office in the Old Executive Office Building to the White House. When you're busy staring at someone, you don't always walk a straight line.

Entering through the northeast gate of the White House, the two presented their credentials. The White House sits on eighteen acres of well-manicured gardens in the heart of Washington, DC. It is prime real estate and the perfect setting for a formal function. The property has an abundance of trees. They are constantly being pruned, grafted, and occasionally, replaced.

There is a tradition of planting a new tree carried forth with each President. As the two walked to the entrance, both stopped to admire the fifty-year-old oaks planted by Mrs. Lyndon Johnson. As they arrived at the door he couldn't stop looking at Anne. He was smitten and it showed.

Once inside, they were ushered along to the State Dining Room. Eric tried not to let Anne see his excitement. This was routine for her. Pentagon brass get invited to these kind of functions like ordinary people go to Kentucky Fried Chicken. No, this wasn't KFC. He was about to go to his first "state dinner" even though it was a luncheon.

This luncheon was being given to honor the President of a now-unified Korea. Eric had little interest in Korea, only that he was going to a White House soiree with his well-thought-of lady, General Hayes. Designed to intimidate, this mansion had always accomplished its task in Eric. Not today. This would be one of the few times business and pleasure crossed. Since Anne was there on business, Eric thought he might as well conduct some himself. There were people at this luncheon that could be very helpful to his project. Certain other JMT-EL folks, and a senator or two, would be there, not to mention the Palestinian ambassador to the U.S. Maybe he could help arrange a meeting.

This part of his government's house always gave him goosebumps. The sense of history is inescapable. Designed by James Hoban for George Washington, burned by the British during the War of 1812, remodeled several times, including extensive renovations during the Truman years from 1948-1952, this estate was a true national treasure.

Eric looked upwards at the large chandelier presented during Teddy Roosevelt's term back in 1902. How could anyone not be awestruck surrounded by this kind of history? As they walked past the fireplace mantle, he couldn't help notice the inscription taken from a John Adams letter. Adams was the first President to occupy the home in 1800. "I pray to Bestow the Best of Blessings on THIS HOUSE and on All that shall hereafter Inhabit it. May none but honest and Wise Men ever rule this roof."

This hopefully wise man was beginning to feel the pressure again. Pressure to finish the team, pressure to begin training, pressure to explain why they were chosen, pressure to—*just pressure.*

And now he was also pressured to find time to spend with his new love. Of course, she had pressures of her own. Hers sprang from the military she had spent her life trying not to offend. There were some who didn't think it wise for her to be seeing as much of a certain science adviser. It was the kind of thing that could end a career. Just ask several former generals who received early retirement when their social life didn't measure up to the arbitrary standards of a fickle military. She was falling in love, too. As the two dined over the toasts to the Korean President, neither heard much of the speeches. All they heard, or saw, was each other.

"Want to go with me to Argentina? Maybe stop in the Caribbean for a little scuba diving? Drinks with umbrellas on the beach, and who knows what else, sweetheart?" raising his eyebrows à la Groucho Marx.

"I'd love to go, but you're aware I can't just pick up and leave. I've got to get B.C.'s okay on it. I don't dive either. Think I could learn? You could teach me," the General's eyebrows raised to mimic Eric's.

"There are a few other things I'd like to teach you," Sheppard kidded. "I'm headed to Argentina to talk to another potential team member. Thought we could combine business and pleasure. If B.C. gives you any trouble, tell him I need your input on this trip."

"We need to get some ground rules set. This is hard for me—for my career. I don't really much care about it right now. But I'd like to not throw it all away just yet. You're wonderful, but what if we're wrong about us? I'm not looking for a short term romance, Eric. Hell, I wasn't looking period," she admitted. "I want to spend as much time with you as you do with me. It's just that it's all happening so fast. We have to be careful."

"Who cares what others think. All I really—"

"I care. And the mission we're both working on cares. And our boss, you remember him? He's the one toasting on behalf of our government. Remember him, the President? I'll bet he cares. And I owe B.C. a lot."

She was right and he knew it. But right now all Eric wanted was to spend time with her, not to have to worry about Jupiter or Genesis or Argentina or anyplace else. He was a realist though. There would be time down the road. It wasn't like they were going on this space sojourn. All they had to do was complete the team, train them, and launch them on their way. It seemed so simple. *Why does life have to be so complicated?* he thought. Simplify. That was going to be his new motto. Simplify.

"Eric, I've got plenty on my plate to get ready for tomorrow. How about working alone tonight? We could both use the vacation."

Was she kidding? He didn't want to take any time away from her. But he had a full plate, too. "Sure. No problem. I've got plenty to do, too," he responded. He did have plenty—a veritable cornucopia of unfinished business that required his attention. Simplify. What a concept.

After the magnificent repast prepared by the White House culinary staff, there were toasts, then small talk, everyone circulating from table to table. Now was his chance, Eric thought. A chance to talk to the ambassador from Palestine. Ambassador Aswari was a tough veteran of the decades of on-again, off-again fighting in the Middle East. He had a tendency to bring any and all conversations back to his portion of the world, and to view problems only from the perspective of the Palestinian cause.

In the early twenty-first century the Israelis and the Palestinians were still locked in a protracted clash.

Palestine had been granted autonomy in the 1990s. Now they had an actual country in the 2010s—a country whose demographic bubble of young radicals made it difficult to maintain order. This was one of the enduring battle lines in the world; it had been since Israel's creation in 1948. It was a geographical, historical, and cultural boiling point for centuries, a simmering cauldron now, intermittently overheated by one party or the other. There really was no satisfactory solution to tensions in this region as long as each side refused to recognize the other's right to exist. Both gave lip service to each other's rights, but, in practice, they were steadfastly defiant.

Eric was as aware of the problems as anyone in government. That was neither his area of expertise nor his focus today. All he wanted from the ambassador was help getting an appointment with a reluctant Palestinian psychologist, one Mustafa Najibul. He hoped Anne might help. He had briefed her on what he wanted. This ambassador was a previous militia commander during the struggles of the 1980s and '90s. He was still fairly militant and Eric thought a uniformed general might impress him. He was also counting on the charm of *this* general.

"Ambassador Aswari, may I introduce General Anne Hayes, of the United States Air Force. I am Dr. Eric Sheppard, President Stone's science adviser. We were hoping to talk with you about a matter and hoped for your assistance," began Sheppard.

The ambassador's eyes raised as Anne thrust her hand to shake his, then kissed him on both cheeks in the customary fashion of the Middle East.

"Al salame Ali Kin," Anne greeted the ambassador. Eric was surprised when she addressed this old commander in Arabic. She congratulated him on his recent appointment as ambassador and saluted his previous accomplishments. The two were getting on marvelously. The lesson here is that all people feel more comfortable in familiar surroundings. Here was a Palestinian, recently named ambassador, talking in his native tongue to a U.S. Air Force general. After a few more moments of this diplomatic banter, Anne reintroduced Eric.

Aswari was much more receptive and certainly less formal. Both explained in generalities the mission. Aswari knew of it vaguely and seemed honored to have his people considered for inclusion. He would definitely establish contact with Mustafa Najibul. The two Americans promised the newly designated diplomat an evening on the town at his earliest convenience and parted company like old friends.

"We'll be in touch about your introduction to the night life of Washington, Mr. Ambassador," Sheppard closed, both shaking his hand firmly to seal their future jaunt.

"Nice touch, Anne. Where did you learn Arabic?"

"Languages have always come easy for me. During the Gulf War, I picked it up from the waiters, just hanging out in the officer's club. Hope I was helpful," she said, knowing full well she was instrumental, not merely helpful. With the luncheon concluded, they walked back to Eric's office again, making small talk along the way. Neither really wanted to leave the other's company, but they both knew it would be best. As he watched her walk away, Eric hoped it wouldn't be for long.

Each burned the proverbial midnight oil at their respective shops. Neither slept much for several reasons, not the least of which was thinking about where their relationship was going. What sleep they each managed was not the restful kind. It was the wake-up-every-thirty-minutes-or-so, toss-and-turn kind. Ponder and evaluate. Study and calculate. Contemplate and reflect. Meditate and deliberate. Over the mission and each other.

Things were moving quickly on the one hand and not quickly enough on the other. As the sun rose over Washington, each separately wandered to the mirror to assess the night's damage. They had been here before. There's a giddiness brought on by too little sleep. A "damn the torpedoes, full speed ahead" kind of braggadocio. An air of invincibility, brought on by a lack of norepinephrine in the brain.

One can only stay awake a finite period before sleep deprivation psychosis prevails. That's what that scatterbrained stage of consciousness is called when you've stayed up too long. Although not quite psychotic, both were intoxicated with metabolic brain chemicals, verging on craziness. Love crazy, not work crazy. The burden of work only exacerbated the madness. Both of them really did need to get away—to find each other, what they wanted individually and together, to define their futures and that of this mission. And to rest. The perspective allowed by adequate rest is grossly undervalued. Both needed to learn that lesson.

Water is an amazing refresher, and hot water even more so. After a long, hot shower, Eric was putting on a suit again. These JMT-EL types were going to strut into his province dressed to the nines in their fancy uniforms. He'd given everyone on his team instructions to look their best. He opted for a new brass tie clip, a recent gift from Anne. She thought it made him appear more stylish. Also, a new tie and, okay, a new suit, too. All picked out by *his* general. Wouldn't Mad Dog be impressed.

He had also informed his people to be in their places at the conference table at 9:30 sharp. He wanted them in place when the JMT-EL arrived. At ten a.m. on the mark the military task force entered. They did cut quite a swath. Eric thought there'd be enough brass to intimidate his folks. He wasn't wrong. He also knew his team was capable of rising to the occasion and had the capacity for intimidation of their own, too. What he didn't want to happen was this to boil down to a pissing contest between civilians and military. After all, they did have a common objective in the mission.

"Ladies and gentlemen, generals, colonels, and all others of different ranks I don't know about," Sheppard began, hoping to inject some levity into the proceedings. "We come together today for our first joint meeting on issues I believe we can agree are of great significance. My intent is to establish areas of agreement rather than areas of disagreement. No doubt there will be divisions among our various opinions. But I would implore you all to keep the larger objective in mind. That is, we are all on the same team, with the same mission, with our future and the future of our species tied to our mutual success. General Hayes."

"I echo Dr. Sheppard's call for cooperation. Each of you brings a unique perspective to the table. Remember the person sitting next to you does also. To that end, I think we should all spend the next fifteen minutes or so getting to know one another over coffee. No mingling with your own. We are on recess." That should lighten up the circumstances, thought Sheppard.

Over the next half hour, the two mingled with the others and noticed several intense, but collegial discussions already beginning. There was also scattered laughter and a palpably less formal tone to the room. They were reconvened by Houston tapping on a water glass.

"My name is Dr. Houston. Mark Houston. I understand some of you from the Pentagon have intelligence," he paused. "Or should I say, receive intelligence." There was the hoped for laughter. "You probably know that I'm known as *Mad Dog*. As long as you mean it with reverence, feel free to address me so. We have used as our guiding principle in choosing team members the concept of picking the best qualified, irrespective of other factors.

"I know that may have created 'problems'," he remarked, fashioning quotation marks with his fingers in midair, "for some of you, but remember, we are choosing ambassadors to space from our species. No one will remember their infirmities. But we hope to memorialize their accomplishments. So far, we have the following members," proceeding to list on the whiteboard:

Team Member	Country	Sex	Age
1. Clarence Taylor Tatman	US	M	58
2. Xiao Deng Wu	China	M	46
3. Parvathi Natarajan	India	F	40
4. Melissa Anne Sturmbourg	European	F	38
5. Kwasie Mutumba Nkata	Africa	M	55
6. Svetlana Yuryevna Gagarin	Russia	F	47
7. David Anthony Chapman	Australia	M	? 40-50

"We anticipate completing the team by adding the following very soon." He wrote on the whiteboard again:

8. Eva Graciela Mariani	Argentina	F	39
9. Mustafa Najibul	Palestine	M	50

"Why have we chosen these particular people? That is the anticipated question I would like to try and answer," continued the venerable Mad Dog, in true professorial tones.

"Yes, doctor, why a philosopher? And an historian?" interrupted General Grimes. "I can understand needing a physician and an engineer. Even a physicist. I've gotta tell you, this engineer not giving his age worries me. What else won't he divulge? But I don't get the historian and philosopher."

"An historian tells us of our past. They also chronicle the present. How else to prepare for the future? As Santana said, 'If we do not learn from our past, we are doomed to repeat it'. An historian is the objective observer. We all have our opinions about history, but can we be objective in our assessments? A philosopher is the conscience of this new colony. If an agnostic member dies, does their agnosticism die with them? Not if a philosopher is there to remind all of those teachings," answered Houston. For a Mad Dog, he was certainly being scholarly, thought Eric.

"Then why a psychologist?" asked Admiral Leahy. "Why not a minister? I'm assuming you want this person to be a spiritual counselor."

"Because it's going to get mighty lonely out there, Jeremy," answered B.C. Adams, the Pentagon's newest expert on counseling. "It'll take more than just listening. It's gonna take a lot of insight into feelings and emotions. Everything will be new. New to the team and to this poor shrink who's got to keep their heads on straight. The one I worry about IS the psychologist. Who shrinks him?" mused B.C.

"I think once the team realizes they are totally dependent on each other, they'll take care of each other. Not just verbalizing it, but living it, in the void of space," this from an anonymous civilian, one of Eric's more junior players.

"B.C.'s right," supported Sheppard. "These people realize they are the start of a new humanity. They are also potentially the end. If they fail—and the new humanity on Genesis is no different than the present here on Earth—there's no second chance. Their training, their psychological makeup, their stamina must reflect that. They will learn to help each other and learn each other's skills. Cross-training is of paramount importance. What if someone dies in route? What if it's the physician? We can give them all the data in the world to survive but it ultimately comes down to their individual willpower. That human spirit and drive to not only survive but to thrive. To live life to its fullest extent, not just survive. They are the first generation. Survival itself will be their top priority. But if it were the only priority, if they don't provide for the needs of the second generation, none will survive. We are jump-starting civilization on another world by giving the first generation five-hundredth generation knowledge and skills."

There was an uneasy quiet in the room as each reflected on Eric's brief monologue. "Then…since everyone will be teaching everyone else their unique skills…why do we need a teacher from Argentina?" came the question from "Colonel" Jim Dupree.

"Because a teacher's first priority is not content. Her skill is how to teach, not what to teach. The physician is responsible for medical content and so on," answered General Hayes. "Also, adult education is different from children's education. This member will be responsible for overseeing how well the content is being conveyed to the team initially and, ultimately, to the next generation, testing the successive achievements both now and in the future. How do you learn best, Colonel?"

"I'm an observer, General. I learn from observing my surroundings, other people, and the cause and effect of things. I'm not much of a book learner. But I guess if there are gonna be kids, we'd better find an educator who can deal with rug rats as well as grown ups, too, huh?" responded Dupree. After a brief chuckle, there was quiet again.

"Why can't they come back? Who made that dumb-ass decision?" The question clearly came from a civilian in the middle of the table.

"The President of the United States," B.C. answered, staring at the accuser.

"Well," came the slow response. "I, for one, still think that's stupid. People need to belong. Their self-worth stems from their appreciation by their group. I don't think it will be enough to be appreciated by their team members when they know there are seven or eight billion soulmates back on Earth."

"Well said, son. But if your space hero doesn't concentrate on establishing a new world, nobody will survive the trip to their new home. They'll die of homesickness," B.C. snickered.

"Geez, General. Give 'em a break," the civilian retorted. "We're picking people who are dedicated and committed to going for the duration. But to hang them out there forever arbitrarily isn't fair."

"Why don't we let them choose what the options for return should be?" came a compromise offer from another civilian.

"Why the hell not?" B.C. grunted, disapprovingly.

"When does training begin? And where?"

"Currently the 'where' is classified," B.C. answered. "The 'when' had better be soon. Eric?"

"We should have the team completed within the next few weeks." Sheppard was guessing. B.C. was right. It had better be soon.

"I think we're forgetting someone very special," tentatively spoken by a second lieutenant aide to General Hayes named Drake. "Who's going to take care of the pleasures of the crew. I mean, life isn't all work. There's supposed to be down time, too. Reading, art, drama, music. What makes life worth living, not just surviving."

The kid had articulated the same thing as Chappo, Eric thought. "The lieutenant's right. Who pulls the artist out of each of us? And who determines who or what makes each of us happy? It's probably someone working in concert with the psychologist. So are we agreed we need another member? An artist, for lack of a better word?" queried Sheppard.

"And shouldn't they take along a lot of art and music anyway? I mean, twenty-three months in space, training and getting there with no music. Bummer," from another back-of-the-room participant on the civilian side.

"Archiving mankind's artifacts won't be easy," answered Houston. "We've already begun trying, with a lot of help from the Library of Congress and the National Archives. The tough part isn't what to take. It's what NOT to take. Who's to say what's important? Remember, 'one man's ceiling is another man's floor.' And what is 'art', or 'music', anyway? Remember rap from the 1990s? That isn't music to me, but it is to someone else. What don't you take?"

Five hours later much of the agenda hadn't even been brought up, let alone discussed. Eric knew this was time well spent, but he was impatient. "People, it's three o'clock. Let's conclude for today. I think we all have a lot to think about."

That was an understatement, now recognized by everyone. There would need to be many more meetings, but, for the time being, each had plenty of food for thought.

While their respective teams were thinking and ruminating, Eric and Anne would be off to the southern hemisphere. B.C. approved her going. Eric figured Adams thought he had a spy in General Hayes. His intelligence had been spectacular to date. He had known Eric's every move. No, Anne Hayes wouldn't be General Adams' G-2. But she would make a better traveling companion than Major Conroy. At least, he predicted, Anne could hold her beer. She was certainly better to look at.

As everyone left, B.C. summoned Major Conroy, and began whispering in his ear. Sheppard paid little attention. He was sure Adams was only giving Conroy operational details for their next excursion.

XVI

Andrews Air Force Base was becoming as familiar to Eric Sheppard as it no doubt already was to a certain Air Force general named Hayes. It seems she had certain base privileges he hadn't previously been aware of. Some because she was Air Force. Some because of her two stars. His almost personal T-43, the "Mad Dog II," was fueled and ready for take off. Major Conroy seemed a bit formal today, probably because of General Hayes' presence.

Eric made a mental note to loosen him up. He wasn't sure about protocol and didn't really care much about it. His woman was traveling today, not an Air Force general. As expected, the major viewed things differently. Stiffly saluting her on their arrival, he stood at attention until relieved by General Hayes. Eric made another mental note not to tread on military convention. He had as much to learn about her life as she about his.

Their first destination was the small south Caribbean island of St. Lucia. Two hundred and forty square miles of difficult terrain inland surrounded by the most beautiful underwater diving Eric could remember. He'd been to St. Lucia many years before with Mad Dog and Billy Sipes. Down near the southern end of the island, near the town of Soufriere, was a hotel, the Anse Chastanet. It was their destination, or, more precisely, the hotel's attached private chateau. After the very bumpy ride from the airport, the three travelers arrived hot, tired, and very dry. Dry, in the "I need a foo-foo drink on the veranda" sense. Three travelers, because with them was their attaché, Tom Conroy. At least he would be in a separate bedroom.

From their balcony window rose the twin Pitons—Gros and Petit— peaked mountains rising directly from the Caribbean. They were very anatomical and that point wasn't missed on Eric. They had three days here and he planned to make the most of it. First, occupy the major. Conroy hadn't advanced to major by hanging around generals and their new lovers. He was nowhere to be found. Nor was their housekeeper. Providence or luck? Who cared?

The villa had a 150-degree view of the bay, with shutters for stormy weather, if needed. They were open, revealing the full expanse of this fairy tale tropical island. Scuba diving for later. Love for now. As the two sat on the large cabana kissing and fondling, drinking their sweet, fruity beverages, their kisses became more passionate. They were soon completely naked in the midday sun, clenched in the bonds of love on the deck of their government-requisitioned villa. God, Eric hoped the governor or somebody didn't come by. He was lying next to his general, and they drifted in and out of passion and sleep over the next hour.

Fortunately, they quickly became aware of their skin and how hot they felt. If these two rookies to the tropics weren't careful, they'd wind up in the midst of a major league sunburn in no time. Passion always seems to end too soon. A sunburn is forever. Running directly to the shower, also looking out over the island, they rinsed away the afternoon's amour with cool, cleansing water. The next thing they knew, they were lying on the large, old, canopied bed, shrouded by mosquito netting. Having fumbled their way through the maze, they fell into each other's arms again.

So much for washing away the afternoon. Her skin was warm, from the sun, and from the small beads of sweat beginning to ooze from her every pore. Their breathing quickened and seemed to synchronize. Together, in each other's embrace, they were an orchestra playing a passionate symphony. A symphony in three movements.

First *Accelerando Allegretto*, then briefly, *Largo*. And, finally, faster again, *Vivace con Allegrezza* to conclusion. Their rhythmical movements replaced by bodies slumped in exhaustion. It had been a long time for both. Sometimes waiting makes it better. They decided not to wait again.

Yes, this was certifiable love. No turning back. No second thoughts. No letting work get in their way. No—

The phone rang, suddenly interrupting the thought. *Hell, I didn't even know we HAD a phone*, groused Sheppard, silently. It was the dive shop reminding him of their scheduled diving lesson, his a refresher and hers a first. They were late but the master said, "No problems, mahn," in an English more closely resembling the French patois of the Caribbean.

They scurried to find their various articles of clothing so quickly discarded earlier, now playing hide-and-seek with their owners. They dressed in a nouveau Carribe style. His shoe on her foot, a T-shirt on backwards, and not enough sunscreen, or at least, not in the right places. And the mandatory island hat. The kind woven tightly from hemp and sporting a brightly colored band of local cloth. Yes, they painted a unique picture, these two American tourists. And when you throw in brand new, color-coordinated, top-of-the-line, latest and greatest scuba gear, yeah, they screamed tourist—loudly!

At the beach adjoining the Anse Chastanet, there is a long dock which serves as a water taxi stop on the way to the capital of Castries. Travel on this island is best done by water. Although they had a rental car, the hotel pointed out that they were responsible for wear and tear. They were also informed them that tires are changed about every six hundred kilometers because of that wear and tear. Lots of bumps and bad roads. So water was the better way. Below the dock was a cave that extended back into the rocks several hundred yards. It was only thirty or forty feet deep, perfect for a beginning diver and a good test for a rusty one. This was their destination.

In diving, the first thing to do with a new diver is to discover their swimming skill and confidence level. She might be a hot shot pilot and a general, but this was a new environment. After a briefing on equipment and a few basic rules, they were off to the water. The briefing was also in Patois, with rough translation by Eric on the fly. Anne was familiar enough with the concepts.

Only now she would be going down, whereas it was her custom to go up. Air compresses one atmosphere every thirty-three feet, meaning one must constantly breathe while under water or suffer the consequences of that compression. If you take a breath at thirty-three feet, hold it and surface, the air expands, doubling in volume. But you don't know that because you are dead, having ruptured the alveoli in your lungs or some other horrid result. So one must breathe. Regular and normal. No holding one's breath. *Breathe!*

They walked into the minimal surf wearing thin Lycra suits. The temperature was around 80 degrees. No need for wet suits. After testing the equipment in the shallows, they began a gradual descent into a foreign environ, beautiful, colorful, and quiet. There was movement everywhere, undulating coral fans, small fish darting in and out of crevices, crustaceans scurrying about. A new world for Anne, a reacquaintance for Eric.

Quiet. All you hear is your own breathing. Pause to listen more closely and you can hear the parrot fish gnawing on the hard coral, later excreting it as sand, or even the sounds of cleaner wrasse nibbling parasites from larger fish. Still, it is a quiet unlike any on the surface. Anne soon recognized the similarity with that of soaring in a glider.

This was a paradise with no phones, no video linkups, no telecommunications of any kind. They drifted down to about thirty feet. The master and Eric put Anne through the paces of equalizing, clearing her mask, correcting her buoyancy. As she was in the air, she was a natural under water. They swam slowly toward the entrance to the cave below the dock. The dock was only a few feet away, but the dock was on land far away from their new circumstance.

As they got closer to the cave the light faded. They turned on small handheld lights. They were attending an underwater festival, like a rock concert where everyone holds up a lighter in the dark. The lighters today were the bug eyes of the crustaceans. The lobsters and crabs like rows of tiny orange-yellow, flickering lights against the darkened stage of the cave. Wavering back and forth, moving occasionally.

Glancing at their regulator gauges more often than necessary, like most new divers do, they watched their air supply slowly decrease. They had been underwater for forty-three minutes. Time to begin the gradual ascent back to reality. A reality with noise, pollution, dust, team members to worry about, and a major to locate. The least they could do was take Conroy to dinner. Or not! This was their vacation. Their three days. Their paradise. Let him find his own.

Over the next three days, they briefly saw the major in passing. He appeared alive and breathing, albeit obligatorily sunburned. He had that white-to-red-to-peel look covered by gallons of white-lathered lotion. SPF-400 wouldn't help him now. Goodbye, major. Write if you need us!

They stayed in bed late into the morning each day, sometimes even sleeping. Sleeping a lot, actually. Both needed to recharge their batteries in preparation for the coming weeks. Their routine included a light lunch, followed by diving, then sunning—with sunblock mutually applied, and a late afternoon "nap." Finally, a large dinner with local rums and imported cabernets. The Port of Castries is naturally deep, allowing large container ships to disgorge their contents onto the docks. Excellent imported wines, even in this Lesser Antilles nirvana, were common. They consumed their fair share over dinners of shellfish prepared in the local tradition.

They ventured into Soufriere the last night in search of a party. What they found were friendly and curious black locals, speaking completely incomprehensible Patois, smoking a musty local hemp, dancing to Rastafarian music, and generally having a ball. They were the only whites in the crowd of sweating, gyrating bodies. Welcomed like brothers, however, they danced and drank until three in the morning. About the only thing neither could quite bring themselves to try was the hemp. Probably not a good thing for a White House civilian or an Air Force general to be trying anyway.

Next morning, reality intruded. The phone rang, and Major Conroy's voice came through the earpiece. Sounding fully rested, and acting the same, their patriotic attaché reminded them of their two p.m. departure. Patriotic, because his blue uniform now covered his crimson skin, except where too much lotion had dripped leaving small white blotchy areas. Red, white, and blue.

The two untangled themselves from each other and, slowly, regrettably, began dressing—paradise soon would be lost—pausing every few moments to embrace again. Were three days really over? Couldn't they spend just one more day? They were 1,900 miles from Washington. Nineteen hundred miles…and a lifetime.

Disappointed at having to leave, they gathered their belongings and began the rugged ride back to their T-43 and the remaining 4,000 mile trip to Buenos Aires. Their need to refuel along the way required a diversion to Rio de Janeiro, adding 700 miles and several additional hours to what would only have been a 3,300 mile flight in a larger aircraft.

"Major, I think I'll fly the first leg, if you don't mind."

"Not at all General," a startled Conroy replied. "Will you need me to co-pilot?"

"No, Eric...er, Dr. Sheppard will sit right seat for now, thank you. That will be all."

If Eric could show her how to scuba dive, turn about seemed fair. Flying this transport was child's play to this decorated ace. It used to be that to fly a plane of this complexity required two pilots. Not since the advancements in computer guidance systems and autopilots. Now, one pilot would suffice. But she still took about thirty minutes to reacquaint herself to an aircraft she hadn't flown in several years. Probably wasn't regulation, but what the hell. She was a general and a pilot, and who was going to argue with her, Eric? The major? After takeoff she leveled off at 28,000 feet. She gestured to Eric to take the yoke. He immediately placed the small jet into a steep dive.

"Eric! what the *hell* do you think you're doing?" Anne screamed, quickly grabbing the controls. Dozing in his seat in the cabin, the major missed the excitement.

"That's the way Svetlana taught me," Eric blushed.

"Svetlana? She let you fly? Fly what?"

"A MIG-31. While I was in Plesetsk."

"What else did she let you do?" Anne was a mixture of exasperation, confusion and bewilderment.

Eric wanted to try flying again. To take back the yoke now would require an act of Congress. Anne wasn't going to give it up again. It had taken a real act of Congress to authorize women to fly in combat. She had the wings. He had some explaining to do. And now, Anne wasn't particularly conversational. All business. No more pleasure. For the moment, it was 2,800 miles across the sea to Brazil's second largest city and by far its most cosmopolitan. A veritable playground and twenty-four hour party city, but not today for our travelers.

Under different circumstances, they might have been tempted to take in the beaches of Ipanema or Copacabana. Instead, a mostly silent general—and the autopilot—flew the six-hour leg to Rio de Janeiro for fuel. Fuel of both the jet and sandwiches varieties. After a one-hour stop, they were airborne again for the remaining 1,200 miles or so deeper into the southern hemisphere, to the Argentine capital and their educator.

During the "silent" flight to Rio, Eric had ample opportunity to refresh his skill with his computerized translator. Their candidate spoke English, but, they were informed, wasn't comfortable in this foreign language. No problem. Since the early-2010s, a computerized translation program was available and had quickly become invaluable. In diplomatic circles it was revolutionary. The speaker talks into a microphone and the recipient hears within a matter of moments in their native language.

The breakthrough in this technology came when computers made the leap from discreet-speech to continuous-speech applications. This allowed the computer to analyze the spoken sentence in context before rapidly translating it. No more problems of whether you meant *to*, *two*, or *too*. Or, *their* versus *there*. Patterns were analyzed contextually, then translated. Markedly improved semiconductor speeds also helped immensely.

These translators were still a bit disconcerting to use—if you looked at the screen. There was just enough time delay to make you crazy if you persisted in staring at the display. Also, speaking in one's best "disc jockey" voice with no *uhhhhs, duhhhs,* or *well-ums* was important. One must speak distinctly, clearly, and with one's best enunciation.

So while Major Conroy concerned himself with the logistics of the trip from Rio to Buenos Aires, Eric took Anne to the back of the cabin.

"Nothing happened, Anne."

"Right. I've seen that sex kitten. She—"

"She was very accommodating. She wants to go to another planet. That leaves this one for us. I love you."

"Okay," Anne responded reluctantly. "Let's practice being honest with each other."

In the back of the cabin, while Conroy flew, they practiced. Practiced using their mouths in unusual ways. They practiced their linguistic skills. Anne may have spoken Arabic, but her Spanish was rusty. She needed to brush up on her translator skills, too. This concluding portion to their ten hour excursion would provide the proper time. Time, if they could stay focused on rehearsing instead of on each other. Only ten hours from St. Lucia and paradise to business in Argentina. Reality is a harsh mistress.

Arriving in Argentina in the early afternoon gave them time for a night on the town. So where to go for the best local cuisine and a tango or two? No problem. With the United States ambassador acting as their concierge, they embarked on a night of revelry and dance. Neither knew how to tango, but since when did that stop anyone? Prior to leaving the embassy, they watched an interactive video on this derivative of the Argentinean milonga and the Cuban habanera and anointed themselves professionals. Of course, if you want to look the part you have to dress the part. This entailed stopping at several stores to pick out appropriate costuming for the evening. They were ready, and looked the part.

Next morning came way too soon for these *conquistadores del tango.* Many more nights like this and there wouldn't be many more nights. Eric had done more traveling, partying, and staying out late because of this project than ever before, in all of his life. He loved it, and loved her, too. Anne was actually more attuned to this lifestyle. She had traveled extensively in the Air Force.

As he struggled to brush his teeth, Eric asked, "What do you do at JMT-EL anyway, Anne? What do you guys really do?"

"Well, all the SETI projects around the world gather a lotta data. They send it to us and we analyze it. Analyze it, and make contingency plans. Like, what if we're visited by hostiles? Or, what if they unintentionally bring some new, weird bacteria? The American Indians were nearly wiped out by the Pilgrim's viruses and bacteria, not their muskets. Of the ten to twenty million people indigenous to North America, there were only about two hundred thousand remaining by the mid-1800s. Between our European ancestors' bugs and those of their cattle, we made a mess of this place. The same thing could happen to us if some alien visitor brought the space plague."

Anne was on a roll. "What if their intentions are less than honorable?" she noted. "And how do we communicate with them? Our 'universal' translator won't work on an alien race. You think a diplomatic miscalculation is important. What about a diplomatic space miscue? And how do we convey our intentions to them? And what about a habitat for them? What are their environmental needs? Do they breathe oxygen or methane? Helium or argon? Who knows? We plan for as many contingencies as we can dream up."

"Why you, though? Why a military officer? Why so secretive?"

"Because a small misunderstanding by the public or a congressman could be a fiasco," she responded. "The military is geared towards secrets. We're used to handling them. And if someone doesn't do it right, we have ways of dealing with offenders. Again, in secret. This isn't an America-only game, Eric. There are counterparts in several other governments, including the Chinese. There are domestic implications, too. What if these new friends bring an advanced technology with them and one of our not-so-friendly Earthly competitors tries to use it to their advantage. Believe me, the Pentagon has contingencies for the Chinese trying that scam. That's what I do, Eric. That's what my job's about!"

Anne's sermon was cathartic. She had never discussed her feelings about her position with anyone. It was important to her and to the U.S. This was a deadly serious business of truly foreign policy, one that Eric hadn't considered previously. He was starting to understand, and beginning to feel that tight sensation, again. Like when he was initially discussing this mission with B.C. Anne was also wide awake now and definitely in work mode. No morning tryst today, he thought. There was much food for thought here. The more they contemplated their wake-up chat session, the more each realized this mission had broader, complex ramifications.

They didn't say much as they dressed. As they stood next to each other they were drawn even closer. They needed each other. Physically, emotionally, and spiritually. Eric reached out and gently grasped Anne's hand. He squeezed it, guaranteeing his support. She threw her arms around him and they stood there hugging each other like there was no tomorrow. There was a tomorrow and each intended for the other to be a large part of it.

They were now friends. And they had become lovers. But it was this hug that solidified their relationship. This was the symbol of their commitment to each other. There was no turning back. Each was committing their soul to the other. They ordered room service and talked about what their lives would be like after the mission.

"I want to leave the Air Force. I'll go anywhere with you, Eric. But sitting at home sounds really good, too. I'm basically traveled out."

"Even if traveling means going to exotic locations?" asked Eric.

"Maybe after sitting home for six months. I want to get to know everything about Eric Sheppard. And not the presidential policymaker part. I'm tired of flying. I'm tired of it whether I'm the pilot or the passenger. We can travel later. Hell, I might even go to Oklahoma with you. Do the 'roots' tour. We've got a lot of living left, Doc."

Wouldn't that be something, thought Eric. Going back to Purcell, Oklahoma with an Air Force general on his arm. "Yeah, we've got a lot of living left in us. So let's get this damned assignment over with and get on with it. Get ready, General. We've got an educator to visit."

Their driver lurched through traffic to the Ministry of Education building in downtown Buenos Aires. The two were quickly ushered to a conference room on the first floor by a less-than-enthusiastic bureaucrat. As they were setting up their translating equipment, a scholarly appearing woman about thirty-five years old entered.

"I am Eva Graciela Mariani. Your equipment won't be necessary. I've been practicing my English." She spoke in absolutely perfect form. "I am aware of the reason for your visit, but I am surprised you are interested in me. Of what value is a school teacher?"

"School teacher? Hardly, Dr. Mariani. Your books on comparative adult and child education techniques are studied throughout the world. It is your unique approach to education that makes you perfect for this mission," opened Sheppard. As he spoke he couldn't help thinking about the stereotype of a teacher, tightly bound hair, no make-up and plain clothes. Mariani didn't fit the stereotype. With a little makeover she would be quite attractive; if she shed her glasses, added a little make-up, and wore some trendier clothes, she would turn more than a few heads.

"Tell me what the mission is to accomplish. You propose sending people millions of miles? For what purpose, Dr. Sheppard?"

"I see this as an opportunity for the human race to wipe the slate clean. To begin again, but with the luxury of knowledge acquired over many centuries. We've tried various techniques and philosophies. We're sending the best our planet has to offer to begin again the evolutionary process. This time with the advantage of our experiences, both good and bad. Hopefully, we have learned from our mistakes."

"And if not?"

"If not? Will they be any worse off? Only that they are on another planet. I have faith in my fellow man and his ability to survive. Not only to survive, but to thrive."

"Is acquisition of knowledge a good thing, Doctor? Are we better as a species because we can contemplate the future? Are our chances of surviving or thriving not improved because of knowledge?"

"I believe so. I believe we all learn from our mistakes. Not many adults touch a hot stove."

"But every child does, Doctor. They must learn some things for themselves. How do we convey the lessons you've learned to the next generation?"

"That is why we are here, Dr. Mariani. We believe you are the answer. Or you have the answers."

"Dr. Sheppard, the answers are not written in stone. They are within each of us. It is the role of an educator to help their students find not only the answers, but the questions asked in the first place. What if someone you choose doesn't wish to go. You want them, but they don't want you?"

"This is a voluntary mission, Dr. Mariani. I want team members who believe in the mission, who want the challenge of a strange, new environment. People willing to step back in a way, while stepping forward."

"Meaning?"

"The privilege of using knowledge acquired through the ages in a place where there is a limitation to the negative from the start. They can step away from the bad while retaining the good."

"And who determines good and evil?"

"The team itself. Not so black and white as good and evil, but what form their new culture will take." Eric studied the woman sitting across the table. She wore her brown hair piled on top of her head. She wore teardrop-shaped glasses that hid her large, round, dark brown eyes.

Taking off her glasses, she stared straight at Eric. "And what makes you believe they won't make the same mistakes again?"

"Faith, Dr. Mariani. Faith. Faith in mankind to know what is right. But with less peer pressure to do the wrong thing. And less external pressures from society. Less temptations, also."

"So temptation has been mankind's principal problem?"

"Certainly one of the main ones, in my opinion. All the way back to the garden of Eden."

"And how will your team deal differently with temptation, Doctor? How should we instruct them to view and confront temptation differently?"

There was quiet. All three pondered the questions and responses. Eric didn't have all the answers, for sure. Did anyone? Eric could see why she was considered an excellent teacher. She was attempting to discover the purpose and rationale for the mission. Eric was being asked to define it in ways he hadn't considered. If she would only lighten up. Let her hair down, figuratively and literally.

"But what of my family? Will I take them to a strange new world?"

Both Eric and Anne were taken aback. Eric looked at Anne and stammered, "We were unaware of a family, Doctor. Certainly arrangements can be made, I guess we can always find, well, room for..."

Mariani began laughing as she realized they were also unaware of her meaning.

"My cats, Dr. Sheppard. My cats. They are my family. And a large one at that. I collect cats like some would acquire art. I care for forty-seven currently. They are my passion. What of my family, Doctor? Will they be offered passage, too?" There was a spark of mischievousness in her eyes. "They are much like children. I try out many of my theories on my cats first. Did you know that, other than the ferret, the cat is the only territorial domesticated animal? People think they are not trainable because they are territorial and aloof. They cannot be herded like sheep. Because they are solitary and territorial, we have been relatively unsuccessful training them. So, too, with children. General, how do you educate your troops?"

"We demonstrate a technique or skill, and then we train or drill on it—over and over."

"General, you are used to commanding your troops much like our childhood teachers. You command and they follow. Our first teachers acted similarly. Remember your own childhood? We were told what to learn and when to learn it. What was important and why. Do you teach your soldiers to think on their own?"

"We teach them to follow orders from a superior. In the absence of higher authority, we hope to give them tactics and strategies to guide them in making decisions on their own. But we get uncomfortable when too much independent thinking occurs."

"While it is true that children are initially dependent, they rapidly become capable of structuring their own education. If we would only let them. Just as with cats, we give up on them too easily. No, General, even children want to discover 'why' things are important on their own."

"But adults don't learn as easily as children, Dr. Mariani. And it is the adults on this mission who must be educated first, before there are any children. We in the military place a premium on following orders and chain of command. We insist on it. We screen applicants for it and train them to obey orders. Does this not also have a place?" responded General Hayes.

"Yes, General, it has a place. There is a difference between training and learning. Your training uses rewards and punishments to shape behavior. You back that training with discipline. Discipline is control gained by enforcing obedience or order. That is your military. But what is learning, General? Can you define it?"

"I've never tried. But I believe I know when it has occurred. I suspect you have a more enlightened definition?"

"Then how can you be sure your soldiers have actually 'learned' what you taught them? How do you change a behavior that was learned incorrectly? If one of your charges already handles a problem in a way you haven't taught them, and it is incorrect, how do you change that behavior? If you can't define learning, how can you evaluate whether it has occurred? And if you can't define it, how can you change it?"

"We constantly train and drill. I guess the only test of whether someone has learned what we teach comes in battle. Their performance is tested and they pass or fail. Those who fail many times don't live to re-test. What is learning, Dr. Mariani? I assume you have spent a great deal of time testing for it and studying the effects of learning."

"Yes. I would submit that 'learning is a relatively permanent change in behavior that comes about as a result of a planned experience'. Your military teaches by experience, but not necessarily a planned experience. War certainly isn't planned. Contingencies are planned for, but experiences of war aren't planned. No doubt, you would prefer an experienced combat veteran to a higher ranking, inexperienced soldier.

"Why? Because the veteran incorporated those combat experiences. He understood how to survive and also strategies for continuing to stay alive. But were those experiences planned? No, usually not. Hence, the incidents that make a soldier valuable in war, make him antisocial in civilian society. Luckily for most, even these experiences are relatively temporary changes, not, permanent ones. All experiences deteriorate over time. We must reinforce the positive events...repeatedly.

"The hardest thing to do is to 'unlearn' an experience. Even negative encounters remain in our data bank. We revert back to our initial instruction, even if it is negative, in times of stress. In teaching an adult or a child, it is the educator's role to plan that experience. The student's role is to be ready to learn—to have the motivation, the will, to learn. That is the difference between children and adults, the way each is motivated, not the way each is taught.

"An educator cannot attempt to motivate each similarly. The educator must find within each student why they want to learn, or show them why they should. Why it is important, not to the teacher, but important to the student. Learning results from the interaction between what the student already knows, the new information they encounter, and what they do as they learn." Mariani paused to take a breath.

"But surely children differ in their learning from adults?" inquired Sheppard, seizing the opportunity. "What we are talking about is 'jump starting' the learning process. Trying to understand it. And to use it to guarantee learning. Not so much with the content of learning, but 'how' one learns. We are taking a first generation society and jumping them ahead to the fiftieth generation by virtue of life experiences acquired over millennia. Or maybe the five-hundredth generation, I don't know. How do we expedite learning in the second generation? Or in succeeding generations? How do we leap through history with our team? How can we make learning less painful to them by teaching them of the mistakes we've already learned?"

"If we can accomplish that, my friend, we will have done what few generations have even scratched at. You ask for a guarantee. There are no guarantees in life, Dr. Sheppard. It is sad to think how many generations haven't learned that simple lesson. I'm not sure we can make the vault from first to fiftieth generation, but it isn't unreasonable to skip several generations in between. Children enter the world completely dependent. Society then defines the role of a child as a learner. We give the child little choice. We set the rules, for better or worse. Not so with adults. Adults are almost always voluntary learners. They simply disappear from learning experiences that don't satisfy them."

"Are you our educator, Dr. Mariani? Will you bear the burden of such an awesome responsibility? Can you accept the burden of educating a whole society? A new culture, on a new planet? We can bargain about your cats. But are you willing to bargain about the future of mankind on this or any other world? Help us ensure that this new world will have the best chance to learn from history and not be doomed to repeating the past failures of this and all previous generations. You have a unique opportunity to make the ultimate impact on your students. Can you walk away from that, Doctor? I think not," replied Sheppard. "I think not."

The room was silent. No tangos to divert the Americans' thoughts. No theory to debate for this educator, only a decision. A large, life-changing decision for Eva Graciela Mariani, as it would be for anyone.

This should, and would be, a very personal decision. Whether to leave the known for the unknown, the comfortable for the supreme challenge. Anne and Eric quietly slipped out the door; slipped away to allow Eva time to think. Only she could weigh the decision for herself. It would be a personal decision for each member of the team. Each of the other members would also bear a similar, awesome responsibility within their area of expertise.

Lost in her own thoughts, Eva Graciela Mariani didn't even notice their departure.

XVII

Geneal Hayes, there's a scrambled incoming message tagged 'Top Priority, Your Eyes Only,' sir." Major Conroy was uncharacteristically agitated. Hayes immediately became all business. These kinds of messages were not routine. Especially to Pentagon personnel out of the country.

"Major, let's get this aircraft airborne on the double." She reverted back to a command-and-control mode instantaneously. "I'll take the communication in back. Dr. Sheppard, if you wouldn't mind. Please remain in the cockpit with the major. I'll get back to you ASAP."

Anne Hayes didn't like what she saw from the first words of the transmission. As she displayed the garbled words on her computer screen, it was quickly deciphered, then decrypted after she input her top secret encryption password, matching it to her thumbprint, allowing her to make sense out of the previously randomized alphanumeric characters. The dispatch concerned the PRC. 600,000 Chinese troops had launched a full scale offensive across the Kazakhstani border. It was a lightning fast strike aimed at capturing intact the oil fields of this petroleum rich, former Soviet bloc country. After the Straits of Taiwan in 2013, Anne knew this would not, could not be allowed to stand. She knew, too, her quiet retirement to the countryside would be postponed.

In 2013, the United States and the rest of the world were caught off guard by the PRC's reaction to Taiwan's declaration of independence. No one in any country could fathom going to war over a scrap of paper asserting independence. No one could grasp how deeply the leaders of mainland China felt about the issue then and few understood it, even now. But America had gone to war over just such a scrap of paper in 1776. So have many other countries over many similar causes.

There are many complex reasons and issues behind these kinds of declarations. Freedom, egalité, liberty, and other higher values. Mankind has fought over any and all moral questions throughout history. God, Allah, Buddha, and Mohammed have been invoked to help the cause just as much as religion has been cited to justify the slaughter. What it comes down to is simple: mankind is violent. It is in our nature. We were prehistorically. We are historically. And we probably will continue to be in the future. Dispute resolution has not been mankind's strong suit.

And for all the window dressing of diplomacy, one of diplomacy's principal goals is to resolve disputes, preferably to one's best advantage. Cardinal Richelieu practiced realpolitik in the courts of Louis XIII during the early 1600s. Though not the first to practice it, he was the first to label it.

It has been one of man's guiding convictions from the time we began to walk upright. To gain an advantage over our adversary. Walking upright was itself an evolutionary improvement to gain just such an advantage. Richelieu, like his many successors, tried to justify his actions on grounds that the interests of the state are more important than religion, morality, or the law, so called "absolutism." From this, "the end justifies the means" and "I was only following orders" evolved. Justifications that are just as shallow today as they were four centuries ago.

Mankind still grapples with the ethics and morality of war, but also continues to use it as the primary form of dispute resolution. As societies become ever more complex and intertwined, relations between parties become more subtle. We like to believe we no longer fight over land or colonies, but has man really changed? Global power politics and diplomacy, spheres of influence and cultural miscommunications haven't changed through the millennia. Only the weapons and the venues have changed. The "arrows" are more lethal and "economics'"is the "religion" to which we swear our allegiance.

Instead of trying to impose Catholicism on Europe, as Spain's Phillip II attempted, we try to impose our different cultural values on the world as the only virtuous ones. The heathens must be slain in the name of God to save them from themselves. Only our values are noble—human rights, freedom of expression, and the thought that all men are created equal. Life is still trying to teach the lessons of tolerance, respect and appreciation of others to us all. We are, indeed, slow learners.

This most recent conflict was about an all-too-familiar theme. It was over oil. After the confrontation in the Straits of Taiwan in 2013, the PRC had increasing difficulties quenching its national thirst for oil. In 1997, the PRC had concluded a massive joint venture with Kazakhstan to exploit the central Asian country's vast petroleum reserves. Having become self-sufficient in oil in the 1960s, China's enormous economic expansion soon demanded more oil than they could produce. The PRC became a net oil importer again in 1993. At the time of the 2013 conflict, the PRC was importing some 6,000,000 barrels a day—more than 55% of its daily need. With 20% of the world's population, it had only 3% of the world's oil reserves. As it came of age economically, oil fueled its transition—moving from an agrarian to an industrial society. With that conversion came the move from bicycles to automobiles, transportation powered by petroleum, not muscles.

It wasn't only industry that needed petroleum. The PRC military did, too. Embarking on a mammoth military buildup and expansion of its forces in the late 1980s and into the 1990s, the People's Revolutionary Army went on a decades-long building binge, a binge requiring oil. In the 2000s and 2010s they built and launched four large aircraft carriers, the only country in the Far East capable of this kind of power projection. The only country in the world other than the United States, that is. Even the former Soviets no longer had aircraft carriers. Across the board increases in every area of their military made the PRC more belligerent and more willing to intimidate its neighbors. Intimidate, or worse. With the Taiwanese declaration of sovereignty in 2013, the PRC was well-positioned to dispute that declaration. Unfortunately, dispute was not in the PRC's vocabulary. Armed conflict was.

Caught off guard in 2013, the U.S. military was not going to let that happen again. The downsizing budgets of the late 1990s were succeeded by a return to higher Pentagon expenditures after 2013. There were replacement costs for equipment lost during the conflict and allocations for new and improved weapon systems needed to confront the more antagonistic PRC. Peace had its dividend in the 1980s. War exacted its price in the 2010s. The effect on the U.S. and other world economies was apparent.

Higher spending on defense meant less for other projects. It also encouraged inflation. The government spent more on planes and bombs leading to lower unemployment. Employment by the military-industrial complex, so labeled by Dwight Eisenhower in the 1950s, created inflationary price pressures. More spending wreaked havoc on efforts to balance the United States federal budget. Governments can't build more bombs without cutting something, or massive deficit financing.

This came at a particularly bad time. The earliest of the "baby boomers" had reached retirement age, compelling the government to spend even more on promised entitlements. The Congresses of the late 1990s and

2000s not only reduced taxes and shied away from significant entitlement reform, they expanded the entitlements. Now there was nowhere to run. All these factors conspired against our domestic economy. The world's marketplaces caught a cold when the American economy sneezed, and this was full blown pneumonia. Hence, John Franklin Stone's background as an economist was sorely needed.

After 2013, China also had to regroup and rebuild. She did both with astonishing speed. Although isolated politically, the rest of the world ironically embraced China's economy again, with even more enthusiasm. The world needed the cheap labor the PRC offered. The planet was hooked on gadgets and high tech communications gear. China could be forgiven economically. For all the talk of human rights, the world's marketplaces looked the other way.

The one good thing that came from the fighting was that the United States and the rest of the West were forced to be honest about their diminished influence in the Far East. Instead of continuing parent-like lectures which fell on deaf ears, the U.S. had to be more realistic. China set its own policies, not those of the United States. The war painfully brought home that fact to the West. Our prodding and cajoling amounted to little more than rhetoric. No action before, and certainly none since the conflict. We wanted their cheap labor and they wanted our consumer markets. An uneasy détente took hold after the short, one month catastrophe historians soon began calling the Straits of Taiwan War. No long-lasting World War II struggle, but devastating just the same to all parties.

Most of the military damage was inflicted on the island nation of Taiwan. Its outnumbered Air Force held its own against the PRC fighters. Better aircraft and better-trained pilots held the day. But there were plenty of losses. They were unable to prevent major bomb damage to virtually all Taiwanese cities. And this damage was from old fashioned, conventional dumb bombs. Where the United States had come to rely on its "smart" bombs—capable of being guided to their targets with minimal collateral damage, these combatants used less high tech resources with an abundance of collateral damage on both sides.

The Taiwanese managed to dole out their fair share of damage to the mainland cities, especially to the business center of Shanghai. This port city of fifteen million, lying at the confluence of the Huang-P'u and Wasung rivers, became a river of blood from annihilation by carpet bombing unseen since World War II. But the Taiwanese were unable to repel a PRC land invasion on their northern beaches. It took the U.S. Navy and Air Force to halt that advance. Halt it only after incurring heavy losses to both personnel and matériel. Anne Hayes remembered the beaches well.

It was here she became an ace. She was a wing commander flying F-22s. The F-22 *Raptor* had three unique features. It was supersonic, agile, and stealthy. Unlike her stealthy, subsonic predecessor the F-117, the F-22 flew at supersonic speed, could outmaneuver anything in the sky, and was equipped with the latest stealth technology, making the aircraft virtually invisible to radar. Its first test flight in 1991 proved it worthy of the $75,000,000 per copy price tag. It was capable of flight for several hours at over Mach II in "supercruise" mode without the use of afterburners because of its super-efficient M-2 engines.

It easily outperformed the latest competition, including the lighter and faster European ETA 2000 and the Russian Sukoi 37. Delivered to the U.S. Air Force in the early 2000s, the F-22 was the state-of-the-art tactical fighter. The F-35 was more modern, but too few had been deployed by the start of the conflict. This was a classic confrontation of high tech versus low tech. High tech won the numbers game but low tech won the psychological contest.

It was also here that the United States lost a nuclear-powered aircraft carrier, the only time in its history. Besides losing several thousand American servicemen and women, it precipitated the rethinking of the large platform naval dogma. Since World War II, the aircraft carrier was the star of the U.S. Navy. We fought this war with the last war's strategy. Now smaller units and smaller platforms were being considered. The aircraft carrier was no longer invincible. What made it so was the first use of tactical nuclear weapons in any conflict. Because of the protective nature of the assorted ships in a carrier task force, China had no other way of getting close enough to a carrier to destroy one without resorting to their use—and even then is was, perhaps, more by chance than by design, given the anti-missile systmens employed in defending a carrier. The strategic, political and historical implications of this tactic were significant.

Sweeping north and west from underground fortresses in the Tian Shan mountains, more than twenty Chinese divisions quickly advanced north onto the lowlands of southern Kazakhstan. A three-pronged attack divided the country with the northern contingent sprinting toward the capital and the southern pincer protecting others from entering the fray from the south. The central contingent was left to dash to the Caspian Sea, occupying oils fields as they went. It wasn't the people they were interested in. As the tanks rumbled through the southern deserts they encountered little resistance. What feeble resistance they did encounter was brutally crushed.

Eight hundred kilometers beyond Almaty, yet still a thousand kilometers from the Caspian Sea, the People's Revolutionary Army had advanced this far in just a few days, having encountered no resistance of any kind along the way. Cold at night, but searingly hot during the day, this persistently dusty, God-forsaken territory was perfect for long tank runs. Wide open desert and little geography to interfere with maneuvering made the initial phase of the attack a blitzkrieg.

It was at one of these watering spots near Kyzylorda, not far from the Syr-Darya River, where the first atrocities occurred. As the lead column of tanks rumbled to within twenty-five hundred yards of an oasis, the commanding colonel sat atop the lead tank, surveying the terrain. He was hot, dirty, thirsty, and sweaty. An air of kerosene and shell propellant hung over this and every other tank, choking out the breathable air. Each soldier wore a mask to protect from inhaling the mixture of hydrocarbons and dust. Or were they worn to protect from something else? The colonel screamed into his headset, regrouping the tanks from their orderly single-file column into a battle formation of staggered rows. As they approached fifteen hundred yards, he ordered them to fire at will.

The shrill, high-pitched wail of outgoing fire was followed in a few seconds by a plodding, low-pitched rumble as each shell found a target. Even at that distance, the cries of the unsuspecting Kazakhstani victims were followed by the horrific odor of burning flesh. A sweet, pungent, stifling smell that hung in the nose. But not through the Chinese perpetrators' masks. This incident barely slowed their advance.

Since Hiroshima, there was an unwritten rule among governments prohibiting the use of nuclear weapons, until broken by the Chinese in 2013. If the Chinese would go nuclear, albeit tactical, what did this say of their doctrine for escalation in a graver, future conflict? This shook American contingency planners to the bone. Reassessment of U.S. strategies followed. America had predicated much of its post-Soviet military strategy on confronting a conventional threat, even dealing with two clashes at once, confronting those conventional threats with conventional arms and weapons systems. America had superiority in virtually every arena.

But the U.S. was unused to casualties. While the United States was considering going nuclear in response to the Chinese escalation, a tense cease-fire was brokered by Iran—*Iran*, of all countries. The U.S. had been deeply divided over whether to escalate the conflict with the use of tactical nukes. The fear was that one or the other of the two sides would go strategic and destroy the world. Was there any country, Taiwan or mainland China, worth risking that kind of destruction, including ours?

Iran had been struggling to rejoin the world community. Still very fundamentally Islamic, its leaders had become more pragmatic. Beginning with the election of the successor governments to Mohammad Khatami beginning in the mid-2010s, Iran's leaders re-engaged the world after their own nuclear brinksmanship during the 2010s. The world was at first reluctant until the Iranians not only verbally stopped supporting terrorism, but actually stopped funding it, too. It was also struggling to become the leading Islamic voice in a culture that had no modern core state. Unlike the United States in the West, or Russia within orthodoxy, or Chinese culture, twentieth century Islam had no primary country to speak for the culture of its many nations.

Iran desperately wanted to be that core state. So did Turkey. Yet Iran persisted. Her total population demographics supported that goal, but her people were the Islamic minority, Shi'ite. Would the Islamic countries, primarily Sunni, back a Shi'ite state as the leading country of Islam? The Turks thought not. This was what Iran confronted within the Islamic culture. It was a bold step reaching out to two cultures, the West and China. Bold—calculated to win the good graces of both—and intended mostly to serve notice on the rest of the Islamic world.

Taiwan was rebuilding, too. It was independent politically, but highly dependent on the West, now even more than previously. Still not allowed to a seat in the United Nations, it continued to rely on the marketplaces of the U.S. and western Europe for its products and desperately needed western capital now to rebuild its infrastructure. The PRC dogmatically maintained a "one China" policy. The reality was, two Chinas would exist for the conceivable future. As mainland China revved the economic engine, its 1.5 billion people had developed an unquenchable addiction to the oil needed to fuel this expanding machine. It now required almost ten percent of the world's daily supply, and the overreliance on this one foreign commodity drove prices up as supplies could not match demand.

"Major Conroy, we've got a change in plans," Hayes commanded from the back of the aircraft. "I'm advised we are Priority One for in-flight refueling. Plot your course west to 205 degrees. We'll pick up tactical support and fuel en route. I've been ordered to Sydney and then on to the active theater. You and Dr. Sheppard will proceed by civilian aircraft back to Washington. Please send the Doctor back here, Major. Do you copy?"

"Roger that, General. Sydney direct. Roughly 7,300 miles. Probably about fifteen hours. That will require three in-flights, General. I'll coordinate with tactical support out of Hawaii. Dr. Sheppard is on his way," answered the major.

"Why couldn't we have refueled before, Tom?" Sheppard sulked. "I didn't even know we could have."

"Not a priority, sir. Something big must be going on. General Hayes is waiting, Doctor."

As the T-43 reached cruising altitude, Eric arrived to find a stern-faced, tight-lipped Air Force general. She was talking over a secure Pentagon video phone. Out of the corner of his eye he could make out General Adams on the screen. Anne was mostly listening with an occasional "Yes, sir." He knew this was serious. After about seven minutes, the conversation ended and the screen went back to monitoring mode.

"Eric, it looks like I'm gonna be busy for the next few weeks. I'm authorized to tell you a little about what's up. Seems the PRC just invaded Kazakhstan and is making a run for the oil fields. The Russians have come to the border but haven't crossed yet. I say yet. It's unclear whether they will honor their treaty responsibilities agreed to when the Commonwealth of Independent States was formed. Satellites show a lot of fighting, but conventional, so far. The Kazahk forces are overmatched and undergunned.

"The United States is, of course, condemning the aggression. We are moving two Navy task forces from the Persian Gulf to the China Sea to join two others already on patrol there. They really can't directly intervene. They can only make the PRC nervous on their southern flank. We are negotiating with India for basing rights, but to be honest, this isn't our area of the world. It's probably going to be up to the Russians. Up to them, or nobody. Escalation is always a possibility, as the Chinese did in the Straits. We're in a tactical support role for now. I'm ordered forward to Diego Garcia in the Indian Ocean. Fourteen square miles of nothing. Nothing but a damn long runway and a lot of B-52s, B-1s and F-22s. I'll assume command of the unit on my arrival."

"Why Kazakhstan, Anne? I mean, you're telling me the Chinese have invaded it? I hate getting my geography lessons by invasion. You're telling me they've gone into Kazakhstan because of oil?"

"Look. The Chinese are very thirsty for oil. They've got deals with Iraq and Iran to buy it. But they don't control it. Remember 1991. When the Iraqis invaded Kuwait, it was about control. Control of oil. Petroleum fuels every nation's engine. Kazakhstan has some of the largest reserves in the world. And the Russians haven't been very friendly with the PRC since 2013. Kazakhstan is just across China's northwestern border. They're in the Commonwealth with the Russians. Hell, their former capital, Almaty, is less than a day's tank ride away from the Chinese border. They were pumping big quantities of oil to the Chinese until the Straits. Then, they cut way back. I guess quiet diplomacy didn't work for the Chinese. They want control. So they went and took it. Obviously, this can't stand. The problem is, we don't have a lot of viable options at this point."

"So what about us? What about me? What about—"

"What about calming down and letting events take their course for now. I just can't tell you where all this will lead. I'm a general military officer. I cannot concern myself with your issues at this time." She could tell he was surprised. She lowered her voice. "Eric, I know this is sudden. But I'm talking about putting us on hold for a little while. Try to understand I've got a bunch of people counting on me. I don't like it any more than you. But I have a job to do. And so do you. Get back to Washington and finish your team. Before you know it, I'll be back and your mission will be over, and we'll be trying to figure out whether to cook at home or eat out. Give me a little time. That's all I'm asking for—a little time. Now, dismissed. Kiss me and get out so I can save the world from Chinese domination."

As Eric left Anne to her planning, he couldn't help admire her take-charge demeanor. "I love you, Anne. I love you," his voice trailing off. As he left the cabin for the cockpit he saw maps and logistical data coming across Anne's computer. She was clearly in this thing up to her neck. He wasn't about to raise the water any higher. His job was to try and lower it.

The tanks ground to a halt at water's edge. No doubt, the Kazakhstanis were here for the water, too. The PRC colonel slowly dismounted from the lead tank and walked to the small reservoir. Dense smoke from the recent shelling hovered over the region, a purple-yellow haze that choked its victims when inhaled, blistering their lungs. The colonel surveyed the scene, noting about twenty corpses twisted and contorted, frozen in place. Each was drooling copious quantities of pink, frothy secretions from their ruptured pulmonary vasculature.

The colonel seemed amused at the sight. He pointed to the gnarled, charred bodies with their petrified eyes open wide from terror, mouths agape in a desperate last attempt to gulp life-sustaining air into their blistered lungs, smoke still rising from their contracted limbs. One corpse caught his attention. He strode to the blackened torso with no head, its arm lifted to about head level, fingers spread, as if about to make a point.

The colonel studied what was left of this human being and finally flicked his middle finger against the little finger of the corpse. The mangled, burnt finger broke off and was catapulted ten feet. The entire corps of soldiers belly-laughed at the gesture as their colonel grunted a crude obscenity, pushing over the body.

Another soldier spotted a woman about ten feet away, next to the water. She was barely alive, moaning in exquisite pain from the blistering burns. The soldiers were clad in full chemical protection as they slowly made their way to her. They knew she was a victim of chemical mustard gas. She was begging them for water, the translating soldier advised his colonel. The colonel took her head and held it under the nearby water, laughing, "I'll give her water!" Mercifully, she expired in about two minutes, as he kicked her body into the stream. This was just a prelude to the nightmare Kazakhstan would experience.

"Wake up, Dr. Sheppard. We're in Sydney." Major Conroy shook him awake and back to reality.

"Anne?...uh, I mean, where's General Hayes?"

"She's already left for Diego Garcia. Grabbed herself an F-22, sir. I was told to give you this letter when you awakened. We're off to Washington with a new crew. I'll be accompanying you, but not as pilot. We picked up a fresh crew."

He pocketed the message. "Major, I've got a feeling it's time you and I got to know each other better," rubbing the sleep from his eyes and stretching his weary bones. "So what happened to you and me going back by civilian means?"

"The General made other arrangements. F-22s are a hell of a lot faster than T-43s. She'll probably be on Diego Garcia before we take off. Apparently, things are a lot dicier than she thought. The Russians are in a real dogfight. At least they got into it, though. Looks like the Iranians aren't gonna sit on the sidelines either. The Kazakhstanis are Islamic. Allah rules in that part of the world."

"Where do you think this whole thing is going, Tom? You're career military. What's really going on? How about a drink? You're officially off-duty by me."

"Never off in a crisis, sir," he responded formally. "But I don't think I'll be much help from here on an underpowered, unarmed little T-43 headed for Andrews," Conroy stated sheepishly. "Aw, what the hell. Why not. Scotch and soda, Doc. No more of those Aussie beers. No more, ever again. We've been to some pretty strange places over the last few months. And I gotta say, Islamabad was the absolute worst. I've never seen anyone as sick as you were there. About this situation..."

"Call me Eric," Sheppard told him, making his way over to the plane's wet bar to pour himself an eye-opener. "We've got a long trip, Tom."

"Well, sir...Eric...the way I see it, this one's not our fight. No matter how much we want it to be, it's just not our arena. Geography and logistics are against us. We'll be in it, but not directly. We'll be pumping supplies to the Russians and probably to the Iranians now, too. Isn't that a bitch. We support the Shah in the 1970s, send him a shit pot of equipment, then they confiscate it and give it to the Ayatollah. He can't maintain it because we won't sell him spare parts, so it rusts away. Now we're about to send them more stuff, again. I guess it beats us going in face to face."

Conroy sighed. "The U.S.? We're out of it, at least for now. Unless it goes nuclear. I can't believe the Chinese would be that reckless. Why go after a bunch of oil fields if there's nowhere left to drive your tank? This is old-fashioned power politics and regional domination by the bully on the block—not much different, really, than that *Risk* game you guys play...except this is for real. And this ain't Saddam and Kuwait. They won't wait for the opposition to amass their forces. No, these are the big boys beating up on the neighborhood ninety-pound-weakling. This'll be over before anybody can mobilize any significant opposition, let alone retaliation. I'm afraid the Chinese just picked up some new oil wells on the cheap. Our job is to make 'em pay the highest price we can. But it's theirs for the taking." The major chugged his drink in exasperation. "Another scotch, please, Eric."

"Why not, Tom. We've only got nineteen hours until D.C. So, you're an historian. I'm just a dumb doctor with a public citizen's view of World Affairs 101. I know about power politics, but only from afar. I'll admit, I don't understand any of it."

"Doctor, this is *dejá vu* all over again. History is replete with similar stories. Only the time, circumstances, and consequences change. It's still hegemony. Domination and control. Superiority and supremacy. The difference is, this time, if this thing gets out of hand, we could manage to blow up the world. It's one thing for Alexander or Napoleon to try and conquer the world. It's another to attempt it when there are nuclear weapons lying around. So you want to know about history, huh? Well, let me give you the Conroy overview."

Eric learned Conroy was a military historian as well as a pilot. He taught briefly at the Air Force Academy in Colorado Springs before requesting a change in duty because of boredom. After all, he was a pilot and wanted to fly. He was disappointed at not being assigned to combat aircraft. The Pentagon wasn't the worst place in the world. No. Wherever the worst place was, he'd been there with Sheppard.

"Now I need another drink, Tom. And I need help trying to understand the world's stage and a few of the acts currently playing."

"Well, to understand the world of today, you've got to look at the world of yesterday," began the major. "Let's look at the beginning. Mankind stepped from the plains of Africa thousands of years ago. Modern man and the history of mankind only began around thirteen thousand years ago. We evolved into several different civilizations and cultures around various regions of the globe. It was Europe, however, that came to dominate the world—from about the sixteenth through the twentieth century—and, in a sense, still does today."

"Why Europe, Tom? What's unique about them—or us? Why not Japan or Venezuela or Egypt for that matter?" Eric sat more upright and leaned towards his traveling companion.

"There are many factors, not the least of which is plain old luck. Eurasia first developed the original "high tech," with weapons and bureaucratic organization. But why were they first, indeed? Were they smarter? I think not. Were they genetically superior? Again, there is no evidence to support that argument."

"So what was it, Tom?"

"Well, from the fertile crescent area of Eurasia sprang most of the domesticated plants we eat even today. A few were independently domesticated elsewhere later. But the so called "founder crops" of wheat, barley, lentils, peas, and flax—they all came from the fertile crescent. And of the fourteen domesticated large animals, thirteen were domesticated in Eurasia. From this area came three cereals, four pulses, that is, the edible seeds, and four early domesticated animals. That's enough protein, carbohydrates and fat to get any civilization started."

"Fertile crescent, Tom? I seem to remember something about that from junionr high. Refresh my memory."

"The area of present day Iraq along the Tigris and Euphrates rivers extending westward into Turkey. This was, and is, a very temperate growing zone, perfect for crop domestication. The ancients of the region became the first farmers. No longer hunter-gatherers, they stopped being nomadic and planted roots of their own and various roots to eat."

"So the world today is in turmoil because of a bunch of ancient Iraqis? Come on, Tom. You can do better than—"

"Really. Let me finish. Because these peoples became farmers instead of remaining hunters, it took less people to feed the clan allowing specialization to develop. The domesticated animals helped pull the plows and carry the produce to market, meaning even less people devoted exclusively to agriculture. They drank their milk and used their skins and fur for clothing and other luxuries. What evolved were classes, tradesmen, bureaucrats, and…armies."

"ARMIES?"

There was precious little the outgunned, outclassed, and outmaneuvered Kazakhstani Army could do to slow the Chinese advance. Their diplomats urgently sought military support from any and all who would listen. While the Russians, Americans, Iranians, and western Europeans were listening, Kazakhstan was being decimated. Finally, reluctantly, the Russian Naval Infantry—the Marines—were landed along the eastern shores of the Caspian Sea in an effort to protect the oil fields not yet seized.

From the north, near Orsk, a second Russian ground invasion raced southward in an attempt to beat the PRC to the plains between the Aral and Caspian Seas. In the skies above these flatlands, battles raged day and night between the Chinese and Russian Air Forces, with pilots and their aircraft being lost by the dozens on both sdes. Those deaths paled in comparison to the withering battles waged by Russian and Chinese Cavalries, as tank battalions had been titled after World War I—and helicopter squadrons became known as the Air Cavalry during Vietnam, since tanks don't travel well through swamps and jungles. And the Chinese were not the only ones using chemical weapons. CNN was nowhere to be found on these killing plains. The slaughter, the atrocities, the gross abuses by both sides were not being showcased on the evening news.

All armies took their marching orders from their political leaders. The military was nothing more than an extension of those leaders. China's Yang was the instigator, the perpetrator, the aggressor—and the most ruthless. He also possessed the most pawns to move on the chessboard called Kazahkstan.

"Armies," Conroy continued. "Kings and Emperors now had more subjects dedicated to learning and practicing the 'art of war.' With food production requiring fewer people to support the many, more centralized distribution and warehousing also developed. Thus, the rise of urban areas with all their attendant problems like disease and crime. And with trades generated by specialization, weapons and tactics also improved. It only took a few years to go from hunter-gathers to farmers to, essentially, where we are today, a highly specialized group of cultures and societies with conflicts over timeless issues. Issues like food, water, shelter, territory."

"So what motivated these Kings and Emperors to use their armies? And what constrains us not to use them today?"

Conroy launched into a lengthy, professorial monologue: "Are we restrained, Doctor? We still use them, but the consequences of their use are so much more devastating. What motivated these men is the same thing that motivates us today. We fight over religion, economics, cultural values. The first Gulf War was the first modern conflict fought between civilizations, basically—between Western Christianity and Islam. Oh, sure, there were a few renegades back then, like the Syrians, but not many. And they all fell out of the coalition pretty quickly after it was over.

"Would the oil be controlled by the West and its puppets? Or, by the Islamic states hostile to our values? Not unlike the OPEC oil embargo of 1973-74, when the question was, as it is today, would they be capable of holding the Western, or, for that matter, the world's, economies hostage? It was the first, but surely won't be the last. The second Gulf War was merely the final chapter to the first. We humans just aren't comfortable with each other's religions, values, and cultures. We've had trouble coexisting with each other for centuries. What is going on today began hundreds, or even thousands, of years ago. The Crusaders fought Islam in the name of Christianity from 1190 or so. The Greeks subjugated the Egyptians.

"What's really interesting is that we have actually had little civilizational contact throughout history until recently. Until 1500, the various cultures of the world had little to do with each other. When they did make contact, it was minimal. Or one conquered the other, with either assimilation or annihilation of its people the eventual outcome. Since the 1500s, we of European ancestry have conquered for the purposes of domination.

"We want other people's natural resources, be it gold, silver, oil, or labor. Were the French really in Indochina before and after World War II because of benevolent concern for those people? I think they were there for the rubber. Did the United States occupy Panama at the turn of the twentieth century to help Panamanians improve their station in life? No, we wanted their land to build a canal for our own purposes. We shouldn't be surprised by

Chinese belligerence in their neck of the world. We should expect it. They are reasserting their dominance over an area they have dominated for 5,000 years." He came up for some air.

"Colonel, the Russians are fifteen kilometers away," shouted the Chinese communications specialist to his commander.

"They blindly place their neck into my noose," he sneered. "When they get to the town, the lazy Russian dogs will rest for the night." He leaned back in his chair. "We attack at midnight. No prisoners, comrade Captain."

"No prisoners, Colonel?"

"Comrade Yang has given us orders." With that, the colonel closed his eyes, optically dismissing his junior. As he left, the colonel reminded him, "Wake me in an hour."

The colonel was awakened instead by the sound of large-bore howitzers firing in synchronous repetition. They were pounding the Russians billeted in the small Kazakhstani town of Chelkar. He knew they would immediately try to disperse from the town. Lying in wait to the southeast and southwest of the town were two Chinese tank divisions, preparing to decimate the Russians.

As expected, the Russians scattered to the south—and were smmarily annihilated. In only thirty minutes, the colonel was walking through the battle scene, walking past still burning Russian tanks, while scattered small arms fire pierced the night as his troops executed the few survivors in the traditional Chinese method of execution, a single gunshot to the back of the head. As he kicked his way through the debris of war, he heard a faint cry. It sounded like a baby's.

The colonel approached the source of sound with several of his men. They came upon a burning horse-drawn wagon, it's owner having wrongly opted for protection from the Russian tank brigade. A young Kazakh mother whose legs had been amputated below the knees by a mortar round, stared up at the colonel. With arms trembling, she held up her six-month-old infant as an offering to the conquering colonel.

He gently leaned down, accepting the child into his camouflaged arms. He carefully unwrapped the diaper, looked at the child's genitals, and just as carefully replaced the diaper. He then handed the baby back to the mother. As she cradled the child in her arms, the colonel fired his pistol at point blank range into the tiny skull. Blood, brain matter, bone, and cartilage splattered him and several of his troops. The bullet easily passed through the infant, also killing his mother.

"Why colonel? Why kill the child?"

"The son of my enemy is tomorrow's soldier." He holstered his weapon and calmly walked away.

"I've never really thought about where we're going within the context of where we've come from," noted Sheppard. "How do we pass on that lesson to the members of the mission? Hell, how do we pass it on to each other on this planet? We pride ourselves on being an advanced species. We can live in the present and plan for the future. But have we learned anything from the past? If we have, we sure seem to ignore it."

"Now you know why history is my passion. It's also why I'm a pessimist. Pessimistic about Earth and why

I volunteered for the assignment with you. I'm optimistic about the opportunity for fixing our mistakes here, with a mission there."

"You volunteered for this? Volunteered how?"

"I asked General Adams. I volunteered because I believe this mission may be the last hope for a world I see spinning out of control. A world caught up in petty issues. Not only caught up, but consumed. In the military we train for worst cases. I'm tired of worst cases. I'm ready to see something or somebody put their best foot forward, not their worst. That's what the space program of the 1960s was to me. Idealism, courage. A moral quest to assert man's supremacy over his environment, not to destroy it. To conquer the challenges of space, not exploit it. You're offering a chance for mankind to start over. Wash the slate clean."

"The great flood, Major? What makes you think we won't mess it up again? What makes you think we can get it right this time where we failed so miserably before?"

"Because I'm an optimist, Doc."

"You just said you were a pessimist. You just—"

"I'm also a dreamer. An idealist in pragmatist's clothing. I'm quixotic enough to know I have to believe in something. Currently, it's you—and your mission. General Adams must have recognized that, too, or he wouldn't have granted my request for transfer."

"So, you wanted to help more, Tom? You want to be on my staff and help pick the players?"

"They're damn-near picked already, Doc. What I would like to do is help train them. But with this Kazakhstan thing..." There came a pause in their conversation.

"Let me talk to General Adams when we get back to Washington. I think you'd be a great asset to our team, Tom."

The Iranian Navy ships disgorged their assets at Shevchenko (or, Aqtau), Kazakhstan, on the northeastern shore of the Caspian Sea—only to return several hours later with more troops and equipment. Within forty-eight hours, the Iranians had mustered 100,000 elite commandos ready to strike at the Chinese from the south, in the vicinity of the Aral Sea to the East. To do so required crossing into northern Uzbekistan, but without first seeking permission from the Uzbekis, the Iranians were met at first by light Uzbeki resistance.

The Uzbekis, however, also communicated news of the unwanted invasion to the Chinese. And China thanked them by attacking southward into Uzbekistan in an attempt to counter the Iranians. With the aid of the Chinese forces, Uzbeki troops fought the Iranians to a bloody stalemate on the northern plains of Uzbekistan, two hundred kilometers south of Kyzylorda. Exhaustion seemed to be the only winner on the battlefield this day.

Conroy and Sheppard talked for several hours, until both finally fell asleep, exhausted from their conversation and the events of the last few days. Conroy was good company. He was easy to talk to. He also read between the lines and listened well, to boot. Before they knew it, they were on the tarmac at Andrews bidding each other good-bye for the moment.

   Eric drove himself home to the suburbs of Virginia. It felt like he was in a foreign country. Nothing looked familiar. He'd been away one week. Nothing had really changed—except his perspective. St. Lucia was an eternity ago. So was Anne. He missed her, and didn't even know exactly where she was. Diego Garcia? Just a name.

   He found it in an Encyclopaedia Britannica Atlas after getting home. It was in the Indian Ocean. *Diego Garcia.* He wanted to be there in the worst way. He felt something his pocket as he took off his jacket, and rediscovered Anne's letter. He began reading....

XVIII

Dr. Sheppard," an obviously annoyed President Stone began. "I'm not sure what you know about the events of the last few days in central Asia. But, right now, I've got bigger things on my plate than your damn Genesis project. I'm not going to go down in history as the President who caved in to the communist Chinese.

"Now, I'll tell you what. You've had months to dance around the world picking your team. When you're done, then we'll talk. If it's so important, finish it. You were appointed with General Adams to head this project. Well, he's being diverted, so it's all your baby, for the time being. Get on with it, man! Do you think those poor bastards in Kazakhstan go scuba diving over the weekend? They're in a life-and-death struggle for survival. I suggest you look upon your endeavor as life and death, also." The President of the United States hung up without waitng for a response. He had no use for small talk, small actions, or small people. He was currently preoccupied with the possibility of having ro fight another war, and was not in a particularly pleasant mood.

After his telephone conversation with the President abruptly ended, Eric sat down to collect his thoughts. *Okay, Sheppard. You're on your own. Like your President said, "finish it, man!"* No more vacations. No more generals for a while. Time to get focused, to get it together.

So what was left? One psychologist and he was done with the team. Then on to training. Eric picked up the telephone and dialed the Palestinian Embassy. He was immediately put through to the ambassador's secretary and, just as quickly, Ambassador Aswari appeared on the video phone.

"Dr. Sheppard, you look tired. How is my favorite American general, your General Hayes?"

"She is out of the country because of the Chinese invasion, Mr. Ambassador. She's also *my* favorite American General. I miss her already. I was hoping to talk with you about Dr. Najibul."

"Of course, of course. How may I be of service?"

"Well, I was hoping to meet with him in Palestine. However, with the current crisis, would it be possible for your government to arrange travel for him here to Washington? We could include him in that night on the town I promised you."

"If it is your wish that he should come here, so be it. Let Mohammed come to Mecca," the ambassador broke into a wheezing laughter. Eric was relieved by the ambassador's casual conversation. Clearly, Anne had given him his opening with the ambassador.

"Unfortunately, General Hayes won't be able to join us, Mr. Ambassador."

"Never mind, Doctor. No problem. We shall make it—how do you say it—a boys' night out," again howling uncontrollably. "If Mustafa is coming, make sure to include condoms," almost weeping with laughter. Was he serious? Eric wondered.

"It may be best that we begin in my office before invading the streets of Washington," suggested Sheppard, hoping to sound out whether the ambassador was sincere about his last comment.

"No, no, no, Doctor. Don't worry," the ambassador coughed, but still laughing. "Mustafa likes to play games with people and the condoms. To see their reactions. After teasing them in his own way, he asks them whether they would like him to put it on. You must understand, it is only to test their response, both males and females.

He makes more and more sexual innuendos. He won't let them escape," he was seized by the image. "And then, when they are expecting to see his genitals, he puts it on his nose. He blows the condom into a balloon on his nose. Blows them until they burst. Everyone in Palestine knows of his investigations. Your Americans will be fresh subjects for him. I can't wait to see how your sexually inhibited citizens react, especially the men. They are so terrified of their own sexuality. And the possibility of homosexuality. You people are such prudes."

Eric was almost speechless. What happened to the conservative Islamic laws of sexuality? Didn't they still stone people for less? "Mr. Ambassador. If it is condoms and barflies you want, it is condoms and barflies you will get. Nothing is too good for you, my friend," he declared, hoping the lack of enthusiasm wasn't transparent. And he thought Australia was bad. He, too, was seized by the image. How would he explain this if *The Washington Post* got wind of it? Or Congress? At least Lightning Ridge was 10,000 miles from the Congress of the United States. He was considering a return there.

"Mad Dog, get in here on the double," Sheppard bellowed into the intercom.

Moments later, he continued, "I've gotta chauffeur-around Najibul and the Palestinian ambassador, entertain them, and convince the shrink to join our journey. Whaddaya got to amuse them? And make it good, or apparently this guy brings out condoms to blow up on his nose."

"We could send them to Madame Helena's strip joint over on E Street. I hear she's got some pretty bizarre acts. Or—"

"Look, damn it. The pressure's on. I've gotta bag this guy and start training these turkeys or the President's gonna have my ass on a platter. So what can I do that's impressive, but not too public, until we figure out whether he's our guy?"

"Dr. Sheppard, the President's on line one," interrupted Eric's secretary. *Great*, he lamented, *now he's gonna chew on me some more.* Eric immediately reached for the video phone, knocking it to the floor. After fumbling around for the business end, he located it and answered as the blurred vision appeared on-screen.

"Yes, Mr. President. Sorry about the telephone, sir. I was—"

"It's okay, Eric. Listen, I don't have much time. I'm sorry I was a bit harsh with you earlier. This Kazakhstan thing is a burr in the butt. This wasn't what I had in mind. I was ready to save the world economically, but not by fighting another war with the Chinese. Anyway, that's not your problem. What I was calling about was to offer my help in completing the team."

"Thank you, Mr. President. I have one more spot to fill and I feel we're finished. Unfortunately, he's in Palestine. The Palestinian ambassador is trying to arrange a flight here. I thought it best to not be traveling in the face of the crisis in Kazakhstan."

"You mean Ambassador Aswari? What if I picked 'em up—the ambassador and your psychologist?"

"Excuse me, sir?"

"Look Eric, I've got to go to that part of the world to deal with this thing anyway. What do you say I arrange to pick up your candidate and schmooze him a bit. Certainly couldn't hurt for me to wine and dine him on Air Force One, don't you think?"

"Mr. President, I think it would be—"

"I know, I know. There are a few perks that make this job worthwhile. And the damn plane is one of them.

She's got all sorts of gadgets and other stuff that ought to impress them. We'll pick them up, bring your psychologist back to you and wow him in the process. Tell me a little about him. You know, what are his weaknesses? Does he have any idiosyncrasies? What do you want from this guy? Do I need to watch for anything?"

A dilemma. Do you tell the most powerful man on Earth your candidate may be peculiar, or let him discover it on his own? There's a fine line between eccentricity and truly abnormal behavior. Surely he wouldn't pull out condoms in front of the President of the United States.

"We don't have much on him, sir. As a psychologist in Palestine, he has studied and written about frustration and oppression and how to deal with anger nonviolently. He is outspoken among his brethren because of this approach." Eric decided to take the conservative route. What if the ambassador was positively joking. If he wasn't, the President was on his own.

"Tell 'em I'll be in touch. The ambassador will be our go between. We'll contact Aswari. We'll wine and dine your psychologist. Aswari's on our side on this one, a real player. I'm headed for Iran in hopes of persuading them to mediate this thing with Kazakhstan like they did in the Straits."

"Good luck, Mr. President. When do you leave?"

"That's classified, Eric. Aswari's got worries of his own right now. He's a good man."

"Good night, sir." Both disengaged their video phones. Sheppard let out his best imitation of an Oklahoma Indian war cry. "Mad Dog. Change in plans!" he shrieked into the intercom. Houtson shot through the door like a bullet. Eric told his old friend his news.

"So what do you think we do with him when the President gets him back here? Air Force One's a tough act to follow."

"Yeah, but what an act."

"Dr. Sheppard. It's the President, again," came his secretary's call. Eric calmly turned on his video screen.

"Yes, sir, Mr. President."

"Eric, why don't you come along, too. You've never been on my little jet, have you? That way you can wheel and deal first hand. What do you think? You can entertain the ambassador on the flight back. I'll pop in a couple of times to help, but it'll be your show."

"Great, sir! Great! And, no, sir. I've never been on Air Force One. Where do I go?"

"The Secret Service will take you to Andrews. Be ready in two hours. I assume your attaché will be with you? That's eleven p.m., Eric. Don't be late. You wouldn't want to hold up world peace, would you?" He disconnected before Sheppard could answer.

Hell, no! he didn't want to hold up world peace. With Houston's help, he began scrambling around to pack. "Mad Dog, call Tom Conroy. I've got to go home and get some stuff. I can't go looking like this. I gotta start leaving some clothes here, or something."

Less than two hours later, Eric and Tom Conroy were standing at Andrews Air Force Base, with the Palestinian ambassador to the United States, surrounded by Secret Service agents and uniformed military personnel, waiting for the ride of their lives. None of the three had been on Air Force One.

The major snapped to attention and saluted as the President's military attaché carrying the "football" arrived. He was quickly followed by the President's staff, the Secretary of State, and National Security Adviser

Williams. Eric had briefly met Williams during his first White House meeting, which Williams interrupted for his daily briefing. That seemed so long ago, yet it had been only months. Williams was cool and smooth, but always appeared to be mad at somebody.

Williams and Secretary of State, Albright Lynn Richardson, were deep in discussion, hardly noticing Sheppard or Conroy. Secretary Richardson, always the diplomat, did recognize Ambassador Aswari and greeted him warmly. They exchanged bear hugs and made brief small talk before Williams intruded. The two American diplomats boarded and disappeared into the bowels of the giant airplane. The Secret Service finally finished searching Eric and his party's luggage.

Eric, the ambassador, and Conroy were finally hustled aboard, along with the rest of the President's staff, but no President yet. Thirty minutes passed. Finally a motorcade arrived. Quickly, the President, the Secretary of Defense, the U.N. Ambassador, and Joint Chiefs Chairman, General Adams, emerged and boarded. Eric had never been around so much power.

It was also rare that so much of the government was traveling together tonight. After the Kennedy assassination in 1963, by policy, one cabinet officer always stayed in Washington. At the time of the Kennedy assassination, the entire cabinet was on one plane headed to Hawaii. President Kennedy and Vice President Johnson were together in Dallas. The policy was developed to insure against a coup or other nefarious act attempting to control or capture the executive branch of government. Even today, when the President addresses the Congress, at least one cabinet member isn't present. So to have this many cabinet members in one place was exceptionally rare. Not the entire cabinet, but certainly the power players. It also explained why there were so many trench coat and sunglasses types with their little earpieces, talking into their thumbs.

Air Force One was airborne within ten minutes of the President's arrival. JFS gathered the group together for an announcement. "I'm glad you could join us on this historic trip. Ambassador Aswari, as many of you probably don't know, has been acting as a mediator between our government and the government of Iran. He has, and deserves, the mutual respect of both our governments.

"Our destination tonight is Mecca, Saudi Arabia. There, the Iranians have arranged a meeting with the Chinese ambassador to Iran and the Chinese foreign minister, Vice Premier Yang's personal representative. It is my fervent hope we can avert further bloodshed in Kazakhstan. In the meantime, we all have a long trip. Let's have some fun en route and maybe get a little work done. Thank you, all."

To scattered applause and heartfelt wishes of good luck, the President worked his way past each traveling guest, shaking hands as he strode by. All knew this wouldn't be a walk in the park. As President Stone passed Eric, Ambassador Aswari told both men he had arranged for Najibul to meet them in Mecca.

Before long, Sheppard and Aswari found themselves alone at the bar, lights dimmed and quiet music playing. "Come here often?" joked Aswari to Eric. "It is my favorite American bar." He took a long sip and leaned closer to Eric. "Shall we talk about Najibul seriously, Doctor?"

"Please, Mr. Ambassador. How should I approach him? Does he know anything about why I want to talk to him?"

"The world knows of your endeavor, but only in generalities, Doctor. What they do not know are the specifics. The devil is in the details," he whispered.

"Our people have dealt with frustration over home rule from the Israelis, anger at having our religious sites desecrated and poverty because of poor education," continued Aswari. "We have, I believe, a "poor me" syndrome. Though I think there are righteous complaints about the Israelis, much of our plight is of our own doing or within our control. Mustafa has studied our people. He believes we must stop feeling sorry for ourselves and overcome our plight by hard work, education, and nonviolence.

"Like your American blacks, when violence erupts, it is our people who suffer the most. Both burn their own neighborhoods. Who are they really hurting? These outspoken views have made Najibul a target in Palestine. I cannot agree with him publicly. It would be political suicide. But he is right. We must work twice as hard, earn twice as many degrees, and work three times as many hours for our people to show the world we aren't second class citizens. It is the psychology of pride, not shame. Dignity, not ridicule. Respect, not contempt."

"There will be plenty of frustration, Mr. Ambassador."

"Call me Gamal. I was named after Nasser, you know."

"I didn't know that. You would have been born during his Presidency? Say, in the 60s, yes?"

"You are too kind, Doctor. No, in the late-50s. Nasser taught Egypt about respect as a country. Palestine must learn that lesson as well."

"Frustration and anger," Eric echoed. "Also depression and loneliness. Even the strongest of the team are committing to leaving all they know. Their family, friends, planet, and environment. No psychologist will have had more of a challenge."

"Najibul will rise to the challenge. He thrives on adversity. That is why the Israelis hate him. That, and because they could not shoot him like a dog because he would not indulge in their violence. It is time we rest, Doctor. Tomorrow will bring new struggles. We must be rested. Good night, my friend."

As the ambassador wandered off to one of the sleeping areas, Eric finished his Dr. Pepper and leaned back in his seat.

Before he knew it, Major Conroy was jostling him awake.

"Eric, wake up. Dr. Najibul is coming aboard. We've been on the ground in Mecca for an hour. You were sleeping so soundly I let you go for it. We have the conference room. Almost everyone else left with the President."

"Is Gamal...Ambassador Aswari...here?"

"No. He's with the President. The shower's available. Get cracking. You got about five minutes to get ready."

Eric needed to shave and shower fast, and make sure not to have a repeat shaving accident. He seemed to cut himself at the most inopportune times. Hell, this was the Middle East. No need for a suit. He'd throw on slacks and a sport coat and be ready in a New York minute. All he needed was a opening line. What do you say to a shrink? Hi, would you like to lie on the couch? While he had his head under the sink washing off his face, he heard an unfamiliar, laughing voice.

"Well, Doctor. It appears you are not using the sharpest knife in the drawer. Or are you trying to slit your throat to avoid meeting your tormenter, Najibul?"

Through the fog of the mirror Eric could barely make out the face. Standing there with only a towel on,

Eric began splashing the mirror and his face and everything else around him, "Mustaf—I mean, Dr. Najibul. You caught me by surprise. I—"

"In more ways than one it would appear, Doctor. You started to call me Mustafa. Why not? It is my Allah-given name. Since I have intruded, I should not stand on formality. I usually do not anyway. Let's talk while you finish."

"No doubt, you are aware of why I'm here."

"Yes, Eric. You are here to wine and dine me, with the help of your President and my ambassador. Then, Aswari has told you, I will bring out condoms and embarrass you in front of your President."

"Well, I..."

"You had hoped I wouldn't," the psychologist laughed. "Aswari. He loves to tell that story. What he never reports are the circumstances," pausing before taking a deep breath. "We were both fighters in the intifadeh in the 1980s. We were both drunk. I brought out the condoms, but it was his idea to blow them on our noses. Of course, he was too intoxicated to remember. I remember the truth."

"I thought Allah didn't approve of alcohol, Mustafa?"

"He doesn't. Nor does he condone murder. But we are all human. And we were young. Old age causes the fires to burn with less intensity. Still, the flames can be stoked."

"So, what stoked the fires in you and Gamal Aswari then, Mustafa?"

"Gamal did not tell you? I am surprised."

Eric studied the face of his newfound Palestinian friend. The smile was gone, replaced by solemnity. There was ambivalence. And pain. Something from his past, that he hadn't thought about recently. Pain and remembrance. But not denial.

"We were young enough," Najibul started, then sighed heavily and continued. "Gamal was drinking with me to keep me alive." He spoke softly. Not the jovial person who surprised Sheppard.

"The Zionist Jews had just murdered my wife and two children. He made me drink Russian vodka until I vomited. Vomited and slept. That kept me from going after them. That is what they wanted me to do. So they could justify killing me, too." There was obvious anger. Najibul looked up from the floor, his smile returning. "It was at that moment I renounced violence. The rules must be changed. The cycle must be stopped. But I will never forget. Violence begets violence. There are better ways to return their insults."

Eric was putting on his clothes. He hadn't read this version of the condom episode in the briefing book on Najibul. He ushered him to the adjoining cabin and through the door to the conference room. A tall, scruffy man of fifty, with a heavy beard and large protuberant nose, Najibul was not imposing physically. He hadn't missed many meals during his years. Still, he had a presence. It was his eyes. His eyes gleamed with intrigue, dark green, with a hint of blue, uncharacteristic for an Arab.

"I've admired your work on conditioning reversal," Eric spoke, changing the subject. "Modifying long held habits will be critically important in traveling to another world."

"We Arabs have learned our ways over many centuries. We are slow to change, but that change is mandatory to survive in our modern world." He was squinting to see Sheppard in spite of the bright sunlight streaming in through the window. "We have been blaming our problems on others for decades. I am no lover of the Israelis. I hate what they have done to my people and my family. But they have a right to exist, just as we do. Like Pavlov's dogs, Palestinians begin to salivate and prepare to fight when an Israeli talks. We don't listen to what he says. Only that it is a Jew who says it. They are just as bad. They only hear a Palestinian talking, not what he has to say. I will repay the Israeli's by turning the other cheek. I believe that is from your Bible. No more violence."

"So how do you enable both to talk to each other, not at each other?"

"Pavlov was able to teach his dogs to salivate when he rang a bell instead of giving them meat, a conditioned response to a conditioned stimulus. What my people must learn is not to salivate. We must learn to ignore the stimulus, or, failing that, at least not respond to it."

"What do you mean, Mustafa?" They were both now sitting on a comfortable sofa in the conference room of Air Force One.

"We must learn to think about the ramifications of our actions in a more complex way, not just a knee jerk response. They shoot at us, we throw rocks. We must consider the consequences of not only our response, but their initial action. What separates a thinking man from any other animal is that ability to consider the consequences of his actions. Responsibility. That is what makes us different. We have the ability to accept responsibility. It is also the difference between a child and an adult. We have been acting as children too long."

"As have others in the world," answered Eric.

"But right now I have my hands full with changing behavior here. Why should I join your endeavor, Eric?"

"To make an impact on a grander scale. You are trying to alter the conduct of a few. Why not help to shape the actions of a whole new civilization? And why not try and prevent a recurrence of the behavior that led to the problem in the first place? You can have a fundamental influence in shaping the deportment of an entire civilization. You can outline what is normal and what is abnormal behavior. What more could any psychologist want than to be able to create societal rules without historical baggage?"

"But how does one create the behavioral incentives? Yes, we can build the new scriptures, but are not the positive and negative incentives created over time?"

"And by the good examples of their predecessors, Mustafa. Don't you want to teach a new society the lessons of Allah? And God, Confucius and Buddha? Are there not universal laws that govern us all?"

"I will need time to consider your offer, Doctor." They both leaned forward, almost touching. The door flew open and the President of the United States entered followed by several aides, a gaggle of security and a cabinet secretary or two.

"Dr. Najibul. I'm so happy to meet you. Eric tells me great things about you."

"Yes, Mr. President. Thank you for inviting me to join your historic journey."

"May it be as fruitful a visit to Mecca as any haj before," the President answered. "We are leaving for Washington immediately. Will you be joining us on the flight, Dr. Najibul? I would like to hear you views on today's events and about Eric's plans for tomorrow's."

Without waiting for his answer the President moved on, seemingly distracted by the circumstance of the day. Eric and Mustafa were left alone again as the President's party disappeared into the next cabin. Soon thereafter, the aircraft's captain, who was actually an Air Force colonel, turned on the fasten seat belts sign and made a brief announcement indicating Air Force One was about to become airborne. The first thirty minutes were uneventful. Eric and Najibul made small talk. Eric knew his candidate needed to think about an answer. He didn't want to add the pressure of time.

Air Force One isn't your standard airliner. The service and accoutrements are unparalleled. The informality is deceiving. This 747-400 is a military aircraft staffed and flown by the U.S. Air Force. In times of turmoil, as existed today, that fact was undeniable. And fully loaded with communications gear and jamming radar, tracked by the various assortment of satellites and other electronic apparatus guaranteed to insure the safety of the President and his traveling companions. Wherever and whenever she flew, the Air Force had contingency plans in place and was well-practiced in dealing with the unexpected. Most of them, that is.

The command pilot needed verification of the somewhat garbled message. "Say again, Major?" The communications traffic came through his headset, clearly this time. The colonel turned to his co-pilot and weapons officer and coolly advised his crew, "This is not a drill. I repeat. This is not a drill. Prepare contingency plan 'Red Tango'. Get the President on the horn, Captain."

The aircraft went into a steep bank to the right, descending rapidly as she banked, causing stuff all over the plane to relocate. Before the Captain could ring the President, Stone was on the intercom to Colonel Weston, the command pilot.

"What's going on, Denny? Why are we on this roller coaster?"

"Mr. President. We just received traffic from the AWACS out of Diego Garcia. They're tracking a flight of six MIGs out of Al-Hudayah."

"Where? What the hell? I—"

"Sir. Al-Hudayah is in Yemen about three hundred miles south of our position. The problem, sir. is that the Yemeni Air Force doesn't have that type of aircraft. Diego Garcia tracked them from the PRC several days ago."

"Colonel, am I hearing you say these are Chinese MIGs?"

"Yes, sir. That's the CO's assessment in Diego Garcia. The Pentagon's in on it and so is Tactical Air Command. They've scrambled a squadron of F-22s and some F-18s from Medina in Saudi. But, sir, they won't reach us before the MIGs."

"What's your assessment of the situation, Denny? We've been too many places together. I've come to rely on your opinion more than the satellites."

"Well, sir. If these are hostile aircraft, I don't think they will give us a fly by. They will attack us straight away and not give us a second chance. We have to assume that's their intent and take evasive action. That's why we're descending to the deck of the Red Sea. We have some tricks up our sleeve, too. The Eisenhower carrier group's on patrol in the Red Sea. They've put up a squadron of F-18s. The Egyptians have also launched aircraft. And the Israelis. But the Chinese have a jump on them. We've got to head north as fast and low as we can to help them close the gap."

"Keep me informed, Colonel. I'm going to brief our passengers." The President knew this colonel quite well. They had traveled well over a million accident-free miles together with Weston at the helm. Stone not only trusted him, but considered him family. "Good luck, Denny."

The President gathered his staff and Secret Service agents, the various cabinet secretaries, Ambassador Aswari, Eric, Conroy, and Najibul. This was, thankfully, one trip without any reporters on board. He explained the situation to the group as calmly as he could. His tone gave away his concern. "Today, the Iranians agreed to mediate the Kazakhstani dispute with China. So far though, China's response to our overture has been lukewarm. We just don't know their objectives. How far do they want to take this thing. Now, there are apparently some aircraft headed our way. We think they are Chinese. We don't know for sure, or what their intentions are."

"Are you trying to read their minds, Mr. President," asked Najibul. "Because you Americans do not understand the Chinese logic."

"What do you mean, Dr. Najibul?"

"Call me Mustafa, sir. We all may be getting more familiar with each other over the next few hours," trying levity to break the tension. "It is best we understand each other. Strengths and weaknesses. Ours and theirs. Your military will confront the Chinese. You have superiority but they had surprise. Now they have lost surprise, but they still have a lead on your aircraft."

"How do you know that?"

"Your voice is one of worry, sir. You Americans must always control the situation, and now you do not. You are obsessed with control. You do not have it, and that worries you and your military. You may have the tactical advantage, but I believe they have the psychological one. They know you want to avoid all-out war. The U.S. and her allies do not have the stomach for it. You will have trouble convincing your citizens of the value of the fight. Is it worth one American life to save all of Kazakhstan? You and your countrymen think about individual survival, not cultural survival. For them, life is a mathematical calculation. Their country and culture will survive this round. So they lose a few of the People's Army. They have been losing the battle, but winning the war for centuries."

"Your argument would conclude, then, that there is nothing Americans think is worth fighting for, other than America or Americans?" interrupted General Adams, uncharacteristically quiet until now.

"Yes, General," the psychologist continued. "This is not the end, but the beginning of another round. This is nothing more than a game of aerial gamesmanship, Mr. President. Like two cars barreling towards each other. Who will swerve first?"

"Well, Dr. Najibul. If this is a game of chicken, as we call it, then no one will be the worse for wear if we make plans to shoot the turkeys—I'm sorry—the other chicken—out of the sky. We might not swerve, but in case he doesn't blink," grunted Adams, clearly angered by the situation. "if I remember correctly from playing the game as a child, when both sides fail to blink, there's a helluva crash and no one wins," stated in his best Texas drawl.

"True, sir, and the only sure way to avoid losing is not to play."

"Sometimes you just can't help playing, Doctor," the President intervened. "As much as we might like to, sometimes it's unavoidable. So, all of you, please stay in your seats until Colonel Weston gives us the all clear. I'm going to put the radio transmissions on the loudspeaker. You're all entitled to know what's happening as much as I am."

All on board fastened their seat belts and prepared for a bumpy ride. Eric nervously reached into his pocket. He found Anne's letter—the one she'd written before leaving for Diego Garcia. He read it once again. *"Dear Eric..."*

"Unidentified aircraft at one hundred miles and closing," came the punctuated, anonymous, unemotional electronic voice in the cockpit.

A friendlier voice aboard an AWACS was heard next. "F-18s are on afterburners at one hundred fifty miles…They're your closest friendlies, Colonel. They're squawking on seven alpha…Diego Garcia's got satellite confirmation. These are Chinese MIGS tracked last week. Same infrared signatures…" There was a pause that seemed to last forever. "Descend to the deck, Colonel…AWACS recommends five hundred feet, sir. Release your first package when bogeys are at thirty miles…"

When I'm relieved from Diego Garcia, I've asked B.C. to let me transfer to your civilian unit to help train the team…

"Bogeys at thirty miles, Colonel… Altitude 15,000 and scanning… They've gone off afterburners… F-18s are at fifty miles and still on afterburners. You should have radar contact… When you detect missile lock, release your heat signature chaff… Don't wait for them to fire…"

I don't want to leave like this, again. Not being able to say goodbye left me so empty. What is living for if you can't be with the one you love?

"Prepare to engage the RATOs, Captain. Arm the anti-missile missiles. We've got to hold on another minute or two. But, if they fire, release the anti-missiles without my command."

Maybe you and I could sign up for the mission. Anything to get away from the insanity of this world.

"They have missile lock, sir! They've got a lock!" the weapons officer reported.

"Missile lock… Chaff released," Weston acknowledged, calmly but with increasing apprehension.

"No fire yet. No fire!"

"On my mark, engage the RATOs, Captain. We'll wait for them to launch…if they've got the balls!"

"They've fired, Colonel! Anti-missile missiles away, Colonel! Two…make that three…no…only two missiles. Anti-missiles running hot, straight, and normal. No deflection yet!"

"Engage the RATOs, Captain." Knowing what was coming next, Weston pulled back as hard as he could on the yoke. There was a sudden lurch. All passengers were thrust hard into the backs of their seats. A loud sonic-boom trailed them. The G-forces from climbing with extraordinary speed pinned everyone to their seat. There wasn't a sound to be heard over the roar of rockets straining at full capacity. This was no ordinary roller coaster ride. Eric dropped his letter as he was pressed hard into his chair. His head pounding about as much as his heart, he recalled his supersonic flight with Sveta Gargarin.

"F-18s are engaging, Colonel…they've fired…."

"Splash two MIGS! Splash two, Colonel…The F-22s are on scene now also…"

"Look out your starboard window, Mr. President," shouted Colonel Weston. "Those are American aircraft. *Oh, say can you see…!*"

Four F-22s and four F-18s now flanked Air Force One. General Adams was standing in the aisle saluting the pilots. They dipped their wings to acknowledge.

There was a collective cheer throughout the cabin. And a sigh of relief. Only moments ago pinned to their seats, now jumping for joy, most quickly collapsed back into their seats, exhausted from the few minutes of tension. Several poured drinks. Others just sat, silenty staring out the window at the escort planes, contemplating their own mortality.

"General, what the hell's a RATO?" asked the President. All the others were curious, too.

"That's *Rocket Assisted Take Off,* sir. When Weston engaged the RATO, four high performance rockets kicked this baby damn near into orbit! Sir, I don't know what our climb rate was, but we were pullin' 7 or 8 Gs, I'll guarantee it. This plane's built to maintain its initial course for three minutes in case the pilot blacks out from the G forces. *Soooo-weeeee! what a ride!*" B.C. was in hog heaven.

Most on board were just glad not to be in heaven—or hell. Weston turned the aircraft on a northwest heading, to take the plane up the Red Sea and over Egypt on into the Mediterranean. They were back to subsonic speed and level flight with their reassuring complement of F-whatevers. God bless the USA!

How was this going to read in the papers tomorrow or sound on the news tonight? It probably wouldn't. There were no correspondents on board and it was in the United States' best interests to let the Iranians use this episode as a trump card with the Chinese. At least that was the current plan. Stone, Adams, and the rest on board the plane knew the story would eventually get out sometime in the future. After the diplomatic advantage ran its course, no one would care much. What they wanted was to end the conflict at hand. But everyone involved had long memories. This incident might not get publicized, but it sure wouldn't be forgotten.

"So, Dr. Najibul. How do you like the way we play chicken?" snorted Adams.

"Very impressive, General. Very impressive. What I fear is the Chinese will react as the behaviorists predict. A stimulus-response pattern. They have learned that if they attack, they must do so completely, rather than subtly."

"What I hope they've learned is not to attack us at all," responded the President.

"You, sir, are more optimistic about our fellow man than I. You hope they go against their nature. You believe the Chinese received negative reinforcement for their actions. An electrical shock for their aberrant behavior. But, by not publicizing their mistake, are you not rewarding them? You are letting them get away with it."

"Get away with it? They lost several aircraft and pilots," dismissed Adams. "We kicked their rice eatin' butts."

"Replaceable, General. And completely expendable to a country of 1.5 billion people. The cost of doing business. And had they succeeded?"

"Had they succeeded, none of us would be debating this. And a bunch of pissed-off Americans would be flyin' up their communist ass!"

"General. Dr. Najibul is our guest," interjected the President.

"The General is right. That is exactly what would happen. And I submit, exactly what they would have wanted to happen. They believe a conflict with the West is inevitable, and they are prepared for it. But are you? They believe that conflict is winnable, partially because they saw your hesitation to escalate in 2013. They think you will blink again," retorted Najibul.

"Chicken, again, Doctor?"

"Yes, Mr. President. You want to change their behavior and they don't. Confrontation is want *they* want—it is *not* what you want. You are doing exactly what they anticipated. The West must change the way the game is played, or risk losing the game."

"Interesting. What game should we be playing, Doctor?" asked Sheppard.

"That you must discover on your own. But to know your direction is wrong is a good first step." Najibul stood and walked to the door of the restroom. "Knowledge of what your adversary wants and needs—his hopes, desires, his fears—that is the key to finding a solution. Now, I will take my leave."

"Mr. President. My job is to make plans for dealing with our enemies when their behavior isn't what we expect," countered General Adams. "I'll leave you to discuss how to talk to him, while I develop strategies to bloody his nose." With that, General Adams and the military contingency left to assess their options.

"Mr. President. If I may be of further service, I am at your disposal," Ambassador Aswari declared. "For now, I too will take my leave, sir. May Allah smile upon you."

After a few quiet minutes the President spoke. "Eric, your mission is the world's mission. Maybe the Chinese will fight, maybe they won't. Maybe they'll see space colonization as something they can support. I don't know. But I do know Mustafa is right. We must engage them. The stick doesn't seem to work." The President was tired. He stood to leave for his private compartment. "Mustafa would be a welcome addition to your team, Eric. Convince him to join us."

"Good night, Mr. President," and Eric was alone. As he looked around the cabin, his eyes found Anne's letter on the floor. In the excitement of the moment he had lost it. He touched the page softly. *When will I see you again?*

XIX

General, maybe Najibul is right. Maybe we have to change the game with the Chinese. I don't know. What I do know is I will not sit here in the Oval Office, a virtual prisoner, because they tried to shoot me down."

President Stone wasn't angry, but he wasn't of the demeanor to write this incident off. After all, it's not everyday one nearly gets killed, by Chinese pilots or otherwise. Frustration best characterized his mood since returning to Washington. He felt constrained and entrapped, like a caged animal aching to escape.

"Yes, sir," General Adams replied. "We have plans in place guaranteeing your safety. Air Force One will have fighter escort any time you fly. We—"

"I appreciate your guarantees, General. What I had in mind was not needing them. Secretary Richardson, have the Iranians come up with anything yet?"

"Nothing concrete, Mr. President," came Richardson's response. "Mr. Williams and I met privately with Vice Premier Yang after the incident and expressed our displeasure in the most strenuous terms. He seemed surprised by the incident."

"No wonder. The bastard was surprised you were alive, not surprised by the incident. He thought we were all dead!" growled Adams. "I don't trust the Iranians. They—"

"They are our best hope for now, sir," interrupted Williams. "We are close on a cease-fire, Mr. President. We should have that in place within the next twenty-four hours."

"By that time the Chinese'll have what they want, sir. The oil fields," Adams retorted. "What you'll have is a cease-fire after they've attained their objective. That's no cease-fire, that's legitimizing their position on the battlefield."

"That may be true, General. But this isn't our arena," answered Williams, always the logical National Security Adviser. "The Russians aren't going to repel the Chinese. They don't have the stomach for it, or the personnel and equipment. It's to our advantage to stop the hostilities and wait for another day." Williams was near boiling in his seat. He, too, wanted a fight like Adams. But he was more of a pragmatist.

"What if the Iranians can't deliver a cease-fire, Trump?" asked the President. "What then?"

"They will, sir," answered a glum Richardson, instead. "They will, because General Adams is right. Once they secure the oil fields, they will have reached their objectives and a cease-fire is moot. We will, in effect, validate their claim to this "border dispute" and there's nothing credible we—or anyone else—can do about it."

"We could use tactical nuclear warheads on the battlefield," answered Adams.

"Launched from where, General? We don't even have a platform in that part of the world," answered Williams. "I want to get these sum bitches as much as you. But it isn't practical."

"Tactical nukes aren't 'practical,' Mr. Williams? Mr. President, you give me the okay, and I'll find a platform," countered Adams. "They keep choosing the stage. We need to break their nose with a sucker punch from behind. Not in Kazakhstan, but say along their underbelly. Near the southern coast. That would get their attention."

"And the rest of the world's. Then what when they escalate?" questioned Williams. "Korea flares, or the Straits, or Europe, and who knows where else?"

"Sir, we're going to have to fight them sooner or later. With our—"

"Enough, gentlemen," interrupted the President. "Listen to yourselves. You're seriously debating turning a dispute over a few oil fields into Armageddon. For God's sake, they only tried to shoot down an airplane. Admittedly, one carrying all of you—*and me*. And they stole some oil. Both are insignificant in the big picture. Hell, we might not even need oil in a few decades. The internal combustion engine is going the way of the horse and carriage—unless, of course, we nuke ourselves back to those days. I don't think this conflict warrants that kind of consideration."

"We are going to have to confront them sometime, sir," came a soft voice, the contemplative voice of General Adams. "Maybe this isn't the right incident, but what will be? Maybe it isn't the right geography, but where will be? My nature is to take on the bulldog, nose to nose, teeth to teeth, strength to strength," came Adams' slow response. "But, I hate to admit it, what we need is a new game plan. No, what we need is a new game. How can we engage the enemy? First, they have to feel like they aren't the enemy," answering his own question. "They have to see it as in their best interests to change their behavior."

"General Adams, I believe you've been talking to Dr. Najibul in your off hours," jested the President. "I congratulate you on realizing what I believe we all must recognize," he stated more seriously. "There are no second chances in the world wars of our age. No, with nuclear weapons, if we get this wrong, God help us all." The room was quiet. Thoughtful, pensive, almost meditative. Here was a group of men who literally had the future of the world in their grasp.

"Mr. President, I'm volunteering to head a group of your choosing to explore our options with respect to changing the game with the Chinese," offered Secretary Richardson. "I think Williams and I have the most vested interest in solving the problem."

"Rich, Trump. As much as I value your counsel, I feel we need to look at our options from an entirely new perspective," responded the President. "You both deal with these issues everyday. You're too close to them to see outside options. Which is why neither of you are on this one, gentlemen. Of course you'll each have input, but I want a different perspective."

"What did you have in mind, sir?" asked Williams.

"I don't know right now. Sheppard's got the right idea. Find a diverse bunch of people, regardless of their previous political or social baggage. Too bad they're already taken. Can you imagine the Congressional reaction if I presented them as a select committee or something to solve world peace?" The President was chuckling under his breath.

"You may have to present Sheppard's team to Congress, sir," came General Adams' reply. "If the Congress is going to pay for them, they're going to want to see what they bought, Mr. President. Sheppard's had them arriving over the last few days."

"Here in Washington?" questioned Stone.

"No, sir. Out west. It's the first time they'll meet each other, too."

"Thank God he's not bringing them to Washington. We'd never have the time to get them trained in between every Congressional committee wanting to subpoena them. Shouldn't I be there?" asked the President. "You know, to start it off on the right foot. Hell, I want to see their reactions to each other as much as anybody.

I've got an investment in this thing, too."

"Your schedule has already been cleared, sir," answered Williams. "I believe you're the headliner for the opening act. Sheppard's got the details. He's forwarding the timetable this afternoon."

"Let's see if we can come up with another team to solve the world's challenges they get to leave behind," pleaded the President. "Any of you want to join them instead?" the President wisecracked, concluding the meeting.

The group dispersed quickly. Presidential advisers don't have time to waste making small talk amongst themselves. Most are trying to one-up the other much of the time anyway. They scattered back to their respective fiefdoms, leaving Stone to ponder his own last question. He sat alone in the subdued lighting of the Oval office. Alone with his thoughts until being disturbed by the telephone intercom.

"Ambassador Aswari on line one, Mr. President."

"Mr. Ambassador. Good of you to return my call," whispered the President as he turned on the video screen with hopeful anticipation. "You have news?"

"Yes, Mr. President. I have contacted the Iranians. Your 'back channel' negotiations have come to fruition. You will be meeting directly with Vice Premier Yang soon. He, too, is concerned about secrecy as much as you, sir. Apparently he has political enemies, too. I should know more specifics, the when and where, within the next twelve hours."

"Thank you, Gamal. Thank you from me personally, and thank you on behalf of the world. Few people know of the countless numbers of people who have been saved by your unselfish diplomacy. I only hope to make the world aware of your contributions in the very near future," answered a genuinely moved John Stone.

"Thank you, sir, for letting an old Palestinian warrior help world peace. Good night, Mr. President, and, again, may Allah bless you and your house." Both screens flickered to black. The President rose slowly and headed to his White House private quarters. He was alone with his thoughts, again. No children to distract him, no Jennifer to give him personal counsel.

He missed her now more than anything. He missed being able to present all the options and get an honest answer without political or tactical advantage. He still found himself telling her about his problems. Since her death, the questions and answers grew harder. Sometimes in the early hours of the morning, he would awaken, and, if only for a moment, think that he had heard her. He needed to have one of those nights, tonight.

"Mr. President. Wake up, sir, you've overslept. You're due at Andrews in thirty minutes. It's eight a.m."

John Stone couldn't remember the last time he woke up as late as eight a.m. He also couldn't remember a more restful sleep. He felt refreshed and ready to face the problems of the world. He was eager to board Air Force One for the flight to Area 96. He showered in less than five minutes—was dressed and raring to go in well under thirty minutes.

Several aides had to catch up with him this morning. He was, shall we say, *perky*. The trip to southern Utah took four hours. The flight was uneventful. No Williams or Richardson, no China or Kazakhstan, no crisis or fateful decision. Today he was to meet the Team. Today was for meeting the future. Yesterday was for today. And tomorrow...who knows?

Sheppard was already in Utah waiting to brief the President before he met with the nine member team. The various team members had been brought to Area 96 by different Air Force aircraft over the last several days. Each had said their good-byes and hugged their loved ones not knowing when—or if—they would see them again. Although they weren't leaving the planet just yet, they were preparing for it.

There were certainly many mixed feelings. Apprehension, excitement, fear, exhilaration, anxiety, tranquility, resolution. Different emotions coming and going at various times in various members. They were experiencing the total spectrum of emotions. They were also meeting new people, their soon to be associates, their new family. And they were about to do it in a strange, new place called Utah.

Area 96 is the designation for a way-beyond-secret military installation in the southern Utah desert. It was almost entirely underground below a designated national preserve, an area so designated back in 1996, hence, its code name, Area 96. Within the desert region known as the Great Basin, it was actually beneath a plateau—6,100 feet above sea level—flanked by steep mountain ranges on its east and west. If you could drive through it—which you can't—you'd think it was beautiful, but you wouldn't want to stop. Utah's Great Basin rattlesnake has one of the more toxic venoms of all rattlesnakes in North America. And seventy percent of the land in the state, to this day, remains under federal control, making access even harder.

Utah has the largest U.S. reserves of beryllium, ample reserves of uranium, and is a top domestic supplier of gold, molybdenum, silver, lead, and zinc. Vast government-sponsored hydroelectric facilities built over the years generate large quantities of energy, utilizing the 5.8 trillion gallons of water generated annually by her streams and rivers. An additional, 24 trillion gallons of underground aquifers mean water and energy are abundant. Though easy to get close via Salt Lake City's international airport, admission to Area 96 requires a "special pass". That pass had better come from someone with lots of scrambled eggs on their hat or your welcome wagon will be a paddy wagon courtesy of the U.S. Air Force security police.

A new home-sweet-home wasn't what a Russian, Argentine, South African, Australian, German, Palestinian, or Louisiana American were used to, or, for that matter, even expected, let alone a pair of Indian-Chinese transplanted Malaysians. Each was assigned to their respective housing units. They were unpacking and generally making their new living space comfortable. Some were even exploring their new home, albeit stealthily.

Or so they thought. What they were really doing was passing time until they met their future spacemates. One or two had inadvertently run into some of the others. Brief, superficial encounters. Just who were the others, and what were they like? Why were they at Area 96 and what were their expectations? Would they have things in common, or uncommon differences?

So, why a secret military base? Eric knew he would have to answer that question—and many others. This, as he was fond of saying, was a work in progress. On that, he agreed with General Adams. Inasmuch as many in the world knew vaguely of this mission, the specifics were more guarded. These people deserved to learn about the mission, each other, and make their final decision about going, in an environment out of the glare and limelight of the media. There would be plenty of time for that. Each and every one of his designated explorers had the right to bail out of this project at any time. Eric reiterated that frequently.

His staff was here, including its newest member, Major Tom Conroy, now out of uniform. Most of JMT-EL was here, too, also in civilian duds. Eric had asked for everyone to low-key the military connection. Uniforms made him feel uneasy, and he was sure a low military profile would help with the others. The only JMT-EL member not here was their commanding officer, General Anne Hayes. The plan was for her to be relieved on Diego Garcia shortly after the cease-fire took effect. He hoped that would happen before the meeting began. Eric couldn't contain his anticipation. But for now, he needed to concentrate on introducing the Team to the President of the United States and to each other, and organizing their training.

He had decided this first session would set the tone for subsequent meetings. To that end, he wanted the proceedings to be informal and democratic. He had asked the President to participate as part of the group. His plan was for President Stone to give a brief opening statement only. As excited about it as the President and the others were, this was not about them. It was about the mission and the team chosen for it. The room was set as a large circle. Eric had always liked the concept of circular meetings. Everyone could see everyone else. There were no leaders, no ranks, no haves or have nots. Besides, most meetings Eric deemed to be unending, just like a circle.

As the appointed hour approached, Eric was becoming more nervous. No Anne yet, no President yet, and no opening line yet. Most of the military and Washington staffers were already milling around when Sheppard entered the conference room, to his version of an Arthurian-like round table. From their dress, if he didn't know better, Sheppard would have guessed these team members were just a bunch of tourists on vacation. Some vacation, he thought. He wanted to observe the dynamics of the prospective team as they entered. Who was with whom, and how were they interacting with each other? Or had he picked a bunch of loners? Would a leader emerge? Would anyone leave after minimal time? He wouldn't have long to wait.

The first to arrive was Tatman, the physician. Eric recalled his seemingly boundless energy, and his inability to sit still. True to form, he was pacing around the room when he encountered Sheppard, the only person in the room he knew.

"Eric, nice little fortress you've got here," teased Tatman, shaking Sheppard's hand vigorously. "I couldn't find the medical facilities in my wanderings. I was out scouting the place this morning. Introduced myself to some damn serious military types who didn't like me opening their doors. I'm sure you'll show me the way…in more ways than one. Ah, there's Melissa. Met her this morning, too. A fascinating woman." Tatman quickly left to greet Sturmbourg who was half wheeling herself and half being pushed by Nkata as the two were deep in conversation. It was clear Tatman hadn't met Nkata previously. Eric watched across the room as Melissa introduced Tatman. Soon, the three were engrossed in conversation, with Tatman intermittently making wide hand gestures and Nkata and Sturmbourg laughing as he did. This was a good start, thought Sheppard.

"Eric, so good to see you again," he heard from over his shoulder. Turning, Eric found Natarajan and Xiao with Eva Mariani, together like old friends. "I was just telling Eva about our first meeting with you," Xiao smirked. "She tells me you're quite a tango expert. You will have to show Parvathi and me how to dance the tango. We miss dancing from our days in Paris. Malaysia doesn't have the right kinds of music for ballroom dancing. Will we be taking music, Eric?"

"Of course, and some interactive programs to improve your dancing skills, if you like," answered Sheppard. "I'm no expert. Eva, how could you mislead them so?" he asked in mock anger.

"That was not the only skill demonstrated, Eric," responded Mariani. "I fell under your powers of persuasion. That, after all, is why we are all here. Speaking of all, are there others?"

"Yes, Eva. Several others. I—"

"G'day, mates. Where are the refreshments, Eric? You didn't fly me all this way only to lose me to dehydration. I'm dry, mate. Very dry," chanted the one and only Chappo. "How's it goin' people. I'm Chappo," extending his hand to Xiao while simultaneously successfully brush kissing both Mariani and Natarajan. "Welcome, ladies. Step up to Chappo's bar."

"What bar, Mister Chappo?" queried Eva.

"The one Eric had better find me, or I'll build it for him," replied Chappo. "I'm the engineer for this trek. What's your forte, if you don't mind my asking?"

"I'm an educator," offered Mariani. "And my two newfound friends are an historian and philosopher. This is Parvathi Natarajan and Xiao Deng Wu."

"Well, I'll be," Chappo spoke incredulously. "I'm a philosopher, too. Give me a bar stool and I'll preach a sermon on the subject of your choice. Not much of a history buff. Never could remember all those dates."

"Mister Chappo. Dates are only the mile markers of history," responded Natarajan. "History is much more than book marks. By reconstructing the past, we are able to learn from it and plan for the future."

"It's just Chappo, love—no Mister. Well, I look forward to learning something, past or present. Now, look who's coming. If it isn't my new girlfriend, Svetlana," laughed Chappo as Svetlana Yuryevna Gagarin approached. "Have any of you had the pleasure of meeting her? Other than old Eric, of course."

Without waiting for an answer, Chappo threw his arm around Gagarin and launched into his introduction. "This young lady has been to space before, mates. She's a genuine, certified cosmonaut. May I introduce to you Svetlana Gagarin. Svetlana, these are some of our new mates, Parvathi the historian. This is Xiao the philosopher. And Eva. She's going to educate us, one and all."

"Sveta, Chappo. I told you earlier, it's Sveta," shrugging off his arm and moving to Eric. She lightly rubbed against him while addressing the others. "I am honored to be a part of such a distinguished group. My role is transportation. As Chappo says, I am a cosmonaut. And also a pilot. I suppose we will need to move around our new home after we arrive."

"May we join you?" asked a new voice unfamiliar to the group. "I'm Jeremy Leahy, and this is Jim Dupree. Is that Svetlana I see? I hardly recognize you without a space suit. We met ten years or so ago on a space shuttle-*SOYUZ* docking."

"Yes, Yes! Admiral Leahy. It was 2008. How could I forget!" She left Eric's side and warmly hugged Leahy.

"It's Jeremy. Just Jeremy."

"Are you going too? These are new team mates," said Svetlana, introducing Xiao, Natarajan, Mariani, and Chapman to the growing crowd.

"No, not me. I'm on the logistical side of this project, Sveta. But I'd give anything to be in your place," responded the envious Leahy.

The increasing noise and laughter attracted the attention of others. Svetlana noticed others coming to join them—Tatman, Nkata, and Sturmbourg—soon followed by Jack Grimes and E.J. Abraham, the remaining members of JMT-EL, who joined the conversation. As each introduced themselves to one another, Eric gradually drifted away. His hopes for a good start seemed fulfilled.

"She'll get here, Eric," came the reassurance of Tom Conroy. "I've got good intel that says it's so. I'm not sure your cosmonaut will be excited to see her." Conroy's eyes met Eric's. Conroy knew Sheppard caught his message. "Rejoin your masterpiece. Remember, they're my hope to save the world," Conroy advised. The two slowly worked their way back into the group.

"So where's our shrink?" asked Chappo. "I was told there was a head shrinker on the list. Does he know about detox, mate?"

"Yeah, I was told the same thing," answered Tatman. "We'll sure as hell all need one by the time we get there. We all must be crazy for even wanting to go." They all laughed, though there was a certain element of truth to his statement. "So where is he, Eric?"

"He's standing in the corner, over there. He's no doubt been watching all of you, even as we speak," retorted Eric, snickering just a bit. He called out across the room, "Mustafa, it's time to end your experiment. Come meet your compatriots." Sauntering slowly over to the group came a smug Mustafa Najibul. Eric whispered in his ear, "No condoms, please."

"Welcome, Sigmund. I love my mother, by the way," answered Tatman. The whole group literally jumped the Palestinian, ruffling his hair and generally roughing him up. Wasn't it Freud who popularized "free association"? This was surely a freely associating group. They were also pretty well adjusted and not particularly capable of intimidation.

"Alright, you crazies. Allah, save me from the heathens. Who wants to lie first on my couch? Maybe... YOU!" pointing to each of the group as he weaved through them.

"Okay, Najibul. What does the future hold for these people? Psychoanalyze them, hypnotize them. Do whatever it takes, just give us insight into the future," theatrically bellowed Sheppard.

"I see...I see...I see," with Najibul's voice rising to a fevered pitch, "I see...a long and riveting journey. A journey full of unforeseen consequences. And unanticipated challenges. And, I see, I see...we don't have refreshments. Eric. Did you not arrange for mineral water or anything? How inhospitable a host you are." Again, they all laughed.

"Hi, I'm John Stone. Have I missed much?"

"No, John. You've only missed the refreshments, as have we all," countered Chappo. "Who the hell are you? What's your specialty? Or is it a quirk, mate? Are you part of this fiasco of a team, too?" The others chuckled with embarrassment at his not recognizing the President of the United States, standing next to him in a polo shirt and wind breaker.

"Well, no. I'm..." stuttered Stone.

"Chappo," smiled an amused Sheppard. "This is my boss. This is John...excuse me. This is President John Franklin Stone. The President of the United States."

"Well, why didn't you say so, mate. Does this mean you're in charge of refreshments, because someone's made a bit of a mess on that one, eh?" objected Chappo.

"No, Mister Chapman. I'm not in charge of refreshments. But I'll bet I can find someone who is. I'm pretty much in charge of everything else," responded Stone. The President was amused by this infectious Aussie.

With that, Eric decided to begin the meeting in earnest. "If I could ask you to each grab a seat. Mr. Chapman, hors d'oeuvres and drinks are coming soon."

"Good on ya, mate. I knew I could count on him, John. I can't think or design when I'm dry. Did you bring Four-X, Eric? Ever had one of Queensland's best, John?"

"If I could have your attention," Sheppard began, sitting down as he spoke. "A funny thing happened on the way to Utah. My plane was diverted. I made stops in Australia, Argentina, Russia, South Africa, Malaysia, Mecca and a few other places I've never heard of." There were a few polite chuckles around the circle.

"Seriously, our goal was to gather together the best minds in their respective fields in an attempt to better mankind. Not just on Genesis, but on Earth, too. Because as you widen human existence, you will be living examples of the sanctity of life. You will have the unique opportunity through your work and daily living to influence your new society as well as the many cultures on Earth. You can write new rules, try new techniques, and explore new vistas.

"But I believe your most valuable lesson will be to take the philosophies, the histories, the technologies of Earth-bound humanity, and enhance the good; learn from the mistakes, amd blend together the many virtues into a new and exceptional society. An incomparable, unparalleled culture Earth peoples will envy. From your vantage, there are no Americans or Chinese.

"From a distance, our differences pale. From a distance, we are all the same species. And from a distance, maybe, just maybe, by stepping back from the brink, you will find the solutions to peaceful coexistence. Maybe you will discover the secret to emphasizing our shared similarities, not our differences. And then, just maybe, we will resolve our all-too-minor differences with words, not wars."

"Well said, Eric," complimented Xiao. "I share your optimism, but with a pinch of caution. Man has been making the same mistakes throughout our history. We can't seem to learn our lessons unless we experience them ourselves."

"So changing the basic way we perceive things is paramount," injected Mariani. "Can we defy the history of our ancestors? What must we do differently to facilitate the change?"

"What are our goals during our time here in Utah, my friends?" asked Najibul. "How will we spend our time?"

"Well. We have a tight schedule," Eric began. "We—"

"Excuse me, Eric. I appreciate what you have done. I dare say, we all do. The monumental task of assembling this team is to be congratulated. We all applaud you and your people," the psychologist complimented Sheppard. "However, I know I speak for the entire group when I tell you that we, not you, will set the agenda. Gently, my friend, I tell you this, but tell you I must," insisted Najibul.

"Mustafa's right. You can be the facilitators. But we must have control of our own destiny," continued Tatman. "You are our encyclopedia of experts. You have been planning this for months. But it is our destiny, not yours." The physician observed his colleagues and the staff.

"True enough. We must have input," offered Sturmbourg. "But this is a group effort. You and your staff have invested much into this project, as well. Although we're just meeting the experts you've assembled, I'm sure they have ideas about how this mission should progress. What do you have planned, Eric?"

"We've planned to have focus groups for each of you in your area of expertise," responded Sheppard. "An engineering task force for Chapman, an agricultural one for Mr. Nkata, and so on. Each team member would spend as much time with his or her focus group as possible."

"I, for one, would like all of the team to attend these sessions," countered Sturmbourg. "A philosophical perspective on physics or a pilot's view would be helpful."

"Yes, we all have ideas relevant to each of the areas," continued Natarajan. "My husband and I found in our seminars that approaching problems from many disciplines was not only useful but usually provided unexpected insight."

"And...each...of...the...problems...and...solutions...as...well...will...affect...us...all," echoed Nkata. "We...must...share...in...determining...our...fate."

"What are our primary needs, mates?" asked Chappo. "Food, water, and shelter. Those are our first priorities and ought to be our first conference subjects."

"You don't consider health a high priority, Mr. Chapman?" Tatman asked.

"Not really," Chappo waved off the Doctor. "If we don't have anything to eat, or a place to eat it in, we're all dead."

"If I don't watch your health needs, you won't be alive to eat, drink or be merry."

"A classic 'chicken or the egg,' eh, Doc? I'm for eatin' the chicken and scramblin' the eggs, mate!" He turned away from Tatman and hugged Mariani.

"I am interested in observing the interaction of the group," Mariani noted. "If I am to facilitate the learning process, I must study how each of you thinks. Not just what you think, but how and why."

"Your staff could present an initial briefing, then our team expert could lead a discussion culminating in conclusions concerning the issue at hand," proposed Gagarin. "I have more to learn than most. You see, I am head strong and consider things only from my perspective."

"Oh, I suspect you're being a bit too hard on yourself, Svetlana," Eric suggested. "I believe you all have traits that make you obsessed with finding the best solution to a problem. Those traits also mean no problem is unsolvable. No, Svetlana, and the rest of you, too, consider questions from your own perspective, but you listen and learn from others. And you have enough self-confidence to not have to choose your own solutions. You aren't afraid of help or cooperation from someone else. The right solution is the issue, not whose solution."

Eric noticed a slightly risen hand asking for permission to speak. He quickly acknowledged the speaker. "Well, I've heard enough to know this mission is in good hands," President Stone submitted. "I also know you won't need my help on the details of the mission, but if I can be of any assistance in any way, I would be honored. I am a member of humanity first, but alas a politician. There are other issues best left for my kind to handle. I will promise you, not as a politician, but as a member of humanity, this endeavor has my utmost backing and is of the highest priority to me."

"What problems do you anticipate, Mr. President," Najibul asked.

"There are funding matters, and if you think you have control over your destiny, let a Congressman or two in here and you'll all quit. The only reason I may visit you is to get away from them," quipped Stone.

"Who is paying for this, sir?" asked Tatman.

"Well, Doctor, you should finally be happy with your tax dollars. The United States is, currently, although we will accept donations. Seriously, this is a mission for all of mankind, but all of mankind doesn't have the resources of the U.S. It is a mission that must go forth. It is precisely because we have the resources that we are paying for it," he concluded. "In more ways than one," the President muttered under his breath, with his double meaning lost on many.

"Why go to Genesis and why now? Why not in ten years? Or fifty?" questioned Xiao. "What is our moral imperative, sir?"

"It is our duty to expand knowledge. There can be manmade limits, such as budgets, or time schedules. But to not expand knowledge when we have the opportunity is immoral," the President was standing and walking among the team. There was an intensity and a carriage of conviction none had seen in him before.

"I know of no better vehicle for that expansion than this mission. Why not wait for ten years? Because we know it is there now. When the fifteenth century Europeans had the high technology to travel to the new world, did they wait? Once we had the means to go to the moon, did we wait? No. And I predict the size of the expansion of man's knowledge from this mission will be a great economy—what we spend for what we get in return will be minuscule."

As he circulated, the President made direct eye contact with every member and placed his hands on each one's shoulders, like an anointment of sorts on behalf of all humanity. "We also have a duty to survive. We are the only species capable of understanding the problems of the future and the only one capable of correcting them.

We are also the only species capable of destroying ourselves and all other life forms on this Earth. There isn't a giraffe or rhinoceros capable of contemplating his own death or the demise of his species. That is what differentiates man from the other beasts. That is man's burden alone. This must be a mission for all mankind, for all of life on Earth. I believe we have a duty to survive. Because we are capable of thought and planning, as well as our own destruction, we must cover our bets, and what better way to guarantee that survival than by dispersing man throughout the universe?"

"Is there moral value? Are our intentions truly righteous? Or self serving?" responded Xiao.

"Can't they be both? Why can't we take the high ground as well as the pragmatic?" the President argued.

"And what if we spread destruction around the universe instead of our survival?" Mariani questioned.

"That is why we must be careful in choosing our team," Sheppard answered. "Not just that you are aware of these questions, but you are aware you must carry them forth to future generations."

"It is a heavy responsibility. One, frankly, I'm not sure I would be able to bear," the President admitted. "But one which all of you must."

"And what gives you and the rest of humanity, the right to ask that of us? Especially if, as you say, you aren't sure you could bear it?" Xiao probed. "Is that fair?"

"No, it probably isn't fair. I think I can speak for mankind when I say we are egotistical," the President answered. "We have our own best interest at heart when we ask it of you. You are basically asking, 'Why should I be moral when you can't?' Because you must, sir. If it were your choice, who would you choose? We have chosen the best of the best. You have the unique opportunity to set the rules from the outset. To write them without the burden of the past. Oh, you can look to the past for information, for guidance...but you aren't bound by it. If you won't, who will? If you can't, God help us all."

"An interesting question," observed Xiao. "Can we agree it needs additional deliberation?"

"You can discuss it," Stone concluded. "But you must each commit to living by those rules here—and when you get to your new home. The discussion should be ongoing, like a religion. You are unique among your fellow men. Make the most of it."

This first encounter between team and staff, politician and scientist, expert and amateur, highlighted the complexity of a few issues. It would require commitments from everyone in order to find solutions. All could appreciate that many a long day and night lay ahead. It would be fun, hard, intriguing, arduous, absorbing, tiresome, exhausting, invigorating, intense, exhilarating. Anything but boring. There would need to be plenty of reflective time. After intense discussions, time to digest issues was mandatory. Everyone was to consider ideas for their schedule by their next meeting. So much for worrying about it, thought Sheppard. Now he had new partners in misery. Let them do the heavy lifting for a while.

"I see my mate bringing some grog," Chappo celebrated. "I say we adjourn for tea. Any objections? Seeing none, I move John open the bar." Chappo ushered his new mate, John Franklin Stone, in the general direction of the makeshift bar.

Eric and the others drifted over to the table of snacks, with several in small groups continuing the discussions. Eric noticed team members, JMT-EL personnel, and staffers mixing. Even the President was indistinguishable from the rest, engrossed in conversation with Xiao, Natarajan, and Mariani. This was going to be alright. He turned to one of the workers setting up the table. "Al" had been written by hand over the name on his security badge with a Magic Marker.

"So, Al, what do you do here?" Sheppard inquired. "And why'd you write over your badge? Doesn't that mess up the scanners?"

"It's my little way of protesting the advance of technology. The computer knows who I am because it scans my fingerprint. But you don't know who I am. Or, you didn't until I wrote 'Al' on my name tag." He was a rugged man in his late 40s, with a weathered face from time outside. Blue eyes, brown, greying hair and a strut to his step. "Doc, I'm the best thing that ever happened to this place. Why? Because everyone turns to me when they have a problem," Al said. "My title is 'Construction Supervisor.' That's just my day job. The rest of the time, it's storyteller, marriage counselor, gourmet chef, plumber, best boy, and high priest. You got a problem, Doc. Come to Big Al. I'll fix it."

"Well, Al, my problem's a woman problem," Eric answered.

"My favorite kind," Al replied. "And also the most common, and easiest to fix. Go ahead. Give Al a shot at it."

"She's not here. That's the problem. And I miss her."

"Doc, you gotta let time run its course. If she's meant to be here, she'll be here. Maybe it's not time, yet. You seem to be preoccupied right now, anyway. Maybe it's best she's not here until you can give her your undivided attention," counseled Eric's newfound rent-a-therapist, Al. "Is she supposed to be here now, anyway?"

"I don't know, Al. I just don't know. I thought so. I may need your help on other things, Al. Can I count on you?" Eric had learned in medical school that his best source of information and problem solving didn't come from the one with the most pedigrees.

"You got it, Doc. Albert O'Connor Anton is your man. Remember that old James Taylor song from the 1980s, Doc? Well, I'll be your handyman. I fix broken hearts, and a few other things, too." he laughed.

"Al, I think this is the beginning of a beautiful friendship," paraphrased Sheppard.

"Doc. Now let me ask you a question."

"Shoot."

"So how come your team's getting up there in years? They're my age or older. At least, most of them. Think what they'll be like forty years from now. Where are the sweet young things? They're all single, too. Except for the one couple. You thought about the next generation any? When they get there they'd better start doing the bunny rabbit thing pretty quick or there'll be nobody to raise the new rabbits. What gives, Doc?"

XX

Step right up, mates. Chappo's cooked up an Aussie breakfast. Not so fast there, Eva. Let Melissa roll through first. Al, help her out, mate. And you, Nkata. I've got a nice bit of Vegemite for you."

"Vegemite?"

"Concentrated yeast extract. We Aussies spread it on everything. Or maybe you'd prefer Marmite? That's just more yeast spread. Hate the stuff, myself. And for you, C.T., I've got bangers and mash. Maybe with a side of peas? A hearty start to a long day. Al, serve the good Doctor a plate," insisted Chappo. He had enlisted his newfound friend, Al Anton to help.

"No problems, Chappo," responded an appropriately dressed Anton, also attempting his best Aussie accent. He was decked out in complete chef's regalia with tall white, billowing hat, an over the head apron, and large serving spatula. "Big Al's a jack of all trades. Construction guru, chef, bartender, and counselor to the stars. Step right up for the finest cuisine this side of Sydney."

"Najibul, I've got a little something you might like," offered Chappo.

"And what would that be, Chappo?"

"Rack of lamb. Not your normal breakfast fare, but tasty at any hour. Or, perhaps rashers and eggs? What you see before you is a king's feast prepared by Al and me for your dining pleasure. Reminds me of a morning camped outside Brisbane twenty years ago."

"Maybe a plate with a sampling of each," salivated Najibul, not a small man by any means. He clearly hadn't missed many Palestinian banquets.

"And for Parvathi and Xiao. I'll admit I was stymied a bit for culinary choices. Not much on Chinese or Indian food. But Al here managed to whip up some steamed rice with several curry dishes. There's also sweet and sour shrimp. Didn't know if you two were of the vegetarian persuasion or not?"

"No, Chappo. We eat meat, although not often. We have not completely abandoned our roots. We especially like curry," Parvathi answered. Xiao said nothing, but watched with his familiar smirk, amazed that Chapman and Anton spent so much effort on their behalf. Watched, that is, until his wife had been served, then stepped forward to enjoy the treat.

"*Zdravstvujtye*, Sveta, and good morning my lovely. I know you would prefer dehydrated space rations, but Al couldn't bring himself to find such rubbish. So we improvised. How about—"

"Chappo. I could get to like you. Maybe spend the rest of my life with you. But you will cook. And do all the cleaning, yes?"

He hugged her and nodded in agreement. "Of course, love. And for you, Dr. Sheppard? Maybe a Four-X like the good old days in Lightning Ridge?" Chappo queried.

Eric, like the rest of the team and staff wasn't quite awake at the ungodly hour of six a.m. After seeing the President off the night before and his normal nocturnal routine, these early mornings were going to kill him, he thought. The Aussie breakfast was as much a surprise to him as the rest. He'd arisen at *0-dark-thirty* to make this first full day. Risen but not awakened yet.

"Coffee, Mr. Chapman. Just coffee…for now. Black, no cream or sugar. And keep it coming." All he could think of was how early Chappo and Anton must have gotten up to create this feast. Eric hated morning. Over the next forty-five minutes everyone ate, laughed and generally continued the previous day's inaugural introduction session. Chappo had succeeded in putting all at ease. He'd provided an informality necessary for a good exchange of thoughts and ideas. With the President gone, they were now truly equals.

Eric had several items on his agenda today, an agenda not written. Even though the team wanted control, there were issues they knew nothing about. So a compromise had to be found. Sheppard thought that shouldn't be difficult. He respected their right to input. They were merely asserting their position as a team. They were the focus now, where before the focus was on choosing them. What was needed was for everyone to get on the same page. Today and the rest of the week would be dedicated to bringing the team up to speed on the preparations already undertaken, and to set the schedule of training. They could have their input, but they needed to have it from a position of knowledge.

As everyone seemed to be finishing, Eric asked for their attention. "I think we all owe Chappo a big thanks for his surprise this morning. And also to Al. For those who haven't met him yet, stand up, Al. This is Al Anton. If you've met him already, you know his strength is problem- solving. Those who don't know him…you will soon. Because you'll have a problem and you'll go to Al, and he'll find the solution. Thanks again, Al."

There was brief staccato-like applause, mostly from Chappo. Al bowed—then bowed out—leaving the rest to their morning session.

"I thought it best to start by bringing you up to speed on what we've planned so far," Eric began. "I know you want to control the agenda, so after we give you the current schedule, if there are changes to be made we can do that together. Agreed?" With that, Tom Conroy began passing out large spiral-bound books.

"Go on, Eric. Let's hear what you've got," Sturmbourg answered. "The briefing manuals Tom is handing out are just the start, right?"

"A…nightly…conclusion…session…also…would…help," Nkata wheezed.

"All in good time, people, all in good time," Eric continued. "The daily schedule calls for morning didactic sessions and afternoon skills and procedures laboratories. The didactic portion will be divided into two parts: matters concerning the trip to this new moon and issues after arrival on Genesis."

"Such as?" Eva was the first to ask the common question.

"Well, I had originally scheduled the 'after arrival' session first. Life support, exploration, resource acquisition. Initially, we had planned for each of you to be in training with experts in your field. But after yesterday, it seems a group approach is what you had in mind."

"Correct. We are all going to the same place and we will all have to deal with the same problems," Gagarin reminded everyone.

"Your general timetable seems logical," concluded Xiao. "After Chappo's breakfast, knowledge is all we are hungry for, Eric. Forgive what seems to be impatience. It is curiosity."

"History is full of examples of curiosity being perceived as impatience, or worse," murmured Parvathi. "We must all guard against our enthusiasm outrunning prudence. What is first, Eric?"

"To start this morning, I've asked Admir—uh, Jeremy Leahy—to begin your briefing on life support questions. He certainly has experience surviving multiple environments from space to the ocean floor, to Saudi and the beaches of Taiwan. Jeremy, they're all yours," Sheppard closed.

"Follow me, people," Leahy instructed with command authority. Not waiting to see who would follow, he began jogging down a long corridor. As he ran, he talked over his shoulder to his charges, "I believe I expressed my envy to a few of you yesterday. Let me make that a public expression. I would give anything to be going in your place. You will find that many here share that view. Our paramount concern is your safety both going to, and after arrival on Genesis."

After running about three minutes, they encountered a large, metal door opening into a large room. There were individual lockers against the wall with the names of each team member taped to one. As he slowed to a walk, he noticed several of the others were straggling behind at various distances. Bringing up the rear was the wheelchair bound Sturmbourg, a short distance behind Nkata, who was just behind a panting Mariani.

"Find your lockers and suit up. The technicians will help you. Sheppard, over here." As the team members found their lockers, Leahy turned to Eric. "If that's the best they can do on a short haul, how do you expect them to last in space?" Without waiting for an answer, Leahy shook his head, "You'd better hope Grimes can whip them into shape. They're not too old, just too flabby. And the one in the wheelchair, Sturmbourg, get her into that haptic suit quickly so we can see if she can cut the mustard."

"Look, Jerry. You're job is to brief them on their environment. My—"

"My job is to assess the feasibility of the team you civilians picked. If I don't think they can cut it, I'm going to report it out that way. Got it? I'll teach them about the environment, but you better start coming up with some contingency players. Some of these are pathetic."

With help from the staff, the team suited up and was ready. For what, they had no idea. Leahy walked among the group checking out each one's new space uniform, adjusting straps and calibrating gauges. "You'll be training in an actual life support module here in Utah similar to the one that will be lifting you towards Jupiter. It is a closed environmental system. The first of its kind, really. Are any of you familiar with life support systems?"

"Sure, mate," Chappo answered. "I've built and lived in a few places that supported life but I'm not sure it was living. We can talk about the essentials but let's throw in a few luxuries, too. What's your model?"

"Watch your step," Leahy ordered. He led them through another door, to an exterior portal. "This is the life support module. This will be your home for at least two years. Follow me." He turned and activated the opening, leading inside to their new home. "Luxuries you want, Mr. Chapman? Safety is the top priority, not luxury."

As the nine team members and Eric followed Leahy, the door closed with a hissing sound. All could hear, *and feel,* the pressure leaving the module. Within minutes, they were all floating randomly about the living space, crashing into walls, equipment and panels of LED readouts. After a few anxious moments, they all found their space legs, including Sturmbourg. She was adjusting not only to near weightlessness, but to having movement of her lower extremities again.

Svetlana floated into Sheppard, nudging into his back. "What do you see in that general, Eric? You know, I could get to like you," she said, her voice just above a whisper, all the while rubbing her knee against the back of his leg. She was unabashedly public about it and, with mixed emotions, it was making Eric uncomfortable.

"It must be friendly as well as safe," Leahy continued. "With redundant backup systems. And, maybe a few luxuries, as you call them. Let's get the basics out of the way first. You asked what our model is, Chapman. Well, it's Earth. Earth, for all practical purposes is a closed system. Everything is accounted for, no waste. Oh, there may be temporary garbage but not permanent."

They began exploring their new habitat. It was divided into several component modules, for sleeping, work, and another area behind another sealed door. "Let's go," motioned Leahy, as he floated over to that door. As he opened it, all could see a vast array of plants, hanging in various tanks, clinging to wires disappearing into the ceiling.

"But much of what we throw away on Earth isn't recycled," Tatman asserted. "We dispose of it by burying it in the ground, or burning it, or—"

"Or reusing it in a different form," Melissa interrupted. "From high school physics we know that matter is neither created nor destroyed. Only converted. But that conversion poses logistical problems. And energy. The ultimate source of all energy in our solar system is the Sun. Energy cannot be recycled. And energy from the Sun 500 million miles or so away is problematic. What's your solution?"

"Glad you asked," Leahy took the opening. "Because it comes back around to the concept of a closed system. What are the key components to a life support system?"

"There...must...be...food...and...water...provisions...and...waste management," Nkata answered. "And...I... would...hope...some...personal...space...for...each...to...withdraw...and...ponder...the...possibilities...of...this... endeavor. I...can...grow...vegetables...but...I...cannot...not...use...all ...the...waste. Go...on...please."

"As you predicted, the key components are food and water. There are others, as you will soon see. At the core of the system is your power source. Power is energy. Ultimately, as you said Melissa, all energy comes from the Sun. What we are proposing is loaning you some of that energy which was converted here on Earth."

"What?"

"Okay, enough coyness," Leahy responded. "You will be taking fuel from Earth to power your life support systems. It will be in the form of nuclear energy. At the core of your life support systems will be a modular, high-temperature, gas-cooled reactor, or MHTGR."

"Now that's a mouthful, mate. An MHT-what? I'm not keen on becoming a crispy critter in space."

"It's through the next set of doors, in a self-contained area for safety. It can be hermetically sealed from the rest of the module, or accessed through a double entry system. That," pointing through the window, "is a new generation MHTGR nuclear reactor. They are safe and modular, meaning they can be expanded by increments as you need more power after you've arrived and set up.

"I would anticipate this supplying all your energy needs for the first fifty to seventy-five years, maybe much longer. It's safe because it is small. It's designed primarily for after arrival, but in its low power state, it will be the energy source for the trip as well. It will provide the energy for the closed environmental life support system."

"What fuel, Admiral," Svetlana inquired. "Are we taking uranium or plutonium?"

"Both. Although 'taking' isn't entirely accurate. The module will be launched into Earth orbit first. You'll go up separately. Most of the fuel will be on board the International Space Station brought from Earth. Since launching the Deep Space One probe in 1998 without incident, I think we have proved our safety record with respect to plutonium. Both the Russians, the Europeans, and the United States have been carrying it up to the station for other purposes in small increments for several years. Svetlana, you commanded a number of those flights didn't you?"

"True. I never knew how much nuclear cargo, though," laughing as she spoke. "How much plutonium does it take to kill you?"

"Not much," Tatman answered. "Not much indeed. But it has to be inhaled or ingested. For fuel purposes it is normally compressed into solid pellets and encased in concentric shells that can't be broken even by an external nuclear explosion."

"Very good, Doctor. Suddenly, you know a lot about plutonium, too," commended Leahy.

"I don't know much. Only what I read," down played the surgeon. "So I guess I better brush up on radiation injuries, huh?"

"So this is the primary power supply. What is the backup?" asked Melissa.

"Let's step back a bit. What I've just told you about is environmental energy during the trip to Genesis and after arrival there. It isn't the mission thruster power supply. That is a separate, self-contained reactor we've been using for years with our other probes," started Leahy.

"But those have been unmanned, haven't they?" asked Mariani. "I'm no 'probe'. I'm no rocket scientist, either. I'm just not comfortable with all this nuclear talk." Mariani seemed more than uncomfortable. She was fidgeting and restless, and her vital signs were abnormal. "I'm not sure this is for me," heading back to the outer door.

"I understand," Leahy remarked. "It may not be for others as well. You are an educator. As you become more knowledgeable about it, your comfort level should improve." Turning to the rest of the group, "The fuel packs for both systems are interchangeable, making the fuel for each the backup for the other."

"Nothing else, Jeremy?" queried Sturmbourg. "Wouldn't it be easy enough to send us with enough fuel to return?"

"Yes, return," Najibul injected. "Eric, why haven't we talked more about a return? Psychologically, everyone needs to be able to go home, again."

"A return may be possible down the road," responded Sheppard. "What I think is important is that no one contemplate a return anytime soon. This mission is to colonize Genesis, make no mistake. You must be focused on that."

"Why?" Najibul persisted. "Why not a long-term exploration. Many years, but a planned return to mother Earth? You are asking much of this crew, physically, mentally, and scientifically. Should they not be rewarded in this way? Is that too much to ask?"

"I, for one, would certainly be more inclined to go with the abstract possibility of coming back sometime," offered Mariani, still squirming in her suit. "Even sailors return from the sea after their tour of duty. No matter what its length."

"And...prisoners...are...paroled," spoke Nkata. "This...should...not...be...a...life...sentence."

"Times change. I was a Soviet socialist, now I am a Russian capitalist," Svetlana smirked. "Who would have suspected that twenty years ago?"

"Jeremy, they have a point," Eric answered.

"I think this would be a good time for a rest break," answered the Admiral. "Now you get to try eating in weightlessness." He began passing out plastic bags containing an unknown gob of gook. "Find the opening and place your mouth over it. Suck the food through the opening. Notice the bag collapses and is ready for reuse."

"Okay, Eric. You get to tell the President," came Leahy's whispered reply in private. "I sure as hell wouldn't go without some fail-safe point, or some chance to change my mind. The key is making it hard enough so it's not a precipitous decision. It can't be something they decide on a lark."

"Come on, Jeremy," Sheppard grumbled. "Do these people look like they make decisions on a lark? Let's give them credit. They're here and they've committed to going. Not you, not me, and not the President."

"Some are committed to going, some aren't," challenged Leahy. "Others may be committed to the mission, but we don't want them."

"I want all of them," Sheppard rebutted adamantly. "They deserve the option of returning at their discretion. I'll tell the President," he added.

"You don't know the kind of pressure they'll be under," Jeremy countered. "Space is no place for the faint of heart."

"I don't think we've picked any wafflers," Sheppard replied.

"I've got my eye on several," Leahy retorted. "Mariani's uncommitted, Sturmbourg's got a major obstacle to overcome and several others are on the fence. You've got a bunch of individuals, Eric. Not a team. They've got to be able to depend on each other. I don't see it."

"When we reconvene, get back to the life support system," Eric answered, clearly frustrated by Leahy.

After a ten minute break Admiral Leahy continued, "So you want to come back to this heap of gas with all its problems, eh? Well, Eric and I have agreed to recommend that to the President. It not difficult from a fuel standpoint. You will have enough fuel to propel you back. Also, the MHTGR is potentially convertible to a breeder reactor."

"Really?" Sturmbourg sounded interested. "So we could theoretically generate more fissionable material than the reactor consumes?"

"Yes. In theory. Breeder reactors work that way. The theoretical part is the conversion. It would be too dangerous to send you off with a breeder reactor. The conversion of the reactor would have to be made after arrival." He looked at Gagarin, "That's one of the reasons you're taking uranium, Svetlana."

"So we should, how did you say it C.T., 'brush up' on radiation problems also," Gagarin replied.

"Back to the life support system," Leahy continued. He moved the others around the large, botanical room. "I've outlined the energy source. Now let's talk food, water, and oxygen. They are all related. Our atmosphere on Earth is primarily composed of breathable oxygen, inert nitrogen, and exhaled carbon dioxide. What keeps us from using all of the oxygen?"

"The…constant…replacement…of…oxygen…is…the…end…result…of…photosynthesis…by…our…plants," answered their resident botanist. He was examining several of the plants.

"Correct," Leahy responded. "And what do plants need to photosynthesize?"

"Carbon...dioxide...water...and...sunlight," stated Nkata.

"Again, you are correct," Leahy answered. "You have just summarized the basic concept of a closed life support system. Let's explore it more. Mr. Nkata is an expert in hydroponics, the growing of plants in a nutrient medium. No soil necessary. One usually uses a liquid brimming with plant essentials. As the plants grow, that is, as they photosynthesize, they take in carbon dioxide and give off oxygen. This is a never ending cycle. Remember, matter, plant matter, or oxygen, isn't created or destroyed. Converted, but not destroyed. The energy triggering this reaction is artificial sunlight, in your case generated by the nuclear reactor. The reactor also gives off heat, for the benefit of people and plants."

"So our atmosphere during the journey is constantly being renewed," Tatman concluded. "But what about backup oxygen generation? Surely you don't intend us to depend entirely on a bunch of plants."

"You'd better hope Mr. Nkata lives long enough to teach you how it all works," Leahy responded. "You'll have oxygen generators and a carbon dioxide scrubber. We've had those on all space flights. They're the standard. Standard, but not renewable. You had better plan on the biosystem being maintained," Leahy admonished. "So what about the rest of this closed system?"

"The...plants...grown...will...produce...our...food. But...what...about...water?" Nkata asked.

"Water also is recycled. But—" Leahy continued until he was interrupted.

"Wait a minute, mate," groused Chappo. "Are you saying we'll eat nothing but the plants we grow? How about some meat, sport. We're not all veggies."

"Yes, I'm aware you're not all vegetarians," Leahy responded. "During the voyage to Genesis, there will be supplemental meat and other luxuries, as you call them, Mr. Chapman. Again, not renewable. And weight is our primary limiting factor."

"Listen, mate. I don't call steak a luxury," Chappo offered. "I consider that, and a tall, cold one, essentials."

"How long can you go without alcohol, Mr. Chapman," asked Tatman growing irritated by the engineer. "You seem to be fixated on it."

"It's not a question of how long, mate. It's one of why go without it at all?"

"Is that a problem, Chappo?" C.T. glared.

"After arrival, you will be able to raise your own cattle, sheep, or whatever you desire," Leahy interrupted, bringing the focus back.

"How?" Tatman asked. "How are we to raise farm animals for food?"

"Because you will be taking the DNA of virtually every species on Earth in the form of zygotes," Sheppard responded.

"Zy-what, mate?"

"Zygotes. Actually, zygotes and gametes. Zygotes are the combination of two gametes. You know, Chappo. The sperm and eggs of different animals," Eric answered.

"Ah, sex. Animal sex, sport. Now I'm with you."

"So once we are settled in we will have the opportunity to raise our own domesticated animals. Now I see where you're going," realized Tatman. "So we will be taking frozen embryos along."

"Not just animals, Doctor," continued Sheppard. "Human DNA, as well." There was a pause. A pregnant, pointed pause. "You see, traveling with you will be this planet's DNA. Not all embryos. Those are the fertilized products of conception. You're also taking unfertilized gametes. We've been calling it a deep space Noah's ark."

"Is that the primary reason for inclusion of women, to carry the eggs?" charged Natarajan. "Do you really need any women then?"

"Wait a minute," Eric countered. "I think we're losing sight of the goal of this mission. It is to create a second beachhead for mankind. An attempt to correct age old problems by choosing well educated, intelligent, thoughtful people for the team. There is no gender bias. Women were chosen because women are equal members of the human race. Remember, we no longer need the female uterus for reproduction. It certainly has its advantages and pleasures, but it's no longer necessary."

"Not very romantic, sport," Chappo grimaced. "I don't know, mate. I, for one, kinda like tryin' to make 'em the old fashioned way."

"That's still an option, just not a necessity."

"Now I know why you told me about treating kids, Eric," Tatman frowned. "And why you said it wouldn't be for a few years. Hopefully, I'll have trained someone else to deal with the little ankle biters."

"And now I know why you were interested in children's education," Mariani added. "At least I'd have some time, too."

"So back to water," returned Leahy. "Mr. Nkata was concerned about the water supply. In a closed system, the second phase of the carbon cycle is what happens to the plants when consumed. In the first phase, as they grow they release oxygen and store carbon dioxide and water in the form of glucose and starches. In the second phase, those sugars are consumed. The by-product of that consumption, whether by you or another animal, is oxidation with the resultant water and carbon dioxide being released again."

"Isn't there some water loss?" Mariani questioned. "I'm new to this. Maybe I'm missing something."

"No, not really," Leahy continued. "There is minimal loss of water. You water the plants, then eat them and finally you excrete the water. Ninety percent of the water you consume is excreted. It is returned as waste or, exhaled to the atmosphere where it is reused again."

There was a loud blast, as water began spraying from at least fifty nozzles scattered throughout the module. "Sorry," Chappo apologized. "I was just trying to—"

"Trying to get us killed," Tatman editorialized.

"Turn the water pressure intake valve to the zero position. It's to your left," Leahy shouted. As Chappo followed the orders, the water gradually stopped spraying.

"I was trying to figure out where the—"

"Next time, ask someone," Leahy interrupted. In a weightless environment, water goes in all directions. It was clinging to suits, and floating throughout the cabin.

"Wait a minute. Excreted?" interrogated Najibul. "I think you are saying our excreted urine is reused."

"In a fashion," Leahy responded. "It is filtered and distilled, submitted to electrodialysis and reverse osmosis. In the end it is crystal clear and ready for reuse."

"You are asking us to drink our own waste?" Najibul scowled. "That, my friend, is as repugnant to a psychologist as anyone."

"You already do," answered Leahy. "As a river flows down stream, the northern-most city dumps its waste into the river and a southern city treats it and uses it for their water supply. What's the difference?"

"I didn't know about it," laughed Najibul. "And I'm not sure I want to know about it now." The whole team laughed with him. "I can get past this, but must you tell us all the details?"

"These so called details are the key to your survival," Sheppard broke in. "The principles aren't new. Just new to you."

"And I suppose you will be reusing our solids, also?" queried Najibul. "Don't touch anything, Chappo. We don't need solids floating around," hugging the engineer.

"Absolutely. That's the nitrogen, sulfur and phosphorus cycles. Tell us about the nutrient requirements of hydroponics, Mr. Nkata."

"In...addition...to...the...already...mentioned...nutrients...of...carbon...dioxide...water...and...sunlight... the...plants...will...need...nitrogen...sulfur...and...phosphorus. The...nitrogen...can...come...from...the... atmosphere...and...waste. Anaerobic...bacteria...can...utilize...hydrogen...sulfide...to...generate...sulfur. It...is... the...phosphorus...that...concerns...me. It...too...can...be...taken. Taken...in...small...amounts...but... absolutely...a...life...necessity."

"We actually have prepared nutrient packets that supply your plants with not only the sulfur and phosphorus you mentioned, but trace elements as well. Iodine, zinc, molybdenum, boron, manganese, copper, cadmium, cobalt, magnesium, potassium, calcium and iron, Mr. Nkata," Leahy added.

"Sounds like a helluva soup, mate. Not my cup of tea, but—"

"Perfect...for...growing...your...tea...Chappo," Nkata interrupted. "I...suppose...it...will...be...my... responsibility...to...mix...and...control...the...fertilizer?"

"You are the master of this witches' brew so necessary for the mission's survival. And also the manager of the hydroponic garden. Some of it will be algae dedicated primarily for the generation of oxygen. Other areas of your garden will be for food generation as well as atmosphere. You, along with Chappo, are the best suited for being the overall systems managers. You two will be the life support engineers. Melissa will assist you as needed."

"I'd...better...prepare...myself...for...problems...of...eutrophication."

"Eu-what, mate?"

"Eutrophication. The overgrowth of algae because of water too rich in nutrients," Leahy injected.

"Sounds like this Aussie has a bit of reading to do on systems engineering as well. Can we make beer from this concoction?"

"Alcohol, again, Mr. Chapman?" Tatman scoffed.

"Not on the trip. But who knows after arrival," Leahy shrugged.

"Speaking of after arrival, Jeremy," Sveta spoke. "Are these minerals available on the moon?"

"We have confirmed the existence of many. Iodine, zinc, manganese, cobalt, and iron are there. Others are still not confirmed yet."

"Don't need those for beer, chief. Just some hops and malt and—"

"You mentioned anaerobic bacteria," Tatman interjected, becoming more perturbed with Chappo. "Are there medical consequences to taking along bacteria? I mean, are we taking pathogens?"

"One species' pathogen is another's savior, C.T.," Eric added. "First of all, it would be impossible not to take bacteria since each of your colons are loaded with them. They are absolutely necessary for human and other animal metabolism, and that of plants as well. You can't avoid bacteria or viruses or other potential pathogens. You're correct in being concerned about taking along disease. We'll deal more deeply with these problems in the medical briefing, but it is a real concern. They may also be the solution to problems down the road."

"Some colons seem tighter than others, eh?" Chappo stared at Tatman.

"I'm still concerned about water," quizzed a worried Sturmbourg. "If the trip takes about two years, that's a long time to ask systems not to fail. Even with backups."

"You are correct," Leahy responded. "There will be more traditional methods of obtaining water. It can be chemically produced and you will be taking prepackaged water. There are two problems with just taking water with you. First, it does you no good once you arrive since it is a finite resource. Second, it is heavy. Water weighs about eight pounds per gallon. Just getting it into space requires a lot of thrust. Again, we have been stockpiling water on the space station for years."

"Two years? I'll have to keep the team healthy for two years? And what about water after we arrive?"

"Not up to it, mate?"

"Longer, Doctor. We're hoping you keep them healthy after you arrive, too," answered Sheppard. "There are ample supplies of water on Genesis and many of the other Jovian moons, including Ganymede. The trick will be accessing it. We'll get into that more later."

"What about gravity? I've read that prolonged weightlessness is a health problem with bone density deterioration and muscle atrophy," Tatman declared. "Can we take gravity in some way?"

"Yes, you will" Leahy floated over to an instrument panel and pressed a button. Immediately, the entire module slowly began to turn. As the speed increased, each member began to fall to the floor. "I've created an artificial gravity by rotating the space craft," Leahy answered.

As the others were becoming accustomed to manufactured gravity and walking about. Melissa remained a bit clumsy in her haptic suit and this altered form of gravity. "We're trying to finalize the computer model and the program to make it work," Leahy said as trying to reassure her. "Thank God for super computers. You'll also be taking along a lot of computer hardware and software. Melissa, you're the designated computer expert for repairs. We'll get into that another time, too."

"Great. I'm going into space to be a TV repairman."

"'Woman,' love," interjected Chappo. "TV repairwoman. And one of my favorites."

"You have talked about food in a general sense," began Najibul. "I'm curious whether you have given any thought to dietary taboos?"

"Taboos?" Something else Sheppard had inadvertently overlooked.

"Many societies have restrictions against eating certain kinds of foods," he continued. "Pork isn't favored by Jews. You Americans aren't interested in a good monkey brain stew. Throughout history there have been many strong religious prohibitions," Najiibul added.

Parvathi joined the conversation. "Hinduism opposes using garlic and onions, and the higher castes prescribe strict vegetarianism. Buddhists believe in preserving all forms of sentient life. Dr. Najibul knows better than I the prohibitions of Islam. But as I understand them, eating sacrificed foods or animals found dead are prohibited. Like his Jewish brethren, Muslims are also opposed to pork. Mustafa, are you aware that taboo comes from Judaism? That, and several more dietary taboos. You may have more in common with Jews than you think."

"We need to learn of each others beliefs and philosophies, and probably each person's religious beliefs to fully understand taboos," Xiao suggested. "That should be the topic for another session."

"This...may...influence...what...we...grow...on...our...voyage," Nkata concluded. "But...probably...of...more...importance...after...arrival. I...think...we...all...have...plenty...of...food...for...thought...now."

"As does your support team," Eric responded, as he signaled Leahy, who led them back to the module entrance. Leahy turned off the rotation and each person became weightless again, drifting upward, this time, with more grace.

"Grab onto something so you're upright before you go through the air lock," Leahy commanded, poised at the entrance, ready to decompress their module. "After a rest, it's back to the lab for some exercise," he chuckled.

Exercise alright. Survival training in space suits. Since none had been in the military, they were in for a surprise, basic training style. This would be the arena of General Grimes—*Attack Jack* Grimes. He'd survived where most wouldn't even want to go in the first place. This secret base had multiple training laboratories and facilities more than adequate for their needs.

There was also a rather harsh environment outside, with desert heat in the summer and arctic-like "summertime" cold and wind in the winter. Perfect conditions for Jack Grimes' purposes. Though Genesis had atmosphere and gravity similar to Earth's, space did not. And it was through this void their trip would take them. This was what worried Grimes and Leahy the most. None was physically prepared for the journey. Leahy was concerned some weren't mentally prepared either.

There would inevitably be problems necessitating repairs. Repairs that might require space walks or depressurizing parts of their vessel. Familiarity with operations in a space suit would be mandatory for all. Grimes had also decided he would need to train mission specialists, designated experts in extra-vehicular operations. They didn't know it yet, but Najibul, Xiao and Natarajan were to be those experts. With Gagarin at the controls inside, these three would become the ship's "TV repairmen," to use Melissa's term.

Because of the modular design of the spacecraft, removal of defective parts by space walk, repair inside, and replacement after the completion of restoration—the mechanic's "R and R"—was contemplated. This meant the mission also had to take some raw materials and machinery for possible fabrication along the way. Not every nut or bolt could be taken. Sturmbourg would be their primary fabricator with the help of their engineer, Chappo. The two would make repairs, or design, replicate, and replace parts as necessary. "Darning the socks," Melissa called it, becoming another Sturmbourgism.

Then there was the issue of Melissa's disability. In all likelihood, she wouldn't be venturing outside the space craft. But the environment on their new home was inhospitable during that nine month winter. Their space suits must serve them on Genesis, too. Protection from radiation, micrometeoroids, temperature and toxins were design specifications essential for their suits. Not to mention durability, simplicity and adaptability. It must be adaptable to space and Genesis, as well as to short or long activities, in either heat or cold. And relatively comfortable; they likely would be spending weeks in them. Add to that Melissa's unique problem of paraplegia. The military advisers were against her inclusion. Sheppard would have none of it. This would be where technology shined, he believed.

In the late twentieth century, personal computers had fully come into their own with hefty improvements in memory, storage capacity, and general program and computing power. But nothing in comparison to the advances of the early twenty-first century. In the 1960s, Moore's law, named for a founding partner of Intel, Gerald E. Moore, stated that, when it comes to computer hardware, about every two years the number of transistors on an integrated circuit doubles. This, in turn, cuts the price of computers at nearly the same rate. By 2005, eighteen months had become the norm, and even that seemed an eternity—by the mid-2010s, those doublings were now happening in only nine to twelve months. Coupled with improved miniaturization and robotic micro-machines, personal computer applications took on a whole new meaning.

They really were personal, worn on your person as part of your clothes. With retinal video displays, multi-function "watches" that were microcomputers, speech recognition capabilities eliminating many keyboard requirements, non-invasive medical advances, fully integrated programs, and much more, computers were now an integral part of daily life. Computerized bodysuits, so called haptic interfaces, allowed the user to combine human senses with manipulation. This meant Melissa Sturmbourg could "will" her legs to move if she were in a haptic bodysuit. Of course, this new technology was expensive. But what was being able to use your legs again worth? And this mission had nothing but first-class passengers.

Needless to say, there was excitement among the team. Other than Svetlana, none had the vaguest notion about much of the technology to which they were about to be exposed. All nine members were milling around, their ten-minute "rest period" having ended. Chappo continued his nonstop patter while they waited. Jack Grimes was uncharacteristically late—especially for a Marine Corps general. Seventeen minutes late, he entered accompanied by a somber appearing Eric Sheppard.

"I have an announcement to make," Eric began. "We have just received new information from the *Challenger II*. A small unmanned probe originally intended to go to Europa was sent to the surface of Genesis instead. It took some time to reprogram it for Genesis, but it's been there for a few days now. We have a discovery of some importance to you."

"Enough already Eric, why be so melodramatic? Can't you see we've got work here? We can get on to the pub just yet," kidded an impatient Chappo.

"Do you ever stop talking," chastised Tatman. "I'm getting tired of your constant—no, I'm getting tired of you. Is everything a joke to you? We're not here to finish quickly so we can get to the pub. Your alcoholic needs—"

"Doctor, to each his own," intervened Najibul. "Mr. Chapman, C.T., everyone. Let's try to coexist in peace. This isn't the Middle East," he laughingly concluded, trying to lighten the situation.

"Eric, you look positively pale," observed Mariani.

"Well," Sheppard began again. "The probe's just discovered life on Genesis."

XXI

Life on Maui, the second largest island in the Hawaiian archipelago, and a favorite tourist destination, moves at a slow, tropical pace. Not exactly the kind of place for a high powered meeting that could determine the fate of the world. Maybe that's what appealed to John Stone. Who could talk of making war in such a peaceful paradise?

JFS had a soft spot in his heart for Maui. It is where he and Jennifer came for their honeymoon so long ago, before he'd heard of Kazakhstan, Vice Premier Yang, or any of the realities of the day. He'd been back one or two times since, but not since her death. He hoped she would come back, too, in spirit at least. This would be the most important test of his Presidency.

It was also not the kind of place the supreme leader of the world's most populous country would be expected to meet the leader of the free world. But the Kapalua area of Maui on the northwestern tip of the island overlooking Molokai, was the destination for this very secret affair. Several weeks in advance of the meeting, the designated hotel had been cleared of its guests—supposedly to make "annual repairs." The pool needed to have the gunite repaired and plaster replaced, and the roof leaked. Or so the press release read, offering the excuses for its unexpected closure at the height of the tourist season. The President was making several high profile speeches on the West Coast during this last week of the month, with a two-day private recreational break between addresses. It was during these two days he would be slipping off to Maui, directly under the collective nose of the media.

The Chinese leader had far less fear of publicity. That was one advantage of a totalitarian system. He was more concerned about security. Last month's events off Yemen were not lost on this despot. So why was the supreme leader of China only a Vice Premier? It was a throwback to the days of "Vice Premier" Deng.

Titles mean nothing in China; power means everything. And Yang had it all. After the liberalization of the People's Republic in the late 1990s, the military confrontation of 2013 brought the rise of the military to the top leadership positions. The conflict in the Straits of Taiwan had done nothing to make China and her leaders feel more secure. They had a smugness about them that grated on most Westerners—an air of superiority, like they were listening to you, but could care less what you were saying. They had their own agenda and the West had little role in it. Yang was actually General Yang Wuu-Shyong, former commandant of the People's Army.

Short in stature, even by Chinese standards, he was ruthless. He always looked out of place because of his dress. The arms of his coats were always too long, ill fitting, hanging over his knuckles. And he had a tendency to wear plaid jackets. Not your typical Chinese apparel. The kind of plaid that never was in style, but may have come close in the 1970s. He never should have given up uniforms. Or he should visit Hong Kong for reasons other than politics to make an appointment with one of their tailors. At four-feet-eleven-inches, with thick and heavy black glasses, he was not an imposing figure. There were probably many in China who made that same miscalculation. He was cunning, and very focused.

He loved charts. During briefings he had been known to jump from his chair and begin drawing elaborate illustrations with arrows pointing to various boxes and other arrows pointing all over the board. He'd draw and draw, arrows flying from one point to another. By the time he was finished, the board looked as if an early twentieth century expressionist artist had created the masterpiece, *Many Incongruent Lines on Canvas*. If someone tried to change the subject, he simply continued on as if nothing had happened. He set the agenda, he decided the topics, and he determined the Chinese position. This was not a man to be taken lightly. Still, one was struck by his inane antics.

The Americans chose Maui, but the Chinese chose where on the island. Their choice was a resort hotel owned by a Chinese businessman from Nanjing, the capital of Kiangsu province, the same city in which Yang was born and raised. The businessman, Lue Lung-Hsiung, was reputedly his brother-in-law, although no outsider had ever been able to confirm the relationship. There is no security like familial security. John Franklin Stone remembered from his youth how stupid and silly the Vietnamese and Americans seemed when they argued for months over the size and shape of the table where they negotiated the end of that war.

He had a new appreciation for those talks after nearly round-the- clock bickering over similar nuances with the Chinese. What difference did it make? How many representatives each side was allowed, whether they could wear uniforms if they were from the military, who sat where, and so on. How trivial? Yet Stone could not extricate himself from these insignificant details. This was what had occupied nearly every waking moment since his return from Utah. Finally, it appeared he would have an opportunity to meet the Vice Premier face to face.

As the President and his party traveled west, eventually landing on Maui, all he could think about was how important this summit would be. He just wanted it over and done with. JFS dreaded these kinds of confrontations. He didn't consider himself very good at them. He was a consensus builder, not a fighter, a negotiator not a litigator. He didn't like adversarial strategies, he wanted resolution. He wasn't at all sure what the Chinese wanted. His three dueling partners for this round would again be "Rich" Richardson, Trump Williams, and B.C. Adams—his Secretary of State, National Security Adviser, and the Chairman of the Joint Chiefs, respectively. The Chinese had been vague about the subordinates accompanying Yang, but the U.S. had intelligence on their potential counterparts. They were prepared to go head-to-head; prepared, but not looking forward to it.

Air Force One, escorted by a squadron of F-18Es, took off heading toward the Pacific Northwest. This "Air Force One" was a decoy, a diversionary flight to throw any smart reporters, or others with less than honorable intentions, off the track. Risky as it was, the President and his three advisers, and only a handful of aides, took off in an unmarked T-43, the real Air Force One on this mission. Out of visual range was another gaggle of F-18Es, and circling somewhere over the Pacific Ocean, an Air Force Boeing E-3 AWACS.

He was not totally vulnerable. Commercial flights between Hawaii and the mainland had been temporarily shut down under the pretense of an air traffic control computer malfunction. The sky between California and Maui was clear. The Chinese Vice Premier had arrived first, just as Stone's party was leaving California. The American contingent left the continent at eleven p.m., due to arrive in Maui at two a.m., local time. The plan was for all to try and sleep on the flight over. No one really believed that would happen. They would be landing at the Kapalua-West Maui airport, not the main airport in Kahului. Who said all-nighters stopped after college?

World politics aside, Stone hoped to steal a few private moments on the beach in Maui. The sun renewed and refreshed. The change from the cold of Washington and the rain of northern California were welcomed. It was this small ray of hope for a brief respite that allowed JFS to see past the meeting with Yang. A respite, a reprieve, a postponement, but, alas, not a pardon. Stone had no choice but to deal with this tyrant.

As the American contingent disembarked from the T-43 in the quiet of the early morning, the humidity swept through them like a blast furnace. All quickly shed their coats but were moist with perspiration within minutes anyway. They began their short trip down the hill from the airport, first heading westbound, then north on Honoapiilani Highway towards Kapalua. Even in the dead of night Stone could see the blue tiled roofs so distinctive to this part of the island. He cracked the window to hear the surf. Although humid, the air was fresh and smelled of tropical plants.

On arriving at the Kapalua Surf Hotel, the Americans expected to be met by Yang and his associates per protocol. As their vehicles pulled up the circular drive, no one was waiting and no one came out. *No one.* No security, no diplomat, not even a bellman. Stone wanted out, but General Adams, the only person vaguely resembling security, vetoed his Commander-in-Chief for now. He stepped out of the armored car to snoop around. Maybe the President knew or maybe he didn't. Adams was packing one of his fabled 1880s Colt .45s in a holster under his jacket.

B.C. wasn't gonna let a fight go down without at least taking a shot. He was from Texas, after all. He checked out the office, then the surrounding grounds and slowly widened his circle of exploration to the outer bungalows. They were all dark save one. As he cautiously approached the light, he was met by two plain clothes types, obviously security and, more obviously, Chinese. They gestured for Adams to enter the two story building at the water's edge. Deliberately and warily, he opened the front door. This was a helluva way to make a living, he muttered.

"Where is your President?" came the awkward query from Vice Premier Yang, standing in the middle of the room, flanked by three men in olive-hued uniforms with bright red trim. "You are late. Where is your President?" he repeated.

"Since there was no one to *greet us*," B.C. snarled, "I have been looking around for *you*, sir," came the less than intimidated response from Adams.

"Quickly. You will bring him, now. Quickly," Yang snapped.

"No, sir. *I will not*," B.C. returned volley, barely containing his disdain for the lack of diplomacy let alone courtesy. "Not until I have convinced myself the surroundings are safe for my President." With that, Adams began walking around the room pretending to be inspecting the surroundings. He slowly opened a few doors. He could play the game, too. He wasn't about to be hurried by this uncouth, discourteous, ill-mannered bully. He'd had his share of dealing with bullies. From the schoolyard, to the Persian Gulf, to the Straits, he knew if he showed any fear, he'd be gobbled up like a junkyard dog on a stray tomcat. *If that ain't a fact, God's a possum*, he thought.

After satisfying himself that the room was safe and, more importantly, letting the Chinese know the score, Adams briskly walked back to the President's waiting limousine. He smartly held open the door and as John Franklin Stone emerged, Adams crisply saluted his President like he had never done before. And by God, he meant it. This was his President, his country, and his chessboard. He was ready for the game. He held his salute while the President sprinted up the walk to the ocean view bungalow. Stone was followed by Williams and Richardson, with Adams bringing up the rear. As the group approached the Chinese quarters, Adams quickly and quietly relayed the events of the last few minutes to the other three. Intelligence was the key to any victory. Again, Yang didn't come outside.

President Stone and the others entered the room to again find a combative Yang standing across from a rectangular table. "You are late!" he began. "We have been—"

"But Mr. Vice Premier, we *are* here *now*," Stone unceremoniously cut him off. "I believe we have more important issues to discuss than the prevailing trade winds which caused our delay," lowering his voice and sitting at the same time. "Would you not agree?"

"You will not dictate to us concerning Kazakhstan. It is—"

"Mr. Yang," the President almost whispered. "Do you have children?"

"I...yes," stammered Yang, quieter and less stridently. "Why do you ask? Of what importance is this to you?"

"It is of the utmost importance, sir. Because I, too, have children," Stone said, lowering his voice to barely audible, "and I would like to think that it is in your children's interests, and mine as well, that we make our world a safer place for them to live. You wouldn't put a gun to the head of your own child, would you Mr. Vice Premier?"

"In our children, we have a common interest," Yang reciprocated. "We assert the right to control the destiny of China and our borders."

"We do not deny the right of self-determination. We ask only that as we respect your right to this endeavor, you respect this right of other countries, also," Stone quietly countered.

"Never," Yang answered, beginning to raise his voice again. "We will determine what is in the best interests of the region. China, and China alone, has the strength to withstand the West. China, and China alone, will be the benevolent leader of Asia."

"Mr. Vice Premier," the President again replied in a soft voice. "Is Kazakhstan worth the life of your son? For centuries, wars have been fought over resources. Mankind has gone to war over salt in ancient times and oil more recently. And it is oil that fueled this current problem."

"There is no problem. We were asked to intervene by the Kazakh people," Yang asserted. "We are protecting the resources of a neighbor from exploitation by the Russians."

"To your own benefit, sir. I do not deny your right to trade with neighbors or purchase their commodities," Stone continued. "It is the seizure of those resources by military force that we dispute. Necessities change. Salt is a common commodity. No one would think of going to war over salt today. Oil is a finite resource that your country and many others need now. But will you in the very near future?"

"What do you mean?"

"Fuel cells, Mr. Vice Premier, fuel cells will soon make the gasoline-powered engine obsolete. You have invaded a country and brought the world to the brink of war over a commodity that will be next to worthless within the next few decades," Stone counseled.

"What do we do while the West, with its U.S.-dominated oil companies, pays little attention to our oil needs because they are more interested in this new technology? A technology you will utilize to again try and bring us under the yoke of oppression. This time we will not bear the burden. We do not need the West. We do not need your crime and decay, your human rights, or your democracy. China will control its own destiny. We will provide for the needs of our people and the people of our region."

"By going to war over an outdated product and technology?" asked Stone. "Let's work together to convert the world—not simply the West or the East, but the entire world—to this better fuel source."

"And how do you propose we 'work together'?" tested Yang. He was already standing and moved to a large whiteboard behind his chair. Stone knew of his tendency to draw. Stone rose, too, walked to the whiteboard ,and stood close to Yang. Close enough to know what spices he had eaten with his last meal. If he had wanted, Stone could have towered over the much shorter Yang. What Stone wanted was to see eye-to-eye, literally and figuratively. While Yang stood next to the board cradling the chalk in his hand, Stone pulled up a small bench next to the Vice Premier, and sat down, fixing his gaze on the Chinese leader's eyes.

"How do I propose we work together, sir? That is a logistical question for us to negotiate. I am here to implore you to let that happen. I come to you not to dictate, but as an equal asking for your help and your cooperation. This is too small a planet to let such pettiness divide us. With your friendship, no problem is unconquerable. With your collaboration, no obstacle is insurmountable. With your participation, no entanglement is hopeless."

The President paused and his face changed from intensity to one of accommodation. "Vice Premier Yang, will you join us in this noble quest?" He felt he had made his case to the best of his ability. Would Yang be receptive? Would he be interested? Would he conciliatory?

Yang held the face-to-face presence, also fixing on Stone's eyes. He too, was trying to read his counterpart, looking for a sign, a subtle nuance, a hint of insincerity. Finally, after what seemed to be countless minutes he broke the visual duel, quickly glancing away, "We will meet again in one hour. Do not be late this time." And with that, Yang quickly left with his entire entourage, adjourning to another building. He left the President of the United States and his advisers standing there in silence. Did Yang understand what the President was proposing? For that matter, did the President understand?

After the room cleared, the President addressed his contingency, "So, I thought that went fairly well. Did anyone—"

"Mr. President," General Adams interrupted, tapping at his right ear and raising his index finger to his lips signaling silence. "Wouldn't this be a nice time for a stroll on the beach? I believe the sun's coming up."

With that, the presidential party went outside to the early morning sunrise. As the sun appeared over the small mountains to their east, the dawning of a new day was more than symbolic. Stone was cautiously optimistic. "What's the problem, General? Do you think the room's bugged?"

"I don't know, sir. But the beach certainly isn't. I have some control here. And the dose of fresh air may do us all some good." As the four reached the beach, Adams continued, "Can we trust Yang? With all due respect, sir, this is the bastard who tried to shoot us down a few weeks ago over the Red Sea. Aren't we obligated by the Constitution—"

"Don't talk to me about the Constitution, General," snapped a clearly tired Stone. He took off his shoes and socks and began walking at the water's edge. Williams and Richardson followed suit, also taking off their shoes and socks, but not Adams. "I am the first officer of the Constitution, and as such I am fully aware of my responsibilities, not the least of which is to preserve the Union. I take that to mean to preserve it on a viable planet. One that some trigger-happy general hasn't destroyed, either Chinese *or* American."

"Sir, try to get your blood pressure back under control," Secretary of State Richardson interjected, while lightly kicking water onto the feet of his Commander-in-Chief. "The General's role is to be the devil's advocate. He—"

"Devil's advocate, yes, not the devil himself," Stone charged, gently kicking water back at Richardson. Then becoming more conciliatory, "I'm sorry for jumping down your throat, General. But sometimes your suspicious paranoia gets to be too much for me. I apologize. What I need is some help."

"Mr. President. The Chinese aren't going to buy into pie-in-the-sky promises," Williams suggested. The National Security Adviser always seemed to bring things back to logic. He was usually hyperactive, but always logical. "We must present them with specific proposals if we expect them to sign on. Are you serious about partnering with them on fuel cells, or was that an opening gambit?"

"It was no opening gambit. What I am suggesting is a worldwide effort to convert this planet from fossil fuels to electricity. It's happening already. It's just a matter of time. If it has begun in the United States, the rest of the world will soon follow. Look Trump, why not enlist their cooperation and help by elevating this to a global undertaking?"

"It will follow, but over decades," Williams suggested. "What are you proposing?"

"How about a global Manhattan Project?" Stone suggested.

"To develop fuel cells?" responded Williams. "The energy companies are already doing it. What could we do they aren't already doing?"

"No, Trump, I think I see where he's going," answered Richardson, splashing water on the security adviser. "By involving China—"

"And everyone else," Stone interjected, now kicking through the surf more quickly.

"By involving everyone in the project, we not only break our dependence on a polluting, finite resource, but the world shares in its development and uses," huffed Richardson, now breaking into a full jog.

"Look, Rich, I know this may sound a bit anti-capitalistic, but the oil companies have had a monopoly on energy for more than 150 years," Stone continued. "They're starting to use a two-step engine now with fuel cells, but continuing to use petroleum-based fuels to create the hydrogen. What I'm proposing is a major effort to convert away from that first step. No more methane, or even ethanol as, a source of hydrogen. Who knows what new technologies will emerge? Think of the distribution system necessary. No more obsession with oil and gasoline."

"But that's what fueled the Industrial Revolution of the nineteenth and twentieth centuries," Williams stated, picking up the pace. "This will be opposed by some industrial heavyweights, Mr. President."

"Fueled it and made the world go 'round," Stone continued. "But Trump, we're in the twenty-first century now, the age of the Information Revolution. Free flow of ideas and technology are the future. Some may oppose us in the beginning, but this *is* the future. Ours, the Chinese, and the rest of the world's. Najibul was right," the President stopped dead at the water's edge, his adviser's thankfully stopping, too.

"Remember what he said on the plane after the attack, that we need to change the game? He said the Chinese felt conflict with us was inevitable, that they believed the conflict was winnable, and how we needed to change the game. Well, this is the way to engage them, a common interest, a joint goal for the benefit of both. Something that doesn't make conflict inevitable, but undesirable instead. This way, it would be in their best interest to avoid conflict. Gentlemen, it's time to quit going to war over salt. The faster the world converts from petroleum to electricity, the more stable the world will be."

Adams, not convinced, responded, "And a bunch of oil companies will be out of business and a lot of people unemployed, and—"

"Not necessarily, General," Williams interrupted, beginning to splash water on Adams with his feet. "Someone has to build the infrastructure to utilize this new source. There will still be gas stations, they just won't be selling gas."

"And many other ancillary services, B.C.," continued Richardson, also continuing the trend of splashing water on Adams with his feet. "This will still take a few decades to fully develop. All we're doing is speeding up an inevitable process. There's a role in this thing for multinationals, countries, and governments. There will be multiple new industries, some of which we've never even heard of yet."

Adams still hadn't removed his boots, but he was wandering closer to the water line. His uniform trousers were now wet to the knees from his companion's splashes. "I hate to throw water on your scenario," unleashing a barrage of water from the barrels of his two heavy military boots. The three stood still completely drenched by the Chairman, including the President. As the four stared at each other, they suddenly burst into uncontrollable laughter. Here were four of the most powerful men in the world standing in the surf on the northwest shore of Maui, acting like kids, splashing each other with salt water. What the hell were they going to tell the Chinese?

"Go on, General," the President recovered. "It appears you have something to say with your mouth as well as your feet."

"We can't dictate what the Chinese role will be," Adams responded. "We're used to the marketplace dictating the direction a new product or technology will go. The Chinese are a planned society. Entrepreneurs are frowned upon. The state is more important than the individual. What will be China's mission in this worldwide endeavor? And what happens when disputes occur? They have a tendency to pick up their marbles and walk away from the game."

"This isn't about fuel cells...or electricity...or...marbles," Stone continued, slowly and deliberately. "Fuel cells are only the vehicle," he paused. "This, my friends, is about re-engaging the Chinese as a world player. If we can get them to go along by changing the game, maybe we can save the world from the brink. The hard question right now is, as General Adams says, how do we get them involved without appearing to dictate their role? The way I see it, we've got about thirty minutes to figure that out."

There was a brief silence between them.

"About as long as it takes a guided missile to get from China to Washington," Adams stared at his companions. With that cheery comment, the four headed for an outside table around the pool. If it takes that short a time to destroy the world, surely they could save it in the same length of time.

Halfway around the world, Anne Hayes had been given thirty minutes, too. Thirty minutes to pack and board an outbound aircraft from Diego Garcia. Her orders relieving her and reassigning her to Area 96 had finally arrived. She had reached a compromise with B.C. If he'd grant her a temporary duty assignment in Utah helping train the ultimate away team, she wouldn't resign her commission. Adams didn't want to lose her completely—he could ill afford that right now. Besides, the President might even be persuaded to authorize her third star now.

Hayes was the commanding officer at Diego Garcia, where they detected, tracked, and warned Air Force

One about the Chinese airborne attack a few short weeks ago. Everyone on the plane owed their lives to her command. Hayes was now set to jet across the Pacific towards Hickam Air Force Base on Oahu, near Pearl Harbor. *Jet* is a relative term. Her first leg from Diego Garcia to Hawaii was on a C-130. Designed in the '50s, built in the '60s, and obsolete by the '80s, it was downright painful in the 2010s; this turboprop was her only means of escape in the next ten days, so she boarded it, reluctantly.

From Hawaii, she could pick up another military transport to the west coast of the continental U.S., hopefully of a more recent vintage. And then on to Salt Lake City and southern Utah. So much for the privilege of rank. Not when you're departing an isolated base like Diego Garcia. Given this aberrant flight plan, it shouldn't take more than a week to get to Utah, she thought. Unless...she could wrangle a ride with B.C. She knew he was somewhere in the Pacific on some Top Secret junket. Maybe she could track him down.

The best communications in the world are owned and operated by the Pentagon. Flag officers' communications were given top priority. She was quickly able to get through to a secure Pentagon line via satellite uplink. Strange. *No one knew where the Chairman of the Joint Chiefs was?* No way. Of course they knew. They just weren't saying. This, however, was highly unusual, given Hayes' long-standing relationship with Adams. She had never been stonewalled like this before. She left a message with her secure videophone number in case he called in for his messages. He knew her number. So much for a First Class ticket, she thought, settling into a less than luxurious military transport seat.

It wasn't the seating that bothered her. It was the noise. Spending the better part of the next twenty-four hours with the constant drone of the four large engines all revving at 120-plus decibels wasn't her idea of a vacation. Earplugs really didn't help. The stridency of the engines gave her a pounding headache, made her perpetually nauseous, and caused her to sweat profusely. What a combination. She'd arrive in Honolulu smelly, tropically wet, and needing to throw up—one helluva an inspiration to any troops on board. It almost made her want to hide her pilot's wings. *This is what I went to the Academy for? See the world...from the back of a C-130. Yuck!*

As the lumbering giant of an airplane strained to make takeoff speed, her phone beeped. It was the military version of an American Express travel adviser. General Adams would be calling her "soon." Great. Whatever "soon" meant, she thought, lamenting only to herself, *Why didn't I wait on solid ground?* After reaching cruising altitude, Hayes heard a whooshing sound, and the cabin soon got hot. C-130s are notorious for losing their air conditioning.

Between the lack of circulation and the vibration, she would really be ripe by Honolulu. Maybe she should read...no, that made her sick, too, because of the constant vibration. Sleep...same problem. Drink...come on, it's the military. Be miserable...well, there you go. She had a plan!

"Vice Premier Yang, we have a plan," began the President. As the American team entered the room, the Chinese leader was again impatiently standing beside the whiteboard. The President looked closely for a sign of conciliation. Anything that might signal a less discordant Yang. "Conservatively, it will cost several trillion dollars to convert the United States from fossil fuels to fuel cell technology for automobiles, trucks, and locomotive transportation. That is, to develop the infrastructure to refine, distribute, and deliver the energy source. That expense will be spread over a few decades at the very least. Would you agree that the cost to your country is roughly equivalent, or more?"

"Yes, if you say so. I know little of the specifics, but our cost is higher in terms of Gross Domestic Product," snapped the Vice Premier. "We will not divert those kinds of resources."

"The way I see it," Stone continued, "the world will need a cheap source of hydrogen, a lot of pipelines to distribute it and a whole bunch of newly designed engines to utilize it, wouldn't you agree?"

"Yes, yes," an exasperated Yang answered. "We agree with the basic technological requirements. This is nothing new. You said you had a plan. What is your plan? And why should I concede leadership to the United States and the other western imperialists—capitalists?"

"You will not concede leadership or be dominated by the United States or anybody. The Chinese should be involved in this for the same reason they should be involved in any project. Only if it is in their own best interest. My goal is to show you that it is in your best interest, in our best interest, and that of the world, for this to be a shared endeavor. Shared development, implementation, and benefits. This will be a worldwide cooperative effort, like going to the moon or the International Space Station. Instead of limiting participation, everyone will be encouraged to join in the undertaking."

"Go on—what will be our role?"

"Well, together, we will develop a timetable for the worldwide completion of conversion from fossil fuels to renewable non-polluting energy," Stone continued. "All countries will assign roughly the same percentage of their GDP to the endeavor. China will be an equal contributor and equal benefactor."

"Who will control the undertaking and who will control the money?" Yang asked, a bit less strident but still not on board. "We must have veto power. China will not be dominated by capitalist governments bent on profit. We have the most people. This means we have the most potential benefit."

"I envision a new world body similar to the World Bank, or the International Monetary Fund," Stone continued. "Like the UN, we must have unanimity. Each country would have a veto. This would protect China's interests as well as other countries. It would also guarantee worldwide standards and consistency. As for who profits, the world would be the beneficiary with new industry, jobs, infrastructure. Someone has to build it. That means employment for Chinese and American workers and many others. In the United States, we are rapidly converting our private and public transportation vehicles to renewable fuel cells. The problem has been the source to generate hydrogen."

"I am aware of the problems," Yang admitted. "We have been researching the technology, also."

"Really?" responded the President. "I was unaware of Chinese interest in moving away from fossil fuels."

"The West is not the only arena for emerging technology, Mr. President," Yang answered with less invective. This was also the first time he addressed Stone as Mr. President. "Like you, we built vehicles using the technology with fossil fuels providing the hydrogen. We, too, have concluded this two-step process is only temporary. Unlike the United States though, we do not have the time or the intervening resources to wait. We are ever-increasingly more dependent on oil—oil we do not have."

"That is why a joint project is in everyone's interest," Stone answered. "This will fuel the economies of the twenty-first century in China, the United States, and the rest of the world. It also dramatically improves everyone's pollution problem. There is another factor, Mr. Vice Premier."

"What? Mr. President," Yang said while pulling his chair up next to the President's.

"I am looking into the eye of the tiger and so are you," Stone said, as Yang stared at him intently. "Mr. Vice Premier, when two tigers oppose each other, there is no victor"—pausing for effect, he contnued—"unless they choose to mate instead of fight," Stone concluded.

"To mate, one tiger must be dominant," Yang volleyed.

"Not if the two agree that to differ is not always bad," Stone replied. "To have differences strengthens the gene pool. The best of each emerges. Strength does not mean dominance. One may be physically larger, as China is, but the other has many attributes, too, as does the United States. I believe, Mr. Vice Premier, tigers mate for life, do they not?"

"Yes. They are also stealthy, nocturnal hunters," Yang countered. "They do not like the light."

"True enough, sir," Stone responded. "It will take a strong leader to step into the light. One who doesn't need to engage in sparring matches with the smaller tigers, such as Singapore or…Taiwan. A tiger with the vision to see far enough into the future to weather the storms of the first days. A visionary confident and able to let other tigers live in his jungle, without a need to lash out simply because the other has differently colored stripes," pausing once again for emphasis.

"A former military commander is a leader with the requisite credentials to partner with the West, just as was the ardent anti-communist Richard Nixon in the 1970s. Our alliance will cause others to reassess their positions. And this project will cause dislocations in many economies. We may share resources during the interim. The Middle East will realize the world is moving away from dependence on a resource they dominate. The multinational corporations will be players, but not in control. Are you willing to be the tiger who stands in the light?" Stone tossed the grenade back to the Chinese leader.

Over the next twelve hours, the four Chinese and four Americans hammered out an agreement in principle. The Chinese had labor and needed the energy to supply their factories. Factories that were old and outdated, labor intensive, not technology intensive. The U.S. would open their markets to the Chinese. Both would benefit from the renewed trade and information exchange. What was about to emerge was a new way of doing the world's business. Less constraints from artificial borders. Borders, like fences, kept ideas in as well as kept ideas from others out. The twenty-first century would have fewer borders. Fewer barriers the result of politics, culture, or trade balances. The future lay with cooperation, sharing and less confrontation. For the first time, Stone felt like the Chinese agreed. For the first time in a long time, he felt optimistic about the fate of mankind.

Twenty-four hours after landing on Maui in the dead of the night, the Americans were back at the Kapalua-West Maui airport, this time with a markedly more buoyant mood. They could hardly contain their exuberance as they boarded the small unmarked jet.

"General Adams, I have that call to General Hayes you requested," advised the pilot as the Chairman came aboard. "She's at Hickam, sir. Line one, in the back."

An effusive B.C. leaped over two seats of the 737 to land in a chair in front of a video screen. "Anne, where the hell are you? I thought you were in D.G. Now I hear you're at Hickam? Want a lift back to the mainland? We can be there in thirty minutes. We're ready to party here."

A relieved Hayes accepted B.C.'s offer without hesitation. She was wet, sticky, and hungry. A little confused by the "party" reference, but things were looking up, she thought. Thirty minutes would give her just enough time to shower. B.C. and whoever else was on board would definitely appreciate that.

Within no time she was standing on the tarmac watching the T-43 land. As the small plane taxied toward her position, she could see an exuberant Adams apparently dancing in the aisle. What was he celebrating? *And was that the Secretary of the State he was dancing with?* What's up? thought one confused Hayes.

Ascending the old style stairs, Anne was met at the door by B.C., tie down and jacket off, looking rather Pattonesque with a pearl handled Colt .45 holstered at his side, a scotch in his hand, and the devil in his eyes. "You ready to tango with me, General?" B.C. asked. "'Cuz we're gonna *get down* on this flight back to California." Was he drunk or what?

"Where have you been?" Anne cross examined her boss. "And what in God's name have you been doing?"

"Saving the world," the President of the United States responded as he walked toward her.

Anne stiffened to attention instinctively. What was the President doing in Hawaii? Maybe that explained why there were four F-18s were circling overhead. "Good evening, or is it morning, Mr. President."

"I don't know if it's morning or evening, day or night. Don't much care either, General Hayes. You've hooked up with a bunch of happy *hombres*. Did I say it right, B.C.? Happy *hombres*? Do I sound anything like a Texan? We are certainly pleased with ourselves, aren't we?" in his best Texas drawl. With that, the President wandered off in the general direction of the wet bar.

"Pardon me for asking, again," she began, "but what on Earth are you doing here in the middle of the Pacific? And what's the President doing here? Where's Air Force One? You're not here just to welcome me back state side. Or to take me to Utah. Come on, B.C., what gives?"

"Welcome to our celebration, General Hayes," Secretary Richardson shouted as he drifted by with NSA Williams, dancing toward the President and, more importantly, the bar. "This *is* Air Force One."

"No, I'm not here to pick you up…figuratively or literally, General," Adams continued, laughing as he spoke with a gleam in his eyes. "That damned Sheppard'd be all over me if I did. Aw, what the hell, you'll know about it soon enough." The Chairman sat down and quickly outlined the details of the agreement Stone had struck with Vice Premier Yang. As he became more excited over the prospects of this truly historic agreement, that excitement began to rub off onto a very tired Anne Hayes.

With the Chinese and Americans acting as two very different bookends for this undertaking, the world was about to get a whole lot safer. This would truly be an endeavor for, and by, the world. If these two disparate countries could agree to such an ambitious undertaking, bringing others on board shouldn't be too difficult. Adams reminded Hayes, they were both tigers. What had to happen next was Vice Premier Yang had to sell his country on the idea and, simultaneously, President Stone had to sell the American public and Congress. With peace as the dividend, not to mention jobs and a clean, unending fuel supply, it shouldn't be a tough sell on either side of the Pacific. Maybe humanity had a chance after all.

The flight from Hickam back to the San Francisco Bay area would take five hours. Anne Hayes had hoped to grab some shuteye, but that seemed increasingly more unlikely as "the boys" began telling stories. She might be tired, but who could turn down semi-drunken stories from the President, his NSA, the SecState, and the CJCS?

Williams and Richardson were regaling their audience with fraternity stories from their college days. They

   In the Beginning...

had both known each other since their studies at University of California at Berkeley in the 1980s.

President Stone was waxing philosophic, telling the group about his college days in New Hampshire and graduate school back in Iowa.

"Probably planned to run for something even then, what with getting your education in those two primary states, huh?" Richardson mocked. "Why didn't you just sleep with the governor or something?"

"I did, Rich," giggled the President.

"WHAT?" Williams stammered. "Who...I mean...when? Naw, you didn't—"

"Yeah, Jennifer's father was a former governor of Iowa," Stone reminisced. "I'm embarrassed to say it, but he never thought I'd amount to anything."

"Why?"

"Probably 'cause he once caught me in a rather compromising position with his daughter," Stone sheepishly admitted. "I loved that girl. And you know, old Governor Cooper, gentleman that he was, never mentioned it once. He always thought I'd just stay a professor somewhere. Be very careful, Anne. Even those whom you think are your friends, may turn on you when it comes to affairs of the heart." The President's mind was diverted to an even happier time for a minute, then he rejoined the party. "How I wish both of them were alive so I could tell 'em what we just did. He didn't think I could save myself, let alone the world. God, I hate surprises."

"Guess I shouldn't tell you about the beach then," Adams was aching to let this one out of the bag.

"What beach?" Stone seemed confused.

"The one on Maui. If those Chinese bastards made one false move there were a few dozen SEALS fifteen yards offshore."

"What good would a bunch of seals have done us?" Stone asked, confused—his usually sharp mind now dulled by the alcohol.

Adams was really laughing now. "Not seals, sir. SEALS. You know, Navy commando-types, underwater." The whole group laughed at the President's faux pas. They were all laughing hard enough to burst a seal.

"Another scotch, sir?" Anne chuckled.

"Sure," Stone sheepishly answered. "We're in First Class aren't we? The drinks are free." They were all laughing now, but there would be hell to pay in the morning. "The Governor would be turning in his grave if he knew what this Republican economist was gonna have to sell. This'll make FDR's New Deal look like no big deal." His speech was beginning to slur as Stone stared off into the blackness outside the window for a minute, his mid reaching for that other time, again. The other four knew he was thinking more about Jennifer than her father.

"So, Anne, I never got a chance to thank you for saving our butts out over the Red Sea last month," Stone smiled. "And now you're off to Utah, B.C. tells me."

"Yes, sir," Hayes acknowledged. "With your news, there won't be any need for us military types anyway."

"Don't you believe it, General," Stone cautioned. "Don't you believe it for a New York minute. We're not out of the woods yet. This is going to be a tough sell for Yang. A lot harder for him than for me. His big advantage is he's from the military and he's in charge of a political system that will allow him to dictate policy. Dictate it until, or unless, he's replaced. Sometimes I long for that kind of a system."

The intercom from the cockpit suddenly buzzed. Adams got up to answer.

"This will be the seminal event of our century," suggested Williams. "We'll help the Vice Premier sell it any way we can. He's got to have our—"

"Mr. President..." General Adams interrupted. He was standing now, his expression somber and his face uncharacteristically pale, stricken by the moment. His body language reflected his emotions; he was completely drained of the high spirit he'd had just a minute earlier. "I have just been informed by AWACS that a submarine-launched surface-to-air missile shot down the Vice Premier's plane approximately fifteen minutes ago."

Adams slumped into the chair as the aircraft's only sound was the muted noise of the engines. This was too similar to their own near miss last month over the Red Sea to be a coincidence. The parallels were not lost on the President and his advisers. They had just been with this man and his party a few short hours ago. They were making history. They were saving the world, avoiding catastrophe.

What could have happened? Now what would they do?

"There is debris scattered over a large area," Adams' voice, beginning to waver with emotion, broke the silence. His hands trembled visibly. "Mr. President...I regret...to inform you...there are...no survivors."

XXII

L ife?"

"Life."

"Explain."

"I can't."

"Eric. This affects everything."

"I'm aware of that."

"What now?"

"You all keep training."

"And then?"

"And then, what?"

"What do we do about pre-existing life on a moon we're going to colonize?"

"Look," Sheppard countered. "I just don't know."

"Well, maybe it's about time you found out, mate."

The nine team members, along with Tom Conroy, some staff, and Jack Grimes stood there, staring at Eric.

"This doesn't change the training schedule," Conroy finally spoke, restoring order to the brief pandemonium. "Put on your helmets and follow me. General, we'll be ready for takeoff in five minutes."

"You heard the major," Grimes shouted. "Let's step it up. Sheppard, you're not on this trip. We'll see you at thirteen hundred hours. That'll give you a few hours to sort some things out, right, Doctor?"

With that exhortation, Grimes opened a door to the tarmac where a C-130 with camouflage paint, props turning, dust swirling everywhere, was waiting for them. "Hustle up, people," Grimes thundered, in a booming voice heard over the roar of the propellers. "We need to be airborne without delay. Hurry up! Hooh, yeah!" he bellowed.

"Double-time, Sturmbourg. You too, Nkata. This ain't no Sunday school picnic. No telling who's got a satellite looking down." What a sight the nine presented, hustling the fifty yards in their awkward gear and up the aft ramp of an airplane ready to take off into the cold Utah sky. The plane quickly reached airspeed necessary for flight and climbed steadily until it reached thirty-five thousand feet.

"Anybody ever made a parachute jump?" Conroy asked over the headset. He didn't need an acoustic response. The terror in the eyes of all nine and the fierce head shaking gave him his answer. "Piece of cake," he shouted back.

"Why, Tom? Why are we doing this?"

"Relax, Melissa," Tom yelled. "You're each testing an escape system, not really jumping."

"What!?"

"Tom's right," Grimes jumped in. "You don't have to do anything. The whole thing's fully computerized. You only have to get comfortable with getting into the pod."

"Turning to zero-niner-zero, General," crackled the intercom. "Prepare your quail."

"Why? We can't jettison into space. I don't—"

The entire team was suddenly floating near the ceiling of the aircraft as it made a steep dive toward the ground. This caused a simulated weightlessness, brought on by the rapid descent, causing everyone to just as rapidly ascend. Ascend in virtually every direction, with no sense of control, dashing themselves into the walls, each other and the ceiling.

"Oh," Grimes added. "You need to be able to find the pod in weightlessness. You've got thirty more seconds." The nine scrambled, crashed into one another, and randomly levitated to their designated stations. As they sat down, a seat belt automatically snapped closed, and a few seconds later, they each heard a loud, hissing sound. Then each was abruptly catapulted away from their mothership. Instantly, there was quiet, like a cannonball shot toward heaven. So quiet. Then, within about a minute, their vessels began screaming back to Earth. Each had a window with a view to observe their freefall.

"This is Big Sky, do you copy?"

"Uh...Big Sky...this is...uh...Sturmbourg," a shaken Melissa answered. "I hear you...loud and clear." Melissa had been the first to be ejected. She was afraid to look out the window. When she did, she was terrified, ecstatic, frightened, and elated. "What...what do I...what do I do, now?"

"Sturmbourg, this is Big Sky. Wait for your 'chute to deploy, then a guidance computer will take control and land your pod at the designated coordinates."

"But—"

"But nothing. Enjoy the ride, Sturmbourg. Big Sky, out."

This was the same message each of the others received over the next fifteen minutes. The view was spectacular; the freefall graceful. And the landing.... As the computer engaged, each pod was thrust in varying directions and at various altitudes. As each approached the landing zone, the gyrations slowed and decreased in severity until they hit the ground, skidding across the runway they'd left less than an hour before. None was thinking about life on another planet. Their thoughts were about life on this one.

All nine made it to the ground, some more deftly than others. Mariani and Xiao had to be pushed into their pods. Najibul barely fit into his. Natarajan had no intention of getting into hers until informed the airplane would stay aloft, diving repetitively until she did, as it was her only way off the aircraft. Tatman, Chappo, Gagarin, and Nkata made the descent uneventfully. Once on the ground, all nine shared a bond. The bond of terror, exhilaration, horror, and excitement. Of course, the most resistant to going were the first to suggest they go again.

"Another time, people," Conroy coolly advised. They made their way to a small outbuilding leading to their underground hideaway. There seemed to be a certain new swagger in their stride. Even Melissa in her haptic suit. Tom had seen it before in flight training school. There's nothing more obnoxious than someone who's just made their first solo flight. And this was one hell of a flight.

"So what was that all about, Tom?" Xiao asked.

"It was a test."

"Measuring what?" Xiao was confused.

"Your courage. Your ability to handle the fear of the unknown. Your—"

"Stupidity," growled Grimes, clearly perturbed. "Do you jump off the side of a building just because someone in authority tells you to?"

"Look, sport, you didn't exactly give us much choice."

"And you think the unknown of space is any different?" Grimes shook his head.

"You're going to be confronted with multiple similar scenarios," Conroy cautioned. "The lesson is to think before you leap. Explore your options. You may have to jump just the same. Maybe not."

"Curious," Xiao smirked. "We were like sheep being led to the slaughter."

"We trusted you for guidance," Parvathi protested.

"Trust yourself and each other," Conroy counseled. "Study your environment. Think about why you give someone your trust. Learn who you can trust. If you can't trust each other, there won't be any others."

"Speaking of curious," Grimes interrupted. "Aren't you curious about this life discovered on Genesis? Let's double-time it back for your next session."

After cleaning up and a brief rest, the group reassembled in the lecture hall for their next session.

"What about it, Eric? What about life on Genesis."

"I don't know much yet, but I'll tell you what I do know," Eric began. "It is microscopic, bacterial life, not macroscopic. We really don't have direct evidence. What we have are chemical changes that occur from the presence of life forms and their metabolism."

"What...if...someone...develops...an...infection...from...the...life...forms...already...on...Genesis?" queried Nkata. We...are...taking...along...DNA...of...many...fungi...and...bacteria...that...also...may...harm...this... pre-existing...life. How...will...we...deal...with...this...problem? Do...we...not...have...an...obligation...not...to... damage...the...environment...we...find...on...our...new...home?"

"Your question can't be answered simply," Eric answered. "At least you are anticipating the problem, which may provide the solution. Your awareness of the impact you might have on the environment is certainly more enlightened than previous explorers. However, the specifics are just not predictable."

"Throughout history, more people and civilizations have been decimated by diseases to which they lacked immunity or hadn't been previously exposed than by war," Natarajan interjected. "Syphilis was a pustular, generalized rash on the entire body killing many people in the eleventh century. Its victims all died within six to twelve months until the bacteria adapted to its host, man, and the host adapted to it. This allowed not only the host to survive but the bacterium as well. Most diseases and plagues throughout history ravaged its victims because of close proximity. Certainly we will be in close proximity during the journey. Our immune systems will positively be unfamiliar with the new life forms on Genesis."

"As they will be just as unfamiliar with us," Xiao insisted. "Who is to say that we have the right to dominate or exploit it? What if it were we who were threatened by them? Do we have the right to annihilate them to preserve our species? Are we not both created in God's image? Or do they have a different god?"

"I say we should isolate our habitat from the environment until we can assure ourselves that neither is a threat to the other," Chappo answered. "That shouldn't be too difficult as long as we all observe some rules as we come and go. The life support module is already designed to have laminar flow and filtered air.

Assuming the Genesis life forms aren't too small to be filtered, our source of contamination will be from our suits. They should be washed down and irradiated in the air lock before one takes them off, then left in the outer area before we step into our little home away from home. As to the philosophical questions, Xiao, I'm just a poor Aussie engineer. You tell me who has the right to live and all that dinkum oil. What about sex, Eric?"

"What about it, Chappo?"

"You may be happy with the test tubes we bring along, but I'm betting someone pairs off, if you know what I mean?" Chappo laughed raising his eyebrows.

"He's right," Najibul supposed. "Sexuality is a normal characteristic of mankind, though we keep trying to suppress it. Besides, I don't see us sitting by the fireplace on a cold Genesis night, stirring the Petri dishes."

"This is obviously an area we won't plan," Eric insisted. "It is a long trip and things, well…things happen."

"Well…" Xiao began slowly. "Maybe they already have. Parvathi—"

"I am pregnant!" exclaimed Natarajan. "I found out yesterday. About six weeks."

"Guess I'd better brush up on obstetrics now," C.T. sighed. "The first birth in a brave new world."

"More likely on the way there," Eric corrected him. "This changes a few things. It—"

"It also helps answer the sex question," Najibul suggested. "We will all be the child's godparents. I predict it will be the first of several. As in ancient times, the community as a whole will have child-rearing responsibilities. Eva will guide us, no doubt. What about genetics?"

"What do you mean?" Eric frowned.

"Should we be tested for genetic defects," Najibul answered.

"It would be advantageous to know if someone had a gene for an inherited disease before the problem arose," Tatman agreed. "I don't propose anyone be prevented from going because of it, but wouldn't you like to know if you have a higher chance for say, colon cancer, before the problem arises?"

"No," Chappo quickly answered. "No, I wouldn't. I—"

"Well as the one who will have to deal with it, I would like to know," interrupted Tatman showing his frustration with Chapman again.

"You're the one who would deal with it, mate?" Chappo frowned. "What about the poor bloke who has it? Don't they have to 'deal with it'? Don't they have a say? It's not my colon you'll be dealing with. It's me!"

"Look Chappo, everyone's health will be my responsibility. Sure, each person has a role. A primary role, actually," Tatman answered. "Each of us will be an open book to the others by the time we leave. We'll know more about each other than our own colons. There may be unanticipated substances there or on the way that enhance the possibility of developing disease. Radiation alone makes knowing one's predisposition necessary."

"Bug off, asshole!" screamed Chapman. "Let me rephrase that: Leave mine alone!" he was now pressed against the physician, chest to chest, eyeball to eyeball. Tatman pushed back at Chapman as hard as he could. Chappo clenched his fist and cocked his arm, ready to strike.

"Enough!" Najibul quietly spoke, thrusting himself between to two, while raising an open hand.

"I don't want him telling me what I have to do," insisted Chappo. "Look, mates. I don't like the idea of knowing what's coming in the future. It takes all the mystery out. Maybe it's alright for you to know about what my future holds, but I don't want to know."

"That is an interesting question," Xiao speculated, moving closer to Chappo. He placed his arm around him and gently guided him toward Tatman. "Is it desirable to know your fate? And if you do, how does that change the way you live your life, which may then also influence your fate? Rather circular, isn't it?"

"What if one of the offspring has more than just a genetic defect?" Mariani asked, picking up on the moral questions Xiao raised. She, too, moved toward both the antagonists. "What if one has a congenital defect? Mental retardation or a life-threatening physical problem?"

"Do we believe in the sanctity of life?" Xiao asked, looking at Tatman, then at Chappo. "This may mean a choice between the rights of the group versus the rights of an individual."

"Meaning?" Tatman asked. He was staring into Chappo's eyes.

"What if survival of a mentally retarded child threatens the survival of the colony?" Xiao continued. "Is life, any life, precious, or is our first priority to survive as a group? It is a slippery slope when one starts playing God with life. Who lives and who dies. If we elect to sacrifice a 'defective' child, upon what moral authority do we have the right to make that decision? Virtually every religion of this world celebrates the inviolability of life, especially innocent life. It is easy to take the moral high ground unless one's own survival is threatened. Then, and only then, will our moral compass be tested."

There was a pause as each considered the implications just discussed. Most people don't flesh out their beliefs until confronted with choices that demand answers. Or, maybe they feel they know their own beliefs, which are usually untested. Only when specifically called upon to address their convictions do most come to grips with their true faith. Morality also asks us how we deal with those who are less fortunate, the downtrodden, or the defective. That is the true test.

Can we be compassionate, benevolent, and charitable at the time we could also be domineering, tyrannical, and totalitarian? Rights are intended to protect those who are incapable of their own protection. Our history in this regard has not been stellar. Hitler, Stalin, Selassie, Pinochet, and many others immediately come to mind. Yet, it isn't only these men who were responsible. Each of us has known, or should have known, what they were doing, many times with not only our knowledge but our acquiescence. Who bears the responsibility? Only the perpetrator or those who silently allow the perpetration? Each of us has a moral obligation to prevent a recurrence. That is what this mission was about.

Tatman and Chappo stepped back from the brink of confrontation. The incident reminded everyone of man's problem with conflict resolution. Wasn't that a key reason for going in the first place? To avoid our past mistakes by starting over. The incident also reminded everyone just how far mankind still needed to go.

"E.J. Abraham will be coordinating today's discussions," Eric broke the silence. "I know you've all had a chance to meet E.J. over the last few weeks. He's a physicist and in the military. I'd like to tell you something a little more personal about him. It's why he's leading the medical portion and not me. During the war in 2013, a tactical nuclear warhead was launched and destroyed the nuclear-powered aircraft carrier, the *USS John F. Kennedy*. There were a fair number of radiation injuries. The physicist assigned to the medical teams for that incident was E.J. Abraham. Because of his experiences then and his background as a physicist, he decided to do a little extra homework on the subject. During his spare time he received an MD degree but didn't have the time to do an internship or residency. Right E.J.?"

"Correct. The Pentagon has a way of occupying my time since they felt I was their property," Abraham smiled.

"He is the Pentagon's preeminent expert on radiation injuries," Sheppard continued. "He's been to Chernobyl, Fukushima, the Straits, and he's also been aboard the International Space Station. A bit after your time there Svetlana."

"I've spent some time talking with Dr. Tatman about his medical concerns," Abraham began. "I must tell you, I echo his concerns about testing, Mr. Chapman. It is not about predicting the future. It's about preparing for it with as much knowledge as you can obtain. You'd better be more than an open book. You'd each better memorize what's in every chapter of that book. Your lives may depend on it." He was staring a Chappo.

"What about motion sickness?" Svetlana wanted to know, but was also trying to break the tension.

"By creating atmosphere, there shouldn't be any long-term motion sickness, so-called Space Adaptation Syndrome. We will simulate the 0.89G of Genesis. So weightlessness won't be a problem unless this system fails. In that case, weightlessness, really microgravity, would exist. What do you know about microgravity?"

"We are all susceptible to the gravity of the Earth out to about one million miles," Sturmbourg responded. "Not really weightless in space, but an offsetting of two forces. The force of gravity equaled by the velocity of the craft, creating continuous freefall. If this artificial gravitational system fails, what are the medical consequences?"

"Bone density decreases with possible osteoporosis-like findings," Abraham responded. "This is correctable once you reach Genesis or restore gravity, unless someone sustains a fracture prior to that time. Also, cardiac output decreases and fluid loss is different than on Earth."

"We have the capability of handling fractures and other possible surgical scenarios on board and after arrival," Tatman added. "One loses about 0.5 to 1.0 percent total body calcium per month in microgravity. Unless we lose gravity right out the box we shouldn't have a problem. We also have structured exercise to prevent cardiac deterioration, general muscle atrophy and bone loss. What about the immune system and infections, E.J.?"

"There is some evidence that the immune system is weakened with prolonged space travel," Abraham continued. "T-cells decrease and susceptibility to infections potentially increase. Obviously, you are taking antibiotics for infections. We are hoping to send along a module for microgravity replication of new biologicals. The Russians did research in this area in the 1980s and '90s."

"But will they work?" Tatman wondered. "It's been postulated that the effects of antibiotics and other drugs given in the space environment are different than on Earth."

"Just as bacteria develop resistance here on Earth, the susceptibility of bacteria may either change or be different from the start in space. You will probably have to develop new medications or modify existing ones. The other alternative is assistance from here on Earth."

"Resupply?" Gagarin asked. "This would allow us not only communication with Earth but let us utilize the Earth's scientists to help solve unexpected problems."

"Help with problem solving, but the timing may not be as helpful as you'd like," responded Abraham. "Resupply is possible. But remember that if you encounter a problem it will take at least two years for that resupply vessel to reach you. And don't forget, that's in addition to the time it takes to determine what you need in the first place. Realistically, the first opportunity for a specific request to be fulfilled is closer to four years than two."

"C.T. mentioned radiation," Sturmbourg reminded them. "What are the medical consequences we're talking about?"

"First some background on radiation," Abraham continued. "On Earth, eighty percent of the radiation humans are exposed to is from natural sources. The other twenty percent is man-made. We can decrease the man-made exposure for you by controlling your living space on the journey. That leaves two primary areas of concern. Exposure during the trip from cosmic and solar radiation. Then, after you arrive, from the same sources, but with different exposure profiles as well as unknown sources on the new surface. The lifetime limit of acceptable radiation is between 100 and 400 rems, depending primarily on age."

"Explain rems, E.J.," Mariani asked.

"Rems stands for roentgen equivalent man," Abraham explained. "It is a measure of the biological effect of radiation on soft tissue. Depending on the quantity of exposure and how spread out over time that exposure is, a prediction of the effects of that exposure can be made. Different tissues tolerate radiation at different levels. Rapidly reproducing cells are most susceptible. The blood forming cells and the gastrointestinal tract are good examples of rapidly reproducing cells that don't do well with radiation. Exposure in the 100-200 rem range causes, among other things, bloody diarrhea and vomiting."

"Leave out the graphics, E.J.," Mariani pleaded.

"The problem of exposure has been greatly improved since the prolonged flights of both the Russians and the Americans. With the most recent improvements in shielding, we anticipate a total exposure of only 35 rems or less during the journey. This is significant radiation, but it's also spread over the two years of travel. It is cause for some concern, not so much acutely as over the long-term. We just don't know what to predict. Genetic and late somatic effects are the primary difficulties."

"I understand the genetic effects. I assume that is why we will be taking the world's genetics with us in our Petri dishes." Sturmbourg shifted uncomfortably in her wheelchair. "What exactly do you mean by 'late somatic effects'? How are the gene samples protected from radiation during the journey?"

"The biological specimens are in shielded containers and essentially unaffected by radiation during transport," Abraham answered. "They're small, so we can protect them. The first samples have already been sent to the space station. As to late somatic effects, that is a fancy way of saying you may have a higher risk of developing cancer."

"How much higher, mate?"

"I can't say exactly," Abraham was hedging. "It's dose dependent. Possibly several times higher. That is why frequent physical examinations will be mandatory."

"What happens if it's me that gets cancer?" Tatman asked. "Who takes care of me?"

"You will all be taking care of each other," Eric interjected. "This is another reason why cross-training is absolutely critical. E.J. has given you the downside of radiation. Let me try and put this in perspective. Astronauts on the International Space Station had an annual exposure level of 35 rems per year, initially. Because of their experiences that exposure level has been greatly reduced. They have exhibited no untoward effects. If you stayed on Earth you would still receive about 1 rem annually just from background radiation. There are some places on Earth where the background radiation is higher. Their cancer rates aren't higher as you would expect, but are actually lower. That's because there are other factors involved, like pollution. Factors you won't be exposed to. So there is a trade-off. Back in the 1970s, the American *Skylab* astronauts received around 17 rems to their skin in only 84 days. Their cancer rate was no different than the general population, and most of them lived to a ripe old age."

"It's not particle radiation," added Abraham. "Alpha and beta particle radiation from say a nuclear explosion stays around and gets inhaled or ingested."

"Why would anyone eat radioactive material?" Mariani asked.

"Because they don't know it's radioactive, or think they have no other choice," Eric responded. "You can't see radiation, or taste it, or feel its effects. Alpha radiation can be stopped by paper and beta radiation by plastic or thin metal. Still, you can't see it so when you open that can of peas and don't wash it off first, you're potentially ingesting those radioactive particles."

"Also remember all radiation is not ionizing radiation," Abraham continued.

"Ionizing?" Mariani questioned. "I've got some studying to do on all this radiation."

"Radiation is energy in transit," Abraham spoke slowly. "In the form of particles and electromagnetic waves, ionizing radiation is radiation with enough energy to cause an atom to become charged when the two interact. This is the type of radiation considered potentially dangerous. Gamma rays and neutrons are examples of this type of ionizing radiation. And x-rays, too. Non-ionizing radiation doesn't have enough energy to cause atoms to become ionized, or charged, when they interact. Microwave ovens, ultraviolet and visible light, radio waves— they're all examples. You're not frightened by them. Still, they all emit a form of radiation."

"So, how does all this radiation actually cause cancer?" Mariani asked. "If I'm to teach about it, I'd best understand it myself."

"Good question," Sheppard replied. "There isn't a simple answer. There are several theories, each with some degree of evidence backing it. First, radiation damages the genetic material in cells. By altering the chromosomes; when they reproduce, they do so incorrectly, causing a genetic defect leading to abnormal growth of the new cells. Think of some of those old 1950s sci-fi movies with giant ants or grasshoppers coming out of the Nevada desert. A little over the top, but not without a few grams of scientific truth behind it.

"Second, radiation impairs the immune system, allowing existing viruses to multiply which, in turn, damage cells. New viruses, which would probably not get past the body's immune system, are able to penetrate the cell wall because of the decreased resistance.

"Third, radiation activates viruses which attack normal cells causing them to grow abnormally. It's probably a combination of all of the above. In any case, it takes many years to manifest. So, C.T., your concern about being the first victim of radiation-induced cancer is a roll of the dice. But a roll at least twenty to thirty years down the line."

"And we've made great progress in understanding how to treat and prevent cancer as we unlock the workings of the normal cell," Abraham added.

"That may be," Tatman scoffed, "But I'm the one who will deal with the consequences."

"Of this and our other indiscretions, both controlled and uncontrolled," counseled Najibul. "We are all obsessive compulsive personalities. We want to control everything. C.T. wants to control our every medical problem, Chappo the environment, and so on. Flexibility and the ability to shrug off some things is equally as important. We are not going to be able to control everything."

"True enough, mate," answered Chappo. "It's the things we can control that worry me. The things we can control but do so poorly, or erroneously. Control alright. But who controls what and for how long? It's a constant struggle." He was staring at Tatman, again.

"All of history has been a struggle," Parvathi offered. "History is an argument without end. Crisis encourages greatness. We will be in constant crisis. How exciting to argue for or against a course of action. We will be masters of our destiny, for better or worse."

"Will we?" Xiao asked rhetorically. "Who will master whom? What happens, E.J., if all the technology goes away?"

"I'm not sure I understand your question," Abraham responded.

"What I think Xiao's asking is, aren't we very dependent on technology," Najibul intervened. "Modern mankind has grown overly dependent on technology. In the process we have forgotten techniques that are no longer needed. Children don't learn to tie their shoelaces because of 'hook and loop' tape. What happens if, suddenly, the old ways are needed again. We may have to relearn them, and can we do that in a timely manner? Or will we jump backward instead of forward?"

"Will we remember the lessons our fathers and mothers learned?" Mariani added. "Some of the lessons may not be positive."

"Does the loss of technology change anything?" Abraham asked. "If your mission is about rekindling mankind, what does technology have to do with that?"

"If you are dependent on it, it has a lot to do with it," Melissa countered.

"Will…one…person…try…to…dominate…the…others…because…they…think…they…know…what…is…best…for…all?" inquired Nkata. "I…have…some…experience…in…man's…inhumanity…to…his…fellow…man. The…lessons…of…our…forefathers…are…not…at…all…encouraging. We…must…keep…a…constant…vigil…to…guard…against…oppression…persecution… and…abuse. We…truly…must…be…our…brother's…keeper.

"It doesn't take much loss of all this technology before we can't provide for ourselves, let alone any future offspring," Mariani observed.

"You mean before we start fighting among ourselves?" Chappo asked. "We already do."

"But we haven't killed each other," Tatman looked at Chappo. "Not yet, anyway. Do we really want to go so far away only to encounter the same basic problems? Or should we try and solve them here before going?"

"Because our societies haven't solved them here is part of the reason we've even considered going," Xiao countered. "I've asked the questions but I'm not sure of the answers anymore than the rest of you. I want my child to inherit a better world. Isn't that the hope of any parent? I believe his chances for that are better if I can have more control, more input."

"But she must ultimately stand for herself," Parvathi argued. "We can counsel her, educate her, celebrate her triumphs, but they are her triumphs, not ours."

"But they *are* our triumphs," Najibul countered. "He, or she, will be a reflection of his parents. And of the community that gave its values to the child. Your child is not only your future, your legacy, but ours as well. We all have a stake in the success of the next generation."

"Lighten up, mates." Chappo hugged Parvathi. "Your little kangaroo will be fine, what with the likes of all of us. It's us I'm worried about. All this heavy talk of radiation, and history, and philosophy. Life is for living, chaps. It's about enjoyment. Celebrating the good life. And I say we start right now. Anyone bring any games, or playing cards? Chappo'll beat the pants off C.T. in poker."

"That'll be the day, mate," Tatman scowled.

"Or darts. Anyone bring darts?"

Eric was watching his team and couldn't help worrying. He'd hoped for them coming together. It seemed they were ripping apart. So, with an air of circus shill he barked to the team, "Have any of you ever played *Risk*?"

Risk helped Eric bridge the gap from fantasy to reality. There was plenty of both over the next few weeks. Training progressed, as did conflict and acrimony. *Risk* became a nightly ritual. It allowed each to yell and scream at the others within the context of a game, a fantasy. The venting decreased in the real world. He wasn't at all sure he could control events. That was taking its toll. This night was like most other nights of the last few weeks. Eric flopped into bed, tired but wired, adrenaline and caffeine being the only things allowing him to function. It was almost eleven p.m., the end of just another eighteen hour day, when his phone rang.

"Say, Doc…" it was the familiar voice of Al Anton on the other end, "I was thinking…" It hadn't taken Eric long to learn that when Al was "thinking," he meant scheming. "Can I come by and talk to you for a minute?"

"Sure, Al," Eric replied. "But let's not make it another one of your patented all nighters. I've got another big day tomorrow. I've got another early morning briefing."

"Yeah, I know," Al answered. And no doubt he did know. He knew that—and just about everything else that was going on, too. "I promise it'll only take a minute." Sheppard presumed that this was a typical Al minute.

In "Anton time," however, a minute was a unique phenomenon of the universe. It was expandable or contractible to the events of the moment. It bore no resemblance to anything. It wasn't matter, although matter was usually created by an encounter with an Anton minute. It required energy, though not necessarily yours. And the inevitable result was light. Light in the form of knowledge, or a change in perception, or a new way of looking at something. Al was a rare commodity. A one-of-a-kind individual Eric and most others had come to depend on. So what was on his agenda tonight? Eric knew he wouldn't have long to find out.

Within a few seconds, he had the answer. "So Doc, have you been outside? Have you seen it?" Al began. "You're going to need a local on this extreme environment trip you've got them going on."

"You know I haven't been outside. Nobody's been outside for weeks. What in the world are you talking about?"

"The weather," Anton responded. "I was out earlier today. It's twenty below zero and the winds will knock you down. If you're going to send the team out there, you need a local to go along."

"How did you…Never mind. I suppose you're *that* local?" questioned a skeptical Sheppard. "Have you ever been in a space suit? You know the whole idea is to simulate a bad environment to test how they handle the situation. What if you get into trouble?"

"I'll make a good experiment on how to manage an emergency," Al quickly answered. "The way I see it—"

"Stop! You're in. I can't take another debate tonight!" Eric caved. "Besides, maybe you *can* show them a thing or two."

"You can believe it, Doc. I'm getting worried about you," Al admitted, changing his voice to a counselor's tone. "You've been more edgy lately. I know it's about not having the general here yet. And it is 'yet,' Doc. I'm working on it."

"Whaddaya mean working on it? You got a source on what's happening outside, Al? Come on, spill it."

"Al's got a source on everything, Doc. Listen," he began, lowering his voice to conspiratorial level. "I've got a friend who's been talking to one of the security guards, who knows a guy—"

"Just get on with it, Al!" Eric was exasperated.

"Doc, every story takes time. Nothing is that simple. There are always multiple layers to things, especially in this place. Besides, what else do you have but time, huh?" Al took out a small cigar with a plastic tip and fired up a match, slowly puffing on the contraband substance.

"Yeah, yeah. Out with it. Do you really know anything? And where in the hell did you get that? Don't you know you'll set off a smoke detector or something?" Sheppard was getting impatient, not to mention increasingly tired.

"Well," Al continued, lingering as he took another draw on the cigar. "From what I hear, there's big time trouble brewing with China. My guy didn't know exactly what, but there's all sorts of troop movements and rumors flying all around. You know, in the military when we hurry even faster just to get somewhere so we can sit around doing nothing, something big's gotta be up. They're moving planes and other hardware, too. I'll bet that's where your general is. These things usually blow over pretty quick. I remember during the Gulf War—"

"So did your friend say anything about what's in the papers or on TV?"

"That's kinda interesting." Al seemed baffled while exhaling the acrid smoke directly into the ventilation system. "Not much is in the air on all this. Hell, those bastards at CNN usually know about good stuff before the President does. Nothing can happen until they get their damn cameras ready. And another thing, it doesn't take a genius to know he hasn't called you recently either."

"Who? What? What'd ya mean?"

"Look, Doc. I know your schedule. You get a call from 'the Man' every Monday night. Except you haven't the last few weeks. Now you tell me. Doesn't that mean something's up? Man…you better get some rest. We've got a big day tomorrow. You look tired, Doc."

With that, Al left Eric to ponder the significance of their discussion. He had to laugh. He was a creature of habit. Even Al knew his schedule. He put his hands behind his head and leaned back on the headboard of his bed.

"Doc, wake up." Al was shaking him hard. Eric was no longer comatose, but still in a daze. Where am I? What the hell? What's going—.

"Come on, Doc. You've done it again. You dozed off in your clothes again. You've only got ten minutes to get to the ready room. The away trip. Remember? Wake up, Doc! Come on! This is my first space walk."

"Uhhhhh…" Eric stared up at Al. He just laid there unable to move.

"No time to shower, Doc. Let's just throw you into a clean uniform." Al was wrestling Sheppard from his bunk to his feet.

"Uniform? I don't wear uniforms." Sheppard was dazed. He was beginning to come around. Uniforms... Jumpsuits...Overalls. Standard issue at Area 96. Now it was coming back. Christ! was it! *I'm in charge of a space mission and I'm late!* This morning was the team's first encounter with the elements in their space garb. And this afternoon. More medical issues. "Oh, Geez!", he muttered. Now Sheppard was up and throwing on clothes. Al was witness to a cyclone getting dressed. It wasn't his first time seeing this curiosity.

By the time Eric made it to the lab, the entire team was already assembled and starting to don their suits. They'd all become familiar with the intricacies of their artificial life support systems. All had been in the pool with the suits and in a simulated zero gravity module. They were fast studies, but both were controlled environments. There was extra staff on hand to assist in case of problems. And whether water or zero gravity, both were a regulated milieu.

Jack Grimes wanted an uncontrolled atmosphere. And he was actually hoping for some unplanned events to test their problem solving abilities. A harsh winter storm—seemingly permanently stalled over this part of Utah—would provide an opportunity to test Grimes' charges. It wasn't Genesis, but it was an uncharitable, stormy environment just the same. The nine members of the Team were eager to try out their developing skills, too. Eric, Al Anton, and Tom Conroy would suit up in the extra suits the team would take as backups. This was the contingency if any of their regular suits needed repairs. In the event of defects or damage, they would have the three extra suits. Conroy was an old hand at survival. Eric had been in the pool and zero gravity with the team. Al was definitely a rookie. But he knew the local area in a way others, even "locals," did not.

Most thought this little trek would be a typical test run. Say, a few hours then back to the hot chocolate. After all, they had a scheduled afternoon session on medical issues. That was not at all Attack Jack's plan. He wanted to test them under extremely adverse conditions. Their plans were not his plans. When they had completed dressing, Grimes sent the team through their checklists in preparation for their mission. Communications, life support, rations were all satisfactory. With that, Grimes ordered Gagarin to open the outer doors.

This portion of the lab was built to simulate how they would exit their spacecraft in the event of needing to make an space walk. There was an isolation chamber which could be pressurized or de-pressurized. It was sealed from the main living space by an inner door. From this chamber was an outer door leading to whatever particular environment they were to encounter. On the journey to Genesis that would be space. After arrival, depending on the time of year, that might be an inhospitable climate or a nice one.

As Svetlana opened the outer doors, she was driven to her knees by the raging weather of a winter blizzard in the unfriendly southern Utah highlands. It was cold and windy, and both were felt through their suits. After walking what seemed to be forever, but actually only about three-quarters of a mile, they could no longer see their adopted home.

"Gather up, people," came Conroy's familiar voice. "Today you're all in for a treat. Listen to your headsets. General Grimes has something to tell you."

"You won't be out there for a few hours. There's been a change in plans," Grimes warned. "Guess you'd all better get used to that kind of flexibility. You'll have to live out there for the next two days. That shouldn't be too hard. You've got our local expert Al here to show you around...a little wintertime sightseeing."

There was a muffled murmur of disbelief spreading through the group. "At least we know we are getting back," chuckled Najibul. "Why not. Let's make the best of our situation."

As they hiked further away from familiar surroundings Chappo spoke. "Our first priority should be limiting the effects of exposure," he grunted, sounding less jovial than his normal. "I've been stuck in the outback in the mountains for weeks. These suits are good protection but we shouldn't rely on them exclusively."

"Dehydration and heat loss are our two primary medical considerations," Tatman added. Both he and Chapman seemed to be on the same page—for the first time in weeks. "We'll be able to regulate heat loss principally with the suits but everybody remember to drink plenty of fluids."

"What about food?" Mariani was anxious. "Did we bring enough food?"

"We'll deal with that later," Svetlana snapped, reverting to business mode. "We can go for weeks without food. It is lack of water and shelter that will kill us. First, we must scout the area and make provisions for shelter."

"You may be able to go for weeks—"

"We should divide into three teams of three each," Gagarin interrupted. "Stay focused, Eva. Eric, are you part of this exercise, too? And Tom, are you and Al just along to observe or what?"

"No way," Al was vehement. "I'm in this all the way. So's Tom," Anton answered, not waiting for Conroy to give his own thumbs up or down. The only one not really excited about this field test was Sheppard. He'd always hated the outdoors in general, and winter in particular. *My ability to get out of bed is proportionate to the temperature outside,* he was fond of saying. Not today. Or tomorrow....

Apparently Jack Grimes anticipated Eric's lack of enthusiasm. As the rest were dividing into search parties, Conroy approached Eric. "General Grimes didn't think you'd be very comfortable out here, Eric. Don't worry. I'll take good care of you. This will be a picnic compared to Islamabad. It'll give you a chance to see them under field conditions."

"Yeah, and it'll give them a chance to see me wither away," answered a glum Sheppard. "Why didn't you tell me about your little surprise? You're supposed to be on my side."

"The General swore me to secrecy. Besides, flexibility and adaptability are keys to survival," Tom added. "You might have tipped them off. You're not the only one I'm concerned about. Mariani needs some toughening. You heard her food comment. Sturmbourg may be enthusiastic about her newfound mobility, but she's untested, too. What about the physical strains on Natarajan's pregnancy? Have you considered what you're going to do if somebody can't cut it, Eric? Or decides they don't want to?"

"Just get them through your survival course, Tom," Sheppard teemed with annoyance. "And don't worry about me. I've been through worse days than this. Nobody's dropping out. Not Mariani or Sturmbourg or anybody. Just get them through it, damn it. And from now on, you work for me, not Grimes."

"Yes, sir, Doctor. I think you may learn something about each of them and maybe yourself, too."

With that, Eric turned to find Al Anton. That was who he was staying close to. Eric didn't like surprises. He was getting too old for this kind of nonsense. What he wanted was a warm beach somewhere with a certain retired Air Force general by his side. Until then, he could tolerate a few days in the elements.

"Voice recording...testing...one, two, three," Natarajan spoke clearly into her communication headset. She then pushed playback and her exact words were repeated.

"Perfect," Xiao exclaimed. Voice recognition technology would make recording her observations easy. With large vocabulary, continuous speech technology perfected several years earlier, all she had to do was talk. The backpack computer she was wearing would be her chronicle of events. She wasn't recording her thoughts, she was dictating them into a computer. As an historian, she wanted to record her observations contemporaneously for later analysis and discussion. Historians should try to be objective, but objectivity is always tempered by one's own beliefs. She thought spontaneous reflections evaluated after the fact would foster objectivity.

Xiao was helping her adjust the backpack. They were both thankful they had stayed in shape with daily exercise sessions at a gym in Kuala Lumpur. Area 96's gymnasium was top notch. Both had continued their work outs. Xiao found them to be a stress reducer. Parvathi couldn't go to sleep without tiring herself at the end of the day. The payoff was being well suited for carrying backpacks. The backpacks would be lighter in the 0.89 gravity of Genesis and weightless in space. Xiao made a habit of watching others and recording questions he was thinking. These observations and reflections would be fodder for later discussions and ruminations. Things like: *Is this what you expected? What drives this exploration? Are you or some other force in control?*.

"Parvathi," Xiao whispered into his headset. "Look at Melissa and Kwasie." Sturmbourg and Nkata seemed oblivious to the wind and the snow. They were quite a sight. A short, bent man and a haptic-suited paraplegic both quite animated. Nkata kept making wide circles with his arms. Melissa was drawing in the snow with her reinvigorated legs. Xiao and Natarajan approached them, switching to their local communication channel.

"I am in control. Not another human being or a god," Sturmbourg proclaimed. "I made the decision to take the risk that caused my accident. You decided to take a stand that resulted in your imprisonment. No one, God or otherwise, forced me to take that risk."

"I took that stand because I believe in a higher morality," Nkata argued. "A higher morality dictated by my conscience. But a conscience based on principles and ethics given by my God. Life is about taking risks. My God gives you the right to make choices. Your choices aren't predetermined—you have free will to make them. And my God doesn't force you to abide by his morality. He offers you those ideals hoping you will accept his wisdom as your guiding light."

Xiao was fascinated by the discussion for several reasons. First, the voice synthesizer in their communications gear had been tuned to improve the gaps in Nkata's speech from his previous injury. Nkata was more lively than his norm, but not enough to overcome his speech impediment. Secondly, the two felt comfortable enough in their hostile environment to be discussing philosophy rather than where they could find relief from the elements or when was their next meal. Thirdly, finally someone was considering the moral, philosophical and ethical implications of the mission.

To Xiao, that meant the logistics and training were becoming mundane to the team. Now they were ready to deal with his issues. *Should they be going? What were the consequences for mankind? For life? For belief systems in God, or Allah, Buddha or Satan? And the ramifications for the universe?* To Xiao, they were ready not only to survive but to flourish. Maybe not everyone yet. In his mind the real mission had started.

"Eva, come join us," Eric called out. Mariani worried Sheppard. She seemed to be the least comfortable with this field trip. Eric echoed Grimes' concerns. Sturmbourg, Xiao, Nkata and Natarajan were off in one direction. Svetlana, Chappo and Tatman in another. Najibul was tinkering with his outfit helped by the ever present Al

Anton. Only Mariani stood alone. She was ignoring Eric's invitation to join him. "Eva," he called again as he jogged over to her. "I'm concerned about you."

"Eric, I have a problem," she began.

Here it comes, he thought. Claustrophobia, vertigo, disorientation? What was it? His mind raced through other scenarios. What were his options? Was she ill? Was she thinking of quitting? Now what? What would he—

"Eric," she said again. "I didn't realize we were staying out for so long."

"Nor did any of the rest of us Eva," Eric sympathized. "Except for Tom," glaring at Conroy through his visor.

"Yes, but that's not what bothers me," Mariani continued. "What do I do about it? I don't know if I have enough provisions."

"Grimes made ample food and water available in your backpack," Tom consoled.

"Yes, but that's not my concern," she paused. "You see...I...I brought two cats with me in my suit."

"What?" came Eric's incredulous answer. "Cats? Where did...you smuggled cats into Area 96? And managed to bring them on this away trip? What the...Do you know what I thought? I thought you were ill, or backing out of the mission. Or—"

"For God's sake, no!" she exclaimed. "I've gotten used to all this space stuff. I'm not sure I accept it yet, but I'm used to it. I just needed something warm and cuddly, so I brought two of the cats. To be honest, I don't know if there's enough food for them."

Sheppard couldn't help laughing. "Well," he began, looking at Conroy. "A key requirement of this mission is flexibility. And contingency planning. I don't think a couple of fluff balls will present an insurmountable problem. You've got to tell the others, though. I'm not breaking this to them."

"Couldn't it be our little secret?"

"Not if you want them to eat," Tom smiled.

The remainder of the two days was uneventful. The weather was horrible, the food was, well, quantity isn't quality and the ground was hard. Real luxury. They slept in a cave and even built a campfire, though they didn't need it for warmth. The environmental suits functioned perfectly after adjustments for more heat. Perfectly, except for a few minor glitches that were duly logged for repair and improved design. The campfire was for Xiao's discussions.

As a group, they began to explore questions most hadn't previously considered. If they had, it was from a new perspective. As they broke camp two days after venturing into the mountains several miles or so outside Area 96, they decided to make this a once a week trip. Just to get out of doors, a change of pace, made it worthwhile. As they stood on the last overlook staring down on the entrance buildings to Area 96, they were all invigorated. Even with the wind and snow, it gave each of them a fresh perspective. Not only of their mission, but of the Utah outback. They had gone out about seven a.m. two days prior. Although they returned two chronological days later, they had advanced months as a team.

Sheppard collapsed into his bunk, dead tired, barely able to remove his clothes.

"Doc," came Al's familiar voice over the intercom. "I left something for you on your night stand."

Eric kept reading Anne's communiqué over and over again. It arrived when she hadn't. The note was encrypted and cryptic. What the hell was going on?

Radical change of plans. Will write or call ASAP. Three stars involved. Can't say more. Much love, Anne.

XXIII

Give him a damn *Risk* card!" C.T. shouted. "You low rent piece of—"

"Hey!" returned Chappo. "Australia's my homeland and my continent now, thanks to your stupid play."

Eric was never sure if they were joking or serious. He was sure they were seriously playing. He'd introduced the team to his favorite board game and they had all become obsessed. There was a nightly game or two with alliances changing as quickly as they do in real life. That's probably why Eric liked the game. It was about real, geopolitical life. Besides, a little world domination never hurt anybody. Frustrations were relieved, steam vented, and hostilities simulated rather than acted upon. As long as it remained a game, who could argue.

"Roll the dice, Eva," Svetlana challenged. "Looks like you'll be stuck trying to defend Europe," she chided. "No one ever wins from Europe. They haven't in my lifetime and they won't in yours."

"Don't be too sure, Sveta," Mariani taunted. "Your beloved Asia has been no more easy to defend throughout history either. Your Russian ancestors made a mess of that region long before you."

"Yes, but if I do hold it, there are seven extra divisions ready to attack Ukraine and boom! No more European continent. *Do svidaniya.*"

Sheppard marveled at how bellicose they could sound and laugh at the same time. The game would take place without Sheppard tonight. Planning and training for this planetary jaunt took his every waking minute and a fair number of his sleeping ones, too. Life on a top secret military base was about control. Control of people, control of information, control of everything. Nothing came in or went out without strict security. Even this top secret base's protection was heightened recently. Their mail was restricted and communication with the outside world essentially reduced to zero. Eric knew something big was up on the outside. But what? Did this have to do with why Anne hadn't arrived? Was it mission related? Was it something completely unrelated?

It was tough staying a step in front of his team members. Mariani joked with him that a good teacher only has to stay one lesson ahead of her students. Not with this group. Eric wasn't sure whether he was one lesson ahead or one behind. There were so many issues, and there were more of them to think up questions than there was of him to answer them. The discovery of life on Genesis threw everyone off track for a while. It also created several new obstacles and posed many new questions. Some were logistical, others philosophical. All were complex. Eric fell into his bunk each night and contemplated the days events—usually a mixture of nine (or more) sentiments.

Laughter and humor, when watching Melissa Sturmbourg nearly float away the first few times she got into her haptic space suit. Joy and pleasure at seeing her experience tactile senses again with the suit. And movement of her lower extremities. How she was able to "think" her legs to move, awkwardly at first. Then, how incredibly fast one can adapt to a new motor skill. Eric smiled as he lay in his bunk, remembering her first steps. Like a junior gymnast, her right leg nearly went over her head, as she did a partial somersault onto her posterior. Tatman was so worried she'd broken her hip he almost wouldn't let her try again. Yet, in less than three sessions, she was walking like anyone else.

How glorious technology could be when harnessed for the right purposes. How frustrating it was when it malfunctioned all too frequently. What was all too frequently? Once a year, once a day? If you can't walk without it, perhaps once a lifetime? How to guard against that malfunction at a critical juncture. How to build safeguards and backup systems to allow life to go on during repairs.

Anxiety and consternation over the increasing combativeness between Tatman and Chappo. The two were like water and oil, soap and dirt, heaven and hell, and Eric wasn't sure which was which. They just didn't mix well. It wasn't so much what one said but the way it was said, or to whom. Their personalities just grated on each other. If one took a position, the other opposed it. Eric's initial inclination was to intervene, but he changed his mind. These people were going to have to find their own resolution to problems, without a mediator or outside arbitrator.

This was the beginning of the group's social organization, the politics of the mission, the politics of their new society. A change in conflict resolution was a prime reason for this colonization so he couldn't interfere with the natural course of events. Still, Eric occasionally felt like slapping one or the other up the side of the head.

He wasn't going on the mission. He could still act out his anger. But was it really anger, or merely frustration over Anne not being there? He was constantly fighting the urge to join the team, emotionally, if not physically. He couldn't really avoid the emotions. He was there every day, feeling the same pressures they did, yet in a different way. He wasn't going. And for that reason alone he had to let things play out among those who were.

Najibul and Xiao were the best mediators in the group although everyone was starting to get involved. Svetlana seemed increasingly perturbed by the two. Nkata went about his work as if nothing around him mattered. He was probably used to it from his prison days, or was he just not interested in the pettiness, Eric wondered. The two reminded Eric of his own problems initially with B.C. Adams.

Eric thought back to his first experience with B.C. He'd just been named science adviser and was being introduced to the press and the rest of the White House staff. There were several other appointees present. Beauregard Calhoun Adams, the Chairman of the Joint Chiefs of Staff, was there, but clearly bored stiff. He didn't have time for political niceties and cared even less about this new science adviser, or any of the other people also recently appointed. No, B.C. only had time for people and things he deemed important to his military or to himself. Sheppard prided himself on being able to get along with almost anybody. But his relationship with Adams was soured from the start. He couldn't get past the ego and the arrogance of this soldier. He knew about the legend of B.C. Adams. But what was the truth?

Truth was, as much as he had despised Adams in the beginning, he had slowly developed a grudging respect for the man. Adams was loyal and trustworthy—and didn't play games. You always knew where B.C. stood, which was usually in your face. He wasn't vain, and he wasn't an empire builder. Why should he be? He was in command of the best empire anyway. Once the two were forced to work together on this Genesis project, Eric came to see, and appreciate, the deeper side of this warrior.

He was sensitive, though he'd deny it. He was caring, though if you said that, he'd probably do something to show he wasn't. And he was dedicated to doing the right thing. He was actually an idealist tempered by the pragmatism of an old soldier. He wasn't afraid of falling on his sword if it was what he was ordered to do. He'd do it with a "don't threaten me" attitude. But he wouldn't do it foolishly. He was also quite altruistic. He was committed to protecting the interest of his military and was fatherly to his subordinates. That is, those who met his standards. God help the ones who didn't.

Luckily for Eric, Anne Hayes was one who did. So, Eric wondered, where did B.C. have Anne now anyway? Where, and doing what? That's what he asked himself over and over until he fell asleep each night.

There were other emotions. Apprehension and fear about the information blackout. Something big was going on. At least that's what his paranoia told him. Did it jeopardize the mission? Was the President ill? Surely he would have heard. Was he having congressional problems? Doubtful. If that were the case, a publicity campaign would be more likely than a blackout.

Was it Kazakhstan? A cease-fire had gone into effect. That was why Anne had been relieved. Or had she? After all, she wasn't there. Or did B.C. and the Pentagon just want to guarantee that there would be no distractions. No outside extraneous diversions to steal focus from the objective. Maybe it was actually calculated to acclimate the team to life without Earth news.

Or was it something else? Who could tell? Sheppard was a newsaholic. He loved to read the newspapers and watch the evening news on TV. His routine was *The Washington Post* each morning and *The New York Times* on Sundays. Since coming to Utah he hadn't seen either. He needed to know the latest sports scores, who'd been caught with whom, who topped the music charts and best seller lists, and what the rest of the world was doing, in general, while he was off planning a space mission. Then there was cable news. He kept his office television in Washington tuned to it as background. With the advent of high definition television and the wedding of that technology to the computer Internet, he was hardwired to any breaking current event. *Was* being the operative word here in Utah. He was in definite information withdrawal.

In the intervening weeks since they began playing *Risk*, training had proceeded, including several more trips to the outside. They looked forward to inclement weather. It meant they would get out of their sterile, underground habitat for awhile. Everyone's mood changed as often as the scenery. Al Anton was their nature guide. Jack Grimes and Tom Conroy taught more about outdoor survival. Xiao, Parvathi and Nkata concocted an herbal tea the group had taken a fancy to. Eric wasn't sure why they liked it. It was strong, bitter and reminded him of something his mother made him drink when he was a kid. Chappo drilled into a frozen lake and managed to catch a fish or two. He'd built a rather intricate shelter in the cave they had discovered that first trip out of the mountain. Svetlana built a crude ski mobile using an old motorcycle engine Al found. Maybe it was escapism. It was also a test of ingenuity. Eric wasn't sure their newly developing skills would have any use on a strange new moon. Their creative juices, on the other hand, most certainly would.

"Who ever heard of a Chinaman in Brazil," Najibul exclaimed. "Out, out, sweet prince. Parting is such sweet sorrow. And get out of Venezuela while you're leaving. Card, please."

"My love, I'm afraid you are not wanted in the Western United States either," Parvathi comforted Xiao. "Or in Alberta, for that matter. You are still my prisoner of love. Card, also."

"Can it be that I am left with Africa again?" Xiao was exasperated. This philosopher had a competitive streak. He tried to remain above the fray, detached, with his air of indifference. It wasn't working lately. He was as cutthroat as the rest of them. "There is no comfort in defeat. No honor either. And no fun!"

"What is the lesson learned?" Mariani asked, mimicking Xiao. "That only victory produces honor? That only domination is fun? That—"

"Enough philosophy," Xiao snarled. "It's a game. That, is the lesson."

"I was just reminding you," she laughed. "And by the way, Africa's my domain. You're out of Africa. Card, please."

Xiao was now the first player defeated in this game. As such he joined Eric in observing the entertainment from the sidelines. He was frustrated, but resigned. It wasn't his first time in this position. He'd been here in almost every other game, too. "So Eric," he asked, settling into a director's chair, with full view of the board. "As much as I love being kicked around the world in almost every game it seems, Chappo asked about real entertainment before. Have you thought about what we do for enjoyment?"

"There are logistic problems," Sheppard whispered as an aside. "Originally, I agreed with the idea of adding another team member. An artist, or musician. The extra weight of provisions and life support considerations necessary to add a tenth person are prohibitive. It is the nine of you who are going to Genesis. No others. I suspect you will all find a way to entertain each other."

Xiao was quiet. After a moment he continued. "It is the purpose of the diversion I'm concerned about. Najibul said we are all obsessive compulsive types. He's right. Will we make time for diversion?"

"It's a long trip," Eric reminded him. "After the initial excitement wears off, it will become mundane, even tedious. That's the way life is. We all train and plan, study and cram for something, then when we attain it we get bored. We need new challenges."

"You aren't saying we'll run out of challenges in this endeavor?" Mariani couldn't help overhearing their conversation. "A good educator knows how to keep the material fresh."

"Since our lives depend on it, I hope nothing becomes that routine." Najibul, too, had been listening.

"Space never becomes routine," Svetlana stated flatly. "There is something new each minute to occupy your time."

"But does it keep your interest?" Najibul asked. He had put down the dice. Only Chappo, Najibul and Natarajan were left on the board. Tatman and Nkata were off to the side in conversation. Xiao, Sheppard, Mariani, and Gagarin now engaged Najibul in the debate.

"What is it about life that keeps you interested, Mustafa?" Mariani asked. "When you have that answer, you will have the answer as to whether space will hold your interest. What is it about life that holds your interest?"

"Where's Melissa?" Chappo asked. "Maybe she'd be interested in watching me conquer the world. None of the rest of you seem to care. Only Parvathi stands against me."

"What about me?" Najibul asked.

"You aren't interested, remember?" Chappo was gloating. "Or does the game no longer hold your attention because you're doing so poorly?"

"I love a poor winner," Parvathi spoke, in an obvious Chappo put down. "History is full of them. No one recalls those who were noble in victory. Only the outrageous, the butchers and despots."

"Are you calling me a despot, Parvathi?" Chappo feigning surprise. "Or a butcher?"

"Neither, just a—"

"Eric!" Al interrupted the discussion. Whispering in Eric's ear so the others couldn't hear, "The President's on the line. He sounds hassled." Al hustled Eric to a videophone in an adjoining office.

Sheppard instinctively stood, as he usually did when talking to his boss. "Mr. President! Good to hear from you again. I—"

"I know you've been busy, Eric," the President began. "So have I. I'll be brief. I'm sure you've heard all about what's been going on here and around the world." For some reason, the video was completely scrambled.

"Actually, no I haven't. What's—"

"Anyway, enough about my problems," Stone continued. "I called to find out about your progress and to advise you about the time frame." Eric was still fiddling around with the monitor, trying to get the picture unscrambled.

"Training's going well, as expected, sir. We—"

"You need to have them ready to fly ASAP, Eric." Sheppard wanted to know why—but couldn't get a word in edgewise. And still no video.

"I'm depending on you, Sheppard. Just so you believe me, General Adams is sending Anne Hayes along at the end of the week. She's been a big help to me, Eric. You're a lucky man to have such a wonderful woman. She's one helluva a general, too. She reminds me of Jennifer. Anyway, that's a story for another time. You take care, Eric. It's crazy here in Washington. Hell, it's crazy in the world. I'll be in touch."

With that, the line was dead. Sheppard stood motionless. Why hadn't the video portion of the transmission worked? He'd wanted to see the President as well as hear him. Maybe he could have discerned something about what was going on from his face. He was no more aware of the trouble fomenting in the outside world than he had been before the phone call. He slumped into a nearby chair, resting his chin on his hands. He was staring ahead, a blank, vacuous stare. Al didn't know what the President had said, but could tell Eric was perplexed by more questions than answers.

"Anything I can help with, Doc?" Al politely asked. Eric waved randomly into the air in a combined gesture of "no'" and "go away." Al slipped out the door, closing it quietly behind him. Sheppard was left sitting in the dimly lit room contemplating the brief call from his President. The good news was Anne would be here soon. Why did the President call for such a brief message? A message whose only apparent purpose was to advise him to move up the training schedule.

But why? What did moving up their schedule have to do with the outside world? He was alone with his thoughts, or, so he thought. Sheppard was startled by a small cat jumping into his lap, one of Mariani's stowaways. This independent-minded furball snuggled into his arm, nudging its nose into the crease of his elbow. As he scratched the little feline, she softly purred. "Guess we'll know what's up when Anne gets here, little one," he muttered.

The door slowly opened, the glow from the hallway casting light into the dimly lit room. Through the doorway, Melissa wheeled herself to Eric's side. "Glad I found you in here. I see you've found another one of Eva's little darlings."

"No bother," Eric said in a voice that Melissa knew meant he was being courteous, not truthful. "I've got a few unsolved problems on my plate."

"Like why our routine's changed in the last few weeks?" Sturmbourg stared at him. "Or, why we haven't heard from anybody lately?"

"You noticed, too?" Eric wasn't sure if he should open up to her. What the hell, he thought. She had as much right to his thoughts as anybody. "I just talked to the President. He wants us to speed up the training."

"Why?"

"I don't know." Eric sighed and then took a deep breath. "I don't know what's going on. But I'll bet moving the schedule up and the information blackout are related. I guess you guys haven't been as busy training as I thought. None of you has mentioned it to me. Any ideas?"

"Everybody agrees something is happening on the outside," she acknowledged. "There are several theories, but no real consensus. It's got to be about China. Life goes on, Eric. We're all just trying to do our best with the mission at hand. That's really why I came to talk to you. I've got two issues."

"Fire away, Melissa."

"Funny you should say 'fire away'," but she wasn't laughing. "We've been talking. Should we be taking arms on this mission? What if there are unexpected creatures there that are less than hospitable? At least that's what some are thinking. Personally, I think the chances of us using them on each other are more likely."

"I haven't given it much thought. But you're right. We need group unanimity on a question like this," Eric answered. "Do you really think weapons are necessary for defensive purposes?"

"Of course not," she responded. "On the other hand, who knows what the future holds?"

"What's your other issue?"

"It's my haptic interface." There was concern in her voice. "Najibul was right about all the technology. We are very dependent on it, me in particular. When you first approached me I was dazzled by the technology. You know this suit will require constant tweaking and tuneups. Going back to not having it would be awful. But can this new colony tolerate such technological dependence? In the absence of the technology, I'm a burden on the mission."

"Hardly a burden," he reacted.

"Eric," she hesitated. "I've been approached by several people about dropping out."

"What? By whom?"

"That doesn't matter. They're right. Who am I fooling here? Tom proposed a support role here on the ground. I was thinking of going back to my SETI project."

"I don't know whose idea this is, but they haven't run it past me," fumed an angry Sheppard. "Stay for now. At least until I get some answers from General Hayes. Besides, aren't we becoming just as dependent here on Earth? Think what would happen if the electricity went out for a day. There'd be paralysis in the world marketplace. No money, or other financial transactions would move. Even if you had cash, you couldn't buy anything because the store wouldn't know the price of it without a scanner. What if you didn't have your personal computer? You couldn't begin to do your work analyzing the stars or anything else that has to do with your passion, let alone balance your checkbook. And dinner. Does anyone actually know how to cook without a microwave oven anymore?"

"Alright, enough," she laughed. "So we're already dependent. I get your message. But when the power goes out, there's someone from the power company to turn it back on. We depend on it. Maybe in a day or an hour, but eventually. If our power goes out, who will be there to turn the power back on, Eric?"

"You've got some pretty sophisticated people going. I'll bet one of them knows how to turn the power on. And if not, at least how to figure it out. Remember, Melissa. You're not alone. The whole world's going with you. We can communicate with each other. It's not like time and technology stop. And there'll be resupply...eventually.

It's not like you're developing these technologies from scratch."

The two sat there for a moment letting the conversation sink in. Both had good points. Reality probably lay somewhere between what both had said. Guns and technology. She brought up tough issues. No question was an easy one on this mission, he thought. There was another knock on the door.

"May I come in?" Eva Mariani asked. "Oh, Melissa. Did you tell him about your decision?"

"Sort of."

"Eric. I've made a similar decision," Mariani hesitated. "I do not think I should be going. I—"

"Wait a minute. Let me—"

"You said it was up to each of us to decide whether to go," she persisted. "I'm sure it is best. I don't fit in, physically or otherwise."

"Both of you, listen," Eric pleaded. "Just give me until Anne gets here. Will you hold off your final decisions?"

"It's late. We could all use the sleep."

With that, Eric bid Eva and Melissa good night and wandered off toward his room, his newfound feline friend jumping to the ground and running to a hidden sanctuary as he stood. His team, mankind's best, was falling apart.

Time is a strange curiosity of nature. Physicists insist it is finite and inflexible. None, apparently, have gone on an all-too-short vacation, or waited for something they really wanted. Time can be fleeting, or imperceptibly slow. Eric lived the next few days waiting for Anne to arrive in the realm of imperceptibility. Though distracted by the training, it wasn't enough to help him sleep well, drink less coffee, or generally be less of a pain in everyone's posterior. They were scheduled for another away mission outside Area 96 during the last two days before her arrival. Most members of the team were torn between leaving him behind, or taking him along...then leaving him behind.

As did the nine team members, Tom, Al, and Sheppard hiked to the high point overlooking their base. There, they all stood at the ledge studying the landscape. Area 96 wasn't much to see. Situated in a valley surrounded on all sides by mountains, there was a 12,000 foot runway that seemed out of place next to a few small buildings. One of the taxiways led to a steep ramp that disappeared underground. Now they knew it was swallowed by a huge subterranean hanger where top secret experimental aircraft were tested and housed.

The small structures scattered around the runway were security shacks and entry ways to the real base below the surface. It wasn't particularly deep, hardened for explosions, or fenced. The natural defenses of this isolated environment coupled with the lack of access made accidental intrusion unlikely. Within a radius of fifty miles, and in any direction, there were no public roadways, and what roads there were, were constantly patrolled by the military, in civilian clothes on the ground, and in fully armed jet fighters in the air. So what if a spy satellite looked down on it? All it would see was a 12,000 foot runway and a few shacks. By all appearances, this was an abandoned facility. In short, the powers that be had a truly isolated fortress.

It was on this unimpressive piece of real estate the twelve turned their attention from this vantage point to another about two miles away and several hundred feet higher up the mountain to the southwest. The route was familiar to all even when the weather wasn't cooperating. Since the first time coming out, they'd been out five other times before this. Today was beautiful, with crisp temperatures in the zero range, no wind, and bright sunlight.

"See you in two days," Sheppard declared to Grimes over his radio, in his voice was a detectible combination of hope, expectation, frustration, and anticipation.

After hiking about three miles, they came to the entrance of "their" cave, now mostly covered with snow and barely visible. Nature takes back what isn't used. And in such a short time..less than two weeks. The day passed quickly with exercises designed to measure their equipment and their skills. Ten hours later, the twelve were ready for discussions around the campfire, a favorite nightly ritual during these outings.

"So," Eric began after dinner and casual conversation, throwing out his question to the group as a whole, "Melissa tells me you're thinking of taking weapons?"

"Discussing, Eric, not a decision," Xiao corrected him. "We're not sure of the need or the purpose."

"The two options are basically these," Najibul continued. "Taking weapons protects us from the unknown, and not taking arms seems more attuned to the philosophic nature of the mission."

"I guess you're not planning on shooting any Jovian rabbits," Al commented, taking out another of his small cigars, rolling it between his fingers. He couldn't smoke inside a space suit, so fondling it would be his only vice. "Or slaughtering any of the cattle you'll be raising for food. I won't say it's necessary, it's not high tech or anything, but guns aren't only for defense."

"There are other ways of slaughtering cattle." Chappo countered. "We'll have knives and electrical shocks. Al makes a good point though, mates. Might make it easier."

"You're taking all this high tech stuff, but it doesn't change your basic needs." Al continued, "You may not like the idea of taking weapons, but I'll bet you'd like the idea of not eating meat even less. That's what I like about you intellectuals. You sit in your castles making policy without any firsthand knowledge of what it is you're deciding. You oppose weapons and war, fine. But it isn't the intellectuals that fight and die in wars, it's poor grunts, like me. How many of you have ever fired a gun? None of you, I'll bet. Maybe Chappo. None of you think about it when you eat a steak though. I'll bet you're all for humane treatment of animals. Well, try killing one for food with a knife and tell me that's more humane than shooting it quickly. Intellectuals. You're all alike. You may be smart, but none of you think!"

Al got up and walked away, clearly angry. He took off his helmet in the cold Utah night and lit up his cigar. He didn't care. To hell with the damn intellectuals, he thought.

The group sat silent, stunned at what Anton said. After about five minutes, Al came back, more indignant than before. "And another thing," standing without helmet, puffing on a cigar, blowing smoke into each of their protected faces. "Who's gonna build all this stuff and fix it when it breaks? You intellectuals think you've got it all figured out." He was using intellectuals like it was a four letter word. "Who's gonna kill your food and butcher your livestock? Hell, who's gonna make your beds in the morning while you're all out exploring the universe? I hate to say it guys, but you are all high maintenance. None of you could find the bathroom if I didn't hold your hand. You need someone to take care of you." He took another drag on the cigar and exhaled. "Someone like me."

Ah, now the truth was coming out. Al had his points, but what this was really about was a ploy for him to join the mission.

"Al, you've got some good ideas," Sheppard calmly spoke. "But you're not going. There are all sorts of logistical reasons. You're just not going. We all appreciate your help and assistance." He looked him straight in the eyes. "Who are you anyway?"

"You don't even want to know," Al answered with resignation. "You gotta admit, I took my best shot." He was looking up in the general direction of Jupiter. "Where exactly is Jupiter?" His arm was waving across the night sky.

"You did take your best shot, mate," Chappo put his arm around him. "I have fired a gun, sport. But I'll bet you're right about the others. So what'll it be, mates? Are we going to ignore this part of our technological development? Or are we going to take weapons?"

"Just because we take them doesn't mean we use them on each other," Natarajan stated quietly. "We are supposed to be changing our behavior. There will always be temptations. We must change our behavior in the face of that temptation, whether it is weapons or something else."

"What we are doing is outlining the purpose and rationale for taking weapons," Mariani added, sounding more like a politician than an educator. "And setting the rules for their use. What if the rules need changing? Change is inevitable, that we can be sure of."

"They're not for dispute resolution." Sturmbourg was adamant. "And they probably aren't for protection, since it's unlikely there is any life on Genesis developed to that extent. And little chance of being visited from elsewhere. So we are left with taking weapons for convenience, to maintain domination over our livestock, and for unexpected needs."

"We cannot ignore a technology already developed." Nkata too, was reasoning out loud. He was whittling on a large piece of wood, fashioning a walking stick, and his voice synthesizer made conversation much more natural. "But that doesn't mean we have to take the final product of that technology. We have the knowledge to make any number of weapons, if necessary. After all, we're taking Earth with us on computer and in our minds and experiences. Since we don't have the need for weapons in the foreseeable future why not take the technology without the end product?"

"That is a good compromise to my way of thinking," Gagarin remarked, nodding her head in strong agreement. The others also liked Nkata's solution.

"When we have livestock to slaughter or that unexpected need, .then we can decide whether to build a weapon. Tea anyone?" Nkata had been brewing his specialty Utah concoction while offering his suggestion. "It will help you sleep. Tomorrow we rise with the sun." The group gathered around to taste this botanist's brew of local herbs. Tomorrow, like all the others before and after, would be a busy day.

They all settled into their minimally padded spaces on the ground. Al had replaced his helmet. He wasn't going, but he wanted the full experience while he could. Since no one had been to Genesis previously, the exact end of the winter wasn't known, it was only an estimate. So working outside of their living space would definitely require the suits in the beginning, until summer blossomed. Their various trips into the mountains had lasted from two to five days with the team remaining in the suits the entire time. Surely, they all thought, any tasks necessary could be completed in blocks of five days.

The next morning, they were awakened by C.T. and Parvathi, both excited.

"Come quickly," Natarajan coaxed Xiao and the others. As the others traveled deeper into the cave, their way was lit by Tatman's light source attached to his arm. He had requisitioned it for exploration of this cave prior to leaving Area 96. He had gradually gone deeper into the cave on previous trips, but lacking a light source hadn't made it further than about one hundred yards. He'd told Parvathi about his exploration attempts and the two had decided to ask Al to get them lights. This time, they had gone about six hundred yards into the cavern when they came upon their discovery. There on the walls were handmade drawings, clearly from earlier natives. The sketches depicted a simpler time.

"These predate horses in the Americas," she exclaimed. "Horses were domesticated in about 4000 B.C., but didn't make it to the Americas until the Spanish brought them in the 1500s."

"The American Indians didn't always have horses?" Tatman seemed puzzled. "I thought they would have come across from Siberia with the first indigenous peoples."

"No," Parvathi continued. "The horse came with the conquering Spanish. Wherever the horse has gone, domination has followed. From its domestication in what is now Ukraine in 4000 B.C. until World War I, nothing challenged the cavalry. After they were devastated by European diseases, there weren't enough American Indians left to challenge the whites. Even though the Indians quickly became better horsemen, they, like other civilizations in the world, were initially overcome by that advanced technological wonder...the horse."

"What will be our horse?" Xiao wondered aloud. He and the rest studied the drawings. None understood the exact meaning, but each knew these drawings were the historical record of an ancient people. "Will it be the computer or the environmental suit? Or something else?"

The twelve slowly emerged from the depths of their cave, toward its more familiar opening, to prepare for the new day. As they arrived back at their campsite, the one thing none could really get used to was the hygienic part. They could eat, sleep, and survive in their suits. They could sort of brush their teeth. And they could go to the bathroom and scratch most places. What they couldn't do was bathe, shower, or shave. There was a recycling system that recirculated and cleansed the captive air of carbon dioxide and odors, and air freshener could even be added. But there was no substitute for a long, hot shower.

Today would be more of the same routine, like yesterday. Testing, training, and survival. Eric had convinced Eva not to bring a cat or two this trip so she wouldn't be distracted. The others seemed to be on automatic pilot. All systems were functioning to specifications. Sheppard was antsy for tomorrow. Anne was scheduled for arrival. That night the team again came together as a group to assess the day's events. All looked forward to the meetings. They were stimulating and, for Eric, the only time he could really have any influence anymore.

"So Eric, when do we leave? What's the timetable?" Melissa was jogging in place in her haptic suit. Since regaining function of her lower extremities she was a perpetual motion machine. She claimed she was only testing the equipment. Everyone else felt she was making up for lost time.

"Your timetable has been advanced." Eric wasn't sure he should divulge everything. Hell, he didn't know everything to divulge.

"That's great. Praise, Allah!`" Najibul shouted. "I was beginning to wonder if we would die of old age here in this Utah. But why the change?"

"Here's what I know," Sheppard hesitated. "The President called and advised me of a crisis on the outside. We all knew something was happening. He also asked us to move up training as fast as possible."

"What is the crisis, Eric? What d'ya know?" Tatman didn't like the hesitation in Eric's voice. "And how much are we moving it up? Are we ready? I'm not real keen on advancing the schedule. What's that do to safety and preparations?"

"I wish I could tell you the specifics of the crisis, but I just don't know," a perplexed Sheppard responded. "Hopefully, Anne—er, General Hayes—will have some insight into all this. Al tells me it has something to do with China. As to the schedule, tentatively you were scheduled to go to the space station in two groups in six months for advanced training. I'm not sure what they mean by moving it up. Do they mean a month, a week, two months? Who the hell knows."

"So are we going to the space station or not?" Svetlana snapped. "If you don't know, who does? This lack of knowledge is unacceptable."

"Are we in danger of not going at all, Eric?" Parvathi was confused. "Is this about money, or China or… what is this really about?"

"I just don't know. Can't you all see I'm in the dark as much as you." Sheppard was venting. "Basically, I'm spinning my wheels, your wheels, until I get some more information from General Hayes. They aren't sending her here just to make me happy. She's Grimes', Abraham's, and Leahy's boss, too."

"Just so I'm clear on this," Tatman spoke slowly. "We actually go into Earth orbit and rendezvous with the interplanetary vehicle there? Or, is this just a training mission to the space shuttle?"

"Originally, there were to be two missions to the space station for training. Then you would leave from the station and dock with the mission vehicle, which will be launched into orbit separately." Eric paused. "This is a heavy liftoff. In order to not jeopardize your safety on the most difficult part, the module is launched from Vandenberg and the crew goes up from Cape Canaveral. There are to be several dockings in order to transfer supplies and equipment, and ultimately, the nine of you. I just can't say what the change means. Now," he hesitated, "several of you have expressed your desire to drop out."

"Who?" Najibul was incredulous.

"I thought you already knew," Eric was surprised. "You seem to talk about everything else among yourselves. I guess it's not my place to say who it—"

"It's me," Melissa interrupted.

"And me, also," Eva added. The others sat quietly for several minutes.

"I'm not surprised," Eric finally added. "It's unrealistic to think all of you haven't thought about it at one time or another. Hell, it isn't fair for mankind to place this kind of weight on anyone's shoulders. It's just that I'd hoped—"

The communication channel from Area 96 crackled to life, "Sky leader, this is Big Sky. Do you copy?"

Eric switched his communication channel so the group could hear. There was nothing to hide from them. "This is Sky leader. I copy you five by five, Big Sky."

"We have arrival information on your party. This message is encrypted. Say, again, this message is encrypted. Your outgoing transmissions are not guaranteed secure. Do you copy?"

"Understand. We are not secure. Only your end."

"Touch down scheduled at 0600 hours, MST. Repeat, 0600. Big Sky, out."

"Well," Eric spoke while switching his channel back to local. "Maybe we'll get some answers tomorrow.

Until then, I can't take anymore stress."

"Will you reconsider your decision, Melissa?" Xiao asked. "And you, Eva?"

"Nothing is written in stone," Melissa looked at Eva. "I think we both will give it some more time. Eric has asked us to wait until General Hayes arrives."

"Who knows?" Mariani smiled. "Maybe she's bringing some replacements."

"How about a little entertainment?" Chappo jumped up.

"We could play pin the plutonium on the slowest," Melissa laughed as she took off running a short distance from the group.

"You're just showing off, Melissa," Svetlana teased. "We could give Xiao another chance to be dominated."

"You brought the *Risk* game?" Xiao was surprised. "I'm in. Anyone else?"

"I'll make tea," Nkata offered. "I'd like you to try a new brew I've put together. I couldn't possibly win without it." He went to get his stash, walking smartly with the new cane he'd recently completed.

"You won't win with it, or without it," Parvathi scoffed uncharacteristically. "I am due. And if not me, then Xiao. Life is full of balances. It is time for the balance to shift from the Europeans and the Americans to Asia."

"Don't forget your current ruler, darling," Chappo insisted. "Say, Nkata, this new drink of yours isn't bad." Chappo slugged down a pint or two in less than a minute through a portal in his suit. The others concurred with his assessment, slurping the tea through the internal straw. They played on through the early evening. What they didn't know now, but figured out quickly, was Nkata's new drink was a home brew he'd concocted. He'd basically gotten his fellow shipmates tipsy.

As they set up the *Risk* board Svetlana had smuggled in her backpack, Eric got up and walked over to the cave's lip and went outside. He'd had enough of world politics for the day, enough of politics, in general. What he wanted were some answers AND a general. He hoped tomorrow would bring both.

He sat alone staring out at darkness, the only light coming from the stars. When the sun went down, Area 96 was blanketed in the shadows of the surrounding mountains. The only light came from their campfire at the cave's entrance and the internal glow of their suits. He'd placed his environmental suit's air supply on circulate from the outside. The air was cool and clean and there were no nocturnal clouds. He took several deep breaths, inhaling the crisp mountain air. The stars seemed close enough to reach out and grab with his hand.

Oh, that it was that easy to touch the stars. Or to travel to them. To slip away from earthly problems and view them from a distance. How petty and insignificant they would seem. How irrelevant and pointless. They jeopardized everything. The mission, his newfound relationship, and maybe the rest of his life as well.

XXIV

Lieutenant General Anne Hayes' T-43 was descending through 12,000 feet, thirteen miles from Area 96 on final approach to runway 36R. This was a landing she had looked forward to for four weeks. Or was it six? Too long, but then, who can remember. A lot had happened in those few short weeks. No doubt, she would have some explaining to do.

The President had authorized full disclosure to the team on her arrival. She had mixed feelings about her arrival. She missed Eric, but for the last few weeks she had been preoccupied with her military assignment. Her new command, and it was a command, was to take control of Area 96 in its entirety, including the isolated personnel responsible for training Eric's team, the Genesis mission. Everything was being transferred to U.S. Air Force Space Command, under its new commandant, Lieutenant General Anne Jeanette Hayes.

With her third star came new stories, added responsibilities and more stress. She had been doing some serious soul searching about her two relationships, the one with Sheppard and the one with the Air Force. As much as she wanted to commit to him, it was her career that pulled at her. She still had a strong sense of duty and wasn't ready to walk away from her country, her career, her President, or B.C. She was all business, very serious business, deadly serious business.

"On two-mile final, General. We'll be on the ground in one minute," squawked the pilot over the intercom. Anne's stomach was in knots. She was dressed in pilot's flight gear, dark blue-green, with a top coat, winter-weather parka, and smartly polished combat boots. The three stars on her shoulders seemed extra heavy today.

Anne tightened her seat belt just in time to feel the light bounce of the aircraft touching down on the south end of the runway. She was only a few moments away from her next command. As the T-43 taxied down the tarmac, she looked out the window and had to smile. Stumbling down the hill a half mile in the distance was a curious sight. As she gazed into the distance, she saw twelve helmeted, silver-clad figures descending from the mountainside. This was definitely a bizarre welcoming party. She guessed who they were, trying to figure out which one was Eric. The sun was barely up and she was entering the twilight zone.

The small jet pulled slowly to an awaiting staircase. The strangely suited away team was not to be her only greeters. There were several others in dress uniforms standing at attention in the morning cold waiting for their new commander. Eric and the others had not been in contact with most of the base personnel. They were kept isolated from the other base functions as well. There was a sprinkling of permanent base personnel assigned, like Al, but they were few and far between. Only Al recognized the brigadier general at the head of the greeting party, clearly the current commanding officer.

Eric had never quite decided if Al was active-duty military, retired, or exactly what. He knew the military rituals, but chose to participate or not on an as-needed basis. The military types were unquestionably nervous about their new boss. Eric and the others were unfamiliar with military protocol or changes of command formalities. They were going to get to the plane after Anne descended the stairs anyway. Close enough to view the spectacle, but far enough away to not be involved directly. As they trudged through the snow, Anne Hayes was coming slowly, carefully down the stairs. The brigadier and the four other soldiers all snapped salutes to her. After she returned their salutes, she then extended her hand to the brigadier in greeting. She was hustled away into a nearby door leading down into Area 96. Eric's reunion would apparently have to wait as would the remainder of the team's introduction to his true love. She was all business.

The Genesis team entered the underground compound about fifteen minutes later through another of the clustered small buildings. The beauty of an underground facility is no one knows how big it is, where it is, or whether there's another base right next to it you don't know anything about. When they were in the complex they knew it was large, but just how large, only Al and his cohorts were aware. Eric hoped to pass Anne in the halls after they had cleared the recompression and biological isolation outer chamber and re-entered the living quarters. That whole process took about twenty minutes. Twenty minutes for Anne to disappear into the bowels of this maze of tunnels, corridors, halls, meeting rooms, and offices. His chances of a random reunion were remote at best. He would have to wait for her to find him. All good things in time, he reflected.

By the time they had completed clearing the outer room and were back in their on-base coveralls, it was only seven a.m. In their rush to meet the plane, none had eaten breakfast. The hike in from the mountains was enough to set off anyone's stomach clock. Al arranged a typical Anton meal: high in carbohydrates, calories, and quantity, with plenty of variety for each and every different gastronomic desire. He had radioed ahead with an estimated "tee-off time" as he called it, of 7:30. By the time they had showered and cleaned up, his estimate was right on the mark. They sat down to eat, not sure of their day's itinerary.

"I was looking over the medical records and I noticed your immunization for tetanus has lapsed, Chappo." C.T. had made it a daily ritual of reviewing each of the team's records. They were usually directed toward a specific goal, such as immunization history, childhood illnesses or chronic medical conditions.

"So you think I'll contract tetanus, eh, mate? Well I don't. But I suppose you can stick your needles in me this time." In his own way, Chappo loved to needle Tatman, even when he didn't care. C.T. was so compulsive that Chappo knew he could get him going at any time, on damn near any subject.

"Parvathi, your prenatal blood work is normal. I'd like you to have an ultrasound now, and about every month until we leave."

"I think I'm beginning to show," she giggled. "Xiao thought he felt her kick last night."

"No way," C.T. disagreed. "You're too early for that."

"What do you know about obstetrics," scoffed Chappo.

"More than you," C.T. shot back.

"Not much more, sport." He was right about that in the beginning. But Tatman was a fast study. The challenges he thought he was getting into when he signed up for this trip were not exactly the ones that came to fruition. Still, he accepted them with the enthusiasm of a first-year medical student. He was spending his spare time with E.J. Abraham and his staff learning as much about radiation medicine as he could. And brushing up on embryology for the DNA samples, tropical medicine, and unusual infectious diseases—not so much for the specifics, but how to think like an epidemiologist. Tatman spent time on biosystems and nutrition, too.

"Come see me this afternoon, Chappo," Tatman advised.

"I'm busy."

"This is important."

"Not to me."

"It's your health. I won't—"

"Look, sport. I'll get by to see you when I'm good and ready." Chappo and Tatman were both standing, moving closer to each other.

"I'm ready now, 'sport'," Tatman mocked. Chappo charged him and the two locked up, pushing, shoving and then Chappo threw a wide swing. It nearly landed on Tatman's left jaw, missing by a few hairs. C.T. grabbed the Aussie by the front of his hair and jerked him to the ground, then dove on top of him. The rest of the seven jumped into the fray, trying to pull the two apart. Eric had been late arriving. As he opened the door, the two crashed into his legs, taking him to the ground with a perfect football rolling block. Tatman returned fire, swinging at Chapman, but striking Sheppard squarely on the face.

"Damn it," C.T. screamed. "I think you broke my hand."

"What the hell is going—"

"That's it!" Chappo bellowed. "He goes, or I go."

"Can't cut it, mate," Tatman jeered. "You can't go…you couldn't find the door."

"I built the door, you tight-assed bugger. Needles and probes won't—" Chappo was interrupted by his chin suddenly pushed upwards, closing his mouth.

"Enough," Nkata quietly demanded, his walking stick being pressed harder and harder against Chappo's mandible. His right foot was on Tatman's chest. He stared down at Eric, holding his position on each for a full minute. Finally, he lessened the pressure on Tatman's chest and Chappo's jaw. "These…are…the….best…man… has…to…offer?" He shook his head, and extended an arm to Sheppard, helping him to his feet. Eric had forgotten just how strong this diminutive man could be. "Maybe…neither…of… you…should…go. Better…yet…maybe…we… should…all…leave…and…let…you…find…out…who…is…the…better…man. That…is…what…this…is…about…is… it…not?" He was glowering at both.

"Who…is…stronger…who…is…right…more…often…who…is…tougher…who…is…our…leader. You…both… should…be…ashamed. Look…at…what…you…have…done…to…yourselves…and…the…mission."

The entire room was silent. The two combatants picked themselves up from the ground and brushed off the dirt. It would take more than a light dusting to remove their hostility. Tatman stormed out of the room, leaving the rest to finish breakfast in hushed silence.

Eric motioned to Al. "Find Tatman," he whispered.

"And say what?"

"I don't know, you'll think of something. Just get him back in here."

Eric's team was falling apart and he felt paralyzed by uncertainty. After slogging down his food as rapidly as possible with the accompanying dyspepsia, he finally stepped to the podium. "The staff and I notified the President by letter about the new contingency plan for the mission returning in the event an emergency and your concerns about permanent versus long-term colonization. I'm waiting to hear back. I'd expect—"

"Excuse me, sir," Tom Conroy interrupted. He was in uniform, not the standard issue jumpsuit, but his U.S. Air Force Class-A uniform with a new lieutenant colonel's silver leaf on each epaulet. "General Hayes is coming to talk to your team, Doctor." Everyone noticed the formality, the promotion, and the uniform. Then he held open the door and Anne quickly walked through it.

"Good morning," she began. "No need to stand." None had, being unfamiliar with military protocol. "I'll dispense with introductions other than to say my name is Anne Hayes. I'm sure Dr. Sheppard has told you something about me. I'd ask that you keep an open mind," smiling nervously. "I'll get to know each of you in greater detail as our time here goes by. Are we missing someone? I only count eight."

"Bathroom break, ma'am," Conroy covered. He'd passed Tatman in the hall, nearly colliding with him.

"As I was coming in, I overheard the comment about hearing back from the President." She paused and took a deep breath. Her posture became more erect, her back stiffened and her eyes narrowed, focusing straight at Eric. "Effective immediately, this base, including this team, has been transferred from civilian control to the United States Air Force Space Command. Dr. Sheppard is to be congratulated for bringing this mission along in spectacular fashion. The President sends his heartfelt thanks. Dr. Sheppard will remain in day-to-day operational control. However, any communications with the President or outside this base must go through the chain of command—through my office."

She stepped away from the podium turning her back to say something to Colonel Conroy. The room's previous white noise returned with more intensity as the team consulted on what she meant and why. Good to see you too, Eric mumbled sarcastically. Couldn't she have at least told me first, he groused. She turned back to her audience. "I know many of you don't understand what all this means or why. I have been authorized by the President to brief you on an as-needed basis." She had certainly gotten their attention. Now maybe they'd all find out what was going on. All eyes were on her. Conroy began passing out briefing notebooks. Eric's ego had been bruised. He didn't mind not being in charge. It was the way it happened.

"I will try and bring you up to speed on what's been going on in the world outside your isolated compound. First, as background, and second, its impact on you and your mission." White noise muttering again. With a rising voice and a bit of annoyance, "I would appreciate your undivided attention."

Welcome to the military people, Conroy thought to himself. Not only was General Hayes going to educate them with respect to their mission, but to the military and its protocols as well. Good luck, he thought to himself, again finishing with the notebooks.

"The world is a dangerous place these days. Six weeks ago, the President of the United States and the Vice Premier of China, Mr. Yang, met in secret in Hawaii. Their agenda was to make the world a safer, more unified community. They agreed on a joint cooperative effort to develop, produce, and market alternative fuel sources for the world. The Chinese would become re-engaged, making world peace a reality. Unfortunately, the opposite has occurred. On leaving Hawaii, approximately two hours west, the Vice Premier's plane was targeted by a sea-to-air missile and destroyed. There were no survivors."

"Who did it?" Najibul asked. Like the rest of the room, he was incredulous, astounded and dismayed. "Who would do such a thing? And why?"

"In a moment, Doctor," she continued in a tone all knew was just the beginning of the story. "As I recall, Dr. Najibul, you have some experience in being shot at yourself. Frankly, it doesn't matter who actually did it, because the new Chinese leadership concluded America was behind the attack. In support of their claim, they point out the United States has been doing this throughout history.

"Japanese Admiral Yamamoto's plane was ambushed during World War II. The *Maine* in Cuba, at the turn of the twentieth century, was actually sabotaged as a way of precipitating war with Spain and gain control of the island. The multiple assassination attempts that the U.S. has always denied—Castro, Saddam, and the ones that didn't fail in Iran and Guatemala in the 1950s, and bin Laden in Pakistan in 2011, to name just a few.

"For the record, the United States did not know about, or participate in, this criminal assault. We initially believed the Taiwanese were responsible. Our efforts to determine what actually happened are ongoing. Because of the Chinese response, finding the perpetrator took a back seat, although resolution with the Chinese may ultimately depend on proving who did do it."

"Their response, General?" Mariani was puzzled. "They started up again in Kazakhstan?"

"Or with Taiwan, I'll bet," Chappo advanced his theory. "Those little bastards started up there again." Again, the room hummed with white noise.

"Watch the Chinese slurs, 'mate'." Xiao was troubled. "There are always two sides to every story."

"That's right, the right side and the Chinese side. I wouldn't give a—"

"People!" Hayes exclaimed, then lowered her voice. She was in charge and the tone of her voice demanded that respect. "I've just come from a war zone. I don't need to see it again from you. You will listen and listen well, with apologies to Dr. Mariani for teaching technique. You are adults, scientists, and soon-to-be explorers. I expect you to act like it. I will not lie to you. But you must listen. Hold your questions until you have the intelligence to ask valid ones."

Just how did she mean, 'intelligence', Sheppard wondered. He'd seen this side of Anne coming back from Argentina after she was ordered to Diego Garcia. She could be all business with some double entendre thrown in. How many caught that, he reflected to himself. He was torn between being proud of her, mad at her, relieved, indignant, flattered, and insulted. He remembered their trip to Buenos Aires to recruit Eva Mariani and Anne's debate with her over military leadership. She was putting her methodology on stage and the final test would be whether she was effective.

Al nearly pushed Tatman into a seat, but at least he was here, Sheppard thought. Tatman and Chappo were on opposite sides of the room. There was no eye contact. All eyes were on General Hayes.

Anne was a quick study of her audience. A good teacher has to know the level of her students, their requirements and concerns, and their ability to grasp the issues at hand, then tailor the presentation to meet the needs of that audience. She had to bring them up to speed with the facts, then give them her analysis of the world situation and let them draw their own conclusions. She certainly had drawn her own. Her other priority was getting them ready to fly as quickly as possible. She would need Eric's help assessing where they were in their training. She also believed in seeing and assessing their performance for herself.

"Let's continue with respect for each other, AND..." she paused for emphasis, "listening, before we speak. You are all intelligent people, yet rather naïve in world politics. After the downing of Vice Premier Yang's plane, the United States was in the dark as much as the rest of the world. The Chinese immediately decided the United States or one of her allies was behind this attack. Frankly, I can understand why they would think this. Who else could contemplate such a thing?"

"Who else had the intelligence to know his airplane was going to be where it was," Gagarin asked.

"Now that...is a good observation, Svetlana," Anne responded. "Who indeed. And what would be the motivation? Any ideas?" She would engage their minds but not their emotions.

"The Kazakhstani's are the obvious choice, but they probably wouldn't have that level of intelligence." Melissa Sturmbourg was pondering the world's players. "But their previous surrogates, the Russians would."

"Of course the Russians have the intelligence," Svetlana almost indignantly replied. "But what would be our motivation?"

"Aiding a country geographically proximate to the Russian border. One they just attacked." Xiao was pensive and appeared dejected. "All this jockeying for position. Why can't we discuss our differences in the open and come to some resolution without resorting to military confrontation?"

"Why indeed," Anne answered. "Dr. Xiao, you may not like it, but your current world doesn't do things that way. So until you are off to another, I suggest you concentrate on how to make this one a better place. The first step is to understand it. To understand your adversaries, your enemies, and your options. Think historically. What has driven mankind to war throughout all of history?"

"Religion," Natarajan quickly answered. "Religion has marked our civilizational territories since the beginning of our time on this Earth. It—"

"Iran."

"What?"

"Iran," Najibul quietly spoke with a tone of despair. "It was Iran who shot down Mr. Yang's plane, wasn't it, General?"

"Why would you say Iran?" Anne prodded.

"The Kazakhstanis are Muslim, as are the Iranians," he continued. "They were coming to the assistance of a Muslim brother, but they did it in a way to deflect responsibility from themselves. No doubt, they too, blamed the Taiwanese."

"Very insightful, Dr. Najibul," Hayes complimented. "And right on the mark, we believe. Although there is much circumstantial evidence to support your intuition, the Iranians certainly haven't admitted their complicity to date. What they didn't calculate into their considerations was the Chinese response. After the shoot down, there was a void in the Chinese leadership. It was filled, and filled rapidly, by the hierarchy of the Chinese military. They immediately blamed the U.S. and Taiwan and instituted action in the Straits of Taiwan. Our navy was attacked and the Taiwanese islands were heavily bombarded as a prelude to invasion. There were multiple air encounters and several retaliatory strikes by the Taiwanese against Chinese mainland cities. The Chinese weren't afraid of a two-front conflict. One in Kazakhstan and one in the Straits. That, the Iranians anticipated, and relished."

"What about the rest of the world?"

"Well, geopolitics doesn't like a vacuum."

"Meaning?"

"Meaning several countries took the general instability and the lack of attention to their particular age-old disputes to settle old scores," General Hayes responded. "New regional conflicts rekindled along the fault lines of our ancient religions. In the Middle East, Israel and several Muslim countries exchanged insults and massed their forces along their borders. Iraq blocked the Straits of Hormuz, paralyzing the flow of oil out of the Gulf in an effort to hurt Iran. There were a few border skirmishes which diverted Iran's attention from Kazakhstan. There were also a few aerial dogfights, but the Middle East—in particular, Israel and her neighbors—was relatively quiet compared to other areas."

"What others?"

"Bosnia became a bloodbath once again," she continued, in a matter of fact way that hid the severity of the conflicts and her concern. "Without the various combatants' senior partners to reign them in, these surrogate parties returned to their centuries old religious struggle. Orthodox against Muslim against Christian. The rest of Europe and Russia were preoccupied with the Chinese in the Pacific and Asia, ignoring their own backyard. The Catholics and Protestants in Northern Ireland briefly tried to return to their divisive skirmishes, though they really didn't have the stomach for it. Then there was Kazakhstan. How many even knew where this isolated country was?" she wondered not waiting for an answer. "This unfortunate country became the focus of a four-way confrontation."

"Four-way? What four?" Chappo seemed puzzled. "I thought it was only the oil the Chinese wanted there? Where the hell is this little gem of a country exactly anyway?"

"Kazakhstan virtually no longer exists," Anne glumly reported. "Where it was, was at the crossroads of four cultures. This little gem, as you call it, is almost seven times the size of California, bordering on China, Russia, and several Islamic republics, including Uzbekistan and Kyrgyzstan. The Caspian Sea to her west and Iran to her south, this country of about eighteen million is in the middle of a cultural conflict as well as petroleum dispute. Although oil is the resource precipitating the conflict, none of the regional cultures want the others any closer or more powerful.

"Russia already had problems with Islamic militants trying to dominate the Kazahk government. The Chinese not only wanted her oil, it also needed a puppet on her western border to guarantee security to the west and with Russia to the north. Iran was pushing for a more fundamental Islamic state, or, at least a reliable ally against the other two. Kazakhstan's fertile southern central plains were ideal for tank battles. That's exactly what the Chinese did, taking the entire central—and ultimately western—region within days. The oil fields in and around the Caspian Sea out-produce the North Sea, and are the world's third-largest resource. Rich and ripe pickings for a country thirsting for oil, like the Chinese."

"That's three powers," Mariani noticed. "I suppose the fourth is the U.S.?"

"You suppose correctly. The U.S. and her European allies along with Japan increasingly utilized Kazakhstani oil. This created a dilemma for them. The Chinese also wanted it, but after the Straits in 2013, the United States and Russia convinced Kazahkstan to halt sales to the Chinese. The Kazakhstanis were negotiating re-instituting shipments to the Chinese when they invaded. China apparently couldn't get what it wanted through negotiations, so they took it by force. The Iranians brokered a cease-fire and the U.S. was willing to give up the oil since we were rapidly moving toward an alternative fuel source.

"Our allies weren't as willing because they weren't as far advanced in moving away from petroleum-based energy. Still, with American backing and subsidies, they agreed. After Yang's untimely death, most agreements fell apart and the conflict renewed. The difference was that the intervening aggressor now was Iran, under the pretense of aiding another Islamic brother state. The Iranians attacked Kazakhstan from the south through Uzbekistan. They gained the offensive when the Chinese leadership was 'beheaded' as the result of Yang's death and, in disarray, was taken by surprise. What wasn't known initially was that it was the Iranians who orchestrated the shoot-down, killing the Vice Premier."

"They appeared to be taking the moral high ground, but in fact, were treacherous," Najibul concluded annoyingly. "Damn Iranians. They are just a different breed of Muslim. Not of my kind."

"And the Russians?" Svetlana asked.

"In the initial invasion, the United States tried in vain to get them to intervene," Hayes continued. "They made feeble efforts, but they weren't enthusiastic. In the absence of significant Russian intervention, frankly, the U.S. was in favor of a cease-fire, although not excited about legitimizing the Chinese occupation of the oil fields. After the Iranians invaded, following Yang's death, the Russians jumped in with both barrels."

"Typical," Tatman frowned. "Just like the end of World War II. Let someone else do the dirty work and come in at the last minute to take the credit."

"Your past history is accurate," Hayes corrected, "but not this time. The Russians and the Iranians had initial successes, but the Chinese recovered. They bloodied both the Russians and the Iranians. They basically fought them to a draw. Most of the other Asian tigers, Singapore, the Malaysians, and Indonesians also settled old territorial disputes to China's detriment and stepped up their persecution of their Chinese minorities. The Chinese fought well on all fronts, exacting a toll the rest of the world was unprepared to accept. The Chinese just don't look at human life the same way."

"Now you're into my area, General," Xiao responded indignantly. "Just what do you mean about looking at life differently?"

"What I mean is that because they have so many more people, the value of each individual is lessened," Anne answered, noticing Xiao took offense at her characterization of his brethren. "We never learned that lesson in Korea in the 1950s and the Iranians and Russians fell into the same trap in the late-2010s. The Chinese leadership believes, by virtue of their superior numbers, they can survive any conflict with any opponent. We in the West just don't think that way."

"Is a Chinese life of equal value to an American's, General?" Xiao asked. "Are you saying China would willingly sacrifice her citizens in great numbers in order to outlast her opponents? Cannon fodder, General? Or, is it not true, that you in the United States also place different values on life?"

"That is my premise, sir. Please explain yours."

"In the first Gulf War, you valued your 148 coalition dead more than the 50,000 or 100,000 Iraqi dead," Xiao reasoned. "I would presume that wasn't the case with the families of the dead Iraqis," he quietly concluded. "Did you mourn for their dead soldiers? I think not. It could have been worse. You could have massacred many thousands more. You didn't have the stomach to continue the slaughter once the journalists publicized what they called the 'turkey shoot' on the 'highway of death'. You in the United States put resources into technology that preserves life. American life, not Iraqi, or Vietnamese, or Chinese. Losing a seventy-five million dollar airplane has less impact on you than losing one pilot.

"Other countries don't have the luxury of your resources. Their resource is their people. I submit it is you who are out of step, not us. A fairer characterization might be that neither culture understands or values the other's. We take a more long-term, historical view. One life is much less important than the life of our culture.

We value life, but the life of the whole, not the individual. China has endured five thousand years of famine, war, oppression, and pestilence. Until we both change, conflicts will continue to be resolved by wars because neither understands the other's perspective. Neither takes the time to consider the opposition's viewpoint. Or we choose to disregard it."

"Isn't…that…change…what…our…mission…is…supposed…to…be…about?" Nkata asked in a hushed voice. He was slowly walking around the room using his newly carved walking aid. He paused first beside Chappo, placing his hand on the engineer's shoulder. "With…all…due…respect…General…one…of…the…principal… reasons…I…choose…to…go…on…this…mission…is…because…I…have…little…faith…in…mankind's…ability…to… change." He had moved over to Tatman. "And…even…less…tolerance…for…the…excuses…mankind…gives…for… why…we…can't."

There was silence. Nkata had finally said what others felt, but hadn't verbalized. It was clear he had little regard for the petty, trivial, insignificant superficialities of this world. He was going because he'd had enough. He knew there had to be a better way. Chappo and Tatman threatened to bring along that pettiness. Xiao had expressed the bitterness of the "have-nots". Several secretly cheered when the "haves" were bludgeoned. Most were embarrassed to realize that during this briefing they chose sides like it was a sporting event, even though none had a direct interest in the parties. "Go China, beat the Americans! 2-4-6-8, who do we obliterate?" This was what each professed to hate, yet each fell victim to it in such a short period. The threshold for Tatman and Chappo's physical confrontation had been low. That was the heritage all professed wanting to leave behind. But could they? Could they change where others could not?

After several minutes of silence, Mariani spoke. "General Hayes," she asked in a hushed voice. "What now? Are we up to speed? Or, is there more?"

"There's more," Hayes answered, recognizing the consternation of the group. "It seemed the world was on the verge of total cataclysmic war. I was dispatched secretly to China by my superior, General Adams on behalf of the President. I'll admit I felt like a sacrificial lamb being led to the altar. My orders were to find a way to get all parties to take a breath, a step back, and consider the consequences of where everyone was headed.

"The Chinese could have shot me down in retaliation without ever hearing what I had to say, but they didn't. The Iranians could have ignored my pleas for an audience, but they didn't. The Russians did dismiss my overtures initially, but curiosity finally brought them to the table, too. Or was it paranoia, I don't know. Taiwan at first refused to participate. Then, their paranoia got the best of them, also.

"There were several other parties involved over several weeks. A very secret, tough, protracted bargaining table, where all parties vented their fears, jockeyed for position, accused the others of treachery and deceit, and generally laid their respective cards on the table. Gradually, after living with each other day and night for four weeks, a mutual, grudging, painstaking respect evolved, with a realization that the fate of the world was in the balance."

"Making a fight personal, looking into the eyes of your antagonist, facing him directly makes one think hard about what one is doing," Najibul asserted. "It is harder to stand face-to-face and poke your enemy in the eye than to drop a bomb on him from thousands of feet away. That is death in the abstract. But close and personal, requires a detachment few have without training."

"And do we really want to train people to be that detached, not to care?" Xiao carried the concept forward. "Someone once said that to end war, all we had to do was eliminate the weapons—force combatants to kill each other face-to-face, hand-to-hand."

"That's wrong," Anne reestablished control. "That is precisely how war began. "Maybe you can change that next time, but in our history it has not been the case." Maybe, or maybe not, given Tatman and Chappo's recent tirade. She was unaware of the timeliness of her message. "The role of a soldier is to be prepared to fight, but to avoid it at all costs. That was my role in Beijing, and it appears I have been successful."

"So how are we involved?" Svetlana was perplexed. She was sitting next to Eric. She unconsciously began rubbing his right thigh. "I have wanted to be in the military for years, but the Russian military, not the American one."

"If I may continue," Anne responded curtly. "I would appreciate all of your attention," staring at Gagarin. "Currently, there is a truce in place, but a shaky one at best. My personal belief is that because all parties suffered such horrendous casualties they are hesitant to resume, at least for the short term. The various militaries were all too eager to stop. Casualties numbered in the hundreds of thousands. The cease-fire left the battlefield with three foreign armies in Kazakhstan—the Iranians primarily to the south, the Russians in the northwest, and the Chinese in the central and eastern zones. Kazakhstani forces and her civilian population were cut to pieces.

"The inhumanity of this conflict is particularly disturbing. Each side slaughtered their opponents with total disregard for non-combatants and the environment, brutally, without hesitation—and in violation of many conventions signed by all to prevent such an occurrence. It seems the concept of mutual assured destruction really doesn't act as a deterrent.

"Another factor is the world's economy. The oil fields triggering the invasion are in rubble and unavailable to all parties. War devastates economies and even short term conflict inflicts severe wounds on the best of them. Governments, whether totalitarian or democratic, are responding to their populations. Those people are saying, 'Enough!' to their respective governments, 'it's time to get back to work.' To that end, my role is to get you to work in a renewed, reorganized fashion. Who knows how long we have before someone strikes a match again?"

"So where does that leave us now, General?" Najibul asked with anticipation. "We're stepping up the schedule. But how? What does that really mean?" Just then, one of Mariani's cats jumped onto the podium. Startled, Anne uncharacteristically let out a shriek while stepping back from the podium. Both the jump and her reaction broke the nervousness.

"Well," Anne smiled sheepishly. "I see someone else is ready to pounce back into training, too. My orders are to have you ready to go, and I mean go, not on a training flight, but go, in one month. Whether you can meet that timetable remains to be seen. I've scheduled a briefing with the staff to apprise me of your progress this afternoon. I hope to have a better feel for whether we can make it after the briefing. As to why you have been placed under my command, I can only speculate. I would guess that the higher-ups feel they have better control if it is a military operation. If you don't meet deadlines, my head rolls."

"Have we missed any deadlines to date?" Eric asked pointedly.

"Not that I'm aware of," she snapped. "Doctor, you know how Washington thinks. They want someone they can lean on, and I guess you didn't bend to their liking." She paused to let the group think about the tale she had just woven for them. If Anne hadn't been a key player, she wouldn't have believed it herself. After a few moments of white noise she brought the group back.

Svetlana leaned directly into Eric's ear. "What do you see in this General?" she whispered.

"I hoped my future," Eric answered. He stood and began slowly pacing.

"That is all, for now," Hayes concluded. "Please continue your current schedule this morning. If I could see Dr. Sheppard in my office in fifteen minutes." With that, she walked briskly out of the room, with Tom Conroy trailing. What had been white noise was now at a decibel level of a buzz saw. Eric slipped out the room and headed back to his room. He had fifteen minutes to sort out what he had just transpired. He needed help. That meant Al.

Eric flung himself on the bed, Al standing in the door. "I suppose you heard."

"Al knows everything."

"What am I supposed to say to her?"

"You've got bigger problems than the General. Let's see. You've got two team members rolling around on the floor in a fist fight and two others who want to drop out. That's four out of nine."

"To hell with all of them," Eric moaned.

"And did I mention the General couldn't help but notice Svetlana," Al frowned. "Who could miss it."

"I'm not interested in her."

"But she's interested in you."

"Thank God she'll be millions of miles away soon. It's Anne I'm interested in."

"Doc," Al cautioned and counseled, "she's in a tough situation. Appeal to the woman in her. Let her talk and remember. Let her run the show. She's the alpha female."

"The what?"

"The alpha female," Al continued. "The dominant member of the wolf pack." He paused to light a cigar. "Damned military. Probably the last one of these for a while," blowing smoke into the vent.

"Svetlana didn't make things any easier."

"Women are competitive, chief. If it's the General you want, you've got to let her know that. Remember, she's got troubles of her own," Al counseled. He took one last drag and left Eric's room, snuffing out the cigar while closing the door. Sheppard went to the bathroom to freshen up. Might as well look as presentable to the General as possible.

He knocked on the door and heard Anne say "come in." As he entered he surveyed the room. There was no one else present. Anne was sitting behind a standard government-issue gray metal desk. "Don't start with me, Eric. I'm under a lot of pressure, here. I don't need you undercutting my—"

"Anne," he interrupted, then changed his comportment and posture to a submissive one. "I understand," he said calmly. "It's just a job. One I hope will be over soon." He stood shuffling his feet. "I missed you." He gently kissed her lips, but she wasn't returning the passion. "What's really happening, Anne?"

"I've made some decisions, Eric. They concern you and me," she took a deep breath. "I can't divide my attention anymore. I've decided to put our relationship on hold."

"Just like that?"

"This is hard for me. "I'm not ready to end my service to our country yet," she stated flatly. "I once told you

I was married to the Air Force. Well, he's not willing to divorce just yet. Besides, it looks like you and a certain Russian cosmonaut are on more than first name basis."

"I'm not interested in her. She's a tease. It's you I'm in love with."

"Are you?"

"Any other bombshells you want to drop on me?" Sheppard slumped to a nearby couch.

"The President's worried about your mission on several fronts." She was clearly worried, too. She sat next to him on the couch. "He's worried about funding drying up because of the hostilities affecting not only the American economy, but most of the world's. And if fighting starts up again...God only knows what that will mean."

"Is it, Anne? Is the funding going away? Are hostilities going to start up, again? Are—"

"Slow down, Eric," she broke in. "First of all, you're asking me to predict the future. Who knows whether fighting will resume. As to the funding, I think our President is concerned. And if he's concerned, you should be, too. That's one of the reasons for transferring you to my command. So Eric, how ready are your folks?"

"They're ready. And willing. At least I thought they were," he answered. He filled her in on the recent ground combat, Eva's decision and the military pressure on Melissa.

"You've got another problem," she added. "I hear one of your crew is pregnant?"

"That's right."

"I've got written recommendations from several sources strongly advising dropping her because of the pregnancy," Anne responded. "It's too risky in transit."

"Great," Eric slumped further. "That means two, not one. They're a husband and wife team. So six of my nine have problems."

"I'll advise you if there are more."

"What does that mean?"

"It means you have operational control, but the final decisions on this team will be my decision."

"You mean it's a military decision, not a civilian one?"

"Correct. If we determine your people can't make the grade, we—"

"How dare you pull the rug out after all my work. I won't—"

"You won't do anything! Is that clear," Hayes shouted, then lowering her voice. "You said, 'My work.' How about the world's work? This isn't about you, Eric. It's about mankind. Can we do better? And with whom?"

"But—"

"But you've done so much? Get real. Without Tom Conroy, you wouldn't have closed Chapman, Xiao, or Natarajan. And I convinced Mariani. JMT-EL picked the winners on your team. Tatman, Najibul, and Gagarin. I'm sure you're upset about her going, aren't you? I've got to give you credit, though. You chose a cripple and an aging fossil of a botanist," shaking her head. "Look, Eric. We've been reviewing current astronauts for replacements. We've got—"

"Stop! No more, please," he begged. "You've ruined the last two and a half years of my life."

"I ruined it? You haven't needed much help, Doc," Anne jeered. "Look, I like you, Eric. Hell, if it weren't for my career, I probably could love you. But—"

"This isn't you talking, Anne. This isn't the caring, sensitive woman I came to know and know quite intimately. I'm not going to tell these people," Sheppard was devastated. He could barely talk. "Any other surprises?"

"Not currently. I'll tell them in due course."

"Let me ask you something," Eric volleyed. "How do I know your space jockeys will have the equipment ready to go so soon? Are you cutting corners? And what about the proper window for launch? Why are we being transferred? What's really going on?"

"The launch vehicle was ready to go six months ago. All we needed was the module to be launched. The Pentagon tells me the real thing, not the mock up you've been training in, will be ready next month. They're doing final testing now at Vandenberg. We've been assembling pieces and equipment on the space station since this whole thing began."

"So? What's with the military show? How come you know so much, and I don't? What if I quit? What then?"

"You won't. This is your pride and joy. We'll start rebuilding your team after I determine who goes and who stays during the next field trip." She was looking at Eric, sympathetic to his position, but focused on her orders. Still, she softened. "Have you ever heard of the NRO?" Anne cautiously asked Eric.

"Another rifle organization?" he sarcastically answered. "Why?"

"Let me tell you about it." Eric could see another surprise coming. "The NRO stands for the National Reconnaissance Office. It was so top secret its existence and even its funding was denied publicly until the 1990s. It's the agency responsible for coordinating all space activities. It began in the early 1960s. Ever heard of the Corona Program?"

"No."

"Those were the first super-secret spy satellite systems, the early KH-1 and its successors. Now we're putting up modified KH-17s. They can photograph you picking your nose through a thick cloud layer and see the booger. That's the NRO. We laughingly call it the 'Not Referred to Openly' agency. I'm the Deputy Director of NRO for Military Support. It's a fancy title meaning I report to the Director of the CIA and the Secretary of Defense. I'm the top military person. JMT-EL is part of NRO along with the spy satellites. It was no coincidence I was sent to Diego Garcia."

"Why are you telling me all this now?"

"Because it impacts your mission," she continued. "You've probably never heard of 'Joint Vision 2020' either. That's the unifying military policy that acts as the model for current and future warfare. Under my command, the Air Force coordinates development, testing and launch of secret and not-so-secret space vehicles. We've got space hardware you've never even dreamed of. We also are responsible for space-based spy satellites, the old KH-11 series with all her modifications. Those are the KH-17s I mentioned. The one's that tracked the Chinese bogeys that tried to shoot down the President. We keep at least two on line at all times. They don't last very long though. Only about five years. Our funding still remains pretty much secret. And our activities are still in the shadows, too. That's why your mission has been shifted to us, as a way of trying to control both funding and to keep snooping Congressmen out of your hair."

"So why am I finding out about it now instead of six months ago?"

"You're lucky to be finding out about it at all," she responded cavalierly. "It was B.C. who pressured the

President to tell you and to make the transfer. He feels like you should know what you're up against. There are a lot of people who oppose spending the money on your project, given the current unstable world we live in. B.C. and I feel that is exactly why it shouldn't be opposed, or slowed down. Who the hell knows what will happen next week, let alone next year. You don't really think the President would let a science adviser commit these kinds of resources without having some control? Believe it, or not, B.C. actually likes you, Eric. And I think he respects you."

"That son of a bitch, he's been holding out on me all along. What would you do without the pressure cooker, Anne?" Eric pleaded. "Can't you deal with Mai Tai's on the beach and getting up a the crack of noon? Or, diving all day, and dancing all night? You're choosing this over that?" There was a sharp knock on the door.

"Come," Anne hurriedly rose from the couch she shared with Eric. Colonel Conroy opened the door and entered, carrying a large stack of paperwork in his arms.

"Colonel, you look inundated," Anne cracked. "Just leave that stuff on my desk. Tom's been my spy assigned to you from the beginning. Right, Tom?" She didn't wait for his answer. Conroy was fourteen shades of red with embarrassment. "And, Colonel, show Dr. Sheppard to his new quarters." What did that mean, he wondered as he stood to leave.

"Will I see you later?"

"Doubtful," came her terse reply. Eric left with Tom. Once outside in the hall, he could barely contain himself.

"Alright, Colonel," asked an angry Sheppard. "What gives?"

"Don't get excited, Doc. It's not what you think." Conroy turned the corner to a hall Eric hadn't been in before. Tom pressed his hand against a plate which quickly recognized him as on the 'A' list. The heavy metal doors opened down another long hall. Tom then opened a door into a spacious office with an even larger adjoining sleeping quarters and bathroom. There was a sauna, a hot tub and an oversized shower.

"What's this?"

"New digs, Doctor."

"Why?"

"So you can concentrate completely on the mission," Conroy answered.

"I trusted you, Tom," Eric was disheartened. "I believed you when you talked about this team being your hope for the future. *Et tu, Brute?*"

"I meant it, Doctor. They were and still are. But I'm career military. You just don't get it," shaking his head. He sighed hard and spoke. "You're a double-A player who got called up to the majors. Just because you were called up doesn't mean you've got big league stuff. You thought you could compete, but you were wrong." Tom stared off, "I had my orders."

"Keeping tabs for the Pentagon?"

"Not the Pentagon. Generals Adams and Hayes."

"So what now...Colonel?"

"Eric, you've been distracted by the General and she by you," Conroy continued. "I won't respond to your disparaging remarks. It's time you demonstrate some leadership and finish your work here. That's what she wants, that's what General Adams wants, that's what the President wants, and those are my orders."

"Great."

"You're isolated from the rest of your team."

"What's left of them," Eric flopped onto the bed. "Is this near Anne?"

"No, sir. Location of her quarters is classified," Conroy quickly answered. "The General's quarters are restricted and off limits to all personnel. They are guarded in the event of intruder activity."

"Come on, Tom," an exasperated Sheppard answered. "Do I look like an intruder? Who the hell could get into this underground fortress, let alone get to her? And who'd want to? Someday, I hope to never see this place again."

"Look, Eric," Tom quietly responded. "I have orders to assist you in any and every way towards successful completion of your mission. She is off limits, let me repeat, off limits. This is a military base and she is its commanding officer. Until this tour is over, it's cold showers for you." Tom closed the door leaving Eric in his new digs. Al opened the door a few seconds later carrying most of his belongings.

"Not bad, Doc," Al approved.

"Yeah," Eric sarcastically replied. "Great. Fantastic. It's just what I ordered."

"By the way, Doc," Al disclosed. "The General's scheduled another away trip. You report in fifteen minutes. She's going with us this time."

"Great," Sheppard answered, rather depressed. "Another camping trip. I can't wait. Can I soak in the hot tub 'til we leave, or is that against military protocol, too? Don't answer. When I get back, all I want to do is soak in hot water until I drown. I don't want a turncoat attaché or any generals anywhere near me. Got it? Until then, I get to live in the wilderness with a team that isn't really a team because two-thirds are being thrown out or dropping out with a general who won't....Why do you know all this, Al? Who the hell are you?"

XXV

Saddle up, cowboys. It's time to ride," Jack Grimes barked to his troops as they donned their environmental suits. Nkata, Mariani, Natarajan, and Xiao were already dressed. Gagarin was helping Sturmbourg get from wheel chair to haptic suit. Chappo was downing a beer he had smuggled out of the kitchen. He was usually the last to start dressing but always caught up. Melissa, of course, had the most difficulty. Until she was in her suit, her earthly disability slowed her substantially. Al was accompanying them as usual. He was a help on the outside. Besides, no one had the heart to tell him he couldn't go. Najibul and Tatman were half finished dressing and deep in conversation. Eric was the last to arrive. He absentmindedly went through the motions of getting suited up, his thoughts clearly somewhere else.

"Aren't you coming, General?" Anton asked Grimes.

"Not this time. Conroy and I are staying here. My ticket's been purchased by another customer. I'll catch you next trip. They're all yours, Al." Although there were always technicians around to help, Grimes had told them not to help much lately. He wanted the team to be able to solve as many problems as they could. After all, the technicians wouldn't be going. They were now consigned to standing around awkwardly, with nothing much to do other than look busy. Still, it was a high tech locker room. There were computer touch screens everywhere, various monitors and sensors sounding more like an intensive care unit than a locker room. Into the fray walked Jack Grimes' replacement for the day, Anne Hayes. Eric was ambivalent seeing their temporary teammate.

"Thought I'd see how the government's spending its taxes," she quipped. "Hope you don't mind. I promise not to get in the way." She was struggling a bit getting into her suit. The suits were designed to be used by a variety of people and were readily adaptable to the individual user's physique. Its last user was Grimes, so it was currently "tailored" for him. Eric attempted to help Anne contend with the suit. It needed to be adapted to her body. Jack Grimes and Anne Hayes definitely had different physiques, he observed.

"You'll be learning about some new equipment this trip," Grimes smiled. "When you get to the surface, as you know, initially you won't have shelter. Until your temporary shelter is built, discovered, or transported to the surface, you'll be susceptible to the elements. Wind, temperature, radiation, that sort of thing. So far, you've trained at surviving in those harsh conditions—as best as can be created here on Earth.

"What you aren't familiar with is the equipment necessary to measure the levels of those potentially harmful factors. You may know it's cold, but how cold? You'll feel the windchill even through your suit, but how much is it? Radiation can't be felt. You need instruments to measure the presence or absence of harmful levels. In your backpacks today, you'll find a collection of instruments to that end. We'll see how well you figure them out on your own. If you can't, and you're not too embarrassed, you can radio us for help." Grimes laughed as he walked away. He'd thrown down the gauntlet. A challenge to their ingenuity.

Eric noticed Al fiddling with a handheld module that looked familiar. "Why are you taking a GPS?" Sheppard asked. "There aren't any positioning satellites around Genesis."

"I've got another project going while I'm out. It's not related to your mission." Al was being elusive. "I've gotta find something when we get out there. This will help."

"Just don't wander off too far." Eric wasn't concerned about Al getting lost. This was his territory. He was still curious about what Al's role at the base really was. And what was it in relation to this mission? Today, however, he couldn't concern himself with that. Today, it was the Team he was worried about. There had to be a final resolution to the question of who was going and who was dropping out. Leaving the underground confines of Area 96, they emerged into bright sunlight, with no wind, and a crisp air temperature of 14° Celsius. In short, an absolutely beautiful Utah day, perfect for showing the new boss around. With all the excitement of the last few months, Eric had forgotten that Thanksgiving, Christmas, and New Year's had all passed since he last saw Anne. When she'd left for Diego Garcia, it was mid-2018; it was now February 2019.

The Team quickly trekked to their now familiar base camp and made their cave home presentable to General Hayes. They set up the recording devices to document their use of the environmental scanners and monitors they would be testing during this expedition. Throughout the remainder of the day they were occupied with learning to properly use the new equipment in question. As night fell, they gathered for the evening meal of rations taken through their suits, and anxiously looked forward to the "campfire" with General Hayes. Al was nowhere to be found. No one had seen him since early afternoon. No one seemed overly concerned yet, though once the sun set, the light disappeared and the temperature quickly dropped about ten degrees.

"I'd better go look for Al," Anne commented, standing to leave.

"Want some company?" Eric was following, as she moved to the cave's entrance.

The others were beginning their nightly ritual. Eric jumped at the chance to be alone, even if it was to find Al. He was tired of *Risk* anyway. Anne would kick their butts at *Risk*. He couldn't have her showing up what was left of his team, even in a game. The two left the cave in search of their supposed guide. "Any change of heart?" Eric asked Anne as they trudged through the snow.

"Sheppard, you're persistent, that's for sure," Hayes was unmoved.

"You know what? I thought you'd made the choice to be a woman, not a machine of a general. That's who I was attracted to. You stay with B.C. and his kind. That son of a bitch has sabotaged me from the beginning." Eric walked on sadly, quietly. "You know the real tragedy, Anne? You've got so much more potential as a woman than the incredible General you already are."

She sped up, moving ahead of Eric. As he caught up to her, she realized he wasn't going away. "Okay, Eric. Here it is. If and when this is over, there will probably be a fourth star for me pretty quickly. I might even have a shot at Air Force Chief."

"Tropical drinks…"

"B.C.'s due to retire next year."

"Beaches without cares…"

"Hell, who knows. Maybe even be the first female Chairman of the Joint Chiefs. I'm fifty years old. It's all I ever wanted. All I ever knew. I'm no good at this retirement thing. I'd get bored. I've committed to protecting the world from itself."

"Is that really what you're committed to, Anne?"

They ventured east, several hundred yards away from the cave, then descended about half a mile into a long, narrow ravine. Anne wasn't paying any attention to Eric. She had a secret weapon. Al was wearing a transponder, a small device that electronically guided her toward his location. Anne tuned the receiver to Al's electronic signature. No major hide-and-seek to this game. This wouldn't take long, she thought.

"Who wants Nkata's nectar?" the little man rasped, holding forth with a large pitcher of his now famous home brew. He sloppily portioned out his concoction for all takers.

"So, who will be my first victim tonight, mates," Chappo inquired. "Maybe you, my fair Svetlana? Or perhaps you, Parvathi?"

"Why not me?" Eva asked. "Or are you wise enough not to take me on?" Tatman wasn't playing tonight. He was in the back of the cave, taking inventory of his emergency medical supplies. He hadn't spoken directly to Chappo since their fight, not much caring if he ever did again. The others bantered with each another until the pieces were divided, then settled into a protracted struggle to master the world.

If only problems were so simply solved. Reshuffle the deck, choose up sides again, or declare the whole affair hopelessly deadlocked and put the board away, ready to play again some other day. Just start over. Life in the real world, on the other hand, gets too complicated. We lose sight of real values, life's virtues, and the precious nature of life itself. Instead, we are consumed by the insignificant, the irrelevant, the ordinary.

Eight of the nine space-suited "aliens" on this cold Utah night sat playing their game of world domination, laughing, taunting each other in jest, drinking Nkata's witches' brew. In the flickering campfire light they could barely see the game board, or was it obscured by the concoction conjured up by their hydroponicist-mixologist.

Without warning, there was a cacophonous screech in their headsets. It was the radio. A transmission was coming in on the universal channel so that everyone in the group could hear the message. "This is Big Sky to Hayes. Big Sky to Hayes. We have emergency traffic. Do you copy?"

"This is Hayes. This channel is not secure," she responded. Even though Eric and Anne were out looking for Al, the entire group heard this communication.

"This is the President, Anne," came the return. "I'm so sorry...I just can't believe they would do this." The President's voice was as depressed as any had ever heard. He sounded like he was actually sobbing. "Why did it have to come to this? Don't they understand?"

"Understand what, Mr. President?" Anne's voice betrayed bewilderment.

"It can't be. It's too unbelievable," he was mumbling. "I never thought—"

There was a loud, high-pitched wail. The tone blasted their eardrums for three or four seconds, then only a steady stream of static.

Suddenly, through the entrance to the cave, night was transformed into day as a light previously unknown to any of the team flooded the darkness. And then another, both of which, in turn were followed within seconds by a tremendous rumbling of the earth, more powerful than any earthquake, throwing all to the ground. The mountains shuttered with a force unlike anything anyone had ever experienced.

Moments after the light had vanished, and as the ground continued to shake, though not as violently, the nine team members struggled to regain their footing, only to be knocked off their feet and hurled to the ground once again, this time by a horrific pressure wave that swept not only into their cave, but across the entire mountain range, uprooting trees and snapping others as if they were mere toothpicks. A fortunate few were left standing, but even those had many broken limbs and were stripped of nearly all their foliage. Hundreds of massive boulders were dislodged and careened into the valley below.

The *Risk* board, precariously perched on a metal container with its fifty or so game pieces—oriented in a way to capture the minimal ambient light—was wiped clean by the blast wave. There were multi-colored pieces and cards strewn throughout the cavern, some as far as fifty feet from where the board had been. The board itself was blown onto the damp floor below—landing face-up, it, too, survived the onslaught in one piece!

Mercifully, the Team had been spared from the ensuing carnage, protected by both their meager shelter and their suits—they were rendered temporarily unconscious.

As the entire team regained consciousness, and struggled to find the wherewithal to stand, each was vaguely aware of having been unconscious, in a fog, now trying to remember.

Trying to remember what?

Only a moment earlier, each had been lying on the cold ground, awakening in an environmental suit. A pounding headache was all each had as a memory of the most recent events. Surely there was more. Each member of the team gradually became aware of the others.

What was going on? What had happened?

As each one's mind slowly cleared, realizing the presence of the others, they fumbled to just touch one another—confirming their own existence, confirming they were alive.

Alive, but where?

One by one they found their feet and, soon, also found their way to the entrance. Jockeying for position, each squinted in an effort to see through the opaque night. All anyone could see was smoke. Thick, acrid, dense, particulate-matter smoke.

Opaque? Not exactly. The exterior was a swirl of winds, intermittent lightning and thunder, and just plain noise. No, this wasn't opaque. It was becoming more and more clear, as each member began to grasp the view. Their instruments quickly began to scan for radiation, temperature, winds—atmosphere. All their devices were working, but the team didn't like the readings. There was radiation, higher than expected. And winds…with occasional gusts over 150 miles per hour. And the temperature was considerably lower than anticipated. But mostly, there was smoke.

"Everyone make sure your helmets are fastened correctly!" Tatman screamed into the headset communicator. "Let's not deal with things we can prevent. Anyone break anything?"

"Look over there! Nkata's not up." They stumbled over to Nkata. He was conscious, but dazed. Tatman began surveying him for injuries. The trauma surgeon's work ethic obscured any need to deal with thinking about what had happened.

"Everyone! Listen," Svetlana commanded. "We need to check out our equipment and each other. Melissa, is your haptic interface working properly?" she asked, fumbling with the suit in an effort to help. "You and Chappo check out the instruments. We have to confirm that the readings are accurate. They must be out of calibration. Then, we have to go outside."

She was right. They *had* to go outside. There was no escaping it. That was what they had to do and each one knew it, no matter how hard they individually tried to put it out of their mind. Each member checked his own suit, then checked someone else's. Then, they checked another—they checked and checked again for at least thirty minutes. To check was to postpone. They needn't check each other's pulse. Racing didn't describe the pounding, or the empty feeling in the pit of one's stomach, a gnawing, hollow sensation, as they prepared to enter their new world. As each stared into the stark, barren surroundings, together they were a composite of emotions. Confused, disoriented, exasperated, angry, scared. But fear of the unknown is the worst of fears.

"The instruments are calibrated correctly. The readings are correct. Radiation levels are way above baseline." Melissa Sturmbourg's matter of fact scientific voice hid her fear.

If there were radiation out there, what caused it?

"Nkata's got a broken arm, but he's alright otherwise," Tatman notified the group. "Where the hell are Eric and Hayes? And Al? They were..." His voice trailed off. He'd nearly verbalized what the others were thinking.

They were what?

"Before we go outside, I think we all need to get our heads on straight," Najibul broke the momentary pause. "I think we all know what happened, or have a pretty good guess. If the three of them are out there, we're no good to them in here. But we're no good to them unless we deal with some realities."

"The first reality is we have to concern ourselves with the main objectives," Chappo began. "Those remain the same. Food, water, and shelter."

"With one additional complicating factor," Melissa added. "My haptic interface works now, but who knows for how long? We are all incredibly dependent on technology. I don't want to be a burden—"

"We are most dependent on each other," Mariani corrected her. "Without each other there will be no technology. Life is about people, not technology. Machines are replaceable or repairable. People aren't."

"People are repairable, too," Tatman added. "To the limits of our technology and knowledge of how to apply it. There is a—"

"Excuse me," Xiao interrupted, perturbed by the conversation. "We can debate philosophy later. Right now, we need to find our three missing comrades and see just exactly what we are dealing with. You're all jumping to conclusions. We need facts, not speculation." That meant they had to go outside.

"Help...me...up," Nkata insisted, in the haltingly, hoarse voice the team had long ago become used to—his voice synthesizer was not working at the moment. Tatman had splinted his arm and placed it in a makeshift sling. "I...did...not...come...this...far...to...be...left...behind...because...of...a...broken...arm. I...want...to...see...for... myself...what...new...prison...we...are...confined...to."

The first person to step out of their cave, Chappo, was blown to the ground by the unexpectedly strong winds. The next, Svetlana, learning from her predecessor's mistake, grabbed onto something, but she, too, encountered problems. The unexpected cold penetrated her suit; so cold, in fact, as to cause her gloved hand to stick momentarily to anything hard and smooth she touched.

And so it began. Each person finding a tentative new bearing in a new, foreign surrounding.

But was it really foreign?

One by one, each scanned the horizon looking for something—something usual. The supposedly familiar, now unfamiliar. The hoped- for ordinary, extraordinary. The common—prayed for, but found to be uncommon.

As each of the nine found a place on the ledge overlooking the land below, they gently held hands. Not only to steady themselves physically, but mentally as well. What they saw was a vast wasteland, devoid of vegetation, in the midst of a perpetual, but stationary, tornado—and cold, so *very* cold. As far as one could look, there was darkness, but a visible darkness, an illuminated darkness. The smog of all smog, the haze of all haze. And the wind. Blowing in a swirling, pulsing, random pattern. Then, suddenly, a lightning storm—but very much unlike "normal" lightning. The billion-volt-plus electromagnetic pulses, with surges reaching peaks well-above 50,000 amps, were arcing across miles of sky, rarely striking the ground, and left eerie, luminous trails in the sky—oddly similar to those irridescent trails left by meteors.

How would they survive? How could they eke out an existence?

"I've got a reading on the smoke. It's actually fine dust. Particle sizes of less than one micrometer in diameter. The average number of particles in the atmosphere is in the 2.7 grams/cm^2 range." Sturmbourg's calming voice helped.

"Can't...grow...anything...in...that."

"What do you mean?" Najibul was neither being accusatory nor questioning Nkata's statement. He, like the others, just didn't know what Nkata meant.

"With...that...kind...of...optical...density...sunlight...will...be...filtered. That...will...drop...the...temperature...below...what...it...takes...for...plants...to...photosynthesize."

"So we need to find temporary food and shelter until I can set up a hydroponics lab for you." Chappo wasn't going to let his mates dwell on the negative. He was an engineer. There was a solution to every problem. All he asked for was time. "Any sign of the others, mates?"

"Why is the temperature so much colder?" Mariani trembled.

"It is down more than thirty percent," Melissa answered her query specifically. "I'm reading -23° Celsius. The windchill makes the effect of the temperature worse."

"How long will the cold stay around?"

"At least four weeks." Tatman answered. "Then much cooler than normal, with continued subfreezing temperatures, for at least several more months."

"What about radiation?" Natarajan had been quiet through the entire catastrophe, until now. "Where are we on exposure now? And what can we expect?"

"Our immediate threat is gamma radiation," Tatman explained to his fellow travelers. "Without the suits our exposure would probably be in the 50 rem range from gamma radiation and another 50 rem from ingestion of beta and alpha particles. With the suits, we should be able to minimize that exposure. Right now, I'm measuring minimal internal radiation. The problem is in the environment. We have to keep it that way."

"And chemicals? There are probably toxic chemicals." Gagarin checked her scanners. She was right. "The atmosphere is a veritable soup of pyrotoxins including cyanide and carbon monoxide."

"We've got high levels of dioxins and furans as well as bizarre organic compounds," Tatman added.

"So no one eats or drinks anything until it's checked," Chappo added. "Everyone stays in their suit for the foreseeable future."

"And what is 'the foreseeable future', Mr. Chapman?" Xiao had more than a tinge of irony in his voice.

"The foreseeable future is our only future." Nkata was emphatic. And his voice synthesizer was once again working, too. "We have to decide here and now. Do we want to try our damnedest to survive or do we roll over and let God or whomever do with us as they please? Right now, sir choose. All of you! Choose now! What will it be?"

"My love," soothed Natarajan to Xiao. "None of us would pick this as our future. But apparently it is. Not only ours, but our child's." patting her growing abdomen. "What has changed? The future is still our history to live, our rules to write and our legacy to create." She grasped her husband's hand. "This, for better or worse, is our destiny."

What hath God wrought? Or was this man's folly? What heaven or hell had they found? What had they gotten into?

They were of one mind.

"Look!" Najibul shouted. "They're coming! Through the haze over there," pointing in the general direction of the east. Through the dust and the winds three figures were slowly coming into view, one being supported by the others. The Team gingerly made its way along the obscure path toward their three wayward compatriots. What was once nine, was now twelve. Tatman immediately turned his attention to Eric as the entire entourage retreated to the sanctuary of their cavern. This former base was now their refuge.

"He was blinded by the light," Hayes advised Tatman. They propped him against a wall as C.T. began to look into his eyes using an ophthalmoscope. Trying to look at someone's eyes through two helmets was next to impossible.

"*I can see!* It's just I can't see clearly," Sheppard said with some degree of truth—and a larger degree of denial. "I'll probably get cataracts in thirty years."

"You should live so long, mate." Chappo was surveying his three lost friends, as were the others. Each couldn't help seeing Eric's dilemma. Hayes seemed none the worse for wear. Everyone soon noticed Al had a rifle slung across his shoulder. The .270 caliber Remington made some nervous, and others secure, but all curious.

"So Al, what's with the artillery?" Tatman broke the impasse. "Are you hunting or being hunted?"

"We don't exactly know," Hayes answered on his behalf. "Al was coming back from a little cabin he's kept secret from you. It's rustic, but Al's stored food and bottled water there."

"I used it as a hunting cabin in the summer," Al chimed in. "I was making sure it was tolerating the winter when..." Like the rest, he couldn't bring himself to say the obvious.

"Who are you Al?" Eric asked again. "How do you fit in here? A hunting cabin on a top secret base? Come on, Al. This time, the truth."

"Well, I'm not a construction foreman," Anton conceded. He sat down, held his helmeted chin in his hands, propped on his knees. "I'm CIA," he sighed. "Assigned to the base as a plant. The cabin's also where I keep my communications gear. I channeled intelligence directly to the Joint Chiefs and to my boss, the Director of Central Intelligence."

"Did you know about this, Anne?"

"He's news to me," she confessed.

"Well, you're one of us now, mate," Chappo stated flatly. "Whatever we are," his voice trailing off.

"We met up with Al coming back from the cabin," Anne continued. "It's about a mile and a half down the trail to the east. It might be very important to us. Luckily, the GPS was turned off so its electronics weren't susceptible to the electromagnetic pulse from the blasts. I don't know exactly what happened anymore than you do, but I'll bet my guess is reasonably accurate."

"Go on, we're all ears," C.T. pressed. "We felt two tremors in rapid succession, preceded by blinding light. Then winds and—"

"The two blasts were a ground burst and an air burst from separate nuclear warheads," Anne quietly, but ominously, advised them. "The fact that there were two means this was an all out exchange. Area 96 was a military target, that's the ground burst. But the air burst is a nuclear explosion designed to detonate in the air usually over urban areas. A one megaton air burst will level a 250 square kilometer area. You escaped serious injury because of the suits and the cave. We were luckier—we were down in a ravine at the time. If they sent an air burst too, this was no surgical strike. My reverse calculations lead me to believe this was an exchange in the 10,000 to 15,000 megaton range. That assumes we shot back. And I'm sure we did. Use 'em, or lose 'em..." Her voice trailed off as her depressingly detached statistics sank in.

"So...what is our future?" Natarajan asked again, sobbing as she spoke. "General. You have studied and trained for this eventuality. We have not."

"I may have studied this scenario, but I never trained for it," Anne answered, shaking as she spoke. "It was all so theoretical. So unreal. After the tactical nukes were used in the Straits, we figured nobody would be foolish enough to risk this. How could they? How could they precipitate this nuclear winter on all of mankind?"

"Who is 'they', Anne?" Eric asked. "Who did this?"

"The Chinese are the only credible player with enough hardware." Anne was despondent. "Why? What could they have hoped to accomplish? Wh—?"

"They did, General. That's all that matters now. And so did the West. And probably all the other nuclear powers, large and small. Well, they are all powers no more. Our job is to survive. Survive and educate our children. This can never be allowed to happen again. Never." Mariani was shaking inside her suit. Her fellow humans were shaking also.

"Will my child ever see the sun?" Natarajan asked, still sobbing. "Will any of us?"

"*Our Father...*"

Nkata, Gagarin, and Tatman had fallen to their knees. Through their headsets the entire team could hear the three softly praying.

"*...thy kingdom come...thy will be done...*" they whispered in unison.

"What?" Xiao struggled to hear, then kneeled with the others. Natarajan joined him.

"What has been done? Parvathi—"

"Quiet, Xiao," kneeling beside her husband alongside the others.

"*...give us this day...*"

"And give us tomorrow," solemnly Najibul added, joining the five.

"*...forgive us our trespasses...*"

"I...will...I...I will never be able...to forgive...whoever caused...this...this..." Mariani fell to the ground, weeping uncontrollably. Sturmbourg knelt over her, consoling her as best she could.

"*...lead us not into temptation...*"

Chappo leaned over, gently touching Tatman's shoulder. "I'm sorry, mate." He was barely heard. "We have all been so...foolish...so...childish...so...," his voice trailing off.

Sheppard, Hayes, and Anton had also joined the nine, bowing their heads. At first they listened. They joined the others praying in unison,

"*...but deliver us from evil...*"

All twelve fell silent. There was noise surrounding them overloading all their senses. Electrical noise, acoustic noise, olfactory noise, and visual noise. Everywhere they reached, they could touch the effects of the cataclysm with all the grit and grime, dust and detritus. They once again slowly, solemnly, walked to the ridge just outside their cave. They were each pulled back to stare into the abyss.

They scanned the horizon from the crest over the valley that once was Area 96, in the state of Utah, in the United States of America, on the North American continent of the planet Earth, the third planet orbiting the G2 dwarf star known as the Sun, its solar system being part of the larger galaxy known as the Milky Way, an otherwise insignificant speck in the vastness of the universe. Squinting, one could make out a huge crater in the belly of the rock below. An opening so large that none could see across it. It was in the vicinity of the runway they used to be able to see from here—the runway that any orbiting spy satelling could also have seen.

For weeks, the dust rained in both directions. Down in gritty walls of pollution and up in sporadic swirls. The winds raged and the lightning crackled, followed by terrific thunder. Their suits provided sufficient insulation and warmth, yet the cold occasionally cut through each one like a razor. None really felt the elements. They had trained for a landing on a strange new world. They had volunteered to be celestial pioneers. They had chosen to be explorers. And now they were here.

What they now realized was the new world they would be colonizing was not named Genesis, but, rather, *Earth*.

Epilogue

It was the kind of day we all dream about. The sun was blazing brightly set against the bluest of skies. No clouds to obstruct the cleansing, radiant rays of sunlight licking the sandy beach as a gentle breeze blew. Blowing just enough to dry the tropical sweat generated by the life-sustaining conversion of hydrogen to helium by fusion reaction we know as solar energy. The air temperature was a pleasant 28° Celsius and the water temperature a comfortable 23° Celsius. The beach was three hundred to four hundred yards wide and stretched as far as the eye could see in either direction, the view unobstructed by structures save for the small cluster of buildings grouped together several hundred yards from shore. As the coast gradually gave way to rocky lowlands, easily seven hundred yards inland, the foot high grasses undulated in the light breeze coming off the water.

What at first glance appeared to be wild growth of plant life, on closer inspection revealed weaving rows of a variety of crops, domesticated for the benefit of this idyllic seaside community. Behind the greenery extending up the hillside from the rocks were crude, but effective corrals, currently empty. Scattered across the expansive pasture were several cows, a few horses and various other four-legged animals grazing intermittently, generally avoiding the midday sun. Above the corrals, if one looked carefully into the distance, there were scattered white dots punctuating the landscape, like paint flicked onto canvas with a brush, each representing a sheep lethargically foraging on the slopes. Every so often a hyperactive dog began barking feverishly at the flock, trying to bring order to their disorderly feeding. Atop the crest, facing into the wind blowing eastward from the shore, were several clusters of stone placed by the hand of man, but whose configuration wasn't immediately recognizable.

This small village of about one hundred humans buzzed with activity, yet, still was tranquil. A tranquility borne of contentment. Of people who were secure in their various stations in life and with life itself. A simple life, fulfilling and gratifying, and filled with the pleasures of family, friends, and community. Each member of the tribe knew he or she had a place and a value. There was no division of labor by sex. What mattered was an individual's skills used to the advantage of the community at large. There was dignity in completing individual responsibilities which, taken separately, meant less; when taken as a whole, for the good of the community, corporate responsibilities were indispensable.

Individually, each could be proud of his or her unique contribution to the well-being of the community. This was not nirvana. As surely as mankind existed, particular men and women had disputes and disagreements. They fought hard for their opinions and beliefs—but they had been taught to fight with their minds, not their fists. This tribe placed a premium on logic and reason, consequences of an emphasis on education and the ability it gave its members to articulate the options for problem-solving. Still, on occasion, two intelligent, reasonable parties with legitimate differences were unable to resolve their disputes. Those disputes were taken to the larger community as a whole. Inevitably, one side wins and the other loses, but whatever the outcome, each gained a greater respect for the other.

These were not battles and there was no sense of victory, only resolution. There was no gloating, but a renewed commitment to get along. Each party to the dispute, win or lose, was required to give something back to the community. It was the community that suffered from the conflict. Individuals would not benefit at the expense of a detriment to another.

On the sands below the village, a cluster of children was gathered around a stooped figure of an old man. They sat at his feet, carefully listening, hanging on each word, looking to discern the full meaning of his ploddingly slow voice, straining to understand his every expression. He was slow, but animated. He was dressed in a flowing, off-white linen robe that billowed with each gust of wind. The old man's body was failing him, but not his mind. Sitting on a makeshift chair, his long, thin shoulder-length hair was whiter than his one-piece, loose-fitting garment. He seemed over-dressed for the beach, yet his skin was reddened in the few exposed places it was visible. Reddened and leather-like, with heavy age lines chiseled into his face, the old man came alive with each of the children's questions.

"Why are you telling us this story, Grandfather?" The question was posed by a thoughtful twelve-year-old boy with blonde hair and deep blue eyes. "Is it to scare us?"

"No, no," smiled the old man. "Not to scare you. To enlighten you. There is a different meaning for each of you to find."

"Where will we find it?" asked another child, a thin dark-skinned girl of seven, with olive black eyes and a curious, constant twisted mouth. A mouth with one corner turning up and the other downward in a continuous smirk.

"Look within your heart. And look over and over. Each time another birthday passes, think about its meaning in your life for that day and the next year."

"When did it take place?" The question came from the oldest of the children, a fifteen-year-old girl with kinky black hair and dark brown skin. She was athletic in appearance and was constantly writing notes. "Or, did it really ever take place?" she challenged.

"It happened, child. Believe me, I know," the old man nodded his head, then pointed his gnarled index finger at his own chest. "I know, because I was there. It happened not so long ago. Time is not important. Open your thoughts to the views of others. Do not be swift to draw conclusions. There are at least two sides to every story. Search for the truth, whether it is spoken loudly or softly. Many times the truth is not spoken at all. But it is always there."

"Who were these people?" The green eyed boy of eight asked the old man.

"It doesn't matter who they were. Only that they sacrificed for you those many years ago. From their victories—and even their defeats—there is meaning for each of you and for all of your children's children." As he spoke, a thirty-something-year-old man had quietly slipped in among the children to the old man's left. He was strong and muscular, gentle yet firm, with compassionate eyes that literally drank in whomever else's eyes met his. They captivated the looker; they did not frighten or turn one away. Just the opposite. They communicated in a language not spoken, yet clearly understood: *You are always welcome.* His body language said he was open to all in a gesture of inclusion.

"It's time, Grandfather." He placed his arms under the old man's, supporting him as he rose. Standing, the old man leaned on him like a crutch. The children stood and bowed their heads, respectfully, as the old man left them with their thoughts, his final lesson now conveyed. He walked so slow as to make his movement almost imperceptible. His grandson wasn't impatient. The old man could take as much time as he needed to get to the small cart only a few feet away. It took him a full ten minutes to traverse the twenty feet, but his grandson didn't mind the old man's feebleness. As he sat upon the cart, from all directions came men and women, children of various ages, infants in their mother's or father's arms. They formed a slow procession up the hill to the crest.

It was high noon on the last day of the summer month called Solius, the warmest, most life-sustaining period of the year. The entire village steadily and deliberately made its way up the hill. The old man led the way in his cart being pulled by several young men, including his grandson. There was no sadness, just reverence. They weren't totally silent, but only necessary words were spoken. And they weren't going because they had to, but because they wanted to.

It took them thirty minutes to reach the crest. As they climbed, the stone markers at the top gradually became more discernible. There were twelve six-foot tall, four-sided pyramids, each standing atop its own two-foot high pedestal. There were markings etched into each of the sharply carved obelisks, all of which pointed toward today's picture-perfect, aquamarine sky.

Having reached the summit, they all stopped and gathered around the old man. His grandson remained dutifully at his side, helping the old man slowly shuffle to the first of the twelve pillars. The old man could barely see, still, he was able to feel each soapstone edifice. He knelt to touch each one for about fifteen seconds, rising again and pausing to kiss the soft rock before moving to the next. The villagers formed a loose semicircle around the monuments with the old man and his grandson in the center. The only sound was the wind blowing gently between the columns as he knelt peacefully for over five minutes at the eleventh. Then the old man rose and gestured to each stone in succession, speaking in a powerful voice, strengthened now by his memories of the past.

"Nkata, giver of bread. All honor to his spirit. Mariani, the wise teacher. All honor to her spirit. Xiao, giver of right and wrong. All honor to his spirit. Natarajan, chronicler of the past, present, and future. All honor to her spirit. Tatman, the healer. All honor to his spirit. Gagarin, the voyager. All honor to her spirit. Chapman, the builder. All honor to his spirit. Sturmbourg, definer of the universe. All honor to her spirit. Najibul, the counselor. All honor to his spirit. Anton, the facilitator. All honor to his spirit." His hand upon the eleventh stone, his voice quivered, "Hayes, the beacon. All honor to her spirit."

The old man's eyes were full of tears as he turned and knelt before the twelfth obelisk, next to Hayes'. Placing his hands on the pedestal, he broke down, weeping, his words no longer audible. The villagers honored the old man. He had lived a full life. It was his time to rest.

"Soon, Grandfather. You will be with your wife again very soon."

About the Author

Harding McRae was born on the Isle of Skye, off the coast near Aberdeen, Scotland in 1958 to McGregor Ian McRae and Rosalind McRae (nee Wallace), he a groundskeeper to the royal family at Balmoral and she a professional seamstress. Growing up quickly, Harding gave his first piano recital and concert at age 5 attended by the Queen and later matriculating to the Royal Academy, graduated magna cum laude in physics and mathematics at age 14. Completing his medical degree at the University of Edinburgh, he immediately enlisted in the SAS, rising to the rank of Colonel before transferring to MI6. Knighted by Queen Elizabeth II in 2002 for his many years of anonymously serving his Queen and country, he retired to the countryside to pursue his avocational interest of United States history and writing. A frequent lecturer around the UK and in the US, Sir Harding remains involved in world affairs and current events. A life-long bachelor and fitness enthusiast, he now concetrates on his passion for gourmet cooking and collecting Italian Barolo wines, and has become a regular guest lecturer at the Culinary Institute of America. At home, he cooks mostly for himself and his faithful canine companion, Babe, and occasionally for his personal assistant Lynne Richardson.

Harding, age 10 months, and his father, McGregor Ian McRae.

www.ingramcontent.com/pod-product-compliance
Lightning Source LLC
Chambersburg PA
CBHW082054090726

47909CB00010B/3025